AF260452

JOE COLLEGE

BERT J MILLER

Minas Tirith Press

Copyright © 2021 by Bert J Miller

This is a work of fiction. Any names or characters, businesses or places, events or incidents, are fictitious. Any resemblance to actual persons, living or dead, or actual events is purely coincidental.

All rights reserved.

No part of this book may be reproduced in any form or by any electronic or mechanical means, including information storage and retrieval systems, without written permission from the author, except for the use of brief quotations in a book review.

In most books, the I, or first person, is omitted; in this it will be retained; that, in respect to egotism, is the main difference. We commonly do not remember that it is, after all, always the first person that is speaking. I should not talk so much about myself if there were anybody else whom I knew as well. Unfortunately, I am confined to this theme by the narrowness of my experience. Moreover, I, on my side, require of every writer, first or last, a simple and sincere account of his own life, and not merely what he has heard of other men's lives; some such account as he would send to his kindred from a distant land; for if he has lived sincerely, it must have been in a distant land to me. Perhaps these pages are more particularly addressed to poor students. As for the rest of my readers, they will accept such portions as apply to them. I trust that none will stretch the seams in putting on the coat, for it may do good service to him whom it fits.

— Henry David Thoreau, Walden

CHAPTER ONE

This is the happiest time of my whole life, just walking along the tree-lined sidewalk of this college campus with my backpack full of textbooks. I know studying in high school seems like a drag. But when you want to go to college and can't, because you don't have enough money or your family situation prevents it, believe me, that's way worse than anything. Sort of like there's nothing worse than going to work, except needing a job and not being able to find one.

I had to take some time after high school graduation to figure things out and make money for college. I may be late, and a dollar short, but here I am, sauntering among the hallowed stone halls of academia past towering student dorms populated with "normies." That's the name I give kids who go to college the way you're supposed to, right out of high school with scholarships, loans and checks from their parents. I've always wanted to be normal, but I've never quite been able to pull it off.

What's this? That's strange! Every building on campus is labeled with an official looking metal sign out front and as I take a shortcut, I spy something unusual. There appears to be a white envelope taped to the back of the sign for the nursing building. Hmm! See this is a perfect example of what I'm talking about. Normal people don't take short cuts through the bushes so they would never have seen the hidden note. Normal people would figure it was none of their business and leave the envelope alone. But I'm definitely not normal.

No one is looking so I carefully open the envelope. I don't want to tear it. Inside is a small square of plain white paper with the following message printed in block letters, like the sort of penmanship your third-grade teacher used to write on the board. The note says:

GO TO THE FRATERNITY HOUSE WITH LIONS IN FRONT YOUR NEXT CLUE IS BEHIND THE MAILBOX.

OK, so right away the gears are spinning in my abnormal mind. You and I both know this is obviously a clue to a scavenger hunt, right? Like some Greek house or campus orientation group is playing this game with freshman or foreign exchange students to help them get to know their way around the campus with all the famous land-marks. How nice!

So, what would a normal person do? Exactly what that guardian angel in your head tells you to do: *Just - put - the - clue - back - in - the - envelope - reseal - it - and - carry - on - your — way.* Am I not right? But no, something about me you'll discover: I like altering the course of history. Life would be too predictable and boring without someone like me to throw a curve ball now and then. I crumple up the original note, get a piece of plain white paper out of my backpack and as care-fully as I can remember penmanship from third grade, I scroll out the following in block letters:

GO TO THE PLEASURE PALACE AND ORDER A WHIPPED CREAM SPECIAL WITH A HAPPY ENDING.

The new note goes into the envelope and I stick it exactly where I found it, on the back of the sign. Of course, like nothing happened, I just carry on down the sidewalk. I have to laugh though. The Pleasure Palace is a new massage parlor in town, sort of a front for prostitution really. Can't you just imagine some freshman getting totally side-tracked by obediently following the instructions on that new note?

What an insane adventure that will be for them. Hopefully a "pleasurable" experience they will never forget.

I veer off the sidewalk again, leaving behind all the normies scurrying like ants on their way to classes. Instead, I start traipsing down the railroad tracks behind the English/Philosophy Building. It's the shortest route as the crow flies, so I take it. My mind wanders and I wonder what will ever happen to me? Will I graduate from college? What will I end up choosing for my career? Will I get a good job? Will I meet someone and get married? Will I have children someday? What will my life be like? I carefully place my feet on each railroad tie and make a mental note to remember this moment into the future. Someday I want to think back to this instant when I have all the answers to my questions.

I'm going into the gymnasium now. I'm not the sports type but I do love nature and they have an outdoor club on campus called *Touch the Earth*. Students can sign up for various trips such as hiking, canoeing, cross-country skiing, you know, stuff like that. I check the sign-up board. Today is Friday and the outing this weekend will be a spelunking expedition. I have absolutely no idea what spelunking is but I basically like to do anything outside in nature so it should be a good time. I'm down for it, so I sign up. Tomorrow I'll try to remember the instructions written on the board: wear old clothes and bring a flashlight.

I cut through an alley now and leave campus. Behind an abandoned Catholic grade school I have my 10-speed bike hidden. The smell of fresh bread wafts from the giant oven in the old school kitchen where a bunch of hippies are running a cooperative called the Morning Glory Bakery. I stop in to say hello and buy an oatmeal cookie. They have a big bulletin board outside and I survey the local events while I munch down the delicious confection.

Out of my backpack I pull a stapler and a magazine subscription ad that I post on the bulletin board. I'm always looking for a way to make some extra cash. For every magazine subscription someone buys from the ad, I get a small cut from the publisher. Next I start the arduous journey home. I don't have enough money for a place of my own, so I still live with my parents. That's beat, I know, but I'm hoping to move out next year. In the meantime, it's a five-mile ride from campus so I better get going.

I load my backpack onto the luggage rack of the ten-speed, secure it with bungee cords and take off at full speed. I like riding fast but one has to be careful to avoid things like loose sand or cracks in the pavement that might send you tumbling to a hard landing where you'll lose some skin skidding across the pavement. Then, of course, there are the cars, the eternal nemesis of all bicycle and motorcycle riders. Some drivers just don't seem to care and, in a way, I can see why. If they make a mistake and hit me, I could be dead and all they'll suffer is a big bug splat on their chrome bumper.

Just the other day I heard about a bike commuter who bit it at a major intersection. The biker was wearing a helmet and obeying all the traffic laws, but someone made them their hood ornament and the obituary was in the news. I go through that same intersection every day on my way to school. I had kind of forgotten about that accident the morning after and was just riding along when I saw this curving red smear on the cement. At first, I thought a can of paint must have fallen off a construction truck or something but then I remembered the accident report and realized it was someone's blood.

Eventually I pedal out of town and onto a blacktop country road. I'm definitely more in my element here with singing birds perched on long overhanging branches and farm fields full of ripening crops. I finally pull into my parent's drive past an old beater Chevrolet pickup. That's my dad's work truck. So now I know Leroy's home, which is good information to have. I'll try to avoid him. You see Leroy is a blue-collar type guy who thinks college is a waste of time. Since I was twelve I have helped him pour cement foundations. But I didn't want to carry a lunchbox the rest of my life so I quit working with him this semester to attend college and that really ticked him off.

I park the 10-speed in the garage, grab my backpack and enter through the kitchen. The smell of plate-sized tenderloins frying fills the air with grease. Mom used to work as a restaurant cook and she makes amazing meals. She got a deep fat fryer and a milkshake machine when the restaurant went out of business. Around here, it's sort of like dining out every night really. One of the things I'm definitely going to miss the most when I move out of here is her cooking.

I creep past the living room where Leroy is sitting in his favorite recliner with the local newspaper. He has never read a book in his life but he does peruse the printed newspaper, mostly for the ads and any coupons he can use. I notice him peer over his reading glasses, which means he has spotted me and will make a snide comment.

"There he goes. The college student. Buy 'em books. Get smart. No time for honest work. But never late for dinner."

"Howdy, Leroy," I respond, keeping the conversation as brief as possible. I take off quickly down a hallway lined with family portraits and retreat into my room. On the dresser is a sleek stuffed mink mounted on a base of cork. Above that hang the antlers from a massive whitetail buck. My room resembles a small museum filled with glistening rocks, twisted seashells, Indian arrowheads and other natural curiosities I've picked up over the years on my forays into the outdoors.

I throw the backpack on the bed and sit down at my desk to take off my shoes. I have two giant dictionaries propped up in wooden book stands. I do a lot of reading for my classes here and I'm kind of obsessed with looking up the definition of every word I don't know. My delay in attending the university left me fixated with not missing anything. Words are like building blocks, if you fail to look up the definition of one word you don't know that just makes it harder down the line to understand other things.

After washing up I take my place at the dining room table. Mom dishes me up. Besides the massive tenderloin sandwich there are French fries and corn from the garden, as well as my favorite: a vanilla milkshake with real cream.

Leroy breaks the silence, "So, do tell what great insight you gained from your studies today scholar?"

Mom gives him a dirty look so he lays off. When I finish eating I thank her for dinner and head back to my room where I stay up late to complete my homework. College requires a ton of reading and you have to keep up or you're lost. I work through Rhetoric, Psych, Mathematics Techniques, Religion and Culture, and my favorite, Humans and Their Physical Environment. I love listening to the lectures in that class. The professor is a genius, really funny, but serious too, in describing all the effects humans have on the natural ecosystem and how we should be more careful to conserve resources.

When the homework is done I lay out my oldest jeans and shirt for tomorrow. Then I dig out the Lithium flashlight my old buddy Gary Eschman gave me a few years ago. Esch was a total gearhead I hung around when I was in high school, always up on the latest technology. I used to be a gearhead too. In high school, I mean. We worked on cars a lot and raced them when we got a chance. But I've put all that behind me now. I sold my mustang muscle car when I went back to college to get money for tuition and bought the ten-speed instead.

I set the alarm to get up in time to bike to campus for the spelunking expedition. I try, but I can't sleep. Something keeps bugging me that I need to answer. So I get back up and saunter over to my desk to look up the word *spelunking* in the dictionary.

Hmm. It means cave exploration. That could be interesting. I hit the sack again, this time falling asleep to dream of giant stalactites and stalagmites shining glassy rainbow hues in deep underground caverns.

CHAPTER TWO

I wheel my 10-speed into the bike rack in front of the gymnasium. After Mom's hearty breakfast of eggs and sausage I rode hard to get here on time and I'm out of breath. I stand around in my old clothes while a motley crew of strangers straggles in for the spelunking expedition. I glance quickly to see if any of the girls are hot looking. Then I sit down on the ground and lean back against the bike rack. Might as well relax. The leader is probably getting one of those oversized university vans to transport us to the cave. They often arrive late for these outings from the van pool so I'll just chillax a bit.

There are about a dozen of us spelunkers. Most look like students but a couple are older, maybe faculty or community members. Some of the girls look like they are wearing pretty nice clothes, a move I predict they will regret. We aren't going to a style show. The trip description was plenty straight forward about not wearing anything good. The rest of us look like ragamuffins in our worn out threads.

Finally, an elongated van with university lettering pulls up. A strange looking little man with a hairy face gets out. The kid next to me explains that around campus this professor is known as the human mole. He's wearing overalls and a hard hat with a spot light mounted in front. He gathers us together for a trip briefing.

"We will be traveling north," he squeaks. "To explore a newly discovered cave network called The Maze."

The word "maze" freaks me out a bit. Mazes can be confusing. I hope this fellow knows what he is doing. But I gradually mellow out knowing it is an official, university-sanctioned trip. Obviously, it has all been carefully planned and approved by the proper authorities.

"Has everyone got a flashlight?" the mole questions, venturing an odd, crooked smile. Naturally some of the students forgot. What the heck is wrong with people? Seems like there are always a few in every crowd that can't follow the simplest directions. The mole pulls a couple of dirty old flashlights out of a toolbox and checks to make sure they work. Then he hands them to the culprits.

We all pile into the van. I don't know anyone and end up sitting by a young kid, probably a freshman like me. He's the one who tipped me off about the professor's nickname. Now he goes into a rambling recitation about how the human mole is famous in spelunking circles. Apparently, he's an expert in discovering and mapping new cave networks. Some of the caves dip below the water table so on occasion the mole must don scuba equipment. The kid tells me that once the mole got his scuba tank jammed on a rock in the narrow portion of an underwater cave and had to be saved. Apparently the rescue divers reached him just in time before his oxygen ran out. My confidence is waning.

Matters become even sketchier an hour later when the van leaves the highway and we are traveling on an obscure gravel road. Next we turn onto a dirt road. Finally the mole stops the van, gets out, and opens the gate to a deserted old farm pasture. The country is hillier here and the van strains as we venture across the bumpy tufts of over-grown grass. The overloaded vehicle is unable to climb any higher up a green hillside so the mole shifts it into park and we all get out and stretch.

I'm a bit perplexed. It's not like I haven't been in a cave before. Sometimes when my family goes on vacation we stop at little tourist trap caves to see the different rock formations. I've even been in the

Mark Twain Cave near Hannibal, Missouri when I was a kid. My mom thought it would be neat for me to see after I read Tom Sawyer. But there are no caves to be seen here and the land is not even rocky. This is an old cow pasture.

Never-the-less Professor Mole beckons us to grab our lights and follow him on up the hillside. He stops in front of a dirty hole in the ground barely large enough for a person to crawl into. Now I'm really skeptical.

"Stay together and follow me!" he emphasizes and, before anyone can ask questions, he disappears into the mud hole. We all look at each other like WTF but then, one by one, each explorer follows. I'm the last one. This is against my better judgment, but since everyone else went in I can't just stand here, so I turn on my light and squeeze into the hole.

Now Mark Twain Cave has electric lights, and a nice path to walk on, and lots of room to move around as you listen to a tour guide bellow canned dialog. In contrast this Maze cave is like crawling through a long road culvert. Only a road culvert is at least straight. This tube of rock constantly twists and turns. I feel like a worm. Worst yet there are several inches of muddy water on the bottom so my clothes are getting soaked. I hurry to catch up to the woman in front of me. She has wide hips and is struggling to get through the narrow tunnel. Faintly, up ahead, I hear someone mention stalactites. Yes, eventually I come to three dirty little knobs of rock only a few inches long hanging down from the ceiling. They have got to be kidding.

I barely hear mention of a bat. The main group is getting further and further away. Their voices have become faint. Then they disappear entirely. In the beam of my flashlight one small brown bat hangs precariously in front of my nose. The poor creature looks scared and emaciated.

Now the woman in front of me is no longer moving forward at all. She starts swearing a blue streak. I realize she has become lodged in the narrow confines of the rock tube. I carefully crawl up just behind her flailing feet. The tunnel is so tight around me that I cannot move my arms down to my sides. My body is literally encased in rock. And so is she.

I'm ordinarily not claustrophobic. But I feel the blood run from my head. A sure sign you are about to lose it, I know. I'm scared, but I try to hide it and talk softly to the poor spelunker jammed in the narrow passage ahead of me. I encourage her, saying, "Don't panic." This just pisses her off and she begins swearing again. I back away from her kicking legs.

All I can do now is wait for help. I try turning off my flashlight. Fortunately the lithium model Esch gave me is very good. But the light is beginning to fade a bit with time and I want to conserve the battery. My God it is dark in here. I wave my hand right in front of my eyes. Nothing! I can't see a thing. Complete and total darkness.

I just wish I could stand up and stretch. But I'm encased in rock. All I can do slowly inch backward or forward. I begin inching away from the irate spelunker. Unfortunately, the tunnel goes upward behind me making this difficult. I think again. I can't just back out of here and desert her and, frankly, I don't want to get lost on the way out. We passed through several forks and turns on the way in here and after all, this cave is known as The Maze.

I lie in several inches of muddy water that permeates my clothing. As a last resort, if I am dying of thirst, I suppose I can lap some up. I keep my light off and the darkness is freaking me out. The muffled struggling of the trapped spelunker in front of me has subsided. The curse words have ended and what remains is the most complete and total, utter lack of any sound you can imagine. The silence is maddening. I feel like I'm being sucked into a lifeless black hole.

"Are you okay?" I timorously venture after a bit. The query elicits only a short string of profanity laced curses. I wonder if I will ever escape these confines. Or will I go crazy down in this pit before the authorities can find and rescue us. My heart is palpitating in my chest. I can feel it missing beats.

After what seems an eternity I hear a voice. Not the cursing voice of the entrapped explorer ahead of me but a calm voice from further up ahead. I recognize it to be the young man I sat with in the van who was next in line ahead of the trapped woman when we entered the cave.

"I realized you guys weren't behind me anymore. But I couldn't turn around until I reached a larger opening in the cave," he explains. "Are you alright?"

The angry woman blasts out the F-bomb followed by, "No!"

I'm so damn grateful that kid came back. I turn on my flashlight to the sight of a big muddy ass in front of my face. I want out of here, bad!

"OK, give me your hands," the kid states calmly. He begins pulling with all his strength on her outstretched arms. I see her wiggling frantically, from side to side in front of me. I have no choice. I place one hand on each of her butt cheeks and begin pushing with all my might. I realize that ordinarily it would not be appropriate to touch her this way. But under the circumstances, our lives are at stake.

Ever so slowly her body begins to inch forward. The kid and I give ample encouragement. She cusses and complains about pain in her hips. But eventually we are all three crawling again, shuffling ahead in the dank tunnel. Instead of The Maze, I'm going to call this creepy place the Cave of Death.

Finally the path widens. I see many lights ahead. The entire group is assembled in an underground grotto, a rock chamber large enough for everyone to sit together. The group is discussing cave ecology and Karst topography. When we arrive the woman who was trapped begins to complain and then cusses out the mole in front of everyone. He looks startled and without answering, motions everyone to follow him. The way out may be slightly wider, but not by much. I can't believe how bad this adventure has gone. I feel completely traumatized and all I have seen for my trouble is a couple of muddy little stalactites and a dying bat.

When I finally pop out of the cave entrance into the incredibly bright light of day I can literally see nothing. Being the last one out a couple of the other spelunkers hold my arms until my eyes adjust. What an eerie sight. Everyone looks like they have been dipped in chocolate, only we are definitely not chocolate-dipped spelunkers. No, we are coated from the top of our heads to the bottom of our feet with liquid mud. Everyone's eyes look so white when they blink. It's freaking me out.

The woman who was trapped wastes no time in finding the human mole again and she proceeds to read him the riot act. Every swear word I have ever heard comes out, and a few I haven't. Cussing him up one side and down the other her main point being that on an official trip like this they should measure people or something to make damn sure everyone can get through before they descend into the cave. I catch her drift. She has a legitimate point actually. It was a very alarming experience for me too. But I keep my mouth shut.

All the spelunkers exchange grimacing looks. Some groan. Then, without speaking, everyone silently piles back into the van. What a mess. Mud is everywhere. It is the quietest trip home ever. No one says a word. A very awkward, uncomfortable atmosphere I must say. When we arrive back at the gym, I thank the kid who helped us out and say goodbye. I feel like a knucklehead peddling home on my bicycle coated with mud. I get some really strange looks from motorists.

At home I peel out of all the dirt-encrusted attire in the garage. I don't want to make a mess in the house. I hold the clothes carefully in my arms and begin walking naked down the stairs to the washing machine in the basement. My head and my hands are coated with dried mud. Half way down what I had urgently hoped would not happen, happens. I meet Leroy coming the other way. Bad timing.

"What the hell?" he exclaims.

I'm really not in the mood for conversation. I brush past him without an explanation. I throw the muddy clothes into the washer, add double detergent and start it on the highest setting. Then I hit the shower for a warm, well needed scrubbing and say goodbye to The Maze as a brown ribbon of mud swirls down the drain.

CHAPTER THREE

I'm back on campus drifting along the sidewalk in a wave of student bodies. It is the last week before finals so everyone is cramming to get their classwork done. But strangely, I'm okay with the tests. I feel like I'm doing what a kid my age should be doing. I've often wondered what college would be like and now I'm finding out, big time, and I love the experience.

Like half of the other freshman, I've decided to be pre-med. I know most of us will never make it into medical school or become a doctor. But you have to have some goal and why not aim high? If I don't try, how will I ever know who I am and what I'm capable of?

"Excuse me!" I say, as I nearly crash into a coed striding in the other direction. She's a beauty wearing tight-fitting Calvin Klein jeans and a tank top. She smiles wide and gives me a nod as she passes. I don't have a girlfriend now, and one thing's for sure, I hope I meet someone.

A lot of people joke about girls in college wanting to earn an MRS degree. But that's pretty one-sided and unfair. Like me, most of the guys would like to meet someone special too. So why do they only disparage girls for wanting that? It seems sexist.

As I walk along a strange noise grows louder, something like, "mmm ... haireeey ... kreeshnaaaa ... mmmmmm ... rama..." Up ahead reclining comfortably on the green campus lawn, illuminated by bright sunshine, are a half dozen odd looking strangers wearing saffron robes, heads shaved except for one single lock of very long hair.

As the Hare Krishnas chant their mantras a crowd gathers round. I have time before my next class so I stop and take a place in the circle of student spectators. Everyone is in a good mood enjoying the strange novelty and fair weather.

Eventually a tall devotee of Krishna stands up. He looks rather bizarre, but then anyone sporting such unusual attire and hairstyle would. He explains the mantra, "Krishna means the all-attractive personality of God. Rama means the reservoir of all pleasure, and Hare is Krishna's lover."

"Whatever," I think out loud, pondering the nearly infinite possibilities of ideas and beliefs people can make up.

The tall devote hears my comment and picks me out of the crowd. As I stand here, he is looking me right in the eyes as he explains, "Life is an endless cycle of death and rebirth, of reincarnation and of karma, a belief that a person's actions decide their fate."

"So how is it determined what a person will be reincarnated as in the next life?" I query, figuring I'll play along for a while. If he's right, maybe I can learn something that will help me avoid being reincarnated as some undesirable life form like a slime mold or liverwort. Anyway, it is nice to get the attention of the other students, including a bevy of cute coeds standing in the crowd.

"One is reincarnated according to karma. So, a person's actions, desires and essence determine their future life form," the tall devotee postulates, adjusting his golden robes. "So, for example, if a person is sloppy or gluttonous according to the Vedic teachings, such a person may get the body of a pig in their next life. Or, if a person is sedentary and moves little, they may be reborn as a tree."

"What if a person," I reply thinking I can make the coeds laugh. "Desires and engages in sex all the time?"

The attempt succeeds and everyone, except for the Hare Krishnas, bursts out in laughter.

The tall monk holds his chin in his fingers and ponders the question seriously. To him, this is no laughing matter, not a joke, but a serious philosophical and religious consideration. I feel a small pang of guilt at not being more respectful of his beliefs.

But he has not taken offense at all and eventually replies that he thinks a person obsessed with sex would probably be reincarnated as a rabbit or pigeon.

Now the crowd really roars. I'd love to stay but personally I need to get to class. As I start to walk away the tall sage asks me if I would like to come and have dinner with them. Now I may just be a freshman but I'm not knuckleheaded enough to go off to dinner with a group of Hare Krishnas. I've heard the stories of perfectly normal people disappearing for years and then showing up somewhere bald-headed and wearing robes. Anyway, if there really is such a thing as reincarnation, I want to come back as a peregrine falcon. Those suckers can fly over 200 miles per hour.

I arrive and take a seat in the giant lecture hall, then get out a spiral notebook labeled *Humans and their Physical Environment*. I like to take fastidious, extensive lecture notes. After all, anything the professor says is game for a question on the final. I've even developed some of my own personal shorthand to keep up. So for example f/ is "for" or "from" and ~ is "approximately" and @ stands for "at" or "about."

Professor Drake walks in, removes his hat and turns on the screen. Large portions of his lectures on the dangers of pollution involve interesting examples and historical stories, like the origin of the phrase "plumb crazy." Plumbum is the Latin word for lead, which explains why the symbol for lead on the periodic table of elements is Pb. Romans used lead to line their chalices when they drank wine. Acid in the wine would dissolve some of the lead and lead tastes sweet—which is why hungry children in poor neighborhoods often nibble on chips of old lead paint. But ingesting lead causes brain damage, which explains the origin of the phrase "plumb crazy."

I really love Professor Drake. Even though there are hundreds of students in the class he always takes time to talk to me after his lectures. I even went to see his home with a small group of interested students. It was a cabin really, nestled in a virgin timber outside of town and his place runs on solar energy.

I sit now, carefully recording the professor's words in my notebook. Since today is our last lecture the subject is global climate change, a topic the prof is passionate about. He lays out the evidence and explains what the consequences will be if we continue to rely too heavily on fossil fuels for energy. Everyone shifts uncomfortably in their seats, considering the dim prospects. But then the professor provides a brighter vision of what the world, and future, could be like if a transition was made to clean, safe renewable energy sources.

When the class is finished, I grab my backpack and go to the front of the lecture hall to bid farewell. It is strange how someone can come into your life and have such a huge impact on your thinking and then just exit. I shake hands with the old professor knowing I will probably never see him again.

"I really enjoyed your class," I tell him.

"Thanks and good luck on the final," he replies with a smile.

I have one more class today. I hurry down the hill to the English Building for Rhetoric One. I'm a little sensitive about taking Rhetoric One this second semester. I mean you're supposed to take it first semester. But, as you know, I had some financial delays in starting college and so, it is what it is. I just want to fit in. So, if people ask me why I'm a semester late, I just change the subject.

I sit here now in a circle of chairs, everyone facing the middle of the room. There are about twenty of us including some sorority types, a couple of athletes and some nondescript, traditional students. The professor's last name is Krupa, but he is a friendly fellow and says we can just call him Gene. I really hate it when pretentious professors put on airs and demand that you call them "doctor so and so."

Today we go around the circle, each student telling what three books have had the greatest effect on our lives. Most students name popular fiction or recent publications by famous celebrities. Maybe I'm wrong but it seems to me that some of these people are just name-dropping popular authors for status, or to create an image of who they are. Or who they want people to think they are anyway.

I answer as honestly as I can, "Thoreau's *Walden, Black Elk Speaks* and the Bible." Now don't go thinking this is the place in the book where I'm going to try and covert you. I'm not like that. You know, I can see truth in many religious views, including atheism and agnosticism. I just try to be respectful of other people's beliefs and look for the truth in the various outlooks on religion. As to my answer here in rhetoric class, it's just that if I'm perfectly 100% honest, those are the three books that have had the most impact on me. I mean, I can't help it if my mom dragged me to church every Sunday when I was a kid.

At the mention of Walden and Black Elk Speaks I notice a couple of the sorority types look at each other, roll their eyes and smirk. They poked fun at my final creative writing composition too. My paper described how I like to go out in the woods in the evening, just before sundown, and try to catch the exact instant at dusk when the human eye transitions from seeing in color to black and white. I said the experience helps me be "present in the current moment." After class I heard one of them refer to me as "the field hippie." Ouch! That hurt.

When it is time to go I wait until a certain girl packs her things and starts to leave. She has beautiful brown eyes and long shiny hair. She seems to be more introspective than the others in our class and she never disses what anyone else has to say. She smiles as I start to walk alongside her.

Her name is Vicki. She tells me that her family had a bakery business but she didn't want to work in it for the rest of her life. So she came back to college late and that's why she's taking first semester Rhetoric this second semester. I can relate.

I finally ask, "Would you like to study together for the final?"

At this she gets an odd look on her face and replies, "I'm married." Then she walks away.

I think to myself, even if she's married, we could still study together. It's not like I asked her to go to bed with me or something. I wish there was a better way to determine which girls were married, or going out with someone, and which ones were single. I'm not very good at intuition and although I am getting As in my classes, I can be somewhat shy and socially awkward. I probably have a low EQ and would get an F in a class on social awareness.

My classes are done for the day so I trudge over to the Morning

Glory Bakery to pick up my 10-speed. Only I won't be getting an oatmeal cookie there any more since the bakery has been evicted. I guess they posted a notice on their bulletin board about a fundraiser for the local women's clinic. Since the clinic performs abortions the priest from the parish that rents the kitchen in the old Catholic school stopped by and told them they had to take the notice down. The woman who ran the bakery refused and, well, got evicted. Basically I side with the woman and free speech. But in this case, it doesn't really matter what I think and there certainly won't be any more of the delicious oatmeal cookies for me anymore.

I wish I could go home and study for finals but I have a job bussing tables at a pizza place. It is kind of a cool atmosphere—with a salad bar constructed in a real wooden boat. The waitresses all wear halter tops with no bra—something the manager pushed to help bring in male customers. Everybody that works here is a college student desperate for money so no one complained. Some of the girls even like the manager, a tall older guy with a black mustache. They seem to look down on me though. Probably because of my position collecting dirty dishes.

CHAPTER FOUR

I crushed finals! I crammed every spare minute I could, pouring over my copious notes. Basically, for college freshman, finals consist of either 4-foil multiple-choice tests or essays you answer in these little blank booklets. I create mnemonic devices using letters for the first word in major points of possible topics. You know, like ROYGBIV stands for the colors of the rainbow, only by college mine are much longer and more complicated than that. That strategy, and all my reading and note taking, paid off big time. I really nailed the tests.

Some students in my math class wrote an invitation on the board to come to *Joe's Place*, a local pub, to celebrate after the last final. I'm conflicted though. I don't know whether or not to go. Finals week was a lot of pressure and I really feel like letting my hair down and having some fun. I definitely need to vent some steam. On the flip side, I just don't know how to handle the bar scene.

I'm going to let you in on a little secret I don't ordinarily tell people. It's extraordinarily embarrassing, so please don't judge me, but when I was in high school, I was pretty much a party animal, smoking pot, drinking lots of alcohol and working on muscle cars. When I was a senior, I got really wasted one night and ended up in a high-speed chase with the cops.

Basically what went down was this: I'm scooping the loop, cruising in my built-to-the-max Ford Mustang and I stop at a grocery store parking lot to do some burnouts and cut donuts. I know that's stupid but, at the time, I was wasted and trying to impress a cute girl that worked there as a cashier. Well, just down the street, the county sheriff and his deputies were directing traffic for bingo night at the Catholic High School. So they pulled me over and told me to park and wait until they were done with traffic control.

I sort of panicked thinking they were going to make me blow into a Breathalyzer and I'd lose my license, which is a death sentence for a gearhead. So, I made a run for it. My hot car was fast and I outran them to my parent's place in the country, pulled the Mustang into the garage, shut the door, ran into the house and jumped in bed. I figured the coast was clear, that I'd made a clean escape. I even started to drift off to sleep when the ceiling and walls in my room became covered with bouncing red dots of light, an effect I attributed to excessive alcohol consumption.

But when I heard someone pounding on the front door, I looked outside and the drive, and even the yard, were filled with squad cars, lights flashing. I kept quiet and Leroy answered the door explaining to the Sheriff that whoever they were after it could not have been me because his son was sleeping in his bedroom. The sheriff insisted and when my dad came back to my room, which smelled like a brewery, he saw my cowboy boots sticking out from under the covers, and I was busted.

I spent an uncomfortable night in jail with the deputies giving me a hard time, shining bright lights in my eyes and interrogating me with the good cop, bad cop thing, so I would learn a lesson. I'd had a few run-ins with the law before and in the morning the Sheriff just basically laid the cards out on the table for me: either join Alcoholics Anonymous and quit drinking or get sent up to the juvenile detention center. I'd heard rumors of how horrible juvie is and the thought of being incarcerated there scared the crap out of me.

Anyway, the people at AA were really nice. We'd sit in a circle and people would tell their personal stories of abuse and redemption. My gearhead friend Eschman was already a member and he told me I could call him anytime if I felt like I was falling off the wagon and needed support. With the help of the AA folks I quit drinking and stopped smoking pot totally. I've been sober for over a year now. So, I'm not sure how to navigate the college party scene.

I finally decide to go to Joe's pub thinking I'll just order a coke or something. But when I get there everyone is having a blast, sitting around a massive wooden table with huge glass pitchers of beer. They all holler my name when I come in, make room at the table and pour me a tall, cold one. I try just sipping but people keep slapping my back and telling me to drink up. So, I figure just one beer won't hurt. I know it's a stupid move, but I want to fit in. Eventually I start chugging beers and laughing and horsing around, playing drinking games and, anyway, one thing lead to another and now I'm totally plastered.

It's late now and the bar is closing, I'm weaving my way back from the men's room when a couple of the students say we ought to go to a kegger some football players are throwing. We leave the sticky table covered with empty pitchers and spilled beer stumbling out into the dark night. I get into their car and before long we're parked outside one of those run-down rental houses common near college campuses.

The place has a long front porch that is currently populated with big athletic dudes and pretty cheerleader types. I'm a mess, totally ripped, as I wander up the walkway to bum a cup of beer. That's when I see her. An old high school girlfriend of mine named Margo. She's quite a looker, tall and thin with long blonde hair and a crooked grin that makes her look wicked good. She is currently in the arms of a tackle on the football team named Shoderbeck, whose father was an All-American.

I only dimly remember what happened after that. I don't know what came over me. We'd broken up a long time ago. But it made me mad to see her with him. Like a knucklehead I stumbled up to the giant athlete, mumbled something about Margo and knocked a bag of potato chips out of his hands. He reacted badly, punching me hard in the face. The next thing I know I'm on my hands and knees in the grassy front yard with blood pouring out of my nose and an eye so badly swollen I can't see out of it. The lineman was, of course, uninjured.

I finally get up and stumble through the night, pinching my nose to stave the bleeding. When I finally make it back to my ten-speed, I'm unable to balance well enough to ride, so I walk my bike the five miles home. It's dawn and the sun is rising over the farm fields before I get there. I fall into bed and sleep until noon when my mom comes in to check on me and totally freaks out at the dried blood and disheveled condition of my face. I can see why when I look in the mirror. Besides the blood, I have a black eye and my nose is crooked.

Mom insists, so we go to see the doctor, even though I'm still hungover. Old Doc Tegler is nice, joking me about how bad the other guy looked. I never admit he looked just fine.

So here I am now. I survived finals and its summer break. For me that means slaving my butt off working for Leroy pouring cement again. I'm loading one of his dually tired work trucks. The deal is this, pouring concrete foundations in the summer I can make twice what I would bussing tables or any other minimum wage job. My goal is to graduate from college without any debt. You can't get there on minimum wage. The math doesn't add up.

Leroy has his own company that consists of several trucks, construction equipment and an old building he rents from the VFW. The people who work here include Jack, a Marine veteran, martial arts black belt who works nights as a bouncer at the most popular bar in town, *The Field House*. He also occasionally moonlights as an all-star wrestler. That is why he has a triple Mohawk haircut. His stage name is Hatchet Jack.

Then there is Phil, who we call Phildo, a former lineman for the college football team. Phil has a bad knee and likes to go coon hunting at night after work. Both Jack and Phil are physically enormous and both of them take large quantities of steroids to bulk up.

My mom does all the accounting paperwork for the business and my little brother, who we call Hondo, because he reminds us of a character from a Louis L'Amour Western, basically handles customers and day-to-day business. Hondo was a star athlete in high school. He went on to play d-back for the college football team but apparently didn't like studying much and dropped out of college. Still, he has the best head for business I've ever seen and handles all the financial details really well.

Leroy basically tags along with us when we go out on the road. He's getting too old to do the brutal physical work but likes to give orders, an annoying habit that gets to me sometimes. Phil and Jack call him "Flash" and just laugh and ignore him. But me, I get tired of him bossing us around. I mean, I've been working pouring cement with him since I was 12 years old. It's not like I don't already know what I'm doing.

Our crew is loading up the trucks now to go out on a job. I check to make sure we have all the right size forms and the toolbox with trowels and edgers. Phil and Jack are giving me a good ribbing about my shiner and swollen nose. Hey, I know it was a stupid move messing with Shoderbeck, but both of them have done a million times worse, and they know it. So screw them!

What bugs me the most is that I knew damn well I shouldn't take a drink. Alcohol and my brain don't mix. I've been through the 12 step AA program and had successfully quit. Why did I fall off the wagon? What the hell happened? I wake up in the morning perfectly fine and then my brain boots up and I remember that night, and what happened, and I just groan. What the heck is wrong with me?

One good thing about Leroy is that he always buys us lunch when we are on the road. Which is generous of him. Or maybe he just writes it off as a business expense. I don't know. Either way, it helps me to save money for college, so I appreciate that. Every little bit helps.

After battling gnats, sunburn and heat all morning we have the forms set up. It is time for lunch so we pile into the work trucks and head out. The guys on the cement crew know every single all-you-can-eat restaurant in a four-state area. And I can tell you those dining establishments lose a lot of money on this crew. Phil and Jack can eat the equivalent of several chickens, fried with all the fixings, in one setting. Heaped plates of food from smorgasbords disappear into their mouths like black holes swallowing up passing stars.

Today we pull the trucks into an authentic German restaurant, *The Colony Inn*, that is popular with work crews. They have long wooden tables with benches to sit on and they serve everything family style. Generous bowls of mashed potatoes, gravy, sauerkraut, green beans and platters of bratwurst, beef sauerbraten and chicken schnitzel are passed around. The chubby old frau serving lunch yells and smacks the back of my head because I forgot to take my hat off when I came inside. The crews of men in their various dirty work clothes joke, laugh and enjoy the feast.

Back at the work site we get the liquid cement poured into the foundation forms. Then we screen off the top with a screed board and smooth everything over with our trowels. When the job is finished, we drive back to the shop talking about what will go down this evening or weekend. With the trucks unloaded it's time to head home. Leroy offers to throw my bike in the back of his truck and give me a ride. But I insist that I'll bike it.

Everyone thinks I'm crazy biking everywhere but I have been on a mission to reduce my carbon footprint and environmental impact ever since Professor Drake's class. I even pitched a tent on some wooded property my parents own.

"People like you would have us all living in caves!" Leroy protests.

"Fat chance of me living in a cave after that experience in The Maze," I think to myself.

Twice a week I pedal back into town for my summer school night class. I need more science classes so I'm taking a Plant Propagation course at the college greenhouse. I'm determined to catch back up with my contemporary students who are one semester ahead in their course work. I figure if I go to summer school every year until I graduate I can close the gap.

My social life? Well I'm still not dating anyone. Sometimes I go fishing or swimming out at the reservoir. Unfortunately the water there is pretty polluted with farm runoff. But at least it cools you down from the intense humidity and burning summer sun. And I like scoping out the coeds in their bikinis. Hey, a guy can always dream.

I haven't had another drink this whole summer. Some people like me just have to avoid booze completely. I've heard it may be ingrained in some people's genetics. Like historically a lot of Native Americans have had reactions to alcohol. Me, I learned my lesson and plan to avoid all mind-altering substances from now on.

But that doesn't mean I quit the college party scene entirely. I still go to *The Field House* bar every night after my class and on weekends. It's the hot place to be in this college town, always packed with horny guys ogling tantalizing young women. Inside there are multiple levels and a dance floor.

The problem is, for most customers, it's hard to get in the door. There's always a long line of well-dressed prepsters winding out onto the sidewalk and down the street. Plus the cover charge is steep. People scratch their heads and wonder WTF when this hippie looking dude in old jeans with long hair and a beard gets waved to the front of the line. Then the bouncer pats me on the back and I skate in without paying cover. Hey, there are some advantages to knowing Hatchet Jack!

One evening I'm sitting at the bar slamming down orange juices and munching popcorn when this stunning chick comes over and asks me to dance. She has emerald eyes, long jet-black hair and a perfectly svelte body. I can't fathom how I got so lucky. But we proceed to the dance floor.

"Do I know you?" I ponder, squinting my eyes. "You look familiar."

"It's Beth McPhearson silly," she laughs, swaying to the beat of the music.

Ouch! I remember now. She's a girl I dumped in high school. She looks totally different now, like an astronaut's wife. At the end of the song I'm informed that Beth now works as a model in California. Boy, do I wish I could rethink that dumb decision I made in high school. She smiles, kisses my cheek and says, "Ciao." All I can do is watch her walk away.

CHAPTER FIVE

I deposit my last paycheck from Leroy's shop. It was a long summer working sunup to sundown pouring concrete, sweating in the hot sun and humidity with lots of mud, bugs, cuts and bruises. But on the up side, my skin is tanned, my muscles are hard as rock and there isn't an ounce of fat on my entire body. I feel strong and have enough money saved to cover tuition and books.

It's a downer though when I check on the prices of room and board in the dorms and I can't cut it. I really wanted to experience the dorm life but it's too expensive for my budget. I do appreciate my mom and dad letting me live at home, but I'm getting anxious to move out and be on my own. I've been pouring over the want ads for efficiency apartments and rooms but even the smallest, most run-down places are too expensive.

At least the beginning of the fall semester is a fresh start, the promise of a new life. Kind of like the entire universe and all its contents are a giant kaleidoscope. Energy turns the wheel and all the constituent atoms reshape and reform into a new reality, always different and never the same. The past is gone, the future is not yet here, and we live in the present moment.

Being a creature of habit I park my bike in the usual spot. Bikes get stolen all the time in this college town. But no one has bothered mine hidden behind this old decrepit Catholic schoolhouse, so I stick with it. Grabbing my backpack I head off to my first class, Principles of Animal Biology.

Now I know biology sounds kind of interesting and fun, studying plants and animals, and it is to a point. However, at this college the course is very intense, serving, along with chemistry and physics, as a weed-out for all the young students who think they have what it takes to hack medical school.

Personally, I think if they are going to weed people out of the medical track, they ought to do so more on social factors, like who gets along with people and would have the best bedside manner. Or make students study something more applicable to medicine—say jamming their brains full of disease symptoms and cures rather than physics formulae and electron shells. But, that's just my idea.

Are the workings of the universe just chaos, a random set of events or is everything controlled by the laws of mathematics and physics? Or is a supreme being in charge of everything? I can't tell you the answer. But I do know that it sure seems like some things in life happen by fate, like my lab partner in Animal Bio.

I walk into the class at the last minute. The place smells like lab rats. Science tables with two chairs each are lined up in neat rows. There is only one seat left, toward the center of the room, with a very cute young woman already seated alone at the table. She has a fresh perm, beautiful luminous blue-green eyes and is impeccably dressed in a business-like outfit that conforms perfectly to her curvy, girlish figure.

I take a seat and introduce myself. She smiles, sort of weakly. I get that reaction sometimes from sorority types. Like their stock is somehow superior to everyone else. Whatever, I'll just try to be friendly and get along since we'll be working together as lab partners.

The instructor mentions that we'll need to purchase a dissecting kit, in addition to the giant text and lab manual. Surprisingly, after class, my new lab partner walks with me to the local book and crook. We students call the bookstore that because they charge exorbitant prices for textbooks and then when classes are over, they offer to buy them back for paltry peanuts.

From our conversation, and a little deductive reasoning, I have learned that my lab partner's name is Danette, she's a member of the Chi Omega sorority, and she has wealthy parents. That last bit of information I infer because when we part, she drives off in a brand-new Camaro that her father bought her for college.

I've only known her for a couple of hours and, without saying it out loud, it's already understood that I should never attempt to ask her out or become overly friendly. Why? For starters I'm sure she thinks of herself as way out of my league. So there's that. Also Danette has informed me that she has a fiancé who is going to propose to her over winter break. So she will be getting married in the spring.

I must have gotten a rather ponderous look when she said she was sure her boyfriend would be proposing over the holiday because she added that the reason she knows this will happen is that her beau told her he was getting her "one little thing" for Christmas. She surmises it is a ring.

I wanted to say, "Haven't you discussed this in depth?" Marriage is such a major life decision it seems to me like a couple ought to have really worked out more details than that. But maybe my view is just Dullsville and I'm not being romantic or something.

It is a perfect, sunny fall day with a crispness to the atmosphere the French would proclaim, "*Bon air!*" As I walk through the center of campus the courtyard lawn is the usual circus of jugglers and amateur trapeze artists practicing on colorful climbing ropes strung between tree trunks.

There are no Hare Krishnas today, just a few hellfire bible thumpers exhorting the flock of passing students to repent and avoid going to hell for excessive partying. Attracting the most attention are Brother Jed and Sister Cindy who lament a lot about gays and abortion but don't seem too concerned about poor people. I have to laugh when Jed calls sorority girls "whores" and boys in fraternities "whore mongers."

Jed wears a black, three piece suit despite the fair weather and he is sweating profusely as he exclaims loudly, "I don't know how the whorehouses in this town stay open, all of you sorority girls are giving it away for free!" and, "Who are you, Bob Marley?" addressed to a young black man with dreadlocks. Jed continues yelling, "A masturbater today is a homosexual tomorrow."

His assistant Sister Cindy declares that feminists, liberals, and those who listen to rock and roll are destined for Hell, along with homosexuals, fornicators and women who use vibrators. I'm not going to waste my time engaging them in debate. What's the point?

I mean, I think Jesus had a lot of good things to say in the Bible, you know, about being peaceful and loving and forgiving and, like, helping poor and handicapped people. But I figure these confrontational preachers, who really sound more like political fascists than religious counselors, are probably turning off an entire generation of young people to Christianity.

I do stop to talk to some students who have tables set up to display campaign literature. The presidential election is coming up soon and this will be the first time in my life I get to vote. Basically, as I see it, this fall we have the following three choices:

- Candidate #1 – a warmonger and corporate shill who could care less about working people and the natural environment.
- Candidate #2 – warmonger lite, slightly less sold out to corporate lobbyists than #1, who does feign some concern for working people and pollution, but no strong commitment.
- Candidate #3 – third party peacemaker who doesn't take a penny from corporations and who has real passion for helping people and protecting nature—but who has zero chance of winning.

So which one would you vote for? Going for #1? Get outta here! Gonna compromise on your values to have a chance of winning, then vote #2. Or do you go with your hopes and dreams by voting for #3, who you know would actually be the best president? Warning—if you go with #3 just say a prayer that #1 does not defeat #2 by one vote because then the end of the world and life as we know it happened because of you!

It always amazes me how badly adults have screwed things up. The American political process with its winner take all, gerrymandered, Electoral College loophole-infested system brimming with corrupt campaign cash is just another example of an AFU dumpster fire my generation is going to have to try and straighten out.

After I finish with classes for the day I stop by the job board in the registration building. I'm constantly looking for a way to make an extra buck after school. Employers post any part-time work they have on the board and I've had gigs doing everything from yard work to stocking shelves in a health food co-op.

Sometimes I sign up to take part in experiments at the psych lab. There students get paid to be subjects in studies on things like hand-eye coordination or interpersonal bargaining strategies. One time they were paying extra to be in a double blind study on a new psychotropic medication. Lots of students were doing it because you could make like $100 for simply taking a pill that I heard would almost always be a placebo.

Of course, I couldn't pass up a chance to make an easy C-note Benjamin. I showed up at the lab and was led to a room by a woman in a white lab coat. She gave me two paper cups—one with a yellow pill in it and the other with water. After I took the pill, I got ready to leave but the researcher said I needed to stay. Wouldn't you know I didn't get the placebo.

After a while the floor seemed like it was moving around and I started to see double. I had to answer questions and describe what it was like while the psychologist recorded everything on a clipboard. I finally got out of there late with a terrible headache. I had missed my bio lecture—and I NEVER miss lectures!

I hop on my bike and head home. The ride to my parent's house is long and I still feel woozy from the drug. But the sun and fresh air revive me. All together biking to and from school and walking between classes I cover many miles in a day. My legs get worn out but I prefer the human-powered lifestyle to the stress and pollution of commuting by car or bus. And the exercise keeps me in top shape.

I have an errand to do at home, taking down the tent in the woods on my parent's land and disassembling the makeshift camp where I have been hanging out. The nights are getting cooler and I freeze my butt off unless I stay in a sleeping bag or start a fire.

When I bring the camping equipment into the basement Leroy gives me some crap, "Going to hang up the Indian lifestyle now, Geronimo."

I especially resent the comment because I've admired Native Americans ever since I was a little kid. I like to search the nearby farm fields looking for arrowheads. It helps me to feel connected to the people who once lived in balance with nature here.

I think adolescents had some real advantages in aboriginal cultures. I mean, they got married young and could move out of their parents place quite easily since all they needed was a teepee and some bone utensils. Modern culture is just so friggin' complicated in comparison with jobs and money and leases and insurance and a million other things we consider necessities of life now.

Leroy thinks I romanticize Indians too much. The thing about my dad is, I really do love him. And I think in some way he loves me too, even though he's never told me that. It's just a very problematic relationship. We are totally different people. He was orphaned as a kid and attended the school of hard knocks. He's very practical and kind of survival-oriented. Me, I'm more philosophical and enjoy thinking and reading about stuff that doesn't necessarily have to do with making money or getting by.

It is kind of sad that Leroy and my mom never got to go to college. They started working right out of high school to make ends meet. They are actually pretty smart in a lot of ways. Who knows what other career paths and lives they could have had if they had been given a chance. Education is just not valued as much as it should be in this country. I have friends who are going deeply in debt for college. But not me, not if I can help it. I have an aversion to borrowing money. I think it takes your freedom away. For my generation, debt is the new slavery.

I'm sitting here on my bed in my room now, shooting paperclips into the stuffed mink on my dresser with a rubber band stretched between my thumb and forefinger. I have to admit my mind keeps drifting off, thinking about that Danette chick in bio. I have sort of an obsessive personality and I'm afraid I'm starting to crush on her. That would be a very bad idea, I know, but in this instance I don't seem to be able to control my emotional brain with my thinking brain.

Social pressure is obviously a big factor in my feelings. I mean, I would like to have a girlfriend, a steady girlfriend, in a committed relationship. You know, where I could experience a lot of nice, consensual lovemaking. I'm just a guy after all with a normal sex drive. I walk around campus and there are a zillion attractive, cool girls and I don't seem to be able to make a deep connection with any of them. I feel like the ancient mariner marooned in a doldrums sea of undrinkable brine with an albatross around my neck. Water, water, everywhere, nor any drop to drink.

CHAPTER SIX

I hear water gushing through the roof gutters when my alarm goes off. I look outside and the black sky is pouring grey buckets of rain. This won't stop me from biking to campus. I've become a pretty hardcore environmentalist.

Leroy's old truck slows down as he passes me on the blacktop road to town. He rolls down the window to ask me if I want a ride but I wave him on. I can see him shaking his head through the rear window as he carries on to work.

I have a rain suit. But by the time I get to the Zoology Building there is a stripe of mud up my back from the rear tire and my backpack leaked soaking my lab manual.

Danette ignores me as I sit down and get out my dissecting kit. Our assignment today involves using a bullfrog to experiment with muscle contraction. There is a wire cage in the back of the room containing about 40 live frogs. Their slippery skin is beautifully colored greenish-yellow and the ear discs on the sides of their heads diaphragm in and out as they breathe.

I love science but I'm not comfortable with this particular lab. A student from each table is to go and grab a frog from the cage and pith it, which involves inserting a sharp needle through the rear base of the skull and wiggling it around to destroy the brain. Afterwards the frog remains alive due to respiration through the skin but it has no cerebral control to jump away.

I'm not a particularly religious guy, or an animal protectionist, *per se*, but I liked catching frogs with a net when I was a kid and I do enjoy seeing them in the wild when I go hiking. The idea of killing 40 of them to cut out a rear leg muscle and shock it with electricity bothers me. It seems disrespectful of life.

"Is there any way we could just kill one frog and all of us watch the experiment on that specimen?" I ask the teaching assistant.

"And what would we do with the other 39?" he smirks.

"How about we let them loose in the lagoon by the Art Building?" I reply.

The exchange elicits nervous laughter from the other students. Danette rolls her eyes and looks away. Given no choice in the matter I reluctantly grab one of the slimy skinned amphibians from the cage and insert the needle. My lab partner does not want to touch the poor creature, let alone help me strip the skin off the leg muscle.

I conduct the experiment and record data on graphs in my damp lab manual. I notice Danette does not seem to be observing or writing very much. I glance at her manual and realize, as far as this experiment goes, she doesn't get it. When we finish I just hand her my manual and let her copy down my answers.

I figure she can return the favor by letting me see her lecture notes from the day I got stoned and missed lecture due to being unlucky enough to get the psychotropic drug instead of the placebo in the psych experiment. Besides, Danette misses lecture a lot herself and I always let her copy my own detailed notes. She grudgingly agrees and hands me one page of notebook paper scribbled with vague references and doodles. Wow! That's all she got out of an hour sitting in the lecture hall!

At least it has stopped raining when class ends. I bid farewell to my lab partner and cut through some bushes on the way to my next class. That's when I see him, a thin forlorn figure, soaking wet from a night spent sleeping out in the rain. His unshaved face seems wild and desperate.

It is immediately apparent to me what has happened. Emboldened by their election victory the political party of victorious Candidate #1 has slashed funding for mental health. The psych hospital has been forced by budget cuts to release many of their patients. Everyone around town is talking about it, how an entire population of these folks is living outdoors or in steam tunnels below the street.

A twinge of guilt crosses my mind. Along with a lot of other idealistic people, I had followed my heart and voted for the third-party candidate. Thanks to us Candidate #1 had scored a narrow victory. I resolve to be more practical in elections from now on.

This wide-eyed fellow approaches me earnestly exclaiming that he is hungry. I'm not sure how you feel about street people but I'm always in a quandary about what to do. The guy seems harmless and he probably hasn't had anything to eat for a long time.

It's not like I have a lot of money myself. But I just can't leave him here like this. It's bad enough that he's wet and cold. I reach in my pocket and hand him a five-dollar bill. He seems overjoyed and quickly scampers away after thanking me profusely.

It feels good to strip off my wet clothes when I get home. Mom worries that I will catch my death of cold. Leroy thinks I have gone crazy riding a bike in the rain. My bro' Hondo just smiles. He never criticizes my strange behavior.

"Did you hear about Shoderbeck?" he probes, changing the subject at dinner. I look up from my mom's homemade chop suey and stare at him intently, signaling a high level of cautious interest. I never told my parents that it was the football tackle that broke my nose. But Hondo understands and is cool about it, being careful not to mention that detail.

My bro' proceeds to tell his weird tale. Real life is so strange sometimes that if you put something like this in a fiction novel, people would say it was too unbelievable. I mean, you just can't make s... like this up.

Apparently Shoderbeck got dressed up in a blanket coat like Clint

East Wood in the movie *High Plains Drifter* and went into the *Airliner Bar* smoking one of those Swisher Sweet cigars. After getting plowed on beer the massive athlete started lipping off to some locals and got into a fist fight during which all of his front teeth were knocked out.

Now I wouldn't wish Shoderbeck's horrible fate on anyone. I immediately feel really sorry for him. I honestly do. You have to wonder though if the Hare Krishnas don't have something there when they talk about karma. I guess one takeaway from the story is that no matter how big and tough you are, there is always someone bigger and tougher.

I'm off to my room for homework late into the night. Then, too soon, the heavy metal song set on my alarm blares me awake in the morning. It seems odd pedaling along at bicycle speed on this straight stretch of country road where I used to easily hit 100mph in my muscle car a year ago. Times change, and so do people.

Today there is a different venue for zoology class. We meet in the Museum of Natural history. I'm early so I wander among the displays. My favorite is a cyclorama detailing the tropical shore of Laysan Island, a Hawaiian atoll and avian sanctuary, complete with the pre-recorded sounds of waves crashing and nesting birds chirping. I also like the display of extinct species such as passenger pigeons, but it begs the question: might the species have survived had they not killed the specimens mounted in the display case?

Eventually students arrive, and finally the TA opens his brief and beckons us into Mammal Hall. We assemble in front of an exhibit on primates containing the skeletons of a human and a gorilla. Danette is nowhere to be seen. I figure she probably spaced off all the reminders that we'd have a different meeting place today.

We've been studying evolution in great depth, along with biochemistry and taxonomy. All of us students are beginning to feel like blobs of protoplasm surviving only due to a myriad of chemical and physical processes, any one of which gone astray would lead to our hasty demise. The science is so exact, so factual and so carefully thought through, and proven by so much evidence, it is impossible to deny. Just comparing that gorilla's bones to the human skeleton in front of us, it's pretty obvious we're cousins.

Without consideration of any spiritual dimension to life, all of us freshman are looking pretty grim. The TA is actually fairly perceptive of our plight. I'll have to admit that. Or maybe he's just had lots of experience teaching biology and evolution to freshmen. At any rate he digresses for a moment and addresses the elephant in the room no one is talking about, how science can be a challenge to people's preconceived religious beliefs and paradigms of life. It was nice that he tried to console us, but it really doesn't help a lot. I mean, you don't have to be a genius to comprehend the implications of the scientific facts supporting evolution. If you're honest, you just respect and accept the validity of scientists' work.

Danette finally arrives, a little befuddled at being late, but dressed impeccably as usual. She has a fresh perm, fresh nail polish and the exotic scent of fine perfume precedes her entrance. I swear she wears the most expensive clothes and never the same outfit twice. In contrast, I always wear the same old blue jean pants and jean jacket. I figure denim is the modern equivalent of buckskin.

It is good timing actually because the TA now gives instructions for us to open our lab manuals and work with a partner to answer questions related to each museum display. I feel the press of Danette's cashmere sweater against my shoulder. The glint off her shiny, pearly white incisor teeth gives me pause, a brief mental lapse when I momentarily mistake her for the female alpha wolf in the exhibit on predator/ prey relationships.

Now I'm not naïve enough to believe her pairing up with me is anything beyond her desire to get the assignments done. But I'll tell you when a GILF that outlandishly attractive pays any attention to a guy like me you can't help it, your heart just sort of melts and your grip on reality is temporarily suspended. Might I have a shot at going out with her? "God no," gasp the sane and informed. "Maybe," I think.

The two of us now stand in front of a glass case containing an arctic hare and a desert jack rabbit as I try to explain the relationship between volume, surface area and heat loss. Danette's contact lenses magnify the deep, blue-green eyes that stare blankly back at mine. This is her way of signaling to me that she has absolutely no clue what I'm talking about, without her actually having to admit it. I persevere, pointing out how the arctic hare is built like a round beach ball with stubby legs in order to retain heat while the desert rabbit has a thin body and long legs with giant ears that function to dissipate heat.

After spending way too much time tutoring Danette in the museum I'm forced to part with her or be late for my elective classes. I gather my things and dash through the bushes where the shortcut once again brings me face to face with the homeless man. Over the weeks he has taken on the look of a Norse Viking raider with long, wild, golden hair and an abundant, untrimmed beard.

Short on time I simply hand over the usual Abe Lincoln and continue on. At least I did get a promotion to cook at the pizza parlor. Basically for burning my hands in the "authentic wood fired pizza oven", and freaking out when orders pile up and waitresses chastise me over minor details, in return I receive about 20 cents more per hour. But the evening job is the best I can do. I can't go to classes and at the same time pour cement all day long for Leroy, so that's out.

My electives are *Religion and Human Culture* and the *Philosophies of Man*. By "man" I know they mean "humans" but they really ought to update the course title, it smacks of sexism.

While science classes lack any spiritual component or mystic consideration of the soul, I have to admit, studying religion academically leaves me feeling like its proponents sometimes lack any grounding in factual evidence. But I suppose one needs both rationality and spiritual knowledge to live a balanced life.

Our professor describes religious faith as one's "ultimate concern." I'm not sure how to apply that personally, as my ultimate concerns right now are finding a girlfriend, making good grades and paying off my U-bill.

After class I'm off to the gymnasium to check out the outdoor discovery trip options. One in particular catches my eye: sky diving. I figure when you're young like me that is the ideal time to try new things, even if they sound dangerous or challenging. I mean, if a parachute doesn't open and I die like a Technicolor pancake splattered on the pavement at least I won't leave behind a mortgage, wife and kids.

The notice on the board says, *attendance at required class component mandatory for all sky diving participants.* Naturally there must be some important information to learn before jumping out of an airplane. I sign up.

CHAPTER SEVEN

The clouds begin to spit ice crystals in my face as I pedal home. The narrow tires of the ten-speed just don't cut it on the slippery asphalt. So I rummage around in the garage and dig out the old wide-tire Schwinn Cruiser of my youth. It will have to do for a winter ride until spring.

Leroy and Hondo are off hunting deer with their bow and arrows. Mom is late getting home from work and seems preoccupied and worn out. We sit together in silence at the dinner table eating a hastily prepared, but drive-in quality, delicious meal of hamburgers, French fries and milkshakes.

Looking pale my mother finally breaks the silence, "Your brother's girlfriend is pregnant."

Wow, that one caught me off guard. I knew the high school sweethearts were close and spending a lot of time together but I figured they probably knew enough to use birth control. I look into Mom's tired eyes but don't know what to say and retreat into my room to study. The shelves of natural curiosities seem somehow juvenile to me now, in comparison to the adult issues my brother is facing.

Later that evening something odd happens. There is a phone call on my parent's landline, and it's for me. I never get calls on their number but when I pick up the receiver a soft feminine voice purrs my name. It sounds like Marilyn Monroe, but it can't be, she's dead!

It's Danette! Immediately the gears whirl in my mind. She must have called the university operator. I listed my folk's number as an emergency backup contact when I registered. How exactly the operator ended up giving her the emergency number I don't know. However, I do know what the emergency is. Midterms are two days away and I'm sure she is panicking.

I agree to meet her at the student union tomorrow to study for the zoology exam. But a false hope creeps into my mind. I can't help it. I know damn well she only tolerates me for my lecture notes and that's it. But could there be something else between us? Hope springs eternal. Even when it should just stand down.

Love and relationships have always been a mystery to me. I admit that. Take Danette for instance. She and I have absolutely nothing, zero, zilch, in common. In fact, how could any two people be more polar opposites than us? Yet, I feel a strange, irresistible attraction to her. It's like our bodies are composed of giant chunks of rare earth Neodymium with a force field of 50 Teslas. Sometimes in love, as in magnets, opposites attract. Danette and I are completely and totally opposite in everything, so the attraction seems infinite.

The rational portion of my brain understands that we're incompatible and any serious relationship between us is utterly incomprehensible. I don't want to fall in love with someone who doesn't love me back. I want to form an equal, reciprocal and loving bond with someone nice. But when I'm around Danette, my emotions take over. Deep down I know there are lots of fish in the sea, literally thousands of single women on campus. So why am I crushing on just this one babe, against my own will?

Honestly, I should be looking for a hippie chick, not a rich sorority type. But, unfortunately, hippie chicks are hard to come by these days. Or maybe I could find a Native American girl who loves nature to go out with, or a liberal feminist into peace, truth, justice and equality or any normal, average female person for that matter. These feelings I have for Danette are crazy and I know it. At night I dream I'm back in the driver's seat of my muscle car going faster and faster but the steering wheel falls off so I'm careening out of control and bound to crash.

My thoughts are interrupted when I hear Hondo and Leroy come through the door. I listen to their story about the massive buck that just barely got away. Then I follow Hondo to his room. I'm about to embark on what could be called the "big brother talk."

"I heard Tasha is preggers," I offer my unsolicited advice. "Bro', you need to man up and get married. You're gonna be a father."

Hondo looks sideways, reeling under the pressure. Then replies calmly, "You know there are other options."

I just nod and walk away. It was really none of my damn business. I was kind of forcing my own opinion on him. Now I wonder if I should have just kept my mouth shut.

The wide tires of the Schwinn provide more traction in the snow but the lack of gears makes pedaling up hills horribly difficult. Cars fly by plastering me with slush. But I trudge on one pump of my quadricep muscles at a time and even make it to the student union early.

I stop by the student activities center where the group Free the Environment has its office. I'm a member and we are organizing a recycling drive on campus. I support recycling totally but personally I think we need to go way beyond that.

My own project in the group is a writing campaign to request that vendors reduce the amount of packaging they use in the first place. I've created postcards requesting such a reduction for people to send to manufacturers every time they buy a product packaged in plastic or Styrofoam. My hope is that if companies can see that their customers want to reduce or eliminate waste, that may encourage businesses to act more responsibly.

Am I sure my volunteer project will work? Will it have any impact at all? Could it snowball and become a national campaign? I don't know. But at least I'm trying. Hey, if nothing is done the way things are going someday the earth and ocean are going to be covered by several feet of plastic!

I leave the activities center and mosey down to the student lounge to meet Danette. The bottoms of my slush-covered pants are secured with rubber bands to keep the cuffs from getting caught in my bike chain. I have a cement construction vest on over my jean jacket for warmth and a wool stocking hat holds back my shoulder length hair.

Danette arrives with an encouraging smile. Removing a dressy wool coat, her incredibly tight designer jeans and form fitting t-shirt reveal all her feminine assets. Blazoned across her chest are the words, *Med Techs Do It—Stat!* Her career goal is to become a medical technician. Judging from her performance in science class she has a ways to go. That, or some patients are going to get really weird misdiagnosis someday.

I can't help but notice the perky, perfectly shaped breasts bulging out from under her skin tight med tech t-shirt. It's not that I'm a perv or anything. It's just that they really stick out there and are hard to ignore.

Together, side-by-side, we sit pouring over my lecture notes. Danette's incredibly long, curved fingernails are nearly useless so I turn the pages, being careful to ask when she is ready to move on. Her breath smells like mint as she constantly pops Tic Tacs into her brightly lipsticked mouth. We concentrate so intently on studying the time races by and it is lunchtime. Other students are working their way through the winding cafeteria line.

From my backpack I pull out a bag of dried fruit I got at the health food co-op. I get a discount on groceries there for working 20 hours a month stocking shelves. I offer some to Danette but she turns up her nose and seems repulsed. I shouldn't care, but I can't help feeling rejected.

She saunters over to the vending machines and returns with a snack pack of white crackers and cheese whiz heavily packaged in plastic. I think to myself her selection has zero nutritional value and creates a mini-environmental disaster of wrappers that will end up in some landfill. But I keep my mouth shut.

We make small talk over lunch. I mention that Native Americans used to have a camp just outside the student union along the river. It blows my mind that just 150 years ago none of these campus buildings or roads were here at all, just teepees made of buffalo robes.

Danette chimes in that her great Aunt Ruby was an Indian squaw. I study her strawberry blond hair, blue-green eyes and snow-white skin. I doubt it. We've been studying genetics in zoology and her story defies every principal of heredity.

We finally call it quits mid afternoon. My eyes are strained from studying and I desperately need a break. I feel like I've done everything possible to bring Danette up to speed. And, honestly, I have to admit it helped me master the material to explain it to someone else. Plus, just being around someone as hot looking as her was motivational.

I walk for a bit along the river trying to visualize what the scene was like as an indigenous encampment hundreds of years ago before European settlement. Then I head off to the gymnasium for my parachute class. The instructor introduces himself and immediately outlines his background as a veteran of an army airborne division. This impresses everyone and I have to say gives me confidence that he knows his stuff.

He tells us that the university lacks funding for any of the modern, ram-air, wing-style chutes but, not to worry, he has gone to an army surplus store and procured some of the old, round, hemispherical type of chutes he affectionately refers to as jellyfish. This raises some questions in my mind, but our jumpmaster exudes confidence so I listen quietly.

The old parachutes have not changed since World War Two he explains. In my mind I picture D-Day and the Normandy invasion. These chutes rely on drag by catching the wind in their dome and that air becomes pressurized. Creating strategically placed holes in the rip-stock nylon fabric on one side of the dome allows air to jet out and move the chute in the opposite direction. By adjusting this air jet, the parachutist can maneuver the direction of the fall.

I'm taking all this skydiving information very seriously. I mean, by comparison, in my philosophy class everything seems so speculative. If I miss something the philosophy professor says I may get a question wrong on the test. Here in parachute class, if I miss something, I could crash through someone's roof at terminal velocity and be served pulverized on their dining room table.

Our commando instructor has rented a small plane at a nearby airport. The first thing he will do on jump day is take a streamer up in the plane and drop it out exactly over a large X in the runway lawn that will be our landing target. The streamer is designed to fall at the same rate as a human body with a parachute. So, if the effect of the wind causes the streamer to land on the ground say ¼ mile to the south of the target then he will have us to jump out of the plane ¼ mile north of the target and theoretically we should land on or near the big X.

All the physics of skydiving makes sense to me so far, so I'm feeling confident. In case the wind varies, and we need to make corrections to hit the target, Rambo explains how we can use risers to open and close the holes in one side of the parachute's canopy. Doing so will cause the chute to move right or left. Also, we can open up both holes at once and run with the wind, using the jets to propel us forward. Or, conversely, if it looks like we might overshoot the target we can turn 180 degrees around into the hold position, using the jets to propel us back into the wind.

The guy obviously knows what he is talking about. Further, he explains that we will all be wearing a backup emergency parachute in case our main chute fails to deploy or becomes tangled in a "Mae West." He proceeds to draw a picture on the chalkboard that looks like two big boobs. This is what a Mae West looks like. It happens if one of the parachute lines accidentally gets looped over the top of the dome.

We will be using a static line for our jump, which basically connects us to the plane and automatically pulls open the main chute when we jump out in a spread-eagle position. If the main chute does not deploy, or is a streamer not filled with air, or a Mae West, then we are to pull the capewell devices that detach the main chute, roll over on our back and pull the ripcord on the emergency chute.

At the end of the class we go down to the gymnastics room to practice jumping down onto a mat from a ladder at a height that simulates the impact we will feel when we hit the ground with our parachute. We all learn to tuck and roll out of the fall. I'm good with everything until someone asks what to do if the emergency chute also fails to open. Our captain has the person stand with their arms twisted over their head and legs crossed. We all look perplexed. He laughs and explains that assuming this position will cause our body to turn into the ground like a screw. The group erupts in nervous laughter at his joke.

The instructor continues, "Seriously though, if you want to survive your first jump, just bring me a bottle of Jose Cuervo Gold tequila next week before we head to the airport."

The statement makes me uncomfortable. It is exactly the type of macho posturing that generally precedes death and destruction. I've been in enough football locker rooms and hunting cabins and gearhead garages and pool hall bars to recognize that when you get a bunch of guys together such talk quickly devolves into who can be the most aggressive, bad-ass alpha male with the biggest wiener and somewhere, some innocent people, end up getting bombed.

Fortunately there is one woman in the class. Just having one female in a smoke-filled room can usually moderate raging testosterone. This is one reason I think our country needs more women in political office. We would probably have fewer wars.

Class ends. Everyone leaves. Except for the girl and me. We are looking for a little clarification on that last statement. The instructor just smiles as he carefully packs a parachute.

"Don't worry," he encourages. "The reserve chutes have an AAD, a pyrotechnic device that will blow open the reserve chute at a preset altitude if the descent rate exceeds a maximum speed. If the main parachute doesn't open or malfunctions and is not slowing the descent rate sufficiently the reserve will open automatically. You really don't have to do a thing. I could throw a sack of potatoes out of the airplane with an AAD attached to it and it would make it to the ground safely."

Our concerns allayed I walk back to campus with the freshman girl. Her first name is Cindy but I don't catch her surname. She is petite, very cute and nice. We're feeling confident about the coming adventure and even joke about the perils of skydiving. I'd like to get to know her better and look forward to seeing her again.

CHAPTER EIGHT

Midterms went well. I'm excited to see my zoo score. I venture up to the professor's office where he said he would have our results available. Unbelievably our corrected tests are just placed in a cardboard box outside his locked door. With students' entire lives and careers riding on the outcome of those tests you would think there would be another, more official, method of reporting.

Some of my classmates say that professors at this institution are only concerned with their personal research getting published and that they consider teaching a nuisance. I wonder if that's right as I look through the papers for my test.

I'm overjoyed when I find it. The score is near perfect, setting the top of the grading curve for the class. It's really none of my business, but after I check to see that no one is looking, I dig through the tests looking for Danette's. Her exam is covered with red marks and her grade is an F scoring at the bottom of the class. That makes me sad, but, hey, I tried to help. I really did.

Our next zoology class is surreal. At least half the chairs are empty when the TA begins. I'm wondering why he doesn't wait for the rest of the students to show up. Or maybe there's a flu epidemic or something. Then it hits me. By now all the pre-med students have gotten their scores on life changing midterm exams in zoology, chemistry and physics. The weed-out process is working as planned and students have dropped out in droves.

This is not one of those expensive, private, advanced high school colleges where profs hold your hand. Well over half the freshmen at this state institution drop out before finishing their first year of pre med. I guess they only have so many openings in professional programs so the college has to make a cut somehow.

Since so many students in our class have lost their original lab partner the TA announces that we can all realign. What results is pandemonium, something akin to musical chairs at a child's birthday party. Danette seems drained and doesn't say a word. Of course I don't ask her how she did on her test. But, to her credit, she's still hanging in there. Unlike the others who did poorly, she refused to quit. I admire that.

In the class there is a definite clique of the best students. Many are the children of doctors. I call them gunners. One of these with-it kids is named Chip, the leader of the pack. Chip is short for Charles, a name that suits him better because he is one of those guys who looks about 50ish even though he is a freshman. Chip wears thick glasses, dresses conservatively and is a member of the top fraternity on campus. I have to say, he has an engaging personality and seems like a really nice guy.

Chip approaches me, introduces himself and shakes my hand. Then he explains that a friend, Julia, no longer has a lab partner and he invites me to join their group. I realize that one of the reasons successful people do so well is that they network and associate with like minds. By now the gunners have noticed I'm doing well in class, consider me an asset and want me in their circle.

I glance back over at Danette who has been watching this whole episode transpire. She quickly looks away pretending not to notice. I know I probably should have stayed with her. It was kind of mean to leave, but I had to make a snap decision. Honestly, what sealed the deal for me, was the way that she always rejects me personally.

I agree to be Julia's new lab partner, gather my things and sit down next to her. Julia seems nice. Her brown hair is severely pulled back in a bun, she has black glasses, no make-up, baggy clothes and ... is smart as hell.

I glance around the room. Everyone in class now has a lab partner except one, Danette. Our eyes meet and I just can't describe the forlorn look on her face, a combination of anger, shock, fear and sadness.

As much as I hate to admit it, it does feel kind of good, in a messed up kind of way, to see that she is hurt. I mean, so many times she has hurt my feelings without consequence or caring at all. Deep down I know that you should never try to get back at people. Revenge is worthless. But it's a done deal now and there's a new reality in this class. I anticipate having a much different experience for the second half of the semester.

It's kind of sad really how careless people can be with other people's feelings, myself included. Part of the problem is just the way the world is set up with competition and systems meant to sort people out. I'm usually more careful in how I treat people. This doesn't seem like me at all. Who am I?

Wouldn't you know our lab for the day involves dissecting pregnant rats. Danette looks mortified when the TA grabs one of the huge bulging rodents from a wire cage by the tail and begins to demonstrate the procedure.

The problem is the rat is squirming all over the place when the TA tries to stick a needle in its neck to pith it. What ensues is a horrible, gross battle with the rodent flopping around, flinging blood and urine and feces and nearly escaping.

Everyone begins to groan, expressing doubt and displeasure at the awful mess. The most strident voice in the room comes from Danette who yells, "Come on! There's a right and a wrong way of doing things!"

I sort of doubt she has any actual humanitarian concern for the animal. She just doesn't want to attempt the dissection by herself. In fact, I'm sure she's horrified at the thought of coming anywhere near a lab rat.

The bad scene wears on and students continue to grumble. The sweating TA finally agrees that we can all just watch him perform the operation. He makes a cut with his scalpel down the rodent's swollen belly revealing the ovaries, amniotic sac, placenta and a dozen little kits, or whatever you call rat babies.

Personally, I feel kind of exonerated having complained about the frogs and having suggested a similar demo during the first dissection. I'm sure the other pregnant rats in the cage are happy to live, for another day in Ratville anyway.

After class Danette leaves quickly without a word to me. I'm uncomfortable with what has transpired between us. So I'm not in a good mood cutting through the bushes when I encounter the homeless Viking.

The old man smiles holding out his hand expecting the usual 5 spot without any complications. I know I shouldn't have done it. I'll blame my dark mood. But I hold back demanding to know, "What are you going to do to earn it?"

It's like this. My hands are all burned up from the pizza place. When I'm removing a pan from the oven, if I accidentally get burned on the bottom of my hand, my reflex reaction is to jerk it up, thus burning the top of my hand. Sometimes I get as many as three burns per incident. I'm sick of having to work at that restaurant. On nights when business is slow they have me bussing tables again, so I really don't feel like I have been promoted to cook like the manager promised.

I want to find a new job and have been applying all over the place, but haven't gotten any bites. Jobs are scarce. The country is in a terrible recession thanks to the fascist candidate #1 who won the election and currently resides in the White House. And now this homeless dude just expects me to hand over $5 of my hard-earned money every day.

I know it's not nice or right, but I coarsely repeat the demand, "What are you going to give me for my money?"

The old guy gets a panicked look on his face. I can tell he's thinking really hard, racking his afflicted brain for some answer so he can eat today. But, if you think about it, a homeless dude has no possessions of any value to give. It's really hard to find a job nowadays and being homeless, I'm sure he has little chance.

Finally a squeaky reply pops out of his heavy beard, "I'll tell you the secret of happiness and eternal life."

"For five bucks?" I mumble sarcastically. "This ought to be good."

The old Norseman stoops over and shuffles through the thick undergrowth beckoning me to follow. At first I'm hesitant, reluctant to follow. I mean I'm pretty sure this fellow is a former psychiatric patient after all. They only released him from the asylum because the jerk-ass political party won the election and cut funding for mental health.

But I duck below the branches and eventually come to his makeshift camp hidden deep in the brush, a few extra clothes, rags really, hanging here and there, a large cardboard box I assume he sleeps in and a grocery cart full of random containers and pop cans.

"Welcome to Asgard!" he declares boldly, throwing his arms out wide.

"Ok, here's the deal. I don't have a lot of time," I reply hastily. A discouraging comment I know. I immediately regret it.

The old man's look turns from delight to dejection. But he continues on earnestly, as if he has something truly important to say that is worthy of his daily bread.

"This!" he declares pointing to one of those Mountain Ash trees you see around campus with the bright orange-red berries and yellow fall leaves. "Is Yggdrasil."

"Is what?" I reply, thinking I must have missed something. I don't hear that well anyway due to an accident I had when I was 14. I figure I just didn't understand him correctly.

"Yggdrasil!" he yells as if everyone should know exactly what he is talking about.

Now I figure the odd fellow is probably hallucinating. I want to be understanding and kind but I also have no clinical expertise in counseling people experiencing a break from reality. This whole scene could go south pretty quick. No one can see back in this secluded spot and if this guy is delusional he may pull out a knife and dismember me. They could find my body parts in a dumpster or something.

"Alright! Great!" I speak loud and clear holding my palms out encouraging him to keep his distance. "Thanks for that. Now, I really need to go. I'm late."

He stands his ground, ignoring my comment and continues, "You know you people are always in such a big hurry, going to and fro on your important business. But if you could simply stop for a little while and learn to completely appreciate the beauty of this tree and of nature then you would be truly happy."

I have to admit he has a point there. Most people are in a hectic rush all the time and the material things we acquire do not make us happy, so we work harder and harder to buy more and more stuff. In the end our materialism destroys natural beauty, and the one thing that really could make us happy, is lost.

I fork over the $5 and bid the old king of the rowan farewell. The guy did his best. I figure he earned his lunch.

The following week is fun. My old gearhead pal Eschman goes on vacation and asks me to house sit his place, which is outlandishly cool, a geodesic dome home with a heated swimming pool out by the lake.

Classes are going well, especially zoology, where my brilliant new lab partner Julia makes everything so much easier. No longer am I solely responsible for figuring out every single answer to all the questions in the lab manual. Her notes and data are impeccable. In the evenings, I invite her out to the dome to study. She's impressed to say the least. The bachelor pad is outfitted with top of the line everything —wonderful modern art on the walls, a great sound system and a gourmet kitchen.

Esch has two malamute huskies with wolf-like fur and big translucent blue eyes that we take on walks along the many hiking trails through the snowy woods. The trees look like stick figures planted in the fluffy white drifts, their deciduous branches bereft of leaves.

Esch has no concern for energy conservation, having inherited a ton of Chevron stock he keeps the swimming pool at a toasty temp. So, after removing a plastic bubble cover we run through the chilly night air and dive with a splash, sinking into the comfy pool's liquid warmth. The heat from the glowing blue surface swirls steam up into the starry night sky.

On Sunday I go to the grocery store and splurge, buying Alaskan crab legs and the fixings for twice-baked potatoes. I mean, that's a week's food budget for me. But I know I can compensate by surviving on the contents of Eschman's pantry the other days. Julia comes over and after a candle-light dinner, we watch a date movie, then sit back on the leather couch in front of the wood stove listening to romantic music, interrupted only occasionally by laughter as the huskies pile on top and snuggle us with their moist noses.

Late that night, when it becomes clear Julia is going to stay over, the mood deepens. We become sort of amorous and she gives me that look that means an opening big enough to drive a truck through, if you don't completely blow it by saying or doing something really stupid. I try, I really do, putting my hand on her back and pulling her closer for a kiss. But something is missing. I can't help it. After all the effort to create the ambience of a perfect romantic evening, no matter how hard I try to picture it, something just doesn't click between us.

We quietly pile into her Volvo the next morning and drive back to campus without talking. Zoology class is weird. I now feel kind of awkward around Julia. Fortunately Chip and the other gunners keep up a steady banter of conversation while we work through the next experiment together.

Chip mentions that some of his frat brothers have dropped out and there are openings in his house for new members. He looks right at me when he says it. I don't know why. Finally, he just comes out and asks me directly if I would be interested.

I'm flabbergasted. I mean, I'm about as far away from frat material as you can get. I'd never even consider it. Besides the vast, Grand Canyon of social divide, there is no way I could ever afford living in a Greek house. I can't even pay for a room in a rundown rental in this college town.

I don't know what to say. Chip is a nice guy and it was good of him to reach out and offer, if not really, really strange. All I can think of to answer without offending him is, "A fraternity is a little out of my price range."

"It's not as much as you might think," he comes back on a positive note. "Living in one house with 40 other guys really brings the expenses down. I'll talk to the treasurer and get back to you with some figures."

Danette is still working over there all alone at her table. Her mood seems glum. As far as the lab goes she is obviously lost. But her countenance is fiercely determined. She's like an energizer bunny—she just keeps going and going and never quits.

Occasionally she gives our clique a cool, calculating stare. Not with malicious intent necessarily, but like she's plotting something. I know she's a bit of a conniver. She is someone who knows how to use her assets to manipulate people. It will be interesting to see what she has up her sleeve.

CHAPTER NINE

The day finally comes for our first parachute attempt. The sky is clear and sunny, but there is enough wind that it's borderline whether or not we can jump. All eyes are on our instructor as we gather around him in the gym. He debates the options for a while, then he finally relents.

"Hell, let's just go out to the airport and see what happens."

He has no university van reserved for the day so I hitch a ride with another jumper. He is a burly fellow named Don, simple in speech and manner, dressed in work clothes and sporting a heavy beard.

At the airport we get on our parachutes, goggles and boots. Then we stand around for the longest time while the airplane pilot and instructor debate whether or not it's safe to go up. This makes for some tense moments as we already have butterflies in our stomachs about the first jump. I'm sure we would all feel better psychologically on a calm day without any wind issues. The class could just review safety procedures, then go for it and get it done.

Finally the pilot and jumpmaster approach the class. The pilot has already gone up earlier and dropped a streamer that landed quite a distance downwind from the target. Cindy leans hard against my body for reassurance. She looks nervous. I stare deeply into her eyes for a time to get her full attention, then I briefly put my arm around her shoulder and in the deepest voice I can conjure up, state confidently, "Don't worry, we got this!"

Her brow unfurls and she smiles the most wonderful smile, like a spell has been broken.

"Thanks," is all she says.

"After your chute opens and you stabilize up there, you're going to want to quickly adjust your position left and right with the target and then hold the whole way down," the pilot cautions us.

Indicating that the two in charge had consulted and arrived at the same conclusion, that it's safe to jump as long as everyone follows directions, our instructor reinforces what the pilot just said, "Yes! Listen up! That's important! Today you must hold into the wind the whole way down. Don't mess up. Any questions?"

No one speaks so we all pile into the plane. Cindy stays very close, like she's glued to my side. Sitting next to me I notice she is shaking.

"Everything's good," I reassure her, placing my hand on her knee. I'm definitely going to ask her for her phone number when this jump is over. Then I add, "Just remember to hold."

Cindy nods innocently. After achieving altitude we bank sharply and the pilot looks back into the stripped-down aluminum interior of the aircraft to catch the eye of the jumpmaster who is clipping our static lines overhead.

I know when the pilot cuts the engine and levels off that it's D-Day. I've been thinking about everything we learned in class. Like what would happen if the static line doesn't pull open my chute and I find myself being pulled along through the open air behind the plane.

Obviously the pilot can't land the aircraft dragging along a jumper. I try to mentally picture how, in that emergency, the jumpmaster would come out of the plane, slide down the static line until he reached me, and then cut the line and manually pull out my chute. I glance down at the Kabar knife strapped to our instructor's leg understanding its purpose.

"Ok, time to roll. Arch your back, stabilize, then HOLD!" the jumpmaster yells out over the wind noise. He slaps my back to signal it is time for me to climb out onto the wing supports.

I ride along clutching the metal bar for a few seconds, wind blowing in my face, then take a leap of faith, trusting the equipment and training we've received. There is a sharp powerful shock as the opened chute jerks my body upright out of the spread eagle position. The harness tightens firmly into my waist and crotch. I look up and feel a tremendous relief seeing a perfect jellyfish above me filled with air.

The first thing that strikes me is how incredibly quiet it is up here, just floating along effortlessly with the wind. But I have work to do. I look down searching the boxy landscape below for our target. Once I locate it, I pull the risers to line up my position left and right with the big X on the ground. Then, heeding our instructors' warning, I pull hard on one side to spin the parachute 180 degrees around so I'm facing into the wind. I plan to hold the whole way down unless it looks like I'll fall short.

Everything is set now and I can just enjoy the sensation of gliding down through the atmosphere. Getting a bird's eye view of the world gives me a new perspective of the land and the surrounding farm fields that stretch out as far as I can see, like an endless patchwork quilt of earthy colors.

I remember to look up and check on how Cindy, who was jumping after me, is doing. I'm thrilled to see her parachute is open. But then I notice something odd. Instead of holding, she is turned the wrong way, running with the wind. She's pretty petite, so it's even more important that she hold the whole way down. A lightweight package like her could sail far away, off into the distance.

The ground is coming up under me now. Everything seems to speed up. I remember to roll when my boots hit the ground, then struggle to rein in my chute with the wind pulling on the risers. If worse comes to worse, I know I can release the capewells and let the jellyfish go. But eventually, with some help from others who have already landed, I fold the rip-stop nylon into my arms. I'm kind of proud of how close I came to the target.

I quickly take off my harness and prepare to help Cindy when she hits the ground. But when I look up, I can't spot her. A murmur breaks out among my classmates on the ground. Someone points straight up.

I squint my eyes. There she is, a faint speck high in the sky above the target where she ought to be landing. Someone yells, "Oh no, she's running with the wind instead of holding!"

The airport emergency crew piles into a truck. As I watch her drift away over a horizon of distant farm fields, they take off in search of her. I turn and see Don make a hard landing. With several others I run over to help him bring in his chute.

Don is limping and patting his pockets in search of something. I put my shoulder under his arm to help him walk. He laments about losing his wallet.

"God what a lame move," I think silently to myself. "Why on earth would you bring your wallet on a parachute jump? It's not like there's anything to buy on the way down. You can't stop along the way for a burger and coke. Zipping your ID and medical card into a pocket, that's smart, but leaving your whole wallet in the back pocket of your jeans when you jump out of an airplane?"

I feel really sorry for Don. He's obviously a working-class dude who probably doesn't have a lot of money to spare. I hate it when I can't find my own pocketbook, so I have empathy for his plight. I spend my time now searching the airport field helping his desperate search.

Everyone else is down now and the plane lands, taxiing towards us. The instructor jumps out and runs over to his truck. With a couple of other jumpers he speeds off to join the search for the missing coed.

Don is despondent. Trying to find his wallet is like looking for a needle in a haystack the size of the astrodome. He finally calls off the search. I help him to his car and we drive back to campus leaving the others to collect the equipment and look for the runaway parachute girl.

Life is kind of strange. You meet people, and like comets they come into your orbit for a while. Then they just speed on away, or in the case of Cindy, they float away, and you never see them again.

One day, as I'm walking on campus, I bump into a jumper from parachute class. I learn they found Cindy a half-mile away from the airport, hanging in a tree. I'm relieved to hear that with the help of a fire department ladder truck, she was rescued unharmed.

When I arrive at the next zoology class the TA immediately pulls me aside for a private chat. He explains that one of our class members has no lab partner and asks if I would mind working with her in a group of three. Looks like the sorority sister has had a little talk with him.

"Danette?" I inquire.

"Yes, Danette," he replies, awaiting my answer.

"Hmm ... she's really something," I mumble under my breath, thinking it is too faint for him to hear. But I misjudge the volume due to my hearing loss.

The TA smiles a crooked grin and states nonchalantly, "Yeah, she's a real cutie."

For some reason I'm surprised by his reply. The remark seems odd, or inappropriate, from a teaching assistant. But, then, hey, I think, you know, he's just a guy, and like any other hetero human male, he has to have noticed her charms.

I explain the situation to Julia. She and the rest of the gunners don't seem happy with the new arrangement. But I'm ok with it. I actually felt kind of sorry for the sorority sister. Nobody should have to work alone.

Danette arrives to class decked out in business attire with nylons, high heels, the whole nine yards. The outfit is out there, even for Danette. We sit down at a lab table, Julia and I on one side and Danette facing us cross-legged on the other side. A studious, platonic ménage a trois.

I must have been staring. Julia touches my shoulder and points to the lab manual. We begin discussing the day's experiment. Danette gives Julia a cold look. I'm no expert on interpersonal communications but even I can detect jealousy when it's that intense. In a twisted way, it gives me a feeling of having some new power in the relationship. But, making someone else jealous is a horrible romance strategy, that never leads to any sort of positive outcome or loving relationship.

What ensues in zoology class over the next few weeks is what I would refer to as truly "hands on science." I mean, whenever the opportunity presents itself, Danette has her hands on me!

She affectionately clutches my shoulder when she arrives in lecture or puts her hand on my knee during labs. When we are looking over the manual together, she leans into my body pressing her perky breasts against my arm. Lacking any other excuse to touch me, she picks lint off my sweater, always feigning a provocative smile as her attention eventually ventures down to my pants zipper.

Julia rolls her eyes as she becomes more and more excluded in the trio. I'm basically swept off my feet. It's stupid, I know, but Danette and I spend so much time together studying in the union lounge it feels like there really might be something more between us than just homework.

Finally, I get my courage up to ask her out. I figure the worst that could happen is, she bursts out laughing and says something antisocial like, "Hell no!"

It's after class and we're alone together outside the main archway to the zoo lab. Before she can say goodbye, I interrupt, "Hey, I was wondering if you'd like to go to a movie with me tomorrow night?"

She looks surprised, but doesn't dismiss it out of hand. That's a good sign. I'm familiar with her enough to know the gears are whizzing away in her head as she considers various social factors.

Finally she comes back at me with, "Oh, sorry, I can't. We have an exchange with the Phi Delts tomorrow."

I'm prepared for that answer and continue, "Well the movie I want to see is actually playing at the student *Bijou Theatre* in the union all week. How about the day after tomorrow?"

Now the gears are really grinding as she looks away to concentrate, then comes back with, "Well, it's just a movie."

It surprises me that she doesn't inquire about what movie is playing. But, hey, I'm happy, thinking her answer is a yes.

More gear spinning and she comes out with, "Yeah we'll go to the movie and then..."

I hope she says we'll go back to her place because I have no place of my own. It would be totally beat to take her back to my parent's place on my bicycle.

The uncanny beauty finishes her thought, "Then, next week, we'll study for the final!"

CHAPTER TEN

As you can imagine, I'm flying pretty high the day of the big date. To go out with someone as hot as Danette is a real coup for a guy like me.

So, I'm in a good mood as I take the usual shortcut through the bushes by the Physics Building and, as expected, run into the Viking. I greet him with a handshake and ask him, "How you doing?"

He complains of cold in his bones and having to sleep on the frozen ground. I suggest he go down into the steam tunnels where the other mental patients have taken cover but he declines, saying he needs to stay above ground where he can "read the stars."

When I cash my paychecks, I always ask for some fives so I'm ready for him. It's not like he can make change or anything. He hungrily grabs the Abe Lincoln I offer, thanks me and takes off, disappearing quickly into the underbrush as usual.

I start to continue on my way but suddenly feel a tinge of curiosity. Where is this dude buying food, I wonder? In a snap decision I tag along behind him, at a distance, so he doesn't know I'm following.

Eventually he pops into a QuikTrip. I think that is a bad choice because all the food there is heavily processed and costs several times what you would pay in a grocery.

He emerges from the convenience store with a brown bottle wrapped in a paper bag. I duck into an alley so he won't see me. Then carefully, like a sleuth, follow him back to his Asgard in the bushes.

Before long the old Viking is snoring inside the cardboard box. I remove the paper bag from the bottle that is lying on the ground. As I suspect, it is an empty quart of beer.

I try not to be judgmental as I walk away to the registration building to check out the job board. I've been searching and applying for all kinds of positions for several weeks now, but no luck yet. I've come to hate my gig at the pizza boat. But I have a personal code that I live by and never break; I always find a new job before I quit my old one.

At the end of the day I finish bussing dishes at the pizza joint and hang up my apron. Despite wearing it, I have still gotten some stains on my clothes. But there's no time to change. I hop on the Schwinn and race over to the Chi Omega sorority house.

The Tudor style structure is massive and imposing. At least they have a welcoming bike rack. I run my fingers through my hair and remove the rubber bands holding the cuffs of my worn out jeans. The sturdy wooden door looks like something from an ancient castle. The cast iron knocker makes a loud *thud, thud, thud!*

Eventually a little window opens in the door. I can see a coed staring out. Not knowing what the proper etiquette is I smile, bob my head and wave.

"Can I help you?" the preppy blonde asks, looking suspicious.

"I'm here to meet Danette," I reply, trying to look friendly and harmless.

"Does she know you are coming?"

I detect a note of disbelief in her voice. Like I'm proposing something scientifically impossible.

"Yeah. She does."

"Do you want to come inside and wait?" the sorority sister offers dubiously, opening the door wide enough to eye me head to foot, but then adds, "On second thought, why don't you wait outside and I'll go talk to her."

The heavy door closes with an ominous clank. It seems like I'm waiting here forever. But finally, Danette bursts outside. I notice a small cylinder of pepper spray attached to the keychain she drops into her purse.

Danette has amazing mental radar. She's aware that I noticed the spray and states unemotionally, "I take it wherever I go."

Here's the thing. It is hard for a guy like me to imagine what the world is like for a girl. I mean, I just go wherever the heck I feel like going, day or night. I never really think about being attacked.

"I'm not even sure it would do any good," the beautiful coed continues, looking me straight in the eye, expecting a reaction.

It's our first date. I'm actually pretty nervous. The silence is kind of making me look stupid. I need to say something!

"Well, I suppose you could get a pistol," I blurt out.

That remark is so uncharacteristic of me. That's not what I think at all. Why did I just say that?

Danette actually stops walking for a minute and just stares at me. I'm trying to figure out what she is thinking from her look. Then it occurs to me. To her everyone, including me, is a potential rapist. What I have just suggested to her seems ludicrous, like me proposing something that could potentially get myself shot and killed.

She shakes her head and we continue to walk along toward the student union. I wish there was some way guys like me could communicate to girls that we wouldn't rape anyone. I mean, I wish there was some surefire lie detector or rapist radar app for a phone or something. Sadly, there's not and the unknown really confuses and complicates relationships and the process of getting to know people. The jerks who are sex abusers really do ruin things for everyone.

The Bijou theatre isn't crowded. There are some other couples and small groups of students, mostly alternative types. Danette chooses aisle seats, away from the others. We're a little late since I had to wait for her at the sorority house, so I don't have time to buy us popcorn.

Well, hard to believe, but here we are on our first date. The Bond girl is sitting right next to me. I swivel my head to look over at her, but she just stares straight at the blank screen. I sure hope she likes the movie. It is an anti-war, counter-culture film examining gender roles and the relationship of male upbringing to violence in society. The flick begins with baby boys given toy guns and progresses through scenes of rage in football locker rooms and the dehumanizing indoctrination of military boot camp.

I think the movie is brilliant. It's a smash hit with me. I'd nominate it for an Oscar. I sit engrossed at how well the director has called out macho posturing as a dark force that leads to domestic violence and war. I don't see how anyone can watch this incredible indictment of our culture and not be impacted by the need to change the way boys are raised.

Halfway through the film Danette declares, "OK, that's enough of that!"

She stands straight up and walks out of the theatre! I'm stunned. I rush along to find her. Then we walk along in silence back to the Chi Omega house. I judge by her countenance it is best not to mention what just happened.

Danette finally speaks up when we reach the heavy castle door, "I'll see you in class. Let's plan on studying for the final next week."

The enchanting sorority sister disappears into the dark fortress. I grab my bike from the rack and turn on my safety light. There is plenty of time to think things over on the long trek home under the starry night sky. Obviously the date was a disaster. I wonder, what should I have done differently? A different movie, a romantic comedy maybe? Or dinner and a play at the performing arts center? I don't know. She probably just doesn't want to go out with me at all. Duh!

* * *

The next week I get a call from the local public school district. They want to interview me for a lunchroom/playground supervisor associate position I applied for.

I ride my bike to the brick faced Longfellow Elementary School and report to the office secretary. After a while the principal greets me. He is one of those short hair, business suit type of middle-aged dudes who really gives me the once over. I'm sure my beard and long hair send up red flags for him.

But I like kids and have always volunteered a lot. I coach a little league baseball team in the summer, chaperone scout field trips and do guest speaker talks on rocks and Indian artifacts in the local schools. So I have lots of good references.

The associate job would fit my schedule well because I would only have to work over lunch and recess. The hourly pay wouldn't be much more than the pizza joint, but I badly need a career change. The principal takes down my information, says he has to do a police background check and if I pass that, I can have the job.

* * *

In zoology lab we have been using fruit flies to study genetics. The little insects are way too small to dissect so Danette seems comfortable with the procedure and participates. We use binocular microscopes to examine simple traits like eye color.

The whole unit on sexual reproduction gets me wondering about my own procreative potential. I mean, I hope to have kids of my own someday. Two children would be perfect, hopefully a boy and girl. I don't want a big family because I worry about overpopulation. Professor Drake convinced me of that with his warnings about exponential growth.

I surreptitiously grab a clean microscope slide and cover slip and put them in my pocket. Then I excuse myself for a restroom break. In one of the private stalls I jerk off, which is not difficult after being around Danette. I make sure to get some baby batter on the slide and seal it with the plastic cover slip.

Making sure not to slam the door I sneak undetected back into the science room and put the slide on one of the monocular compound microscopes on the back counter. Focusing down reveals a zillion little sperm guys whipping their tail-like flagellum.

Uh-oh! Julia the brain spots me and wanders back to the counter to see what I'm up to. Julia is perceptive and the scene looks suspicious to her because I'm using a monocular scope that is not called for in the fruit fly lab. I must look guilty or something because she starts grilling me.

"What are you doing?" she pries. "Let me see that."

"They are just tadpoles from a miniature frog," I offer a ridiculous mea culpa.

Julia takes a look in the microscope and bursts out laughing. This draws the attention of Danette, who is not cool with Julia and I yucking it up without her.

Danette strides over to our huddle and demands to know what is going on. Julia slides the microscope over in front of her like a beer stein on a bar counter. I yell, "No," but it's too late.

Danette stares into the eyepiece for a while. It takes her a bit longer than Julia to catch the drift. Then she reacts badly.

"Oh my God, that is so gross!"

I feel a bit defensive. I mean those squiggly little guys look pretty darn virile kicking around in that man chowder. Everyone was half sperm at one time in their lives, right? Even Danette.

But now the commotion has garnered the attention of everyone in the room. I grab the slide and head back to the restroom to rinse it off. I don't want the TA to discover what I've done. Getting kicked out of zoology would be a death knell for my career plan. I don't think I could recover from losing credit for all the work we've done in here this semester.

I return unceremoniously back to the lab and take my seat like nothing happened. Julia gives me a wink. But I don't risk a smile. Danette is deathly serious. Using tweezers we finish sorting out the Drosophila melanogaster identifying genotypes by categorizing phenotypes like vestigial wings.

After class two really weird things happen: first of all Chip approaches me with some numbers on what it would cost to live in his frat house. I'm stunned. The price is much lower than even a crappy room in a run down rental.

"And that includes utilities, 3 meals a day and all social activities," he adds.

"Wow! That's amazing," I finally reply, and then add, "Thanks, but unfortunately, it's just not for me."

"Well, if you change your mind let me know," Chip responds enthusiastically. "The fraternities are all having a special winter rush over break. I think you'd really enjoy it."

The thing is, I'm just not the Greek type. Plus, I don't want to admit to Chip that I can't afford even his generous offer. I'll need all my savings and paychecks to cover tuition and books next semester. I have to say though, I am shocked at how reasonable the price of living in a frat is. I mean, I always assumed it was really expensive and that only kids with rich parents stayed in Greek houses. In reality, it turns out, it's the best housing bargain on campus. Figures rich people found a way to get by paying the least.

The second weird thing that happens after class is that Danette makes a pronouncement indicating that we, meaning her and I, will be studying for the final together tomorrow. Julia interrupts to say that she will meet us at the student union. Then Danette gives her a cold hard stare that could melt steel plate.

"No, I've reserved a private room at the Med Science Library. That's where we'll be studying," Danette announces placing her arm around my shoulder indicating possession.

"Well, I wouldn't want to interrupt anything," Julia responds sarcastically, giving me one of those odd looks that elicit a retort.

But I don't know what to say. I suppose I should have objected and insisted that we all study together at the union. But, honestly, I have to admit I'm intrigued by Danette's arrangement. I mean, it feels kind of good to be an object of desire for once. On top of that, the private study rooms at Med Sci have a reputation as make-out rooms.

CHAPTER ELEVEN

As expected I encounter the freezing Viking on my next shortcut through the brush. He appears more desperate than ever with icicles hanging from his dwarf length beard and a raspy cough that sends a puff of frosty breath into the crisp winter air.

"Are you hungry?" I offer, already knowing the obvious answer. I don't know how any human could see another person in his condition and not have compassion for their plight.

The old man is unable to answer verbally, his voice gone with the ice-cold air. But he shakes his head vigorously, indicating he's famished.

I've been thinking it over and have a plan. I'm no longer going to simply offer him cash. I know now that he will probably just buy alcohol and in these frigid temperatures that will only make his condition worse.

So I encourage him to come along and after much jawboning he does so reluctantly. We walk to the *Hamburger Inn,* a local greasy spoon with excellent comfort food.

"You can order anything you want," I explain, and then add, "Except beer."

He gives me a sly, slightly pissed off look, but then smiles and orders fried chicken with mashed potatoes and gravy. The waitress gives me a knowing wink as Viking man wolfs down the warm food. She doesn't even ask, just hands the bill to me.

After lunch I suggest we go to a homeless shelter run by the Methodist Student Center. I've been doing some research on resources for homeless people in the city and there are opportunities. But the old guy wants nothing to do with it. He thanks me for the meal and scrambles away to his Asgard.

I don't claim to be a trained social worker, or a mental health specialist. That is what people like the old Viking really need. But since the funding has been cut for that kind of service, I'm just trying to do the best I can.

Zoology lab is over for the semester and all that remains is the final. I trudge along toward the Med Sci Library sticking to the sidewalk where the snow has been shoveled and avoid any more short cuts through the drifts.

The black water of the river swirls below me now as I pass over the footbridge to the west side of campus. Near the shore, where the current is slow, ice has piled up in the tall brown cattails. It has become sort of a right of passage for freshman during hot humid summers to jump from this bridge into the deep river water below.

But I have a different history with this place. When I was in high school a kid I knew drowned here. People couldn't figure out why because he was an excellent swimmer, even on the swim team. The boy just jumped in and never came back up to the surface.

I was there watching from the bank when the fire department boats dragged the river and finally pulled him up out of the water. His limp body was tangled up in a trotline someone had put out to catch catfish. Several hooks sunk deep into his flesh prevented him from surfacing.

Life can be cruel. I mean most of the time it's relatively safe to jump from the bridge. You just never expect something like a fishing line or a sunken log or something weird to be waiting there to ambush you.

I see people my age risking it all on snowboards and motorcycles doing all sorts of crazy stunts. The survivor's videos go viral but the unlucky ones in coffins and wheelchairs don't get as much attention. I broke my neck once diving into a shallow lake, so me, I already know I'm not invincible. I don't attempt dumb stunts anymore.

Fortunately the steep stairs by the Nursing Building have been scraped and covered with sand and salt. I won't have to take the long away around to Med Sci. I'm anxious to see how this day plays out. As I near the top I hear the clock chimes from the nearby hospital tower. Now, ordinarily, I love the high-pitched chimes, they make me happy and my nearly deaf ears dance with joy as the high-pitched tones drown out the constant ringing I usually hear.

But this day is different. The chimes now sound like a warning bell that time is running out for me. I know it's crazy but I feel incredible pressure. This could be the last time I ever see Danette, and my crush on her has only grown over time.

I look around and it seems like everyone has a partner. My little brother is getting married and is going to have a kid. My older sister is living in Germany with a corporate executive. It seems like all my friends are dating or forming serious relationships with significant others or getting married and starting families. I don't even have a girl-friend. I feel like a hungry artist lost in a funhouse. I don't want to end up in life an old man, all alone, feeling alienated, maladjusted and unfulfilled.

The stakes seem incredibly high as I enter the massive cement panels that form the Medical Science Library. The Picasso-like, stark, cubist architecture boldly states this is no ordinary place. Medicine is serious business. Life and death dance in the volumes on this library's shelves. I sit quietly on a bench in the foyer waiting for Danette.

When she finally arrives she goes straight to the main desk and secures a key to one of the private study rooms in the basement. She barely acknowledges me as we walk down the stairs. The solid metal door bangs shut behind us and we are now completely and totally alone, deep in the bowels of this giant research center.

We spread out our notes and lab manuals on the empty table and begin to study without small talk. The only interruption comes anytime Danette moves. The jeans she is wearing are so incredibly tight the front snap keeps popping open. It seems to me it must be extremely uncomfortable to wear pants that small. Personally, I like wearing my blue jeans on the baggy side. But then, I'm not exactly the most style conscious person in the world either.

We're making progress. I explain the labs and lectures to Danette and, honestly, re-teaching everything to her helps me master the information as well. Plus, it is a great motivator having someone as gorgeous as the sorority sister sitting inches away from you.

Occasionally I remember the rumor I've heard about the study rooms being a make out venue for lovers. But I look into Danette's eyes and she doesn't seem to be able to read my mind for once. I think maybe I might be blowing my big chance, she seems so comfortable with me now. I could make a move on her. But then my rational brain says, "Hey man, she's just here to study, forget it, don't be a lecher."

Finally, after hours of intense, exhausting concentration Danette stands up signaling a break. She arches her back, stretches her long thin arms behind her, yawns deeply, thrusts out her chest, then her pelvis and her pants unsnap. The latex-tight attire reveals all her feminine assets, like clothes alone are unable to contain her voluptuous body. She nonchalantly snaps the jeans shut as if nothing happened and then pulls a diet coke from her backpack. Sitting back down in her chair she eyes me intently. I figure this is as good a time as any to talk.

I've been wrestling with the future, unsure about what approach to take with her. A big part of me says hang it up. She's just interested in passing zoology. Our only date was a disaster. Move on and find someone who likes you as much as you like them, a reciprocated, egalitarian relationship with someone more compatible.

Then I remember every motivational talk I've ever heard, about pursuing your dreams, finding what you want and going for it and not giving up. There are times when I'm with her that I honestly think she too feels some attraction to me. If I don't give this relationship my best shot, won't I always regret it?

I decide on a course of action and nonchalantly ask her if she has registered for next semester yet. I figure I can find out what courses she is taking and then, when I go to register myself, if I want to pursue the relationship further, I'll try to sign up for one of the same classes she'll be taking. Since she's in a medical track, she has a lot of the same requirements as me. The strategy will provide flexibility and buy me more time to win her over.

Now, I know, I have kind of blocked one thing out of my mind that I'm having trouble dealing with. Over break, Danette thinks her boyfriend is going to give her an engagement ring. He has told her he is getting her "one little thing" for Christmas. If that happens, of course, I need to bail.

For some reason the intuitive young woman now seems oblivious to my plan. She pulls her registration form out of her backpack and starts going through her next semester classes. Most are big lecture hall subjects, like chemistry, that I'd probably rarely see her in. The chances we would wind up in the same lab are infinitesimally small. But two of the classes seem interesting. She slowly pronounces "Parasitology" and "Marksmanship."

Parasitology must be a specialized course for med tech majors on intestinal worms and stuff like that. I figure it would work as a science elective for me. Also the class would be small. Maybe I could end up being her lab partner again.

I don't know what the hell is going on with her registering for a marksmanship class. I must have gotten a confused look when she mentioned that because she follows with an explanation.

"It satisfies my PE requirement and I won't even have to change clothes or shower after class. Plus, my boyfriend is a hunter and I thought it might be fun to go along with him on his hunts."

I find it difficult to picture Danette stalking woodland creatures through the brush in her skin-tight jeans and polished fingernails, but whatever. We return to our studies, cramming as much information into our brains as we can for the final. When the afternoon ends, we have covered all the material.

I find it hard to say goodbye. The thought that I might never see Danette again is disheartening. It really was a thrill to spend some time with her this semester. Then I think of something.

"Are you going to the party after the final?" I spontaneously blurt out.

To celebrate having survived zoology the other students plan on hitting the bars after the test. If Danette goes, this could be another opportunity to see her before winter break. She seems like someone who might like to party, so it's a possibility.

"Yeah, I'll go!" she chimes out. "Meet me by the door after the test and we'll walk there together."

"OK," I reply, then without thinking add, "I'm getting you something for Christmas. I'll bring it."

Danette looks a bit perplexed by that last part.

CHAPTER TWELVE

I park the Schwinn behind the old parochial school putting a bread sack over the seat to keep it clear of ice and snow. The cross on the church next door towers over the city like a sentinel watching over the ant-like souls scurrying below, including me as I head toward downtown.

I saunter across the pedestrian mall, a small but welcome oasis for walkers from the busy traffic, and enter a sporting goods store. Strolling among the fishing rods and hunting attire I finally find what I'm looking for.

I pick out a pair of shooting muffs, protective headgear to prevent hearing damage from gun noise. I know it seems weird but when Danette told me she was going to take a course at the rifle range I just flinched. Most people just don't know what it's like to have hearing loss or tinnitus, both of which can be caused by loud noise such as gunfire.

I don't have much money but this is something I want to give her. I'd hate for her to end up like me. I suppose when you really like someone a lot you just naturally feel a little protective. Anyway, the lady at the register takes my cash and even giftwraps the box for free.

The present goes into my backpack and I cut across the ped mall toward campus where I encounter a small group of anarchist punks. Like the Hare Krishna's they have their own distinctive, superficial adornment with studded leather jackets and spiked hair or Mohawks dyed in florescent colors.

As I pass by, a tall punk with multiple face tattoos and piercings takes a large plastic soft drink cup and hurls it against one of the festively decorated holiday trees that grace the ped mall. I approach the group and inquire as to why he just did that. The punk snarls at me some BS about his anger and resentment at "the establishment."

I walk over to the tree and pick up the littered cup. I'm headed toward the student union anyway and figure I'll just drop the thing off at the student activity center where Free the Environment activists have set up a recycling center.

My finals are all going well. In fact, I'm sure I'm crushing them. Today I have two in a row though, which I dislike. I'd rather have them spread out with more time to recoup and study between tests.

My first test today is in Philosophy class. The final is all essay with lots of writing. Immediately after that I head over to the lecture hall for zoology, a final exam I know will be challenging. The competition in that course is fierce so the instructors are forced to create complex questions to sort people out.

It's pretty bizarre how your brain can pick out something you love from a zillion other things. The enormous lecture hall is shaped like a giant fruit bowl now jam filled with students waiting to take the zoo final. I enter the arena with my head still spinning full of Socrates, Voltaire, Kant, Locke and Rousseau from the Philosophy test. But my eyes immediately and instinctively pick Danette out from the enormous crowd in a millisecond.

She is surrounded, so I find a vacant seat toward the back and try to refocus. The professor and TA's march in, give some instructions and start handing out the tests. I should have sat up front, it's hard for me to hear the instructions in the back and we are the last to receive our tests—precious minutes lost while others have already started their exams.

I grind through the test and I'm solid on most of the questions until I get to the section on genetics toward the end. The foils are complicated, like those Mensa quizzes you see in the back of magazines. Ordinarily I would enjoy the challenge. I've always been a good test taker. But now, I'm pretty exhausted.

People are starting to leave. Danette is one of the last to go. I see her disappear into the foyer in her brand-new ski jacket. I finish abruptly, knowing I got a solid grade, but no way will I be setting the curve this time. I could have done better, but between not wanting to miss her and having two finals in a row, my brain is kind of fried.

There she is waiting in all her Vogue glory. Frankly, I'm a little nervous. For the first time since I started college, I actually fretted this morning about what I should wear. I picked out a nice striped shirt and newer jeans, but have on my old lined jean jacket for protection from the cold.

"How'd it go?" I ask tentatively, trying to be upbeat. I'm sure she struggled.

"Well, it's over," Danette rolls her glistening eyes. She wears contacts and I think the devices magnify her irises. Sort of like French high society ladies once used Bella Donna to create the desired big-eyed effect. Then Danette adds, "And I survived."

I have to hand it to her. She did hang in there through some tough times. But I wonder if she will get a passing grade? It would be a shame if she went through all that work and ended up flunking out and not getting any credit.

We walk together through the snowy night toward downtown where all the student bars and restaurants are located. I figure we'll go to Joe's Place, where most of the zoo students will be reveling late into the evening. But in a totally unexpected shift, she wants to go to a different establishment, a quiet lounge frequented more by fraternity business major types.

We end up at a table all by ourselves. She removes her coat revealing a lacey shirt and bright greenish blue Malachite necklace that perfectly matches her glowing eyes. I remove my jean jacket and for some reason notice a loose thread on her blouse. Even the smallest flaw is uncharacteristic of the supermodel. I guess that's why I noticed, it seemed out of place.

For some reason my mind wanders back to the last day of zoology lab. The professor had a saltwater tank flown in from California containing the contents of a tidal pool. Students got to examine and hold all sorts of ocean creatures including starfish, sea cucumbers and clams. Some were still alive, but many had not made the long trip.

It was cool to see all that marine organism stuff, but I thought that lab was a horrible idea. I mean, I asked the TA what they were going to do with all the specimens after class and he wearily admitted they just threw the whole assembly into a dumpster. All that life expended just so we could get to see, and hold, some members of different Phylum.

I feel a little like a sea squirt out of the ocean myself sitting here in this swanky bar. I'm not in my natural habitat. Danette, of course, is right at home, in her element, smiling and laughing. She seems happy, but in a cruel sort of way. Gregarious, yet cold as ice.

The waitress comes and takes our order. Danette gets a Heineken. And I know what you think. That I start drinking pitchers and get into a bar fight or end up swinging from a crystal chandelier. Give me a break. I may be obsessive, addictive, quirky, and even a little crazy. I'm definitely not normal. But I'm not totally stupid either. I order a coke with ice. That raises her eyebrow, but elicits no comment.

We talk about plans for the break. Danette is headed home tomorrow in her Camaro. I don't have a lot to say, just mention my new job as a playground lunchroom supervisor.

"I've got some other leads too." I try to sound positive and responsible.

Jobs aren't too much of a consideration for the beauty queen. With a rich old man she doesn't have to worry. She can get all decked out and arrive in style.

"I got something for you," I remark, grabbing the gift from my backpack.

Danette looks at me curiously. They did a good job wrapping the present at the store. It has an official holiday ambiance. She unwraps the noise protection devices and gets a confused look. I think she thinks they're plastic earmuffs or something. A serious fashion faux pas.

"They'll protect your hearing. I thought you could use them in your marksmanship class. Or when you practice shooting, before you go hunting."

Danette gets it now. She smiles. Honestly, I think she's relieved that I didn't get her anything weirder.

I'm taken aback when she grabs her own backpack from the floor. It has a button pinned on it. I cringe thinking it may be leftover from the election. If it's a campaign button for the fascist jerk in the White House I'm going to gag.

Closer examination reveals the button's proclamation, *I'm a cuddler*. I find this saying interesting. She apparently wants people to know she likes to cuddle. That's nice. But with whom? Her boyfriend? You have to figure Danette is a pretty selective cuddler.

To my surprise out of her pack comes a hastily wrapped gift. She slides it across the table to me. Wow! I didn't see that coming.

I unwrap the gift paper saving it for reuse. My motto: Reduce, Reuse, Recycle. Inside is a book entitled, *Orienteering: How to find Your Way in the Wilderness*. I suppose by now she has noticed I'm an outdoors nature boy. I thank her and thumb through the book to look appreciative. Inside she has included a studio picture portrait of herself. She's a real stunner all right.

Fumbling around I notice she has written something on the back of the photo: *I hope you have found the friend in me that I have found in you.*

Now, to most women, that sounds like a really nice message. But you have to realize that to a guy in love "friend" is the dreaded "F" word. It is code for "I don't find you suitable for a life partner but we can have a casual platonic relationship sometime."

I try not to show any emotion as the sorority sister is staring at me very intently now. I just thank her again and lean back in my chair trying to look cool and collected. We spend some time making small talk about school and studying and stuff like that. Later the waitress comes but Danette doesn't order anything else. I guess she really did just want to go out for "a beer."

It seems like time to part ways now. I should have left everything like it was. But I get to thinking again about whether or not to pursue the relationship any further. I just can't let go. I don't want to be just a friend. I want to be with her forever.

Now I do something really stupid. And I'm not even drunk. I'm just being totally honest. I sort of look her deeply in the eyes and say it, right out loud.

"I really like you a lot."

She sits so still. The only way I can describe it is, she turns into a pure white marble statue. She says absolutely nothing, just stares at me.

I don't know what to do. I'm, like, sitting here, like, "What?" She not only isn't saying anything, she isn't even breathing. Finally I feel compelled to break the silence.

"I guess, I mean, I love you."

Well that was obviously the wrong thing to say, a huge mistake. That saying you always hear about how honesty is the best policy, well, really, honesty isn't ALWAYS the best policy. If you're walking down the street and see someone who is overweight you could tell them they're fat. I mean, that would be true, right? But in this world you have to exercise not just honesty, but discretion.

All I'm getting from the marble statue is a cold stare. I get the feeling she would like to stab me and cut me up into little pieces. This is probably one of the weirdest spiritual experiences I have ever had, to see that kind of reaction, almost cruel or inhuman hatred.

I feel really embarrassed. I don't know what to do or say. I start to get up. She finally flinches. In a rather blunt way I request that she not ever tell anyone I just said that. Her face cracks a crooked smile giving me an evil look.

"I led you on a bit," she laughs, flippantly with a snarky smirk.

I may have my faults. I admit I'm socially inept. But one thing about me: I don't like using people. It gives me the creeps when people do that.

"Ok, bye," is all I say. Then I stand up, grab my things and walk out into the cold night air. It feels warm in comparison to Danette's stare. I know now I'm not going to try to register for any of the course sections Danette will be taking next semester. At least I have some closure knowing I'll never see her again.

CHAPTER THIRTEEN

Hard to believe I have two semesters of college done now. My freshman year is over and I'm officially a sophomore. My grade transcript came in the mail and I got top marks. So, I should be flying high, but to tell you the truth, I feel pretty depressed.

The university has gone on its month-long winter break and most of the students have left town. The snow is over a foot deep outside and the wind is howling. With nothing else to do I've been bundling up in my warmest clothes and walking Leroy's dog so much we have a trail beaten through the drifts in the woods. Leroy loves it when I walk his retriever. He's crazy about that hunting dog and wants it to get plenty of exercise. So at least Leroy and his dog are happy.

I suppose part of my problem is just plain old cabin fever. The wind chill outside is brutal. The roads are covered with a sheet of ice so riding my bike anywhere is impossible. I'd be better off ice-skating to town. There is nothing happening out here in the country. I try reading and watching TV but it gets boring.

I have to admit my deep funk is not all about the weather and isolation though. Mostly I feel really sad about my own social failure and inability to form a caring relationship with a significant other. The whole episode with Danette has me feeling like a total loser.

I know it's impossible for some people to understand this feeling of rejection and despair. They marry their high school sweetheart and never struggle with romantic relationship failures. So they can't relate.

On the flip side, according to Shakespeare, *The course of true love never did run smooth*. So I suppose the "I married my high school sweetheart" thing may not be all it's cracked up to be either. There has to be some spiritual deficit in never having your heart broken. And if you don't search and meet lots of people, how will you ever know you found your true love?

I just keep running the whole Danette scenario over and over again in mind. WTF was I thinking? I knew the whole time she was only interested in me as a study partner. I knew she already had a boyfriend. I should be looking for someone different, someone who feels the same way about me that I feel about them. Why couldn't I control my own thoughts and emotions? What's wrong with me?

I probably should have stuck with Julia. She was so smart and nice and honest. Why didn't I feel a romantic attraction to her? Honestly, I think I have low self-esteem. It's like I would never go out with someone who would stoop so low as to go out with me. Will I always want what I can't have?

These thoughts are psychologically devastating. I feel frustrated, confused, anxious and depressed. I should be more positive. I got good grades. It's true I fell head over heels for the sorority sister but, hey, there are a lot of fish in the sea, right? I just need to be patient. You can't hurry love. The problem is, I can't see these positives through the fog of regret.

I think I need help. I need to talk to someone. But there's no one around here I can rap with. Instead, I start listening to my old pop rock albums. Now, if you are ever heartbroken, I can tell you this with 100% certainty: DO NOT listen to break up songs. Rock musicians aren't trained in counseling and they give terrible advice. The whole "I'll die without this one particular person in my life" thing is fatalistic and to be avoided at all costs.

I lay down on my parent's flowered sofa in the living room. Bright sunlight pours in on my head from the picture window. Mentally and spiritually I cannot handle what is happening in my life. Honestly, I feel like I'm dying of sadness and grief. I fall into a deep sleep, even though it is early in the afternoon.

I dream that I die. I see Leroy and my brother spreading my ashes on an overlook deep in the woods where I always like to sit and meditate watching the sun go down. I can barely make out their faces, but can tell they are grief stricken.

I wake up with a start. I really do feel like I just died in some way. It's an eerie feeling. Like I'm now a different person, or at least a new version of me. When you are an endangered species you have no choice but to adapt and change, or you will go extinct.

I pick up the phone and dial the student counseling number. A sympathetic woman answers. I tell her I'm depressed and unhappy. She asks if I'm suicidal. I answer that I don't know. She says they aren't busy right now as most all the students are gone for break. They can get me right in.

I'm somber as I take a shower and get dressed. With flat affect I tell Leroy I'm going to town for something. He throws me the key to his work truck.

"Here take this. You can't ride your bike on that ice!"

The old me feels like an environmental traitor. I had sworn off the internal combustion engine forever. The new me says, "Hey, this is a survival situation. You have to do this if you want to live. Quit being so hardcore."

I swear the psychologist at the mental health center is a dead ringer for Sigmund Freud. We sit in comfortable stuffed chairs by a fireplace. He asks questions. I'm in no position to be evasive. I just spill everything, even my deepest, most personal thoughts. I look at him for reaction but he never seems phased by anything I say. He smiles knowingly, like he has heard it all before.

It doesn't hurt that the conversation drifts to politics. Of course, with all the cuts in mental health services, the old shrink really dislikes the prick in the White House. We have that in common, and it helps me gain even more trust in him.

By the time I leave I'm feeling a lot better. I set an appointment for next week. Both Sigmund and the receptionist emphasize that I can call, or drop in, anytime if an emergency arises. Their concern and availability gives me confidence that I can handle this.

If you are ever feeling really down, don't give up. It's always darkest before the dawn. The universe contains equal amounts of both positive and negative particles. After the world screws you over for a while, things have to change for the better, just to balance out. The tide will always turn.

I park the old truck in the drive. Mom is frying fat steaks from a champion steer Leroy bought at the 4H Fair last summer. Leroy loves steak. Business was good this year. We got a lot of cement foundations poured. Leroy is packing a positive attitude and a wad of cash.

"Hey, there was a letter for you in the mail today from the university," Leroy grunts as he heaps mashed potatoes onto his plate, next to a juicy T-bone.

This seems odd to me. I already got my grade transcript. I shouldn't be getting a u-bill for next semester yet. Why would the college send me a letter? What gives?

I open the official looking envelope, checking and rechecking to make sure it's addressed to me. Inside, on university letterhead, is a message from the Dean of Students congratulating me on my grade point average. Then a huge kicker, I have now qualified for an honors scholarship that will pay for all my tuition next semester.

In an instant I have gone from barely scraping by, to being suddenly flush with cash. But I'm not going to spend the money I've saved for tuition like a drunken cowboy in Las Vegas on a Saturday night. I need to think over the future possibilities carefully now that I have new options.

* * *

Phildo and Hatchet Jack from Leroy's shop have started a new business venture and ask me to join up. We drive around the industrial section of town shoveling the deep snow off of buildings so the roofs do not cave in from the weight.

The work is dangerous and backbreaking. The roofs are packed with heavy snow and ice. It's slippery up here and we occasionally fall down and nearly slide off roofs.

After a week of shoveling my spine hurts so bad I walk stooped over and in pain. But the businesses, and their insurance companies, are willing to pay big bucks to avoid catastrophic roof failure. My bank account grows like slime mold on warm broth.

I get a phone call on my parents' landline. I know before answering it is someone who called the university operator for my contact number. I don't know why, for some reason they give callers my parent's line. Hearing Danette's soft feminine voice would be too weird. Instead, I recognize Chip's cheerful tone.

"So do you want to come to winter rush?" he inquires.

Ordinarily I would dismiss this invitation out of hand. I'm not frat boy material. But on the other hand, I want to move out of my parents' place and with the money I made pouring cement all summer, and now a tuition scholarship, I can afford the frat house.

You know, the old me would have said no. But I'm no longer that person. I really liked who I was. The nature boy was a really decent kid with lofty ideals, and that will always be a part of me. Maybe that was the best version of me there ever will be. But I had no choice. That version of me was not succeeding socially or leading to happiness. I had to change and evolve. It was a matter of survival.

"Well it wouldn't hurt to check it out," I reply, wondering what the hell I'm getting myself into. Then I think out loud, "I can always say no."

"Absolutely," Chip barks, sounding happier than a puppy turned loose in a meadow. "Meet me at the Phi Psi house on the 30th at 7:30PM."

Ordinarily by now, my parent's indoor Christmas tree is surrounded by presents. I say indoor tree because Leroy also buys a second Christmas tree that he puts on the back porch so mom can cover it with cranberry and popcorn chains for the birds. But this year, the indoor tree gracing the living room is deserted, with only a handful of gifts, most of which are from Hondo and I to our parents.

I'm kind of suspicious, but don't say much. You know, I could understand if it was a bad year or something and my parents didn't have much money and needed to cut back. But Leroy is flush with cash. What's shakin'?

It's not like my parents usually get me expensive gifts anyway. Mostly new socks, a sweater, maybe some binoculars or other outdoor gear. But this year, as we gather in the living room for Christmas, no presents from my parents have appeared under the tree.

I'm munching on some heavily frosted sugar cookies. I give Hondo a look. He shrugs his shoulders. We give our gifts to Mom and Dad. Nothing fancy. A new hat, insulated hunting gloves and a flannel shirt for my dad. Mom gets new pajamas and some kitchenware. Both of them have weird smiles on their faces.

"Well you probably know we had a good year at the shop," Leroy begins, talking slowly. "And this year is our wedding anniversary."

"We've decided to fly to Hawaii for two weeks!" Mom blurts out, unable to contain herself.

"Great," I think to myself. "They had a good year and decided to fly themselves to Hawaii instead of getting us any presents."

CHAPTER FOURTEEN

So I'm sitting here in the living room with Hondo on Christmas Eve feeling weirded out. There are no gifts for us under the tree and my blue-collar parents, who usually scrimp and save, have just announced that they are flying to Hawaii for two weeks!

Not knowing what to say I comment, "Well that's nice. Congratulations. When are you leaving?"

"Not until March," Leroy adds smiling widely.

"What you waiting for?" I question. "That's not your wedding anniversary date."

Without a word Leroy hands Hondo and I each an envelope. I look at Hondo. He shrugs like he doesn't get it either. I rip open the envelope and inside is an airline ticket with my name on it—destination Honolulu, Hawaii. I can't believe my eyes.

"We're flying Hondo and his fiancé over the first week. Then you and your sister are joining us the second week," Leroy pronounces proudly. "We planned it so you can come over during university spring break."

I thank my mom with a hug and give Leroy a firm handshake. Frankly I'm overjoyed. I've never been off the mainland before except to go deep sea fishing with Leroy in Florida. Suddenly my life is looking up. This trip will be fun. The only downside, all the effort I put into riding my bike and walking to reduce my carbon footprint will be negated by that one flight. Oh well, I can't exactly turn down the gift.

* * *

The Phi Psi house looks like a southern mansion with huge pillars out front as I approach for the party. Inside the place is appointed with expensive leather furniture and an annual member composite hangs over the mantel above a massive stone fireplace.

The parlor is packed with preppy looking guys, short hair, well dressed, making snappy jokes. Pretty looking coeds mingle about laughing and sipping beer from paper cups.

I feel a little self-conscious. Everyone in the room is wearing the same brand of designer pants and polo shirts with the same little embroidered emblem over the heart. They're even wearing the same style of boat shoes. Me, I have on my old jeans, a plaid shirt and snow boots.

I'm just sort of standing here all alone feeling uncomfortable. I don't know a soul in this place. I wish Chip would show up. A cute coed in a bright yellow sweater wanders up to me and gives me a quizzical look.

"I'm from Winnetka!" she chirps. "Where are you from?"

I recognize that neighborhood she is speaking of as one of the richest in the Midwest, a lakeside suburb of Chicago.

"I'm from Ford Heights," I reply sarcastically, watching for her reaction.

Sure enough she crinkles up her nose and walks away. I really shouldn't do stuff like that. She was just being friendly and I really yanked her chain to cite a poor area like that on the south side. I just couldn't help it. It's the old political progressive in me popping up again. You know, the old me who disliked it when students asked you where you were from in order to determine your social status. I need to relax and play the game if I'm serious about moving into a frat house.

Finally I hear Chip yell my name from across the room. This causes a lot of people to look my way. I cringe and make a little wave back. I wish he would hurry up and get his buns over here.

Chip arrives offering a paper cup of beer. I accept the cup and pretend to drink, but secretly don't actually swallow any of the brew. The frat boy Chip is so gregarious and cheerful I just naturally begin to lighten up.

Soon he is introducing me to some really hot chicks he calls his "little sisters." I figure this eye candy is here to impress the new recruits. I'm nicer this time talking about our college majors and stuff like that. They seem slightly more accepting when I mention that I'm pre-med.

Chips tosses in an endorsement for me, "He was, like, at the top of the class in zoo!"

"Well for a while," I add, to get it straight. "Until that killer final anyway."

The cuties wander off. Chip gives them a rather incestuous stare, considering they are his "little sisters."

"We have girls like that hanging around our house all the time!" Chip brags.

"Wow!" I speak loudly. The music has been turned up. It's a great song but with my damaged ears I'm having trouble hearing the conversation.

"Well I better go," I exclaim rather suddenly. It's kind of embarrassing not being able to understand people when they are talking to you. I better Audi out of here. I can only read lips so well.

"Tomorrow is winter rush," I decipher from the movement of Chip's mouth. "All the houses will be open in the afternoon. You should check them out."

I get a call in the morning from the director of transportation for the city schools. He wants me to come in right away for an interview about a bus driver position.

At the interview the bus director is friendly. He knows Leroy somehow. He tells me he's desperate to find drivers. I express my doubts. I mean, I'm used to driving big trucks at Leroy's shop so I know I can handle the buses. I'm just not sure how I could fit another job into my already busy class schedule. I've already agreed to the lunchroom playground supervisor position at one of the elementary schools.

"No worries!" the director encourages me with a nod and a wink. It seems this fellow knows someone in the registration department at the university. He can get me into any class and section I need. It always amazes me how these things work in life. Like who you know and their insider connections can get certain favors to grease the skids.

I would need to get up super early and be at the bus barn before 6AM every school day to drive a regular route, which takes a couple of hours. Then I'd have to hurry back to the campus for a couple of classes before I need to be at the elementary school from 11AM to 1PM to watch the students at lunch and recess. After that I'd get in a couple more classes at the college and at 3PM, be back at the bus barn to drive the students home. To top it off, the director tells me I can volunteer in the evening to drive sports teams to their games, if I want for extra pay.

The fellow is so enthusiastic I agree. But honestly, I'm not sure how the heck I'm going to be able to fit everything in. There is no way I can get to work and back to classes in time riding a bike. Even Lance Armstrong couldn't pull it off. But it will help that I can register for any class I want. Ordinarily students like me have to struggle to get into class sections and usually you end up with rotten times or classes that aren't your first choice. Not any more. I've got an inside connection now.

After taking a competency test that includes maneuvering a bulky school bus over a road course and proving I can park the thing, I leave the bus barn pondering how I'm going to fit everything into my schedule. I end up downtown at Stan's Barber Shop. A gregarious hair stylist named Tom snips off all my long locks of hair and gives me a shave with one of those incredibly sharp steel razors honed on a leather strap.

Next I pop into a popular men's clothing store and pick out a couple of colorful sports shirts with the logo I saw at the Phi Psi party. I try on some designer jeans, and select a size that fits a little snugger than I usually wear. A pair of boat deck shoes and I'm ready to check out.

They say, "When in Rome, do as the Romans." I guess the same principle applies to fraternities—when in Greece do as the Grecians. I figure I need to play the game a bit more if I'm going to live with 40 of these guys.

At home I get dressed. My mom says she does not recognize me anymore. I look in the mirror. I don't recognize me either. Who is that prepster staring back at me? He looks like a frat rat!

I make a list of all the fraternity houses on campus. I haven't totally bought into this whole Greek thing yet and I doubt I ever will. I walk around feeling like an undercover agent secretly posing as a new pledge as I walk up to each house and knock on the doors.

The reserved old Greek houses have a lot in common, always a central meeting room with lots of cozy furniture and composites hanging on the walls. You really get a sense of tradition and a feeling that a lot of history (and parties) took place within the walls.

With my new duds I look the part, so mixing with the Greeks is fairly easy now. Each house has a bevy of attractive looking girls hanging out. I ask a frat boy how they manage to round up only good-looking females.

"We send out invitations to be little sisters," he smiles. "Then a whole bunch of girls show up and we throw out the rags."

"So you only invite back the girls who are physically attractive?" I solicit clarification. He looks at me like I'm completely out of it that I don't already know this.

"Man, that's fucked up!" I blurt out, without thinking.

The frat boy gives me an angry look. Oh well, I'll scratch his frat off my list of possibilities. I head out the door and on to the next house.

I feel like an actor in a movie playing the role of new pledge. The Greeks are welcoming, but a little condescending. I suppose until you're officially initiated, they don't really consider you one of them. It is an attitude I don't appreciate, but tolerate for now.

I have to admit it is nice socializing with new people and being introduced to lots of cute girls. At the Pike House I meet a gorgeous

Chi Omega. This could be interesting. I try not to seem too anxious as I carefully pump her for information.

"I had a Chi Omega in my zoology class," I mention nonchalantly. "Her name was Danette."

"Oh yeah, Danette, she's a Neophyte. Bid last fall."

"I wonder if she'll be moving out of your house now that she's getting married?" I drop the bomb.

Everything is casual. The Chi Omega soror just keeps talking like everyone is best buddies or something in the Greek world.

"Oh no! You didn't hear? Her boyfriend was two-timing her. They broke up over Christmas."

"That's awful!" I feign dismay, my mouth agape. But deep inside I have to admit hearing that Danette didn't get a ring strikes me as kind of righteous in an ironic sort of way. Looks like that "one little thing" Danette's boyfriend promised her for Christmas turned out to be just that: one little thing. Probably one little stuffed animal for her to cuddle.

CHAPTER FIFTEEN

After visiting about 15 different frat houses I decided to join the Kappa house. The Phi Psi scene was just a little too hoity-toity for me. I liked Chip but didn't think I would ever fit in with the other members.

At first I had dismissed the Kappa house and nearly skipped visiting there because it had a reputation on campus for the wildest parties. But when I actually met the members they seemed pretty laid back. Some of the brothers actually had jobs and weren't just living off their parents.

My own parents took the news that I would be moving out in stride. Mom looked a little sad. Leroy didn't say much. Me, I just sat down with a city map to figure out some way to get to my jobs and classes on time.

I traced out the route I would need to take from the Kappa house to the school bus barn back to campus to the elementary school, back to campus to the bus barn and then home again to the frat house. It looked like a spider web! There is no way I can make it work riding my bike.

A solution arrives when I hear Hondo is moving out too. He and his fiancé are getting a loan to buy a trailer. Since they are going to be starting a family, and will soon have a little ankle biter crawling around, they need some practical transportation, like a boring 4-door sedan or minivan. So Hondo wants to sell his little sports car.

I always thought his car was a cool ride. It has a 4-speed shift and removable top. Of course I feel like I'm selling out on my environmentalist ideals buying a car. But at least it's lightweight and gets good mileage. I don't really have much choice. I'm old enough, I need to earn my own living and be out of my parents' nest. I've taken the only jobs that were available and in order to make it to class and work on time, I need wheels.

Since my tuition bill will now be covered by the scholarship, I use some of the money I was saving for tuition to pay Hondo in cash for the car. I pay cash for everything. I'm allergic to loans. Next I go ahead and use the rest of my savings to pay for a whole semester at the Kappa house.

I always thought fraternities and sororities were very expensive since many of the members put on an elitist air. But it turns out the Greek houses are one of the few bargains left in housing for students. Having 40 people live in one house and share all the expenses really reduces the cost.

My bank account is empty again but at least my tuition is taken care of with the scholarship, I have a place to stay with meals for the next semester, and I have transportation to get to my two new jobs where I can earn more spending money.

It seems like a good idea to make a clean break with my parents so I get busy emptying out my room. I only pack my new duds and the bare essentials I need into the convertible. Everything else has to go. I mean everything.

It's tough too, parting with things you've had from way back when you were a kid. I've been collecting rocks, seashells and Indian artifacts since I was 5 years old. I donate my entire collections to the elementary school for their teaching units on Indians, earth science and the ocean.

I hike out into the woods and throw a particularly beautiful agate, my favorite rock, into the creek where I discovered it. The massive antlers on my wall I leave in a little timbered valley, the exact place I'd found the deer years ago. My stuffed mink I donate to the Natural History Museum.

All my unfashionable old clothes go to Goodwill. School papers get recycled. I take the trophy I won as a member of the city championship basketball team apart and recycle the metal. Before long my room is bare. All that remains is some hunting equipment in the garage that I sell off with an ad in the local shopper.

A Vietnam Veteran buys my old shotgun. He tells me stories about 'Nam for about an hour when he comes to pick it up. I tell him I don't plan on ever joining the military, but if I did, I'd want to be a medic because I wouldn't want to hurt anybody. I was worried he might laugh or make fun at me, but instead he seems to respect my view. He even says a medic is worth a whole squad as far as he is concerned.

I sell my bicycle to Beevo, an old gearhead friend from high school who is transitioning away from fossil fuels. The last thing to go is my fishing rod. Leroy gets kind of upset, what with me selling everything I own, and he insists that he wants to buy the rod. I tell him I'll just give it to him if he wants it but he forces a twenty-dollar bill into my hand. That's the only money I ever got from him for college.

I have to admit it's kind of tough parting with all my stuff. I feel a little uneasy, even scared, like I'm headed into a strange new world. But it is also exciting and liberating. The last thing I pack into the sports car is a box of fireworks from years ago. You can't exactly donate those to Goodwill. So I developed a plan on how to use the pyrotechnics later. I kiss my mom, shake Leroy's hand and drive over to the Kappa house.

It is just so incredible being in the fraternity. I've been wanting to move out and be on my own for, like, ever, but was always held back by lack of money. Now, here I am!

The social aspect of living with 40 other guys and having lots of girls hanging around is awesome. Basically there are two groups of members here, the rich kids and the middle class working types like me. I meet Jeffery, a mild mannered prepster whose dad is vice president at IBM. Also Joe, whose dad is a union ironworker. Joe's brother works for a progressive senator from our state. I find the diversity in this house stimulating. There is a member from India and another from the Mideast. I always had a pretty negative impression of Greeks but now my opinion is slowly changing. You can never stereotype any group of people.

I'm dragging my humble belongings up to the room I have been assigned. There is a bunk bed, a dresser, a desk and a single closet. A senior has been living in the room all by himself since the house's membership was low. He doesn't seem too pleased to have a new roommate. He tells me in no uncertain terms that he likes to have sex with his girlfriend in the room and I will need to leave whenever she comes over.

"Whatever," I reply, trying to get along.

He repeats the demand, this time with emphasis, so I just mumble something about how I paid my dues and the room is half mine. I don't want to get into any territorial disputes. If he asks nice I'll be happy to leave when he needs the room for conjugal visits. But I've made up my mind before moving in, I won't put up with any bullying or hazing.

I only get about a quarter of the closet, but it is okay since I now have so few threads. I unpack some socks and underwear and fold them into one of the drawers of the dresser. My roommate has already staked claim to the bottom bunk, which sucks, I hate sleeping in top bunks. But I put some sheets my mom gave me on the narrow top mattress and set up two alarm clocks by the head. When school starts I'm going to need to get up at 4:30AM in order to make it to the bus barn on time. I can't afford to oversleep.

Laying here in my bunk this first night I feel excited to finally be living on my own. I'm up late listening to the most amazing tunes rock the entire house. Some of these frat boys have really expensive stereos and they play all the latest albums. All I have is a pathetic boom box that I keep hidden in the closet.

Since it is a few days before school starts the guys in the house are bored. They engage in bottle-rocket fights with the rival Phi Delt house across the street. I'm pretty popular when I whip out the fire-works arsenal from my car. The arms race is won in favor of the Kappa house with my added firepower. They use up all my skyrockets but I hold back the heavy M-80s and cherry bombs. I have a future plan for those.

With the aerial fireworks exhausted the battle escalates to water balloons. The brothers have the biggest surgical rubber bands I have ever seen and use them to lob large, water-filled projectiles whenever anyone exits the front door of the fraternity across the street. Some of the Phi Delts, and their little sisters, get completely soaked.

I have to admit there is an element of "idle rich kids with time on their hands" around here. I've seen a float from the homecoming parade in the backyard made of thousands of Kleenex stuffed into a chicken wire frame. Honestly, who has time for that kind of nonsense?

It's the last weekend before classes start and Eschman asks me to go downhill skiing. He picks me up in his fancy new Grand Am and gives me a hard time about joining the Kappa house. He was a member of the rival Phi Delts back in his college days.

We drive an hour north to the ski lodge and Esch puts on his shiny new boots and skis. I have to wait in line to rent some. I love finally getting out on the snowy slope. The crisp air smells of pine and cedar. I cut a long slow S through the drifts down the steep hill.

Of course with Esch everything has to be a competition. He wants to race and keeps enticing me until I give in. We get off the chair lift and he immediately heads down a black diamond at top speed with me tailing right behind. I nearly beat him to the bottom but catch an edge and go somersaulting into a snow fence. Stupid rental skis.

At 4:30AM the next morning, both my alarms sound off. My roommate in the bunk below moans. I crawl out of bed stiff from the gnarly wipeout the day before, pull on some jeans and head down to the kitchen for a bowl of cereal. Then I zip off to the bus barn, maneuvering through traffic in the sports car like an Italian race driver.

The bus director is glad to see I'm early. He gathers all the drivers around and gives us a pep talk on safety. I'm taking this seriously. The last thing in the universe I would want is for some little kid to get hurt. It is an awesome responsibility really.

I'm driving my route, slow and careful. Only problem is keeping on schedule. Each student's home has a target time when we ought to be there and since it is the beginning of the school year the youngsters are having a difficult time getting out of bed. On top of that many of the parents want a "first day of school" photo of their little ones boarding the bus.

I manage the route timing as best I can. The kids are great. The high school students are well groomed and serious. The elementary tikes are cute. I pull up in front of one house and no one emerges for a long time. I hate to leave but can't wait forever. Finally, a little girl in underwear runs out the front door with a lunch box in one hand and her school clothes in the other. A high school girl on the bus helps her finish getting dressed.

When we are done with our routes the drivers are required to make a mandatory check from the back of the bus to the front to make sure no kids are left behind. Then I hop into my sports car and race back to campus a few minutes late for my first class. What a rush.

After my morning college classes are over, I race over to the elementary school and check into the office, then head down to the lunchroom. There is a bucket of soapy water and one of my jobs is to wipe off the tables between shifts. The students are having fried chicken today. The food looks great but some of the children still throw out their trays without eating much. The principal tells me I'm welcome to grab any uneaten portions. So, I snarf a couple of tasty chicken breasts while I help empty trays. When you're in college on a budget you need to take advantage of any freebies that come along.

It's fun interacting with the elementary kids on the playground. There are some minor injuries and fights. I hand out band-aides and break up any scuffles telling the kids to shake hands. When things are slow, I play hopscotch or foursquare games with the Special Ed students or throw the football with older boys. I'm trying hard to learn all their names.

After every student is accounted for and herded back inside I run and literally leap into the 'vert speeding back to campus where I rush between classes. Fortunately the bus director wasn't just bragging about knowing someone in registration. All I had to do was ask for a certain clerk and they made sure I got into all the classes I needed at perfect times. Otherwise this crazy schedule would have never worked. My day has to go like clockwork right down to the minute.

I don't like the rush here, rush there, pace of my new life. But if I want to finish my undergrad without any loans I have no other choice but to make it work.

After finishing the evening bus route I'm back at the Kappa house. We meet for dinner in the dining room. The older members expect the pledges to tell stories or jokes.

For some reason I've always been able to remember jokes really well. I have an amazing repertoire and have gone on for half a night when camping with friends before. The upperclassmen appreciate my humor but can be demanding. They prefer dirty jokes.

Our cook is an older, grey-haired lady who wears spectacles and a hair net. She makes comfort food in large quantities heaping it on our plates. I think she is kind of religious though because she complains a lot about the off- color jokes.

"How do you eat a frog? Drape one leg over each of your ears."

The cook screams, "Enough!"

Sometimes the seniors tell stories about events that have taken place in the house or happened to members. I'm a little skeptical because their tales often sound like urban legends. Our house president begins a typical piece of work now.

"This a true story. My roommate knew a neophyte a few years ago who was making out with a tri-delt. This soror wasn't on birth control but she said she'd let him do it to her up the dirty road."

"Oh, brother, this is going to be weird," I think to myself.

"So, he doesn't wear a condom and lets her have it in the yazoo. A few days later he's in excruciating pain and his tool swells up. It's so bad he can't even take a whiz."

"Well, maybe he'll redeem himself," I consider silently. "And this will be some kind of moral fable intended to warn the pledges about STDs or something."

"So he goes to student health. And the doctor inserts tweezers into his penis and pulls out a piece of corn."

The whole dining room explodes with ruckus laughter. I just shake my head and digress, "No way!"

CHAPTER SIXTEEN

fter a house meeting to discuss upcoming social events the brothers elect Jamie as our house president. I voted nay. Jamie is everything that is wrong with fraternities. He's a druggie with no scruples and only one goal in mind, to be a rich corporate CEO someday.

I feel tired and want to crash. Our frat has a full bar in the basement and most of the guys head downstairs for a nightcap. But I have a mission. I grab my coat and the box of leftover fireworks and head over to the Chi Omega house. By now all the Chi O sisters have arrived back on campus and are just slumbering off to dreams of marrying rich doctors and CEO's and heirs to vast fortunes that will fix them for life.

The fireworks box is about half full of M-80s and cherry bombs. I create a delayed fuse by rolling up some notebook paper. It will burn slowly giving me plenty of time to leave. I place the box by the front yard of the monolithic sorority, light the fuse and walk casually away.

A couple of blocks later all hell breaks loose. The firecrackers are extremely loud, penetrating the peaceful evening like a war zone under bombardment. I had to get rid of the arsenal anyway. The Kappa brothers would have done something even crazier if they found the explosives.

"Welcome back, cuddler," I mumble. I guess I still harbor some animosity toward Danette. I know I shouldn't have pranked her house. It was a dumb stunt. Better to forgive and forget and move on. But the stunning explosions provide a catharsis and I feel a ton of pain and sorrow flow out of my body with each concussion. No one is hurt and the shenanigans provide a little pre-semester excitement for the soror girls.

I collapse into my top bunk making sure to set the alarms. I'm an anomaly getting up so early around here. Most of the guys in the house sleep in during the mornings. I've noticed they try to schedule their business courses in the afternoon. Half the time they're hung over from partying the night before.

My high school class gave each graduate a one-word description. Mine was "ambitious." I kind of wondered why at the time but it is clear to me now observing these other guys. When I was ten years old I had my first job, delivering the local newspaper. When I was twelve years old, I started working in Leroy's shop after school and during the summer as sort of a gopher or apprentice.

In my spare time I did about anything a kid could do for spending money. I mowed lawns, detasseled corn, shoveled snow, trapped muskrats and cut firewood. Now I'm pursuing an insane college schedule taking pre-med classes and working two jobs. To fit in homework, I told the bus director I would drive athletic teams to evening events. Once I get to the host school I drop off the team, park the bus and pull out my books to study in the cab. This works well because I get paid by the hour to sit in the bus and do my homework. Then after the game I drive the team back home.

These days I have a reputation in the frat as a workaholic. Also some of the brothers think I'm a druggie, which is undeserved. At parties I get a beer and feign drinking, never actually taking a single sip. I don't inhale either. The only drug I take is No-Doze. But my eyes are always very bloodshot from lack of sleep so everyone thinks I'm high all the time.

I'm perennially up late at night driving local sports teams to games or attending frat parties until one or two o'clock in the morning. Then I roll out of bed at 4:30AM to drive the bus. It's amazing what a young body can endure. Older folks can't handle extreme physical duress like young people can. That's probably one reason why they draft 18-year-olds.

I try not to drive on Thursday nights because that's when we have exchanges with each sorority. These are themed events like a Hawaiian luau or librarian/barbarian costume party. The parties started out fine. We had normal events like toga parties and speed dating.

But as this semester has progressed my fraternity is turning into the animal house. Part of that is my fault. I bought some grow lamps because I thought I was getting seasonal affective disorder from lack of sunlight. But the brothers hijacked my lamps and started growing pot in the basement.

Now everyone but me gets stoned before getting drunk at exchanges and the parties are increasingly debaucherous. We've had a rave, Mardi Gras flash, "snow pants or no pants", "straight shots", "girls wear skirts and no underwear allowed" and "anything but clothes" themes. Some of the sororities are no longer coming to our exchanges.

Tonight is a huge night for me because we have an exchange with the Chi Omega house. I talk the guys into toning it down a bit. So we are having a "sex change" exchange where the guys dress up like girls and vice versa, the sorority girls dress up like guys.

We're reading F. Scott Fitzgerald's Great Gatsby in my American Lit class and I feel like I'm playing the part of Jay Gatsby with expectations that his quixotic passion and obsession, the beautiful former debutante Daisy (Danette) Buchanan will show up.

The brothers go all out borrowing dresses and female fashion accessories from little sisters and girlfriends. Someone gets some balloons to stuff the guys' bosoms. Only about half the Chi O's show up since by now our house has a terrible reputation. The Kappa brothers are absolutely plastered acting like, well, hookers hitting on all the Chi O sorority girls who are dressed as macho guys with charcoal beards and work clothes.

By the end of the evening the party has become a fiasco with half naked guys passed out on couches exposing their fancy lingerie. You can hear balloons popping all over the place as the few remaining drunken alpha-male type girls grab guys' fake boobs.

Danette never shows up. Which doesn't surprise me. She's pretty coy and obviously knew to avoid this insane place. I have to admit though, I'm disappointed. In the back of my mind I still harbor some feelings for her and had gotten a naïve premonition that maybe we would have some fanciful reunion tonight, since her engagement fell through.

I'm jolted back to reality the next morning when my alarms go off and I literally fall out of my bunk onto the floor. My roommate complains about my early hours then rolls over, covers his head with a pillow and falls quickly back to sleep.

The bus director is always glad to see me. I never miss a day of work and some of the other drivers have not been showing up on time. That throws the whole school day off for teachers when buses arrive late. I just yawn and try to help out as much as I can. We are headed into vacation and the kids on the bus sing cute songs:

"Hark the herald angel shout, twelve more days 'til we get out!"

Eschman invites me over for dinner in his geodesic dome house to meet his new girlfriend. When I get there I see why. She's a smoking hot nurse and he wants to show her off. She tells me she works for some crack ear, nose and throat doctor who specializes in reconstructive surgery for hearing loss.

When I was 14 years old I was working on a corn detasseling crew. A bunch of us were sitting along the sides of a grain truck eating our lunch. The careless driver didn't remember we were there and he popped the clutch and took off in the truck sending kids sprawling all over the place. I fell hitting my head and the impact dislocated my middle ear bones.

Esch's nurse friend, Diann, informs me that the doctor can perform an operation with a microscope to reconnect bones in the middle ear. That idea gives me a slight ray of hope that I could hear properly again. Being hearing impaired is more of a challenge than you can imagine. People think you're dumb or dull when you have trouble understanding conversation. But my faint hopes for hearing normally subside when I remember I can only afford a crappy student health insurance policy and there's no way I can afford an expensive surgery.

The evening ends with Eschman giving me a hard time about my car and bragging about his new Grand Am model. We're good friends from back in my high school gearhead days but I do find his competitive nature annoying at times.

I finally relent and agree to drag race him on a nearby highway straight away. His nurse friend just rolls her beautiful big eyes obviously unimpressed with our macho lack of common sense. We line up the cars. Actually, I think the engine in my little sports car is superior, but Esch has a big old American V-8 so it's not exactly a fair fight in cubic inches.

We scream away from an even start, tires squealing and my little sports car grabs the lead but not for long as Esch revs up into the V-8's power curve. I'm approaching red line so I have to back off. I can't afford to blow my engine—I need this rig to commute to work. Not Eschman though, instead of backing off the wealthy heir and insurance man keeps his pedal to the floor and disappears down the road. If his engine blows he'll just trade his car in on a new one.

We rendezvous back at the dome. Diann is just glad we didn't kill ourselves. Me too. Of course Esch is bragging about how he blew my doors off. At this point, I really don't care. I shake my head and bid farewell.

Back at the Kappa house I skip dinner. The old cook has quit because of profanity in the dining room. Jamie went out and hired an over-sexed blonde bombshell with zero culinary skills to be our new chef. As far as I can tell the primary job skill that got her hired here is that she's a nymphomaniac. She's already slept with half the guys in the house.

Fortunately I have enough money to grab some fast food when I get hungry. I don't spend as much time around the frat now anyway because things there have been spinning out of control. The semester began with beer kegs, then escalated to hard stuff. Next the house filled up with pot and hash smoke. After that was a period of heavy use of methaqualone, the guys refer to as "ludes." Finally, Jamie scored a load of good rock and people's sinuses are getting all messed up snorting lines of the dust.

I thought about trying coke just to see what it was like. I even purchased a little envelope of it from Buzzy—a legacy who sleeps 24-7 except when he is shagging his girlfriend. I'm aware of their flip-flopping because his room is next to mine and they bang up against the wall when they boink. His girlfriend is also a wailer, giving up a high-pitched moan when she climaxes. Old buzzy is flunking out even though his parents gave him a blank check book for college.

Jamie grabs the envelope of cocaine out of my hand and tells Buzzy to give me my money back. This is because Jamie suspects that I might be a narc. He's noticed that I never get wasted at parties. Since he's the dealer supplying everyone in the house, he's paranoid of getting busted. Actually, it was probably divine intervention that I didn't snort the nose candy. With my addictive personality, and bad track record with alcohol, I could have burned out rapidly on blow and I'd be a junkie by now.

Sometimes I regret not joining the Phi Delt house or one of the other more respectable fraternities on campus. I like the diversity here at the Kappa house but the party atmosphere is out of control. I have trouble focusing on my studies and my perfect 4.0 GPA is beginning to slip going into midterms. That worries me because if I lose my scholarship, I'll be SOL.

I've noticed some of the groupies hanging around here look a little on the young side. One of them, a cutie named Sara, has taken a shine to me. I mean she is literally throwing herself at me, calling me on the phone at all hours of the day and showing up in my room half naked at night. I ask her how old she is and she insists she's 18.

But I'm skeptical. I mean, I like Sara and I'd probably get it on with her, but on the other hand, you know, I don't want to get in trouble with some under-aged jailbait if she's lying about her age. So I make an appointment to talk to a lawyer.

CHAPTER SEVENTEEN

One of the house functions that must be accomplished before spring break is initiation of the new pledge class. Fortunately the Kappa's aren't into hazing. Anytime an older bro' would try to diss me, I'd just tell him to fuck off.

Initiation comes about the same time as midterms so between work, class, cramming for tests and the ceremonial frat activities my life is a giant crunch sandwich.

Some of the initiation stuff is pretty mundane, like learning stupid songs and studying the ancient history and origins of our fraternity. You can frequently hear the pledges around here singing:

"Chi O, Chi O, it's off to bed we go,

A Phi, A Phi, it's off to bed with me..."

With the song continuing to rhyme through all the sororities on campus.

Our fraternity traces its origins to ancient Italy where some students formed a secret society to resist a tyrannical ruler named Baldassare Cossa. I can see where a secret rebel group could have real merit in forming a resistance to a monarch or dictator. But in modern times fraternities and sororities are really more like social clubs.

Throughout history human beings have gathered together to form tribes and alliances. One function of Greek system tribalism is economic, providing connections and landing jobs for members.

Certain major corporations have relationships with particular fraternities and sororities. When a member gets a job at a company or institution they reach out to other members when hiring new staff. In my case, I'm not interested in going corporate, so this will provide no benefit to me.

During initiation the brothers like to do stuff like blindfold the pledges and drive us around so we don't know where we are. One night I take off the bandana shielding my eyes. I see that I have been left in a cemetery under a large black angel statue in the middle of the night. This would scare the crap out of most people but I've worked pouring cement in the cemetery with Leroy's crew so I already know the place and the effect is muted.

I won't divulge our actual initiation ceremony. For one thing the brothers take you to the basement and show you the contents of a secret chest. Inside there is a skull and bones that they claim belonged to someone who blabbed about their secrets.

I have to admit, in the final ceremony, they do pull off a rather mystical experience where you are blindfolded and taken "back in time" to the ruins of an ancient city where our fraternity was founded. Some props, the right music and a fall from a staircase into a blanket held by the other brothers all create a lasting vision in one's memory.

Now that I've been initiated and have "crossed the burning sands" to become an active member, I feel even more confident than ever around the house. I don't take any crap from anyone. For sure I would never harass or haze anyone else either. That's just not how I roll.

* * *

If you ever have any questions as to the legality of something you are thinking about doing I highly recommend talking to a lawyer. People make wisecracks and jokes deriding lawyers but the alternative to a legal system is an anarchic society ruled by violence. Most lawyers are happy to give you a free initial consultation where you can learn a lot.

In my case, I have doubts about shagging Sara. The opportunity is definitely there. Like being the running back on a football team with a great offensive line—the openings are big enough to drive a truck through. Consummation would be a slam-dunk. But I suspect Sara may be too young. When it comes to sex, the only thing that gets me off is a relationship with a consenting adult. The very thought of rape, including statutory rape, makes me ill. I don't want to go there.

There is a storefront near campus with the following inscription in gold letters on the window:

Thomas E. McDonald, Attorney At Law.

I walk in and sit down in the reception area. A stout, jolly man in a grey three-piece suit introduces himself and leads me back to a dusty office full of books and documents. I explain my situation with Sara.

The lawyer's belly ripples as he chuckles, "So she wants to jump your bones?"

"Basically," I reply, in a more serious tone than his.

We have a long talk. The legal scholar lays out the law and age limits on consent in our state. Although Sara is tempting, I decide right there it's not worth pursuing. I mean, what am I supposed to do? Ask her for an ID? What if it is a fake ID? A person needs to be careful. Sex is fun but there is a lot at stake—laws, pregnancy, STD's, people's feelings and so forth.

Now the conversation drifts all over the place. I'm amazed at how willing this lawyer dude is to give legal counsel without any charge. I can tell he's a kind, and very humorous, character.

When I bring up my hearing loss, and the potential surgical fix, MacDonald suddenly becomes solemn and focused though, probing me with questions about when and where the accident took place. He explains that I would have had a legal case for negligence against the corporate, big Ag employer I was working for when the accident occurred but the statute of limitations has run out.

However, in our state there is no expiration on workman's compensation and he may be able to get the operation paid for. The attorney agrees to take my case to court pro-bono. I'm amazed at his generosity, getting involved and spending the time to help me without compensation. What a great man!

* * *

Midterms are here. I'm nervous. A lot is riding on my grades. I can't afford to lose my scholarship. This semester has been a wild ride living in the frat so I'm not as confident as usual. The two things that get me through are: 1) I'm a good test taker: 2) all those nights studying in the bus waiting for the teams to finish their games.

I say goodbye to my playground kids and bus riders. They are all so happy for spring break vacation now. I've become friends with one very smart 6th grader named Gib. We share an interest in outdoor sports. Gib dreams of canoeing in the Boundary Waters someday.

I've also become particularly close to the Special Ed students, one little Native American boy named Troy in particular. We talk about Indian lore a lot at recess. The teacher encourages me to go into special education as a career but I don't think I have the stamina. Spec ed is a noble calling but I'm afraid it is also a burn out profession. The people who work with handicapped kids are amazing heroes.

The next day at the airport I meet up with my sister who is home from Germany. She has married a refrigeration CEO and considers herself high society at this point in her life. Even though we are siblings we are very different people. I wish we got along better but we don't have much in common. I try to be social and converse, but it is a very long flight to Honolulu.

What a sight when the big airliner banks into a turn and we see the lush tropical island below. Leroy and my mom are there waiting to greet us with the aloha spirit, placing leis around our necks. They have a little rental peanut hauler to drive us to their condo that looks out over Waikiki Beach.

I'm very thankful to my parents for this vacation. Hawaii is so incredibly beautiful. Especially so when you leave behind snow and ice back home. The gently swaying palm trees and warm, crystal-clear ocean are like paradise. I go snorkeling with my sister and we see an incredible menagerie of sea life, schools of colorful fish and a red octopus.

My sister and parents have always been very close. I often feel like an extra wheel when we're together. They have gone off shopping together. So I head down to the beach and rent a longboard for the week.

I was first introduced to surfing when Leroy moved our family to southern California when I was five. Leroy tried to make it in the insurance industry but he just isn't the salesman type. He's better working with his hands and has a real talent for fixing machines.

When California didn't work out we moved back to the Midwest but I still got to surf a few times when we went to Florida on vacations. It isn't long before I'm up on the board and riding the perfect waves rolling in on Waikiki Beach. One day we drive over to the north shore. That's a whole different level with waves bigger than a house breaking on coral. I don't even go in the water there!

I've been surfing a few days now and I meet a girl my age named Nikki. She has long blond hair and a bright bikini that reveals a perfect figure. I try not to be too forward. It's hard to know when you can strike up a conversation with a stranger, especially a girl. You don't want to come on too strong.

But Nikki is so open and nice. I ask her if she likes to surf. She says she would like to try, so I give her a few lessons on the longboard. Soon we are conversing like we have known each other a long time. I'm pretty excited that someone as awesome as her wants to hang out with me.

I only have a couple of days left on the island. My new beach baby asks me if I would like to go out tonight. It's really special when a girl asks you out. Ordinarily the pressure is on the guy to ask for a date. We wander around downtown together among booths selling colorful floral shirts and carved coconuts.

She smiles and takes my hand. This whole episode seems surreal to me. Here I am with this kind, stunningly attractive young woman who is equally attracted to me. Nikki actually seems more beautiful to me than Danette, because she has a natural look and isn't all made up. I just contrast the two in my mind. Danette was so unattainable and standoffish. Whereas the surfer girl is so open and welcoming.

I really appreciate honesty and this girl is completely straight and truthful about everything, including sex. I always figured the goal of every woman was to get married and have a monogamous relationship. I guess I'm pretty naïve about that. Beach baby explains to me that she is not interested in having a long-term, serious boyfriend at this point in her life. But the island is such an extraordinary place she would like to be with me tonight.

We find a private spot in the soft sand of the beach under some palm trees. Thank God she has a condom with her because I forgot to bring one. I'm just blown away by the whole experience: the tropical setting, her spontaneous, fun personality and smell of the salty breeze coming in off the vast ocean. I can tell she's experienced and when we make love the feeling is marvelous, almost unworldly.

I dream about my romantic rendezvous on the flight home. We arrive to a snow bound icebox. We're lucky they can even land the plane. I hug my sister and parents at the airport thanking them profusely. Then throw my carry-on in the sports car and slide around on icy roads to the frat house.

It's not long before everything is back into the same old routine. I must get used to waking up early again as I've been sleeping in for a week in the tropics. The brothers are planning the details for spring formal. We have an exchange with the tri-delts and will be paired with them for Greek Week activities.

Greek week is a whole bunch of contests between competing houses that take place once the weather gets nice. The guys in the house volunteer for different teams and challenges. I agree to be in a song and dance routine with a group of tri-delts.

This is very uncharacteristic of me. I was a gear head in high school and was never involved in any extra-curricular activities like drama or swing choir. That's one good thing about the frat—you get to try things that are out of your comfort zone. A couple of the girls compose a song about the *Airliner Bar* on the piano. Then they choreograph a dance routine around a saloon scene backdrop I help build on the stage with a few of the brothers.

Unfortunately it's not long before the house devolves once again into an outrageous, drug and alcohol fueled party scene. I remain completely sober and just observe the unfolding drama of human behavior around me. Sobriety has distinct advantages—no hangovers, accidental falls, car wrecks, STD's, missed work, failed tests or unintended pregnancies.

The house has a file of exams stolen from various college courses over the years but even when they cheat some of these frat guys are flunking out. Irresponsible behavior takes a heavy toll on the brothers. I try to help out when I can but don't see how this movie is going to have a happy ending. The Inter-fraternity Council keeps writing us up for violating the honor code and the college administration placed our house on probationary status for alcohol infractions.

CHAPTER EIGHTEEN

One of the best things about living in a Greek house is meeting lots of different people. That includes almost limitless dating opportunities. The time for spring formal has arrived and I invite Pat, who is the president of our little sister organization.

Pat is considered a fairly hot date and some of the guys seem jealous, which I don't really get. I mean it's Pat's choice who she wants to go out with. If some of these guys want more dates, they ought to sober up, get a job and start acting responsibly.

The dance is held at a Holiday Inn convention center about an hours drive away, which I think is a horrible idea. They ought to choose a venue as close to campus as possible because having these guys drive an hour when most of them will be intoxicated could be disastrous. But the convention center is in Jamey's hometown and he gets his way, as usual.

I don't have any formal clothes so I ask Leroy if I can borrow his suit. He is gracious and agrees. The suit doesn't fit perfectly but I figure it will do for one night.

I've never liked formal dances that much. Pat and I mostly sit at our table and talk. We don't have a lot in common. Almost everyone associated with this fraternity is either from a rich family or aspires to be rich someday I call them working class, rich wannabes. I have other goals and ideals.

* * *

Breaking up is hard for me. Sara was the worst. She just seemed really hurt. I tried to be nice telling her she needs to find someone her own age to go out with. But now, whenever I see her, she just looks away.

Pat was easy. I just quit asking her out. We didn't have that much in common anyway. She's fine with it and we can still be friends.

By far the strangest break up, but probably the one I learned the most from, was Anders. He was a nice guy whose father had died and he was living in the frat on social security survivor benefits. Anders had a good eye for art and culture so we went to a few plays and concerts together. He disliked the fascist in the White House so we could talk openly about politics. But I had no idea he was gay.

I have no problem with anyone's sexual orientation. I enjoyed Anders' company but when he made a pass at me it kind of freaked me out. He was pretty insistent and I was feeling pressured so I just kept establishing boundaries and telling him up front that it was nothing personal, I'm just very hetero.

I guess I don't have very good gaydar. I just treat everybody the same, not really being able to figure out who's gay and who's straight. I talked to Pat about it. We're still good friends. She said some people just don't have a high EQ. It's not like I'm a bad person. I just don't have the greatest social skills.

Being a bit confused I ask her why a gay guy would find me attractive. She just laughs and relates how I'm always ironing my button-down shirts and look very well groomed. She said she thinks I'm nice, smart and act responsibly holding a job and getting good grades, so some people are naturally attracted to me. That right there, what she said, did a lot to boost my low self esteem and help me recover from bad past experiences and put downs.

Tom McDonald, the lawyer, calls. He won our case in front of the state insurance commission. My former employer at the giant hybrid seed corporation will be responsible for paying the medical bill if I get the ear operation. I'm pretty stoked. I haven't been able to hear clearly since I was 14 years old when the accident happened.

I make an initial appointment with the ear, nose and throat surgeon. He is a very old man with thin grey hair and thick glasses. He has me lay on a table and he peers into my ears with a microscope. He tells me that he can see old scars and that the middle ear bones are broken with the incus unattached.

I get a date for the operation at the hospital where Eschman's girl-friend works as a nurse. They can do the procedure on a Friday, so I will only miss one day and can be back at school and work on Monday.

At the fraternity the brothers are having a slave auction. I know this sounds like a barbaric, horrible idea but it's a tradition in our fraternity and not something I made up, so don't blame me.

All the little sisters bring a pair of their underwear. Jamie is the auctioneer making all sorts of suggestive and salacious comments while acting the part of auctioneer. The brothers bid as each pair of panties or bra come up for sale.

I know this is an outrageously sexist event. I suppose I should boycott the debacle. But everyone, including the little sisters, is in a festive mood and the lusty climate is contagious. Ordinarily I don't waste money but I feel sort of independently wealthy now that I've been working long hours driving the buses.

I start bidding on the panties of a cute little sister, a brunette named Jane. People are cheering as the price goes higher than I thought it would, but I hang in there and win the auction. In my defense, I just have her make me a roast beef dinner at her place. I'm hungry for some home-cooked food as our new fraternity cook is a bimbo who can hardly boil water.

Most of the other brothers engage in much more lecherous behavior, like having their female slaves serve them beer and munchies wearing skimpy outfits or bikinis while the guys sit on the couch in the frat lounge and watch sporting events on TV with their buddies.

The day has come for my operation. I'm totally amped, hoping I can recover at least some of the hearing loss I have from the accident. I'm so grateful for my lawyer who helped me get funding. He won't accept any payment so I swing by the grocery store and order their best fruit basket to be delivered to his office.

Thursday evening after work I check into the hospital. I'm taken to a room where the nurse tells me to shower with disinfectant soap. Afterwards I get dressed in a hospital robe and climb into an adjustable bed to watch TV. Different nurses stop by to take my blood pressure and explain the procedure. I will stay in the room tonight and go in for surgery first thing in the morning. The old doc likes to operate very early.

I find it difficult to sleep. Mostly I lay awake fidgeting around, nervous about tomorrow. It seems like forever until morning and just as I finally fall asleep, the nurse arrives to wake me. I'm wheeled down to the operating room and wonder at all the various, high-tech apparatus. It looks complicated. Do I really have what it takes to be a doctor someday?

The anesthesiologist arrives and puts a mask over my face. It seems like I'm in a dream world now. I can faintly make out human voices but can't understand what they're saying. Oddly enough I can feel my ear being manipulated and the instruments inserted, but there is no pain.

The doc cuts out an eardrum and uses a microscope and delicate instruments to reconnect the ossicles. Then he takes some tissue from behind my ear to graft a new tympanic membrane. I awake later that morning still groggy from the anesthesia.

I'm weirded out because my head feels stuffy and, if anything, my hearing is even worse. The nurse arrives and explains that there is packing stuffed into my middle ear to hold the bones in place. This packing will gradually self absorb.

After I get discharged I head out to my parents for the weekend. I really don't want to recoup in the fraternity house. The brothers are always horsing around tackling people, throwing stuff and playing pranks. I don't want my head to get jarred accidentally. That could ruin the effect of the operation.

I mostly lounge around reading my class textbooks or watching TV. Mom makes me milkshakes and chicken noodle soup. I need to eat soft food for a while and not bite down on anything hard. I had forgotten how good the food was at home. I wish the cook at the fraternity was even half the chef my mom is.

The weather is getting warm now. Glorious spring has arrived after a long cold hard winter. People seem happier and more positive. The trees are budding out, tulips and daffodils are blooming bright yellow and red, birds and bees are mating and the campus is full of life.

It is time for the Greek houses to conduct their philanthropies, which are events to raise funds for various charitable causes. Each fraternity pairs up with a sorority and tries to come up with a novel theme like, "rocking against muscular dystrophy" where they teeter-totter for 48 hours and collect money from sponsors. With our tarnished reputation our house gets paired up with the Delta Zetas, who have an undignified nickname, "the easy DZs" and a reputation for loose behavior.

Personally, I think the whole philanthropy thing could be an attempt to atone for bad behavior and partying all winter. Maybe the brothers and sisters think they can thus escape the effects of karma. I realize it is commendable that they are raising money for good causes. There is just a part of me that senses a disconnect in the process, like collecting cigarette coupons to fight lung cancer.

A week later I'm having a check up with the ear, nose and throat surgeon. The old guy peers into my ear and moans. Despite everyone's best efforts, the operation has not been successful. This is a huge let down for me. I start to feel depressed but dig deep and summon every ounce of my will power. I can't give up. I'm not going to let this setback defeat me!

I focus on work and study, losing myself in the daily struggle. The students at the elementary are so looking forward to summer break. Gib, a 6th grader, has made plans to go canoeing in the boundary waters of northern Minnesota during the coming summer with his father and uncle. They invite me to come along.

I drive the middle and high school students to track and cross-country meets in the bus. Instead of studying inside the cab I sit in the bleachers now with my books in my lap. When my eyes become fatigued from reading I pause and watch the students compete down on the field.

It is kind of emotional to say goodbye to all the students at the elementary school. I'll miss them. They tell me about their plans for summer camp and vacations. Some of the parents send along thank you notes and small gifts for me. I feel grateful for the chance to work with their children.

One fantastic aspect of life is the opportunity to remake oneself. If a person can master this ability, your time on this planet is infinitely more interesting and adventurous. I don't mean that a person ought to be fake or fickle, lacking any commitments. But rather accept life as a game to be lived in its entirety, both the good and bad.

The traditional decoration above a Greek theatre includes both a happy and sad mask, symbolizing that in a full life, and a good play, one should experience all the emotions.

So I go about my affairs as an actor in the theatre of life. It works well for me. I meet a new romantic partner, Barb, the president of Kappa Kappa Gamma, the most prestigious sorority on this campus. At times, driving around with her in the sports car with the top off, I feel like we're movie stars in a romantic adventure film, rather than college students.

When you think about it, just one year ago sorority girls were making fun of me, calling me a "field hippie." Now, here I am, dating the sorority queen, and yet, inside, I'm the same person. Life is crazy!

I have to add that Barbi is not your typical sorority type. She's attractive, but not super hot like some of the girls. Being a math major she is more cerebral, probably the most intensely intelligent person I've ever met. Her brain is like a giant sponge, in constant need of input and information.

Together we drive in the sports car to see documentaries in small theatres or attend lectures on campus by visiting experts. Her social calendar is always jam-packed. We avoid my Kappa house. Instead Barbi is invited to the best parties, including the Phi Psi house.

There is golf, tennis and tubing down the river with her soror sisters on weekends. I always feel kind of guilty, all those cute girls in colorful bikinis riding inter-tubes down a river that is polluted with farm and industrial waste. But we survive the filthy water and have fun, bringing along coolers of food and beer.

I actually have trouble keeping up with Barb. It's a challenge. Her mind is so quick and her activity schedule so intense. My back becomes sore from golfing so many weekend rounds. At night she often can't sleep and we work crossword and Mensa puzzles for hours.

Finals come and I squeak by ending the semester with a GPA of 3.55. I guess an inch is as good as a mile when you dodge a bullet or a car wreck, but considering that my scholarship requires a minimum GPA of 3.50 I consider the margin too close for comfort.

I'm in serious need of a makeover, another total life change. The Greek life is just too hectic and disorganized for me. I lose my concentration and can't focus on homework. The writing is on the wall. There's no doubt I have to move out of the frat house. But where can I go? I have my scholarship and 2 steady jobs but any feelings of independence are but a mirage. I'm really just a struggling student barely making ends meet.

When you move out of home there are all sorts of unexpected expenses your parents used to cover. Now with the sports car I have insurance, gas and maintenance expenses too. Boomeranging back home with my mom and dad is not an option I want to take. I don't know what to do!

CHAPTER NINETEEN

I feel a need for a total separation from the fraternity. The crazy party atmosphere here in the Kappa house is simply not sustainable over time. At some point this drunken rodeo is bound to crash, and I don't want to be around when that train wreck happens.

I suppose I could stay and try to wrest the presidency away from Jamey. Would I be able to turn things around and build a house that really does stand for its own stated principles of honor, courage, justice and truth? No! Probably not!

The current condition of this organization is so decadent the task is insurmountable. I could neglect my studies, spend every waking moment of my life in a grand noble effort to reform this Greek house, probably accomplish very little and end up flunking out of college like so many of the brothers have. Ultimately in the frat, I'd be seen as a crusader, not as a friend or brother.

I feel like I'm searching to find out who I am and trying on different roles for size. The Greek life was fun for a while but now I know it's not the right fit for me. So I decide to leave the frat and break up with Barbi, the sorority queen. It's a sad experience, but also a relief. Barbi was challenging and always in the know, but so damn intense. I tell the guys in the house I'll be moving out. I'm a sentimental person so leaving is hard, but also extremely liberating.

This frat was my first home away from home. It gave me the opportunity to get out from under my parents' wings. I did have some good times here, learned a lot and met some amazing people. I wouldn't trade the experience for any other.

When I announce that I won't be coming back a brother approaches me. Ross is one of the more cool-headed members of my pledge group. He says that he and some friends are subletting a house for the summer and wonders if I would like to rent one of the rooms.

The place is close to campus, near the football stadium. The monthly rent would be higher than the frat and not include meals or utilities. But I like the close-in location and, anyway, I have no other options. So, I withdraw what money is left in my savings account for a damage deposit and sign a lease.

The end of finals week means spring semester is over. The weather has shifted to warm and sunny. The college students are fired with pent up energy and ready to party hard. This is the last weekend before I start pouring cement again at Leroy's on Monday. I feel like partying too.

It is pretty amazing really that I've lived here in the frat house attending countless wild bashes and, even with all the peer pressure to fit in, I never imbibed one drink, toke or illegal drug. I feel like a true survivor.

But nobody is perfect and I finally screw up. I randomly meet a couple of dormies downtown. The girls are cute and nice and want to crash a party in the country thrown by the wrestling team, but they don't have a ride.

I agree to take them, somehow cramming all three of us in my little sports car. We get to an old farmstead with a dilapidated barn. In the pasture are hundreds of college students drinking heavily while gyrating to the pulse of a band. Girls are sitting on their boyfriends' shoulders to see above the crowd and some of them are topless.

Stock tanks full of ice cool off dozens of beer kegs. My new friends encourage me to get a beer but I'm upfront about not wanting to drink. They persist, but I'm steadfast with resolve, using the excuse that I need remain sober so I can drive us home.

One of the girls swears that she does not drink herself and offers to be a designated driver. Now I have no excuse. I finally give in and accept a paper cup of brew she puts in my hand and... I take a swig.

I don't know what the hell is wrong with me. All that perseverance and will power to make it through a semester in the crazy animal house without getting wasted even once and now something about the female chemistry of these two, interacting with my current end of semester state of mind and the wild display of instinctual adolescent savage tribal energy surrounding me here just explodes all my inhibitions.

One beer leads to another and soon I have a good buzz going. I have to admit, the high from alcohol is pleasant, at first anyway. I can see why so many people partake. I feel a sense of relief, even euphoria, as if the pressure of finals week has been vented like a vapor cloud from a steam engine.

An airplane appears overhead. Everyone gasps as a man jumps out. The shock turns to relief as a parachute opens. Then a cheer and laughter break out as the crowd realizes the skydiver is completely naked except for his harness.

I recognize my old jumpmaster from the parachute class and take off running across a field to greet him. But drinking so many brewsters has left me uncoordinated. I veer to one side, trip and fall onto the ground.

I realize I've had way too much to drink. I need to blow this scene. The girls arrive laughing and help me up. I explain that I want to go back to campus. Surprisingly, they agree, having heard about a party at their dorm.

I make it back to the sports car with an arm slung over each of their shoulders. We pile in with the sober girl in the designated drivers seat.

"Uh oh," she exclaims. "I don't know how to drive a stick."

"Shit!" I lament. "What are we going to do now?"

I insist that we stay at the party or call a cab. I'm in no condition to drive and neither of them can handle the 4-speed shift. But the girls have other plans.

They talk me into taking the wheel and assure me they will be sitting right there beside me the whole way to monitor my driving. It's a horrible idea but I reluctantly agree.

The little sports car weaves back to campus. I'm distinctly aware that my driving is impaired and atrocious. The ladies just laugh, grabbing the wheel and correcting our trajectory when the car drifts off course.

It's a miracle we're not stopped by the police or, worse yet, have a terrible accident. I look at the cute girls and shudder, remembering the story about how Hollywood movie star Jane Mansfield was decapitated when her convertible ran under a semi trailer. I feel better when we all arrive safely at the dorm. No one is hurt and my car, which is my only real physical asset in the world worth anything, is parked safely out front.

We take the elevator to an upper floor. I haven't spent much time in the dorms and look around curiously at the layout. There is a lounge and long hallway with bulletin boards. All the individual rooms have decorated doors. I use the restroom then find the party with the girls.

The dormies have a huge punch bowl and are playing games like twister and spin the bottle. I sit on a couch with one of the girls on each knee watching the competition. Finally, it's our turn. I try to keep my hands and feet on the game mat's colored dots but end up falling, taking everyone else down with me in a pile of sweaty bodies.

Too late I realize the students have spiked the punch heavily with 190-proof Everclear. We stumble back to the girls' dorm room and they begin to disrobe. They are hot to trot with a threesome. Before I know it, I'm on my back with both of them on top of me, laughing and pulling my pants off.

I don't have a condom with me. I ask, and they don't have one either. This scenario makes me nervous. Everything is progressing too quickly. I engage in kissing and petting. But when one of the girls tries to insert me into her I wrestle my way out of the bed.

She seems disappointed now, sitting there naked, and she asks me what's wrong? I mumble that I have to go, to which she begs, why? If you ever want to end a tryst quickly, I'll tell you how. Just mention that the person you are with has a large bottom. I was drunk and blurted it out and I was soon in the elevator headed down to the ground floor.

Outside I struggle to make it back to the frat. It's a beautiful afternoon, sun shining brightly, birds chirping, fragrant lilacs blooming in purple bouquets and me unable to navigate down the cement sidewalk. I literally have to crawl on my hands and knees.

The Kappa's are having their last party before summer on the frat's stately front porch. As I approach doggy style, crawling on all fours along the sidewalk toward the house, the crowd spots me and a hearty roar ensues as the brothers cheer me on. Exhausted, I finally collapse halfway up the stairs. It is probably the single moment in my entire duration as a frater that I feel totally accepted and understood.

The brothers can relate to my plight. The crowd enthusiastically yells my name with newfound affection. Several brothers come to the rescue, carrying me up the final flight and accompanying me to my room where I fall onto the couch.

The next day when Ross comes to check on me my head is throbbing every time my heart beats. I awoke with the worst hangover of my life. That is saying something too because in my gear head days I tied on quite a few binges. My advice: Beware of Everclear!

I finally get up. It is late Sunday afternoon. I go searching for the sports car, finding it parked crooked in front of one of the dorms, but, mechanically unscathed as far as I can tell. I just look at the hunk of iron, glass and rubber that represents all the collateral I have left in the world and swear I will never drink again. For real this time! Never again!!!

I wasn't able to afford collision insurance so if I'd wrecked that little beast it would have been a financial setback I never could have recovered from at this point in my life. Worse yet, what if one of the girls I was with last night had been terribly injured or killed. Getting buzzed just isn't worth it.

Back at the frat I pile all my scant belongings into the passenger seat and trunk, just some preppy clothes and personal items. Then I remember the grow lights in the house basement. They would be worth something to sell so I decide to head back into the house one last time to recover them.

The old brick structure with all its stories and traditions seems empty now. My face appears, smiling down at me from the current photo composite hanging prominently over the fireplace. I have been part of Kappa history.

Why no one is around I'm not sure. Perhaps some of the brothers have left for summer? Or maybe they are sleeping off hangovers from the party last night? I find out when I descend the stairs into the darkness of the basement.

Through the blackness candles illuminate a skull and bones resting on an altar. Swords clank a stark warning above my head. The gruff voices of the door guards cry out, "Who goes there?"

I have committed a mortal sin having forgotten to use the secret door knock, identify myself as a brother with the secret greeting and then give the top-secret handshake to the guards. Brothers enrobed in black satin grumble and give angry stares as the lights go on. Basically I just unintentionally crashed the solemn, sacred, end of the year ritual.

I back out of the basement and up the stairs. Screw the grow lights. The potheads can have them. This was a bad way to end my life as a Greek. But the way fraters take rituals and secrecy so seriously just seems like errant child's play to me now. I have more important things to do. Adios Kappa brothers! I'm outta' here!

CHAPTER TWENTY

*I*t's a major change moving from a big fraternity house with 40 other guys and their little sister groupies into a small home with just 3 roommates. Our new place isn't too shabby really, a little run down and neglected, like most rentals, but comfy.

The only furniture in my room is a single bed with a lumpy mattress. Ross and I scour the dumpsters and curbs around the neighborhood looking for furniture abandoned by students leaving town. I score a broken, but fixable, dresser and then help Ross carry home an old couch for the living room. The fabric is stained and faded but we throw a blanket over it and, hey, it's functional.

Ross is a true gentleman, studying urban and regional planning. He wants to run for political office someday. I wish him luck in that endeavor but have my doubts. He seems like too nice a guy to win in our reactionary state. His common sense, middle ground, small town charm will be no match for the fascists and their corporate backers.

Ross is active in a mainline protestant student church group. He is kind of a lady's man and I'm amazed at some of the attractive dates he scores pursuing this religious angle. His father owns a lumber company and Ross does odd carpentry jobs for spending money.

My other roommates are Tom and Jay. Tom is a rather aloof dental student who lives in the basement, studies a lot and sleeps on an enormous waterbed. Jay is an international student from Serbia. He is an imposing presence, tall and muscular, a business major who manipulates himself into the master bedroom, then staples centerfolds from Playboy magazine on the walls for decoration.

Work at Leroy's this summer is the same as usual. I have poured cement here since I was a kid so the tasks are mundane and I get through the day listening to rock music on the radio and laughing at the antics of my crew members, Phildo and Hatchet Jack.

Jack has gotten married and is trying to have children but to no avail. The fertility doctor thinks the problem is all the steroids he takes to bulk up for professional wrestling. The drugs have caused his testicles to shrink stopping sperm production.

Phildo is engaged and invites me to his bachelor party.

The event is held in the loft of a local bar. Drinks are on Phil so everyone, except for me, is guzzling lots of beer. Jack uses his connections as a bouncer to secure an attractive stripper. Leroy is present, drinking a beer and talking with the guys, but he leaves in a rush the minute the stripper arrives.

I ask Jack about the arrangement and he tells me that for $100 the girl will go completely nude. He forks over the cash and she seems to enjoy slowly taking her clothes off for the crowd of horny guys. Everything is mellow for an hour or two with her verbally interacting and sitting on different guy's laps.

As the evening progresses the guys get drunk and start fondling her breasts and ass. She laughs and tolerates this for a while but then Jack fingers her from behind and she gets mad and leaves.

Phil and Jack are doing shots the last time I see them. Both do not show up for work the next day. Leroy is pissed. Hondo just shakes his head. I work with Leroy making cement forms and getting ready for some smaller foundation jobs we can work on without the malingering crewmembers.

Hondo is replacing some furniture at the shop. I get dibs on a solid old desk with a plate glass top. Leroy drops it off at my place in his truck and helps me carry it to my room. He comments that the rental isn't half bad. I introduce him to my roommates, then he says goodbye and leaves.

The thing about pouring cement for Leroy is that the hours are long, the work brutally hard, but the money is good. And I'm in need of money! Living in the rental house is going to be more expensive than the frat. So I use my old gear head skills and connections to map out a plan.

First I sell the sports car. Living so close to the college I won't need regular transportation. I'm applying for jobs on campus for next fall as well. I put most of the money from selling the car into my savings account. But I hold back a couple of grand in cash to purchase a broken-down foreign station wagon from my sister's husband that I think I can flip for a profit.

I enlist my gearhead friend Beevo and we get the wagon running. Now the horse-trading really begins. Beevo wants the Mercedes luggage rack off the wagon so I let him have it for helping with the repairs. Beevo's eccentric father likes the wagon and trades me a broken down Harley Davidson motorcycle for it.

We get the Harley running except the loud exhaust bothers my impaired hearing making my tinnitus worse. So Beevo helps me put mufflers on the pipes that I fill with steel wool to quiet the noise.

I take some of my preppy frat clothes to a second hand shop and trade them for old jeans and a distressed leather motorcycle jacket. My style makeover is complete when I let my hair and beard grow out. The world's a stage and my new role is biker. The image is fun, a quantum change from frat boy and I enjoy the different way that strangers interact with me now. Bikers are considered kind of dicey, rough characters, seen as outlaws by some. Life is weird. People give me strange looks but I'm the same dude inside.

This summer I'm taking a field ecology science class in the evenings. After classes I usually head downtown to eat popcorn and watch TV in the saloons. The bartenders give me strange looks when I order a coke or orange juice. Who is this teetotalling biker dude anyway?

Tonight my former life as a frat boy comes in handy. I'm walking downtown after class and notice a pretty young woman stuck in the long line at the popular *Field House* bar. She calls my name and I realize it is Amy, a little sister from the Kappa house. I'm surprised she recognizes the latest version of me with a stubble beard and biker duds. But she seems glad to see me again and we begin talking about old times.

Hatchet Jack is working as the bouncer. When he sees me waiting outside he yells my name, waving my friend and I to the front of the line where we cruise in without paying the pricey cover charge. The little sister seems impressed and we have fun dancing the night away.

When the bar closes she hops on the back of my Harley and I take her home. One thing leads to another and soon I'm in the sack with her. In my room I have a stash of condoms ready just in case and we begin humping away on my rickety little bed. Ross's room is next door and he gives me a ribbing about the noise the next day.

One thing I hadn't planned on was that the little sister is a virgin. I guess I naturally figured that frat house groupies were probably very promiscuous. All the women I've been with before this have been experienced. It was difficult penetrating her and I tried to be as gentle as possible.

I hope the experience was all right for Amy. It must have been okay because she called the next day. I tried to be nice and let her down easily. It was just a one-night stand. I'm interested in a dental student named Juliana in my ecology class and I don't want to lead the little sister on.

Dating and romance are an exercise fraught with peril. People's feelings are always on the line and you have to be sensitive. I know I've hurt people, and I've been hurt before too. So I have experienced pain and disappointment from both sides. You do the best you can and try to leave everyone as unscathed as possible. But it can be tough.

Living in the Midwest we are far away from an ocean or other large body of water that would act like a giant flywheel to moderate the weather. Instead the climate swings wildly from ice-cold winters to hot humid summers. At work I sweat and suffer with the cement crew slaving away in blistering sun and oppressive humidity.

The wind feels good riding the Harley home after work and a shower is heavenly, washing the salt and mud crust from my muscled body. Then I'm off to Field Ecology, a class that is more challenging than I expected. The field part is fun. In the evening before the sun goes down I lay on my back in the woods with Juliana taking data on a clipboard as a pair of woodpeckers fly to and from a hole in a dead elm tree bringing food to their young.

But then, after dusk, we must trudge back to the classroom to crunch the numbers on a calculator for our study project. Thankfully she is better at statistics than I am. The math is complicated: $y\ln(y/n) + (n-y)\ln(1-y/n) - y\ln(p) - (n-y)\ln(1-p) = \chi^2_1 - Z/2$.

When summer school ends, I bid farewell to my field ecology partner. We have become friends and I really think we could have got something going, but for some reason I never asked her out.

I have arranged to take a week off work and travel to the boundary waters with Gib, a former student from my lunchroom supervisor days. Along with Gib's father, Dave, and uncle, Jim, we drive to the Sawbill Outfitters near Ely, MN where we pick up canoes and dry bags.

The Minnesota backcountry is gorgeous but Gib's father and uncle have desk jobs and struggle with the canoes on long portages. Gib's arms are like broomsticks and I move to the center of our canoe to take most of the weight. Fortunately Leroy's concrete work has me in top physical condition.

As we paddle along the Minnesota water is clear and clean, not polluted like the rivers and lakes back home. Under the lily pads I spot giant pike and bass lurking for a meal. I wish I still had my old fishing pole and some bait.

The trip goes as well as possible. There are hordes of mosquitoes and black flies that dampen our joy but the scenery is amazing. During our last day we face a tough portage and stiff head wind. I suggest we canoe a bit out of the way to paddle in the shadow of an island. Gib's father, Dave, disagrees, wanting to take a straight, as the crow flies, path to get back as soon as possible.

I let it go and we are exposed to the brutal wind in the middle of a lake. As hard as we struggle the canoes make little headway and are even blown backwards when we pause to rest. Finally Dave gives it up and we take the alternate route I had suggested, making good headway on the calmer water with the island blocking the wind. I wink at Gib. He smiles.

I made a lot of friends like Gib driving the school bus and working as an aid at the elementary school. I will miss all the kids. But I'm looking forward to having a job on campus in close proximity to my classes so I don't have frantic commutes all over town like last year.

After a summer of applying and searching I'm lucky and land a job at the campus information center in the student union. There is a counter at the entrance to the building where we answer questions from students and visitors. My classes are right across the street and a nice walk from the rental house. It's a perfect gig and I'm looking forward to fall semester.

I can hardly believe it. With the hours from my summer class my sophomore year is over and I am officially a junior. I register for a full load of chemistry, physics and math classes plus some elective classes like "Econ" and the American Political System just for fun. As long as my scholarship is covering tuition, I figure I might as well go all out and take a heavier load, including some elective classes I have a personal interest in.

Work is winding down at Leroy's shop. The Labor Day holiday comes. Everyone on the cement crew wants time off. Leroy goes camping up at the lake. Eschman calls and wants to go backpacking in Wyoming.

I'm happy I've been able to arrange a lifestyle that I won't need to commute anymore. I sell the Harley and put most of the proceeds in the bank. I don't have any fancy backpacking equipment but purchase a beautiful Gregory Cassin pack at the sporting goods store.

Eschman arrives with Diann and two of his former drinking buddies, who are now sober. One of them has a Jeep Cherokee that we pile into and take turns driving straight through to Wyoming.

By the time we arrive everyone has road burn, but it's thrilling to see the majestic scenery of the Wind River mountain range. After a few days of hiking we are beyond civilization. I borrowed my fishing pole back from Leroy and catch hungry trout everyday in the lakes and streams to augment our freeze-dried food. The fish are biting eagerly here away from civilization and are easy to catch.

I've taken some geology classes as science electives and marvel at all the intrusive igneous rock on the mountainsides, something I never see in the flat country back home. There is a small seam of shiny metallic rock in a granite cliff that looks like a gold vein and I chip a sample out to carry home.

I have no tent like the others but sleep out under the open sky. There is zero artificial light here. You can make out the Milky Way disc and swaths of stars you'll never see in the city. One evening I watch a meteor shower fill the sky like celestial fireworks.

All goes well until we attempt to climb Gannett Peak. We rope up and carry our ice axes across a frozen glacier. The terrain requires some scrambling. Just before reaching the summit Esch's girlfriend starts shaking and becomes catatonic. Esch makes some snide comments that sour the mood. With disappointment we are forced to retreat back down the mountain without summiting.

Our first stop back in civilization is a Dairy Queen. Everyone is sick of eating freeze-dried food, which by now tastes like reconstituted cardboard. We have all lost weight on this trip. But we make up for it ordering hamburgers, French fries and banana splits for desert. My next stop is a barbershop for a haircut and a shave. I was beginning to look like Grizzly Adams, the mountain man.

CHAPTER TWENTY-ONE

*L*ife is good! I love my new job! People come to the information desk with a myriad of questions: Where is the English Building? How do I buy sports tickets? Are there any vegetarian restaurants near campus? Where can I find a dump station for my RV? You would be amazed what some people ask!

My classes are challenging and I'm learning a lot. Life is so much less hectic with no commuting. Everything is close by. The rental house is more conducive to organized life and study than the frat. Hey, if I want a party atmosphere, I can just go downtown.

My chemistry and physics profs are geniuses. Really they are. A couple are involved in work for NASA calculating the trajectory of space probes. They engage in intense discussions on the ramifications of pollution and global climate change. Considering their dire warnings, I'm damn glad I've been able to forgo fossil fueled transportation and can walk everywhere now.

Out of the frat and in my new living arrangements, I can concentrate and my grades soar back into the 4.0 GPA range. My scholarship is secure. But money is tight. Living expenses are high and pay has not kept pace with inflation. My new work supervisor, Bonnie, is a kind person who tries to accommodate students' needs. But everyone asks for more hours and the budget is limited.

I may have an ace up my sleeve though, a possible way to score some big bucks. Hope springs eternal in the back of my youthful mind. I take the shining rock sample I found on Gannett Peak to the Geology Lab. It sure looks like gold to me. Maybe I'll get lucky and strike it rich! A friendly professor who teaches "rocks for jocks" smiles, lighting up a Bunsen burner. Held in the flame the shiny rock starts to smoke.

"Sorry. Just iron pyrite," he consoles me. "Fool's gold."

"Shucks," I reply dejectedly. "Oh well, you can't blame a person for trying."

Finances are tight for my roommates too. When the football team has home games we charge fans to park their cars in the lawn, cramming as many vehicles onto the lot as possible. An alumnus teases us about making beer money. We reply grimly, recounting how the cash will actually go for groceries instead.

We split the utilities and rent four ways. But Jay, the business major, frequently cannot pony up with the money for his portion. So late fees add another expense.

I seem to be stuck with the job of collecting from everyone. When I ask for payments, Jay explains that he is an entrepreneur. He is starting up a new business catering Serbian food and will soon have the cash. But he hasn't had a single customer yet. I try to help out arranging for Jay to cater a meal for my family.

The clan is all here now, gathered around my parent's kitchen table: Leroy, my mom, Hondo and his wife. My sister and her CEO husband, home from Germany, are chain smoking and rolling their eyes at Jay's antics. Everyone but me is drinking lots of wine, so the mood remains upbeat.

Jay's appetizer is flaming goat cheese. But he pours way too much brandy in the pan. When he ignites the dish with his lighter the liquor creates a giant fireball that scorches my parent's textured ceiling.

The burned cheese is served with Cvarci, which tastes like pork rinds. Everyone is polite and tastes a bit, without enthusiasm. Next comes Sarma. Thankfully Jay's mother has provided this dish and the cabbage rolls are actually quite delectable.

Desert will be cherries jubilee, which I don't think is even Serbian. However Jay is trying to be flamboyant. To add flair to the meal he has rented a tux and is playing traditional Balkan accordion and violin music on his boombox. But my parents are adamant, yelling an emphatic "No" when Jay gets out his lighter to ignite the sweet cherry confection. They don't want their house burned down.

Back at our rental I'm gracious, telling Jay the meal was great and forking over my own hard-earned money for the catering service, along with a generous tip. Jay smiles, then frowns when I grab all the cash back explaining that he is way behind on rent and I'll use the money for that.

Jay grumbles something about, "Damn Croats!"

Apparently long ago something bad happened between the Serbians and Croatians. So now, whenever things go wrong for Jay, he blames the Croats.

I've noticed humans organize themselves into tribes. Then they like to blame all their problems on another tribe. Like long ago there was a theft or war or slavery or some other transgression and now one group is trying to blame another group long after the event transpired and the guilty parties are dead and gone.

Sorry but one cannot blame the bad actions of distant ancestors on their descendants. No, the son should not suffer for the sins of the father. Every human being is a unique individual, responsible for only their own actions. People ought to be less tribal and not stereotype others. It does not help to lay guilt trips on people for something they did not do.

Jay needs to face the fact that Croats are not to blame for all his problems. I don't know what caused the bad blood between these two groups but they ought to hang it up. I realize that maybe long ago the Croats did something really horrible to his ancestors—but honestly, that was then and this is now and people need to learn to forgive and move on.

The real problem that Jay, and the rest of us college students, are grappling with is that education is underfunded in this country. It makes me mad to see students struggling so hard to survive. Here we are, young people trying to gain skills to become productive members of society, and the government doesn't seem to care. The aid that is offered is mostly loans and the interest rates are not even that good.

My roomies are going deeply into debt. But I have an aversion to taking out loans. In my English Lit class I agreed with the character Polonius in William Shakespeare's play, Hamlet, who counsels his son Laertes, "Neither a borrower nor a lender be."

But my savings account dwindles as the semester progresses. I request more hours at work. Bonnie, my supervisor, looks sad and stressed out. Her boney hands shake when she talks about work hours now. She would like to help, but funding for the information center is tapped out.

Relief for me comes from a strange pair of fellows. Phildo and Hatchet Jack call. They need my help. The two burly men have landed a gig setting up for rock concerts in the campus gymnasium. The rock bands are liberal, insisting on organized labor. So, we join the Teamsters Union and the wages are quadruple the current minimum wage I've been working for at the info center.

We're used to heavy labor at Leroy's shop. Jack drives the forklift. Phildo and I stack the enormous speakers closely following directions from the road crew. Groupies hang around in the shadows. A pretty hippie chick approaches me.

"Hey man. Can you give me some money?"

I give her a dollar, much to the disgust of the other workers who despise the moochers.

"Just ignore them!" the roadies insist.

The rock bands are happy with our work. There are large tips. The university is happy with our take down and clean up afterwards. They offer us gigs as concert ushers.

After putting up the stage and speakers at the next rock concert they give me a flashlight and instructions. When the lights go out, I'm supposed to police the audience making sure no one is smoking pot.

A few riffs blare through the speakers. A cheer of anticipation rumbles through the crowd reaching a crescendo. The lights dim until the gymnasium goes black. The band comes on stage. Then, everywhere at once, tiny lights twinkle like the bulbs on a giant Christmas tree. Literally the entire audience is lighting up. Here I stand with a stupid flashlight in my hand. There's no way I'm going to try and weed whack these stoners' grass party.

The usher gig is a lucrative opportunity getting paid to see great bands. I mean, it just doesn't get much better than that. When one female rock and roll legend comes on stage I can tell she is stoned out of her mind. She wears long, sheer, madrigal attire that lends a mystical, elfin aura to the scene. But she cannot remember the lines to her songs and just spins endlessly like a top.

Mobs of dazzled young men surround the stage yelling, "I love you, Stevie. I love you!"

That's the last concert I work as an usher. I'll continue working with the teamsters on set up, but the actual concerts are just too damn loud. It was an awesome gig but even with earplugs my head buzzes for days and I cannot hear lectures properly.

The people who organize campus activities have taken a shine to me though. I show up for work and don't get drunk or high. When I complain about the concert noise level, they offer me a different gig, pouring draws at the union bar. I give it a try but have mixed feelings about slinging brew.

The organizers explain that if I take a class on how to prepare mixed drinks they'll raise my pay. I reluctantly sign up for Basic Bartending class at the local community college. It's a totally different academic experience than my university classes.

Our textbook is the *Old Mr. Boston Bartending Guide*. We students sit around tables in the lab mixing drinks with the various liquors before us. The instructor demonstrates how to make Golden Cadillacs, Margaritas and Bloody Marys. I notice that he takes a swig to test each drink we make. By the end of the evening he is always bombed out of his mind.

Even though I can use the extra money I decide to quit the bartending gig. There is a moral dilemma in serving alcohol when I know it messes up people's lives. It makes me feel like a legalized drug pusher. Besides, they canceled the bartending course because our instructor crashed his moped driving home from class under the influence.

Two concerns weigh heavily on my mind now. First, I always had a dream of meeting someone special and forming a long term relationship. But all I seem to experience are very short-term romances and one night stands.

I know this is absolutely horrible, but I have to admit it, the one person I would most like to be with is Danette. It's strange how I have never quite been able to shake off my feelings for her. I even called the Chi Omega house once just to hear her voice, but they tell me she has moved out. That's a shock!

We have a campus directory at the information desk. I check it out and find Danette now lives in an apartment not far from our rental house. What a coincidence. Or is it fate?

The second enigma that vexes my mind is how I'm ever going to afford medical school? I'm barely working my way through my under-grad degree. I look into it and find that medical school would cost about $250,000. I certainly do not want to take out a loan for that much money and there is no way I can work my way through a program that costs a quarter of a million dollars! My only hope is winning the lottery! And in addition to not borrowing money, I don't gamble.

CHAPTER TWENTY-TWO

The fall weather in these parts of the country is a narrow window of near perfection betwixt hot, humid summers and cold, snowy winters. I have joined the university sailing club and love going out on the boats, cruising over the lake's glassy surface on sunny days.

But as I hone my sailing skills the lure of adventure hits about the time the fall weather turns blustery. With a couple of daring club members we sail in the worst storms, hiking out far over the edge of the hull to avoid tipping over. The sleek craft rips across the lake, sending spray through the crisp fall air as it bounces over waves. We hit 12 knots on one run.

It's exhilarating and fun until we tip the craft over trying to break our record and subsequently freeze our asses off in the frigid water. It's not easy to right one of these boats either. Grabbing the centerboard of the dinghy we pull down hard, working against the weight of the mast and wet sail on the other side. Then, completely exhausted from getting the boat upright, we sail to the shore shivering in our soaked clothes. Time to call it a day.

Back at the rental house I take a warm shower, wrap up in a blanket and relax on the couch. Jay has become flush with cash lately and he brings me payment for rent and utilities in advance. I'd be happy about the new development, but I'm skeptical about the source of his newfound treasure. It certainly isn't from his catering company. My family was his only gig.

Shady characters are in and out of the house calling on Jay at all hours of the day and night. Things go missing. At first small stuff like clocks, headphones and DVDs. Then larger items like the television disappear. The other two roommates are tired of the disruption. They know Jay's visitors have been ripping things off, but they're frightened to say anything.

Jay can be an intimidating character. But finally, I confront him about his enterprise. As I suspected, he admits he's been dealing out of the house. When I tell him he has to stop, he offers to cut me in. His network can offer me a lot of money if I join "the family."

Well that would be one way to pay for college! But I would rather go hungry working in an honest job, even washing dishes, than be a pusher. Two weeks later Jay is busted downtown for dealing coke. Thank God they didn't raid our house, we all could have been implicated.

When Jay gets out on bail I try to be friendly, but firm. He has to move out of the rental. He's putting us all at risk with his illegal business venture. He says he won't go and becomes belligerent and threatening.

It is a tough situation. My roommates want him gone too but they are scared of Jay and his co-conspirators. I figure someone has to step up. I drain Jay's waterbed and move everything out of his room, piling it all in the garage. Then I change the locks on the doors and wait.

It's a tense few days spent looking over my shoulder. I put a separate lock on my bedroom door so I can sleep at night. Eventually Jay's belongings disappear from the garage. Apparently he got the message.

With Jay gone we need a new roommate. I post ads in the local paper and on campus. Several people are interested including a short, odd fellow named Doug, who is a dead ringer for Napoleon Dynamite. The other two roommates think Doug is too nerdy. I notice he wears hearing aids and that actually makes me want him as a roommate even more. I have empathy for people with hearing loss because I'm challenged with that as well. My other roommates acquiesce to my choice, considering I had to do the heavy lifting to evict Jay.

My romantic life has basically dried up these days. There were always lots of girls hanging around the frat and exchanges with sororities where you could meet new people and find dates. There are a few girls in my classes that I'd like to ask out, but I don't seem to be able to break the ice and ask for their phone number.

I become frustrated and call Cathy, a little sister I knew in the Kappa house. We go out to the bars together a few times. She even invites me to come to Chicago to meet her father and attend the wedding of a friend.

Her dad is a high roller who talks the whole time about financial investments. Not being a business major I fail to understand exactly what people like him provide for society that they are so well compensated. It all seems like a numbers game where they actually produce nothing tangible for their hefty rewards.

Eventually I break up with Cathy. Basically when I go to her place one night to pick her up for a date she doesn't answer the door. I look through the window and she's in bed with one of the other brothers from the frat. That sucks.

Today I'm at a little mom and pop grocery store a block away from our rental buying soda crackers. It's the end of the month and I've run out of money. I resort to an old starving student trick gorging my stomach full of the white soda crackers. They have zero nutritional value but if you drink plenty of water the starchy saltines swell in your stomach providing a feeling of fullness.

As I leave the store with my box of crackers I'm startled to come face to face with Danette. It takes me a second or two to orientate my mind. But if you think about it, living in such close proximity, we were bound to bump into one another sooner or later.

She's wearing sweats and no makeup, probably on a quick trip to the store for some grocery item. But she still looks amazing. When it comes to dating, my entire life has been either a feast or a famine, and right now, I'm in the midst of a desperate famine. To a man dying of thirst, Danette looks like a tall pitcher of ice water.

I peer into her deep blue-green eyes and I'm lost. A huge amount of pent up emotion I had sublimated from the past rushes back into my conscious brain. She greets me and we make small talk for a while. I mention that I live just down the street and she remarks at the oddity of how close her apartment is. I make a move.

"Hey, how about I stop by tonight? We can catch up and talk about old times?"

Danette demurs. She doesn't say no, but doesn't exactly seem thrilled either. I don't know quite how to take her stoic reaction. My poor social skills once again leave me at a loss.

Evening comes and I decide to go for it. I'll stop by Danette's place to just feel things out. I'm uncustomarily nervous. Her apartment is a typical big boxy beehive. I know her room number from the campus directory. I knock on the door. Her soft, feminine voice is unmistakable.

She invites me in. We sit on the couch chatting. I look around. There is a small, very revealing sequined suit hanging from a chair. Its bright red, white and blue colors remind me of something from the chorus line in the movie *I'm a Yankee Doodle Dandy*.

Danette has incredible intuition. She traces my stare and knows exactly what I'm thinking. She explains deftly that she has been to a Halloween party in the capital city.

I wish I'd been at that party just to see her in that skimpy little costume. For this Halloween I was invited to a different bash with a girl I knew in high school that I really didn't care for. But I didn't have any other options so I went.

The girl works at a high-end jewelry store. Everyone at the party has fancy rented costumes on except for me and one other starving college student there, a girl who wears a garbage bag with a piece of green garden hose around her neck. I ask her what she is supposed to be and she replies, "A hose bag."

I wear all the black clothes I have with a Darth Vader mask and lightsaber I borrow from the neighbor's kid. Everyone except for me is doing coke and hash. The owner of the jewelry store comes riding into the party naked on a Harley Davidson motorcycle. It's a surreal scene.

Tonight, sitting on the couch next to Danette, my heart is pounding out of my chest. Just getting to spend some time again with her is a thrill. I can't say whether she realizes how much it means to me. I suppose she knows, what with her high EQ and uncanny intuition.

She smiles but her reaction is vague. I can't tell if she is just being coy, or truly isn't interested. But I can't let this opportunity go without trying. Before leaving I mention how great it is to see her again. And maybe we could go out to the 'Liner for a beer. I remember that the *Airliner* is her favorite bar. I leave it that I'll stop by tomorrow evening and see if she's up for a date.

The next day my lab partner in Human Biology class mentions that I seem distant. We're conducting a procedure to determine blood type. But I have trouble concentrating. All I can think about is Danette. We finally determine that I am o-Negative and my lab partner is B-Positive.

At the info desk I'm distracted. Bonnie has us working on a Rolodex of answers to possible questions. It's a good idea to have such a resource because no one can know how to respond to every question people ask. Having grown up in this city I can contribute a lot of local information. But not today. I'm spacing badly, being distracted and focused on tonight and my rendezvous with Danette.

I have a hard time deciding what shirt to wear. My wardrobe is scant. A few polo shirts and a pair of designer jeans from my frat days and the leather jacket from my hiatus as a biker. I never set an exact time with Danette but figure 8PM would be good. I'm as tense as a coiled-up seedpod on a touch-me-not plant.

I walk down the hall in the drab apartment building. The carpet is dingy Berber. The walls need paint. Pretty typical college digs. Hard to believe a creature as desirable as Danette exists behind these walls.

I knock on the door, one of those mass-produced, hollow wood affairs. There's no answer. Now I really panic. I had high expectations that some feelings between us might be rekindled tonight. But what if she's gone? Did she blow me off?

I knock again. I hear faint shuffling inside. I'm glad there is no window. If she is with another guy it would kill me to see it. Finally, her soft voice calls out tentatively, asking who is there. I reply.

Now her voice takes on a sterner tone. She sounds perturbed. "Why don't you just go away?"

Wow! There's nothing subtle about that dig, rude and insensitive maybe, but direct. The ramifications hit me in the chest like a cannonball. There is absolutely no doubt. I have zero chance with her, ever. I don't say a thing, just turn and walk away.

Strolling home through the evening light I have time to reflect on the rejection I just sustained. It really hurts to get jilted by someone you have strong feelings for, it can send you into a deep funk and cause tremendous spiritual pain. But the upside is, having been through so many relationship failures before, I have discovered the secret to recovering from a painful breakup.

When someone gets dumped, they naturally feel anger and a desire for revenge. Forget that. As King Arthur points out in *The Once and Future King*, "revenge is the most worthless of causes." Next a spurned lover tries to forget, to erase that person who hurt you from your memory. You're working against science there. As I learned in zoology memories are stored as electrical and chemical signals in the brain. Nerve cells connect together in certain patterns, called synapses, and the act of remembering something is just your brain triggering these synapses. Sorry, the neural pathways that code for memory are NOT erasable. You have to deal with the pain another way.

I'll let you in on a secret every lover should know. What is causing your sincere spiritual anguish after a breakup is that you are trying to stop loving the person that dropped you. What you have to do to truly get over it seems counter intuitive. You have to keep loving the other person anyway, no matter how badly they mistreated you. You don't have to be around them. You don't have to do anything for them. You shouldn't let them treat you like a doormat. Just don't try to change your original feelings of love. Those feelings had a reason for forming and were honorable for their own fullness.

An act of love that fails is just as much a part of the divine life as an act of love that succeeds, for love is measured by its own fullness, not by its reception.

—Harold Loukes

If you want to see the brave, look at those who can forgive. If you want to see the heroic, look at those who can love in return for hatred.

—Bhagavad Gita

I resolve to forgive and keep on loving. It's hard to do though. I admit that. Back at the rental I crash onto my bed. My life is a train wreck in a tunnel. I'll soon be finished with my sophomore year and on winter break. Next semester I'll officially be a junior. I have solid grades and a good job but I'm still broke. My dream of finding a committed relationship has gone down in flames. I don't even have a girlfriend. The lofty goal of attending medical school is fading away. I don't have 2 cents, let alone $250,000! But I keep on living regardless.

My roommates struggle as well. One night I hear Doug whimpering in his room. I knock on his door and ask if he is ok. Once inside I see that his hands and arms are covered in a nasty rash. I ask why his hands look burned and swollen. He mumbles something about his new job.

Doug has been searching for employment for weeks now and in his desperation to make some money he took a gig at a salvage yard where the proprietor instructed him to unload 55-gallon barrels of toxic waste from a semi truck and pour the contents out onto the ground. My roomie has obviously gotten some of the nasty chemical waste on his skin. I tell Doug it is an emergency and he needs to go to the hospital.

I know what it is like to be in Doug's predicament, needing money for living expenses and having trouble finding a decent job. I'm so very thankful for my position at the information center. I concentrate on doing the best job there that I can answering people's questions.

After my shift as a university information specialist is over, a girl who works with me asks to speak with me privately. She confronts me about whether or not I've noticed that she has been ignoring me. I explain that I have not. Then she goes into a rambling declaration of how she has decided to give me one more chance at asking her out.

The whole episode is just sad. I've never had any interest in asking her out and how she got the idea that I ever would is beyond me. How can people miscommunicate this badly? She must have a low EQ like me!

I'm pretty depressed about my life and the whole world really. The way everything is set up in the universe seems upside down and crazy to me right now. I'm falling into a deep funk and it is in this vulnerable condition that I hear a voice call out to me like a carnival barker from a table in the union hallway.

It is a military recruiter in a fancy uniform. He has a big smile that I suspect hides something. But I'm tired and I stop to politely hear him out. He explains that the Army can help pay for college expenses. I have never considered joining the military. I just naturally hate war and violence.

But I feel the pangs of poverty like every other struggling student. I mention that I want to go to medical school just to see what he will say. The recruiter opens a glossy pamphlet explaining that, if I qualify, the Army will not only cover all my medical school expenses, they will pay me a stipend while I'm getting my MD.

Wow! That does sound appealing. Not only would I not have to go into debt, I would actually get paid to go to medical school like students in progressive countries get paid to go to college.

"What's the catch?" I quiz the sergeant, figuring they would demand my firstborn child in repayment for such a Faustian bargain.

"For every year of medical school we pay for, you would owe us one year of military service to your country," he replies in a husky voice.

I start to turn away. It really disgusts me how few options poor and working class people have for college. The country may not currently be engaged in military conscription, but there is definitely a poverty draft.

I thank the recruiter for the pamphlet and agree to look it over. But he is very persistent, not wanting to let me go, and he grills me about any possible doubts I have.

"I don't want to hurt or kill anyone," I say bluntly, trying to be honest.

Without presenting any sort of moral counter-argument the sergeant goes into a spiel about how if I were accepted into a medic program I would actually be helping people, not hurting them, and that I could serve my time in a national guard medical battalion that responds in times of national emergencies like hurricanes and earthquakes.

I have to admit it is a very tempting sales pitch, especially to a depressed person with no money and no options who has just been jilted by a girl he loved. I put the pamphlet in my pocket and head home to cram for finals.

CHAPTER TWENTY-THREE

My starving roommates and I get a lucky break. Hondo returns from a hunting expedition in Colorado with an elk he killed. There is no way he can eat that much meat so he gives the rest to us. Doug has a friend from Japan named Yoshio who makes us delicious elk teriyaki.

My roomies have also discovered a government program that gives away large blocks of surplus cheese to low income people. So now they eat surplus cheese omelets for breakfast, surplus cheese sandwiches for lunch then macaroni and surplus cheese for dinner. They eat so much cheese they suffer from chronic constipation. But at least they are no longer hungry.

Hondo's attempt to make homemade wine doesn't turn out well. So he brings milk jugs of the stuff over to our rental house. My roommates are poor and so desperate they love any form of alcohol that is free. We sit around the dining room table in the evening laughing and talking, everyone but me getting drunk on rotgut wine and dipping stale bread in a fondue pot of melted surplus cheese while Yoshio prepares heaping portions of elk teriyaki.

The food gives me renewed strength to pull all-nighters cramming for finals. With a manageable workload at the info center, no time wasted commuting and a positive roommate situation I can totally concentrate and crush the big tests. Before I know it, the semester is over.

I'm now so burned out from studying I would do anything to get out of town for a change of scenery. An opportunity presents itself when Greg and Arvella, two college professors who know my sister, ask me to come along with them to Florida and help watch their youngster Jimmy.

It seems like a good opportunity to get an all expenses paid vacation. But I figure their kid must really be something for them to make such a lucrative offer.

I throw a gym bag with a swimsuit and a few extra clothes in the trunk of their Camry and we're off on the 26-hour drive to Clearwater Beach. I'm stuck in the back seat with Jimmy, who is a nice kid but extremely hyperactive. Most people would pump him full of Ritalin and zombie him out. But not Greg and Arvella.

I read books, play games, tell stories until I run out of ideas in a couple of hours. The kid is bouncing around inside the car. The couple is very intellectual, discussing all sorts of interesting concepts but they become argumentative when their kid won't behave.

This continues all the way to Georgia. The couple is nice enough to buy me lunch and snacks when we stop for gas. But I end up chasing after Jimmy who takes off running the minute the door opens.

Then it happens, at first a small splatter on the windshield builds into a full-blown ice storm. We end up stuck on the interstate highway in the middle of nowhere. Cars all around us are spinning their wheels. I finally get out and start pushing on people's bumpers to help them along. At least it gives me some exercise and provides a break from babysitting.

All the other commuters heed the warnings to get off the road but Greg pulls over onto the gravel shoulder where the car can get some traction and we continue on the perilous trip. I think he figured we would all go crazy cooped up in a fleabag motel with a hyperactive kid.

We are exhausted by the time we reach their motel in Florida. They didn't cheap out though. It's a beautiful place right on the ocean. I grab a towel and head down to repose on the white sand beach.

Before I can catch some Zs the couple shows up with Jimmy and a thermos of rum and coke.

I throw a beach ball and make sand castles with their kid. Then we all go swimming. Jimmy disappears under the surf. Arvella is frantic. I dive in and pull him out. He coughs up a lot of seawater but he's fine, more relaxed and less intense for once actually. The brush with death, and stomach full of brine, have subdued his manic intensity. I think we discovered a cure for hyperactivity: near drowning.

Each day we visit the seafood market. Greg buys huge portions of fresh grouper, snapper and other fish. Arvella purchases citrus fruit, avocados and other farm fresh veggies. The couple drinks a bottle of wine with dinner, then they switch to mixed drinks in the evening. The conversation is lively until they get smashed and start to argue.

Greg is a Russian language prof who tells me interesting stories. For example when Soviet Premier Nikita Khrushchev visited the United States he was misquoted as saying "We will bury you." What Khrushchev really uttered was an idiomatic expression that in Russian means "you'll eat our dust," in other words, we'll out compete you. And I guess when you figure they launched sputnik, while we were still on the ground, in a way they did. Especially considering they started the competition with their country left in an ash heap and 30 million of their people dead from Hitler's invasion while the U.S. emerged from WWII with its infrastructure unscathed.

The mistranslation of Khrushchev's words led to harsh feelings during the Cold War as many Americans thought the Soviet Premier was threatening nuclear war or something.

Greg tells many other insightful stories from his days as an intelligence officer during WWII. It gets me thinking a lot about war. The military recruiter's offer weighs heavily on my mind. In Greg's case, I think serving in the Army was a little clearer. I mean Hitler and the Nazis were obviously a terrible foe that had to be defeated. These days the situation is a lot muddier with the U.S. fighting wars that don't seem necessary or with any clear or legitimate goals. I mean fighting a war for oil isn't exactly a noble quest.

I do like the idea of actually getting paid by the army to go to medical school. So many students these days graduate with huge, crippling debt that burdens them for a lifetime. Also the idea of helping people during crisis like floods or tornadoes appeals to me as honorable. I like the arrangement of doing time in a national guard MASH field hospital where I could serve one weekend a month and 2 weeks in the summer after boot and AIT.

It is a huge decision. I feel like joining the army would be like signing away 8 years of my life. On the other hand, I don't really have any other options besides going a quarter of a million dollars in debt for medical school. I go back and forth in my mind, unable to decide.

The week on the sandy beach basking in Florida sunshine is over and we must bear the trek back home with Jimmy at full throttle. I tell stories and play games in the back seat until I'm exhausted. I think you could put kids like Jimmy on a hamster wheel and generate a lot of renewable energy.

Everything has changed when I get back home. The weather is nasty cold with lots of snow and ice. Leroy buys a trailer and takes off to spend the winter in Arizona with my mom. Hondo and his bride are having marriage problems. Basically, his wife is a practicing alcoholic. Ross and Tom have decided to move out of the rental.

I put up notices and place ads for new roommates. A well-groomed young man named Mark shows up. He works as a full-time truck dispatcher, in addition to taking college classes. So, I figure he'll be able to pay the rent on time.

I help Mark move his scant possessions into one of the rooms. He has some teddy bears he tells me he won in a contest. Mark is a sweeper. He enters hundreds of sweepstakes as a hobby. So far he has only won the three stuffed animals. But he remains hopeful of winning big, a house or car or vacation or a lottery someday.

I wish him luck, but honestly, from what I have learned in my statistics classes, he might as well take a shovel and go dig in the yard for gold, he would have about the same chance as striking it rich in a lottery. Gambling to me is just a tax on people who are bad at math.

I will say Mark is extremely neat and clean. The house is now dusted and the trash is always taken out to the curb on time. He is basically the perfect roommate.

One day I have to move his car and notice bundles of newspapers on the seats. It is an alternative student publication called the Gayly Newspaper and Mark is the editor.

It was a weird way to discover his sexual orientation and I regrettably feel kind of uncomfortable because of the bad experience I had with Anders in the frat house. I don't want to be prejudiced. You can not extrapolate one individual's behavior to an entire group. That is stereotyping. I respect other people's rights and freedom. I just have some anxiety.

I ask Doug what he thinks and he sets me straight.

"What's the guy supposed to do, tell you he's gay when he calls to ask about the room? He probably deals with discrimination all the time in his life!"

We still have Tom's room to fill and Mark suggests an acquaintance, an older, non-traditional student named Charles. Charles is a hairdresser. I help him move his stuff in and it turns out to be an amazing, all day experience.

Chuck has an incredible collection of expensive antiques. We go from having a decrepit couch we found deserted on the curb to an antique French provincial Louis XV Rococo style ornately carved settee sofa. Mark finds a rotten old sandwich that Jay lost under the old couch that he removes from the house wearing latex gloves while plugging his nose.

The rental house is transformed! There are exquisite antiques, oriental rugs, rare china in the kitchen, new curtains, and flower arrangements. Chuck shares his furniture and Doug now sports a deluxe bedroom set instead of sleeping on an air mattress. In my room, I stick with my own original early American Ghetto pieces. But I do enjoy the look in the rest of the house.

Chuck gives free haircuts to the other roommates. He talks me into letting him cut my hair and I have to admit it is probably the best style I've ever had in my life. I can just run a comb through it and my hair falls neatly into place. But I insist on paying him cash. I just feel deep down like work is an honorable thing, and that he should be compensated.

So, what's it like for two straight guys, Doug and I, living with two gay guys? The house is always meticulously clean and well decorated and the bills are always paid on time. Basically, they are ideal room-mates and wonderful people.

In order to keep up my end of the rent and utility payments I land a second position, a peach of a job working as an usher at the university center for performing arts. Along with science and math classes, the information desk position consumes all of my days. Now in the evenings I get paid to watch Broadway musical plays, fine symphony orchestras and the Joffrey Ballet perform the Nutcracker suite. It's a sweet gig.

Life is getting better! I renew my interest in the outdoor club, this time signing up for scuba lessons. The classroom portion is interesting with lots of important information to remember about decompression stops and other safety considerations.

When it comes time to do the pool certification I enjoy breathing underwater with the regulator and everything is going well until we come to a test where I must take off my mask and let it drop 15 feet to the bottom of the pool, swim down, fetch, and then clear it, by blowing the water out.

Unfortunately, grafted eardrums can't take the water pressure at that depth. Unable to equalize adequately I experience extreme pain. So, I'm washed out of the course.

This failure reminds me of the time I signed up for flying lessons. I learned to take off in the small Cessna plane and land without any problems. I could handle 2 axis maneuvers but when we got to three axis bank turns, the plane wasn't the only thing turning. So was my stomach.

In addition to hearing, the inner ear regulates balance and my messed auditory system leaves me susceptible to motion sickness. I guess sometimes in life you have to accept that you have certain challenges that limit what you can do. Such limitations result in both frustration and humility. I'm just thankful for what I can do and resolve to move on and not perseverate about the failures.

The military recruiter calls me at work. How he got my contact information I don't know. I talk with him for a while. I explain that I have thought it over but I'm not ready to make any decision. He suggests that I take a battery of tests that would determine whether or not I would be eligible for the Army medical program.

I agree to take the tests. I mean, I might as well find out if this military avenue is even an option for me. Sometimes major decisions are made in small, manageable, incremental steps.

CHAPTER TWENTY-FOUR

I have taken on a full load of tough classes this semester. I'm struggling in my Math for the Biological Sciences class and I signed up for a computer programming course that is sheer hell.

I'm basically a nature lover at heart who digs the great outdoors. Instead I spend way too much time in a drab, cement-walled, underground computer-processing center that students call the dungeon.

I have trouble getting the mainframe to follow my programs while super-nerds produce innovative results, not only are their data correct, their numbers print out in displays that create cute pictures of animals and cartoon characters. Geez!

Sometimes in life you have to know when to quit. I'm not saying a person should be a quitter, I think you should always try your best and show grit, determination and perseverance - to a point. But sometimes ending some involvement is the right and logical thing to do.

I drop the computer programming class and feel like a ton of bricks has been removed from my back. I relish having a little extra time to actually take walks outside and breath fresh air, instead of the dungeon's stale vapors.

The biological statistics class is another story entirely. I need to know this stuff for the MCAT someday. So I refuse to quit. But no matter how hard I try, I come up with C grades on my coursework. Average does not cut it in the pre-med world and I have to do something to bring that score up.

I explore and ask other pre-med students for suggestions, finally discovering a university program called the tutor referral service. I fill out a form and I'm paired to work with a math grad student a couple of times a week. Never in a million years would I have thought I'd ever need a tutor, but here I am.

The grad student's name is Tom. He is sort of a nerdy geek with a lot of peculiarities, like opening his mouth and rolling his eyes when he thinks. But the guy really knows his statistics stuff and my quiz scores improve.

The thing about Tom is that he's a born again Christian, which he lets you know within the first five minutes of conversation. When we get done studying I always thank him and he corrects me that I should thank the lord because God sent him to help me.

I'm good with the Christian thing. I mean, I basically agree with everything Jesus actually taught in the New Testament, about making peace and helping poor people and not being greedy and so forth. It's just that some of the more conservative religious people emphasize issues like abortion and gay sex that Jesus never said one word against.

Amidst the tutoring Tom mentions that I must bow down to the lord and be born again. I try to explain my own philosophy, that I think God is a kind and loving God that wouldn't really want us to bow down and capitulate. That would be like bowing down in a mirror. I mean, would you want someone you love to bow down to you? I'm not sure that is love at all.

But Tom continues, driven I guess by a compelling need he feels to avoid going to hell by saving other people's souls. One day, as we study, he lays a paper down in front of me from his church that says *I accept Jesus Christ as my personal savior*. I just want to get an A in the damn math class. I sign the thing and he lays off the proselytizing so we can get back to studying. Apparently it is really important to evangelicals that you say the exact magic words they believe in.

Personally I think believing in religion, or not believing in religion, is a personal choice. I'm fine with discussing religion, and politics too for that matter. I don't think any subject should be taboo in honest conversation. I just don't like it when zealous people go fundamentalist on me, acting like they have the only one true belief, and if you disagree with them, that makes you a bad person who is going to hell or something.

I try to find truth in all different viewpoints. I think every religion has some validity, and so do atheism and agnosticism for that matter. I just try to be respectful of everyone's views and not pretend that I have all the answers like some of these people.

The military recruiter is thrilled when I show up at the local National Guard Armory to take the aptitude test battery. With its many different flags and drab green war paraphernalia the place actually gives me the creeps. The whole idea of war and fighting is really foreign to me. I'm not one of those guys who enjoyed playing army as a kid and I was never fooled by propaganda movies starring actors like John Wayne or Sylvester Stallone who never served a single second in the military themselves.

I sit at a small desk with some other recruits, a couple of college students and some kids who appear to be from low income or blue-collar families. The tests are actually kind of interesting—the usual math, science and English stuff but also some engineering and mechanical problems. Having a diverse background as both a college student, and a former gearhead who has worked in construction type jobs, I find every question doable.

I'm not sure if these recruiters get paid a lot of money for every person they sign up, or maybe they get promotions in rank or something, but I can tell you the sergeant is absolutely giddy when he contacts me a few days later. I passed all the exams with flying colors and rank in the top percentile. He has a slot open in the medical track and the paperwork is all ready to go.

I take a walk on the campus golf course wanting to be around nature for a bit. This is one of the toughest decisions of my life, right up there with going to college instead of working full time and taking over Leroy's business someday.

I think I can barely squeak by working my way through my undergrad degree without any loans. But I would have to borrow about

$250,000 for medical school unless I join the Army. I don't want to hurt or kill anyone but I'd be serving as a medic in a national guard MASH unit so hopefully I would be helping people.

All the pomp and adulation that society heaps on soldiers and veterans is tempting, but I can see through that. "Thanks for your service?" Yeah, right. Most people just want someone else to do the dirty work in war for them. But ultimately, having someone else kill for you is morally no better than killing someone yourself.

I don't really like the idea of having anybody else defend me. I'd rather defend myself. Really how fair is it that a large portion of our military forces comes from low income and minority backgrounds? Wouldn't it be better to have a cross section of society involved? Maybe there would be fewer wars if billionaires' children had to fight.

Unless we see things with our own eyes, how are we to know that the government is not just conning us into attacking another person's country for no good reason? Both the Vietnam War and Iraq War were based on lies.

I do support ideals like freedom, equality and democracy. I'm just not sure that the current government really pursues those goals around the globe. Instead of defending the country or lofty ideals, these days the U.S. military seems like more of a bouncer service protecting corporate property rights in other countries and imposing crony capitalism on emerging nations while their labor and resources are exploited.

I'm not the only one having tough choices to make. My brother Hondo is going through a nasty separation and since they have a toddler, a beautiful little redheaded girl, there are custody issues. Leroy and my mom are back from Arizona. Mom wasn't cool with living in a trailer at an over-50 retirement community all winter. So now her and Leroy babysit a lot while the little girl's parents, Hondo and his soon-to-be ex, duke it out.

At the rental our utility bills are getting expensive and we struggle to make payments. But my roomies think my energy conservation measures are too draconian. I put low-flow, water-saving heads on the showers and a timed thermostat on the furnace. I ask them to turn down the temperature of their waterbeds. Sleeping on those sloshy, slip and slide mattresses is like having four water heaters in one house.

The roomies revolt. Chuck says he would rather enjoy a more luxurious lifestyle and pay higher utility bills. I don't push the issue. I'm just glad to have responsible people living in the house who pay their bills on time and pick up after themselves.

The memory of my former roommate Jay is still clear in my mind. He was so irresponsible. I actually bumped into him on campus one day. At least we have buried the hatchet and are not enemies. Jay is working as a wine sales representative. So, I guess he is technically still a drug pusher, but a legal one now.

When I enter the recruiter's office he is practicing his putting on one of those miniature golf holes. He's glad to see me, of course. I was probably an easy mark for him, low on funds, fresh off a terrible jilting and with no other options except massive debt to pay for my dream of attending medical school. He saw me coming a mile away.

"Being in the armed forces is a dog's life," the crew cut recruiter informs me. "You just put in 20 years and then you can retire."

I sort of ignore his self-interested cheerfulness and sign the enlistment papers. I have no desire to be in the military at all, let alone 20 years. But I sign up for an 8-year contract to lock in the medical slot.

Eight years of your life is a long time, and a huge commitment. I try to make sure everything is down in writing. Recruiters make lots of promises. I've heard horror stories about enlistees not getting the training they signed up for. My roommate Charles joined the navy to study computer programming and instead ended up spending four years in the boiler room of a warship.

I raise my right hand and repeat an oath: "I do solemnly *affirm* that I will support and defend the Constitution of the United States against all enemies, foreign and domestic; that I will bear true faith and allegiance to the same; and that I will obey the orders of the President of the United States and the orders of the officers appointed over me, according to regulations and the Uniform Code of Military Justice. So help me God."

I insist on *affirming* rather than *swearing* an oath because in James 5:12 Jesus specifically instructs, "Above all else, brothers and sisters, do not swear, either by heaven or by earth or by any other oath." The recruiter just considers it an oddity, but I mean really, if they are going to include religion in this military oath with the "So help me God" line then why are they ignoring the teaching of the architect of this country's most popular religion?

In the next official act, I'm supposed to take one step forward crossing what the recruiter describes as an imaginary line. After you cross this "line" then you are "officially" inducted into the armed forces. I think to myself there actually may be something to this tradition, sort of acknowledgment that you are crossing a spiritual line when you agree to kill people for the government.

I take the big step and the recruiter cheers. But I'm not that excited. I know from reading about the whole process that I'm really not officially in the Army yet because I haven't passed the military physical, which will take place in the capitol city this weekend.

It is kind of weird, and startling, that as soon as you sign the papers and agree to join up everyone treats you differently. The recruiter becomes less friendly and more demanding. In a bossy tone he tells me where to report for the bus ride to MEPS, the Military Entrance Processing Station, where I will get my physical and official orders.

I board a drab green military bus the next day along with a bunch of other young recruits. No one is smiling. A couple of hours later we arrive at the military processing center, a plain red brick building that could just as easily house a meat packing operation. The sergeants are rude, ordering everybody around in bossy tones.

Medical specialists perform routine procedures like blood pressure and listening to our hearts with a stethoscope. There are also some not so routine procedures like telling everyone in line to drop their pants, bend over and spread their cheeks.

The medical specialists are all men and after they finish performing this group humiliation on the male recruits they head into a separate room to do the same with all the females. They seem to enjoy it and are making jokes and laughing about it.

In the final stage we get to confer with an actual doctor who is a civilian, not a member of the military. The doc looks at my chest x-ray and gives me an inquisitive look. I explain that we do a lot of sandblasting at Leroy's shop. I've breathed in a lot of silica dust over the years and it has shown up on radiological exams before.

Next the doctor explains that my audiology screening shows a hearing loss. I recount that I fractured my skull when I was 14 years old and the crack ran through my middle ear. He asks if I have ever broken any other bones and I describe how I broke my neck once diving into a shallow lake.

The old doc just shakes his head. Then something really insightful happens. He explains that if I didn't want to be in the military I would never have to go because any one of these medical conditions could keep me out. They would never be able to draft me.

Then he asks if I want in or out. Just like that. Which kind of reveals a lot to me about all the movie stars and rock stars and politicians who say they wanted to serve but couldn't because of some minor medical condition like a bone spur. Basically, unless you are blind or missing a limb or have some really major health problem you can get in ... if you really want to. The truth is most of those chicken hawks who are big war supporters, but never served themselves, could have served if they really wanted to.

The civilian doctors at MEPS are really decent people. They are not going to force anyone into the military if there is any possible medical excuse to get out. I tell the doctor I want in. He just shakes his head and signs my physical papers.

There are many more forms to sign. At the end of the day I get my orders that come stapled in multiple copies. I'm to report for support basic training at Ft. Knox, Kentucky in June after school is out. I had agreed to this arrangement with my recruiter. The date would not interfere with college classes and since I was in the medical track, I'd go to support basic which is not as intense as the training received by those who would be going into combat missions.

For final approval I arrive in the office of a top military officer. This fellow is a rude jerk who immediately starts ordering me around. On one of the forms they have a box to check if you consider yourself a conscientious objector. He demands to know if I have moral or religious objections to war.

I ask him to explain exactly what being a "conscientious objector" means. At that, the officer's face turns bright red and he goes ballistic on me screaming something about, "Either you believe in your country or you don't!"

A couple of days later I get notification that my orders have been changed. I'm no longer required to report to Ft. Knox for support basic training. I'm now ordered to report to FT. Leonard Wood for combat basic training in July.

CHAPTER TWENTY-FIVE

I'm busy and the days go by quickly now. Classes are challenging and I'm learning a lot. At work I really feel like I help people out with their questions at the information desk and that gives me a positive feeling of affirmation. At least two nights a week I'm an usher at the Center for the Performing Arts watching plays, recitals, symphonies and other events. Personally, I'm not that artistically talented and I really appreciate the skills and dedication of the performers.

Once a month I attend drills at the local National Guard center. We recruits wear civilian clothes and mostly practice various skills that we will need when we go to boot camp this summer. We learn to march, take M-16s apart and put them back together and memorize the various military ranks and insignia. Since we are a MASH unit we practice putting up the big tents and other equipment used by our Mobile Army Surgical Hospital.

Most of the people in our battalion are decent, just trying to do their jobs and get their time in. There are some bossy jerks who like to pull rank and find some minor fault, or even make something up, as an excuse to force you to do push ups. When they yell, "give me 20!" you just do the exercises and try to ignore their BS.

The motto of our medical battalion is *Save to serve again*. I'm learning a little about triage, which is the military system of sorting out patients according to the severity of their wounds. I understand the need to prioritize care. But I also think that our motto really ought to focus on the goal of saving lives. *Save to serve again* sounds like our main purpose is patching up soldiers so they can get back out there on the battlefield. Leave it to the military to corrupt even something as worthy as providing medical care.

I've added a weight lifting class to my school schedule this semester and work out faithfully at the gym. I splurge on a pair of top quality running shoes, Air Nikes, and hit the track wanting to be in top shape for the rigors of boot camp. After weeks of training I can run the seven miles to my parents place in the country, have dinner and chat with them for a while, and then run seven miles home without feeling exhausted or tired.

My roommates Mark and Chuck are supportive, but skeptical, when I tell them I joined the Army. They wish me luck, of course, but also seem leery of my decision. Both of them had bad experiences in the military. I just want them to know my intentions in advance, that I'll be moving out for the summer, so we can plan ahead and find someone to sublet. I'll miss them.

I go to the post office and get a mailbox. I can have all my correspondence forwarded there while I am away at boot. Then I concentrate on reducing my current inventory of scant possessions even further so everything I own can fit into my backpacking pack, which I'll leave at my parents while I'm gone to Ft. Leonard Wood.

It is difficult giving away, or selling, the last few things I own in this world. But I have always been somewhat of a minimalist, if for no other reason than to reduce consumption. Materialism has a huge impact on the natural environment.

The minimalist lifestyle fits my personal philosophy well. Like Thoreau, I feel it is liberating to own no more than you can comfortably carry on your back. Jesus himself owned little. Biblical accounts say that after he was tortured to death by Roman soldiers they threw dice for his clothing, his only worldly possessions.

The Native American medicine man Black Elk speaks of living the true authentic life in balance with nature as "walking the good red road." In the Indian code of ethics the earth is our mother and we should respect and care for nature. To honor creation is to reject materialism, to take only what you truly need and leave the rest. I want to walk the good red road, but it is hard in our modern society.

I have to admit the one thing I found most difficult to give away was a beautiful picture I had framed in my room of Sitting Bull with his quote *Let us put our minds together and see what life we can make for our children*. I wanted to find a good home for it so I donated it to the Latino Native American Cultural Center on campus.

Spring break is here, and just in time. I have been working so hard in my classes that I need a vacation for my own mental health. A fellow classmate named Gary, who spends hours crunching numbers with me in statistics, feels the same way. We have no money to head off to some exotic beach somewhere like many other college students. So we check out a map of our state and decide to drive to a giant forest on the southern border and go hiking.

We are on the road by 4AM and pass through a small town that is home to an alternative community where people practice Transcendental Meditation, or TM, a form of silent mantra meditation developed by Maharishi Mahesh Yogi. Some of the people in town, townies, do not like the mediators and call them fliers or roos which is short for gurus.

There have been articles in the news lately about how the meditators can defy the laws of gravity and levitate. We heard they even built a dome to float around in. As we pass by the TM community on the highway, sure enough, there is a golden dome constructed in the rolling hills.

I tell Gary I'd like to stop and check it out. His brow furrows with skepticism. We pull off the road and park in the lot near the dome. I want to go inside and see if people are really hovering around in there. Gary does not want any part of it and stays in the car while I walk gingerly up to the front door. It is unlocked.

I'm hopeful I can just take a peak inside and leave. But the front door only opens to an entrance area with cubbyhole boxes filled with shoes. I understand in many eastern cultures it's a tradition to remove your footwear upon entering so I stick my tennie runners in an empty box and proceed.

A long walkway leads to a fancy inside door with *Gateway to Utopia* inscribed above it. I'm tense with excitement as this must open into the actual dome area where they supposedly levitate. However disappointment sets in when I try the handle and find the second door locked.

Just as I turn to leave someone emerges from inside carrying a rug. I slip my foot in the door so it does not shut and then sneak inside. There are people sitting cross-legged on small rugs with their eyes closed. At the front of the room is something resembling the altar in a church upon which rests a large picture of the yogi surrounded by piles of flowers. Except for a few people humming, it is silent.

Being a student of science and realism, it is just as I thought; no one is levitating off the ground. After a bit, some of the transcendentalists notice I'm not sitting or meditating like the others. This seems like a good time to exit.

I quickly slip back out through the *Gateway to Utopia*, hustle down the hall, grab my shoes and sprint out to the car in stocking feet where Gary is waiting nervously in the driver seat.

"What happened? Were they really levitating in there?" he probes anxiously.

"Let's get out of here!" I yell. "There were people floating all around inside there. I'm afraid they'll come after us."

"No way!" Gary screams doubtfully. "Are you kidding?"

"I am NOT kidding!" I blare out frantically. "I mean it, they're actually hovering up to the ceiling in there."

Gary floors the old clunker and we tear down the highway making our escape. I keep insisting that the levitators were real for about a hundred miles and occasionally search the sky to see if any are following us. Gary doesn't know what to believe. After all, there have been articles describing the practice in the news.

Finally when we stop for gas I admit the whole thing is a hoax. Gary breathes a sigh of relief and we grab some drinks and power bars for the upcoming hike.

Unfortunately, before we make it to the forest on our hiking expedition, the old clunker begins to make strange noises. The engine begins to miss. We're in the middle of nowhere with no gas stations or auto repair shops.

The car heaves and jerks. It's obvious something is seriously wrong and the engine is about to quit. We pull into a farmyard, the only hint of civilization for miles. The car backfires, emits a cloud of smoke from the tailpipe and stops running.

Gary and I look at each other stunned. Now what are we going to do? We pile out of the old clunker and pop open the hood.

I know some things about auto mechanics from my old, high school gearhead days. I fumble around checking the engine wiring and gas line. Instead of hiking, we spend the whole afternoon trying to get the car rolling again. Nothing seems to work.

Eventually an elderly farmer in overalls saunters out of the farmhouse and over to our car.

"Having trouble?" he asks smiling.

He seems genuinely concerned, so we explain our dilemma. All three of us gather peering under the hood. The old guy just scratches his head. Eventually the battery wears out trying to start the car. The farmer pulls around in his pickup truck to give us a jump. But then changes his mind.

"Why don't you boys come inside and rest a bit and I'll make a couple of phone calls."

Lacking any better strategy, we follow him into the old homestead. There are ancient looking landscape pictures on the walls and the furniture is heavily worn and faded. But it is warm inside and the aroma of home cooked food permeates the air.

The old man returns from making his calls and invites us to sit down at the dining room table for dinner. A grey-haired woman in a baggy paisley dress, whom he introduces as his wife, uses her apron as a pot holder to bring heaping plates of roast beef, mashed potatoes with gravy and green beans.

I'm worried about getting the car fixed but the old couple are so relaxed, I can't help but sit back and answer their questions. We explain that we are college students on spring break and we came down to hike in the nearby state forest preserve.

Finally, after a desert of pie and ice cream, we head back outside to work on the broken-down clunker. I'm amazed to see a couple of young farm boys closing the hood. The car is running smoothly.

While we were having dinner, they were busy fixing our vehicle. I take out my wallet. I don't have much money but offer them all I have left. The young men smile and decline the offer, explaining that the carburetor had just vapor locked.

It is getting late, so after many thanks Gary and I bid farewell and head home, never having stepped foot into the forest. But we definitely learned a lesson about helping strangers.

My roommate Mark is planting colorful flowers out in front of the rental when I get home. Can you believe that? Most people couldn't care less about a place they are just renting. We've never had any flowers planted around here before.

I tell my roomies about my experience today. "Farmers are the salt of the earth," Mark replies.

"Yep," I agree. Then qualify my statement, "Some of them sure are!"

Kind of depressing when you think about it. After all my hard work and studying I'll be spending spring break going nowhere. The other roomies drift off to visit their parents or go on vacation. I sit on my bed in my room daydreaming of distant beaches crowded with girls in bikinis.

The phone rings. It's Leroy. He's purchased a travel van. I know he is disappointed my Mom didn't want to stay all winter in Arizona. He's bored and looking for someone to head off on an adventure with.

"How about Texas?" I ask. I've been wanting to check out the hospital facilities at Ft. Sam Huston in San Antonio since that is where I'll eventually go for medical training.

Leroy is down for that and before you know it, we're off on one of his straight through, stop only for gas, expeditions in the van. I put my seat back, tune the radio to rock and roll, and stare out the window watching the scenery go by.

When we get to Dallas Leroy finds Dealey Plaza. We head up to the sixth floor of the historic Texas School Book Depository that is now preserved as a museum. I peer down from the window where Lee Harvey Oswald supposedly shot President John F. Kennedy.

Leroy gave me my first gun for Christmas when I was ten years old. I have hunted and target practiced with guns my whole life. I stare down at the X painted on the pavement below that marks the spot where Kennedy was hit. From my own experience with guns, I'm skeptical of the Warren Commission version that Oswald accurately fired 3 shots from an old bolt-action rifle in 8 seconds from this window.

Personally, I've always suspected that Allen Dulles, the former right-wing head of the CIA, who Kennedy fired, may have had something to do with the assassination. I mean Dulles was livid at Kennedy for firing him and Dulles hated Kennedy because the president was going to end the war in Vietnam. But, if a secret agency like CIA was behind the assassination, I figure they're experts in concealing their tracks and no one will ever know what really happened.

Life is strange like that. There are so many things I'd just like to know the truth about. But it's impossible to know everything, and I must accept the fact that many of my questions will never be answered, at least not in this world.

Leroy and I duff around Texas for a few days, staying in small campgrounds and parking lots. I marvel at the pink flamingos prancing around the San Antonio Zoo. We tour the old Alamo and then, in the evening, amble along a colorfully lighted river walk. The next day we drive to Ft. Sam Huston, the Army medical center, where soldiers on AIT march in formations among imposing red roofed buildings.

I have a hard time picturing myself there. I feel an ache in the pit of my stomach wondering if I made the right choice joining the army. But I really had no other option if I wanted to further my education, besides going deeply into debt. I was drafted by my lack of money and opportunities.

Leroy wants to see Mexico so we take the van across the border at Matamoros. There are lots of small, dusty market stalls with people selling almost everything. A man pushing a cart full of freshly butchered animal bones looks down self-consciously as I pass by on the street.

"*Buenos días,*" I try out some of my high school *español.*

The pushcart man looks up smiling widely and replies, "*Buenos días señor!*"

The people seem happy when I speak their language. But I'm rusty and they often laugh at my amateurish attempts.

My dad has become embroiled in a bartering session with a leather worker. It doesn't help that Leroy knows not one word of Spanish. I saunter over to observe.

The old Mexican craftsman has a finely tooled holster. I have no idea why Leroy wants it. What is he going to do with it? Walk down main street back home with a six-shooter waiting for someone to draw on him at high noon?

I determine that Leroy really doesn't want the leather holster, but everyone here is trying to sell us stuff and we have trouble turning people down. Every time Leroy turns to leave the fellow lowers his asking price. Kind of sad really, since the amount of money is not the problem. Finally, the Mexican craftsman says 20 bucks and Leroy dishes over the cash. The holster is probably worth at least a hundred.

Our foray into Mexico is ending and we head back to the United States. On the way Leroy does what I have seen him do a hundred times, he stops to help a stranded motorist. A Hispanic woman, with children huddled at her side, is broken down along the road. Their tire is flat, so we fix it. The woman says *Gracias* repeatedly. There are a lot of things I dislike about Leroy but I have to admire him for helping people out.

I feel a kind of relief I cannot explain when we cross the border back into Texas. It is good to be back in our own country. We're tired of camping out, so I call an old high school friend who is living in Houston. After graduating from college with a business degree Chuck Klasson, who we nicknamed Hucky Bucks, got a job as a systems analyst for Exxon. He invites us to crash at his pad.

We stop a couple of times along the way to walk the beach. The sand seems kind of dirty here in Texas and there are lumps of dried oil mixed in with the usual ocean flotsam. Looks to me like someone sacrificed natural beauty for money.

The streets in Houston are a maze. It looks like they hired a madman for their regional planner. It takes forever to find Hucky's place. The city outgrew the ability of street planners to keep up, my old friend explains. Like so many things in Texas the road system suffers from a lack of even the minimum basic rules and regulations.

I like Hucky a lot but I always feel a bit weird when my friends sell out and go corporate. Our relationship is different now that he works for big oil. Just my bias against the man.

My old pal is gracious though, letting us crash on the floor in his living room. Hucky is about 6'6" tall, tanned and solid muscle. He'll make a good Texan, I figure. He laments how he bought an expensive new Ralph Lauren suit but ruined it by putting it in a washing machine. Now THAT is the same old Hucky Bucks.

Our last stop is the Hotel Galvez on the coast. On informational posters I read about how Galveston Island was destroyed several times in the past by destructive hurricanes. I ask the fellow at the hotel desk about rumors of a hurricane party that no one survived. He told me that never really happened.

The next morning, we pile into the van and head for home. Out on the interstate Leroy floors the engine. The speedometer says 95 mph. A lot of people would be terrified riding at that speed in a top-heavy rig like this camper. I adjust my seat back, tune the radio to rock and roll and just gaze out the window as the world rolls by. Leroy barely graduated from high school, didn't go to college and has never read a single book in his whole life. But he is street smart and a damn good driver. I know we'll get home safe and in record time.

CHAPTER TWENTY-SIX

*B*ack at the college the big story going around is how my old fraternity is being thrown off campus for repeated violations of the drug and alcohol code. It didn't help that one of the guys got charged with sexual harassment at a party. I'm just glad I'm out of there. Looks like 40 young men are going to be looking for a new place to live. But that's not my problem now. I never really fit in there anyway.

Time flies and before I know it, I'm cramming for finals again. All my hard work this semester pays off and I blow through the paper chase without a hitch. I even crush all the statistics problems. My transcript grade report shows all aces, which I don't understand, because I had a C on my statistics midterm before I started working with Tutor Tom.

Most college classes have a midterm and a final that count 50% each toward your grade. In statistics I got a C on the midterm and an A on the final. Wouldn't that average out to a B overall? I go in to talk to the prof thinking there may have been a mistake. I love getting a 4.0 but I want to earn it honestly. The prof explains that when grading he figures in improvement. Since I went from a C to an A during the course, he recognizes that as improvement and rewarded me with an A overall. Whatever! I'm down for that!

To thank Tutor Tom, I bring takeout Chinese food over to his sparsely furnished family housing pad. Like most grad students he and his wife survive on a shoestring. There is no table so we sit cross-legged on the dining room floor devouring egg foo yung while Tom preaches the gospel. I can't complain. I never would have gotten a top grade without his "divine" intervention.

I have a few weeks off before boot camp so I sign up for a rock-climbing course in Baraboo, Wisconsin. It's offered through the university by a mountaineering group and I'll even get a couple of hours of PE credit for having fun outdoors. That's the kind of lucra-tive offer you have to take advantage of in college.

I hop into the university van with the backpack containing all of my worldly possessions. I needed to vacate the rental house so the summer sublet could move in. With a couple of dozen other climbing junkies I set up camp near the crystal clear water of Devil's Lake.

The azure lake is surrounded by buff-pink cliffs composed of quartzite rock that is perfect for climbing. Our instructor, a giant of a man who was a member of the U.S. Army's famous 10th Mountain Division, explains how to set up anchors, make knots and use safety equipment.

Everything about this place is beautiful from the lichen-covered boulders to the pine scent and white cotton clouds dotting the blue sky overhead. I feel comfortable, strong and happy here with the other climbers. The instructor sends us up the cliffs on climbing routes that become increasingly challenging and we take some falls. But thanks to our training on ropes and belays no one is hurt. At night we sit around the crackling campfire telling stories and laughing under the stars.

But on the ride home I have an anxious feeling, like Dorothy in the movie Wizard of Oz watching the sand run out in the witch's over-sized hourglass. Boot camp is looming and my freedom is coming to an end. I feel like I've signed away 8 years of my life.

Somehow, deep down, I still feel a kernel of optimism though. It's a big universe out there. The opportunities and possibilities are infi-nite. I need to challenge myself. I need to find out what I can do. I look at Leroy and I know I'm not like him. I can't pour cement my whole life and be happy. But who am I?

Sometimes the world seems like a maze of different choices. To earn a living a person needs to have a job and a career. I decided I'd like to be a doctor. But I don't have enough money for medical school. Joining the Army is the only option I have, besides going deeply into debt. It's either a military enlistment contract or a student loan contract. One way or another society makes me sign my life away. That doesn't seem right.

I did what I had to do to pursue my dream. Now I just need to relax and accept the fact that I did my best. I feel a sudden burst of energy. I think to myself, "nothing is impossible!" But then my intellectual brain kicks in. If nothing is impossible, it must be possible that something is impossible.

I sit on the vinyl van seat on the way back to the university pondering the question in silence. I reach the conclusion that if nothing is impossible, then it must be possible that something is impossible. But just because it is possible that something is impossible, does not necessary mean that in reality something is impossible. It just means that it is possible that something is impossible.

Life can be confusing. I strike up a conversation with some of the other rock-climbing junkies as we drive along. They are a motley crew. Cheery, positive, hopeful—they all live on the edge of starvation and economic ruin, but are still joyful in pursuing their outdoor passion. They live in the moment. That is a good way to live. Not in the past. Not in the future. But in the present moment. Happy and appreciating what they have, even if it is materially very little. I think I've learned more about life from my fellow students in college than I have from all my professors and books.

Tomorrow I'll leave for boot camp. I'm staying overnight here at my parents. All I own is in the mountaineering backpack resting at the foot of my bed. I've sold, or given away, everything else. Any mail can collect in my post office box while I'm gone.

In the morning I carry the heavy backpack up to the attic in my parent's house. It feels strange leaving it there. Scripture says where your treasure is, there will your heart be also. I don't have any treasure.

My savings account was drained by the last semester of college. Since all I have now is in that backpack, I guess I'll leave a little piece of my heart in my parent's attic.

I say goodbye to my mom. It's difficult. She starts to cry. In her mind she thinks I am going off to war or something. I tell her it's just boot camp. She thinks I might die or come home horribly wounded. I try to explain that I just joined a medical battalion. It is not like I'm going into combat.

Leroy shakes my hand and offers me a ride to town. I decline. I want to walk. It will give me time to think and, because I'm walking instead of driving, it will be a good red road I'm on. Black Elk would understand. Leroy just shakes his head.

I take one last look back at my parents standing there. The looks on their faces are hard to describe. Like they are considering the possibility they may never see me again or something. Then I'm off.

I'm trudging down the black top road now. I have on Nike Air running shoes, shorts, and a tee shirt. My official military orders and a road map are tucked into one pocket. In the other are my driver's license, a toothbrush and paste. It makes no sense to drag along a bunch of superfluous stuff to boot camp. They'll just confiscate everything anyway.

I can identify all the wild plants in the ditch as I walk along the road—Sweet Clover, Queen Anne's Lace, Milkweed, Jerusalem Artichokes and Coneflowers. All swaying in the wind as if they're waving goodbye.

The frogs croak, the bees buzz, the birds sing, the squirrels chatter. In their primordial languages they're whispering, "Don't go. Stay here with us, where you belong." But I must bid them farewell.

I wander around downtown before reporting to the Armory. I'm in and out of various shops looking over the merchandise. The salespersons ask me if I'm looking for anything in particular. Can they help me? No, thank you. I have lived in this city so long everything is familiar. Somehow I feel a part of this place—the buildings, the sidewalks, the street lights, everything.

The usual drab green Army bus sits waiting at the National Guard station. A small group of recruits sit around under the shade of a nearby tree wearing their civvies, that is to say, their civilian clothes. Since I'm a college student, I'm considered an E-3 Private First Class while the other working-class kids are designated E-1 Recruits.

With my rank, the sergeant expects me to lead the others in an orderly march over to board the bus. But I hate bossing people around. The line isn't straight enough. This pisses the sergeant off. He takes over, barking orders. The line straightens.

I grab a seat. No one is talking as the bus leaves the armory. The recruits stare ahead. They look nervous. I take out my road map and start tracing our route as the bus heads down the highway. The map gives me something to think about. So I don't freak out.

The familiar scenery passes by. We're leaving my part of the country. What lies ahead, I'm not sure. I've heard that boot can be tough. I've been lifting weights and distance running for months. I'm pretty confident I can handle the physical part. I'm not worried about the mental part either. It's the spiritual dimension that has me troubled. What if I get into a situation where they order me to do something I know is morally wrong? Would I have the strength and courage to do what is right?

Along in the afternoon, about halfway through the forested Ozark hills on the way to Ft. Leonard Wood, we run into road construction. The signs are confusing. I'm pretty sure the driver made a wrong turn. But I keep my mouth shut and carefully trace the route on the road map.

Yep, the bus is lost. The driver stops to confer with the sarg. But they don't know which way to go. I figure I ought to say something. I stand up and walk to the front, holding my map prominently in my outstretched arms hoping it will lend me some credibility.

"What in the hell do you want?" the sergeant barks.

"You need to take highway 19," I explain.

The angry centurion looks me up and down, glaring hatefully. It is obvious he despises new recruits. He grabs the map out of my hands.

"Sit down and shut up!" he screams, red faced.

The driver and the sarg study the map intensely, turning it one way, then another. The driver speaks softly so no one can hear.

"Take highway 19!" the sarg finally blurts out, stuffing my map into his knapsack.

Eventually we arrive at the Fort. The sprawling base is surrounded by a tall fence topped with razor wire. The barrier reminds me of the cattle fences back home, only this fence is built to restrain humans.

We enter the front gate through a checkpoint. Soldiers with rifles stand guard while our papers are checked. Then a sentry raises the boom bar and waves us on through. None of the recruits say a word. The seriousness of our situation has sunk in, for even the most clueless. This is no movie.

If you have never been in the military, I can tell you, the difference from civilian life is huge. I would say it is like visiting a foreign country, but actually visiting a foreign country, even the most remote, is nothing in comparison. Being a soldier is more like traveling to another planet.

Freedom, equality, democracy, justice—these are ideals our country was founded upon. But in the military there is no freedom or equality or democracy. Justice consists of the *Uniform Code of Military Justice*. People will say that the US military defends a democracy—but it is not itself a democracy. That's for sure! You are subject to being ordered around by anyone with a higher rank—even if they have no clue what they are doing.

We arrive at the reception area for processing. The sergeant screams at us to get off the bus. Unknown people scream at us. There is confusion. Picture the rudest person you have ever met in your entire life. Now imagine a place where everyone is like that. Here we are. Young people who have volunteered to defend our country. And we are being treated like crap.

Some of the recruits have brought along small backpacks with toiletries, a change of clothing, etc. These are confiscated. We pass by the amnesty box. This is like your last "get of jail free" card. If you have any contraband you dump it in the box, or you risk getting detained. Guns, knives, illegal drugs, porno, music CDs, cameras—you name it, it goes in the box, never to be seen again.

We sit in rows of school desks, filling out paperwork while the reception office workers yell and scream. If anyone makes a mistake on their form, the sergeants pull them aside and make them assume a stress position, like leaning against a wall with your knees bent. This is a subtle form of torture actually. I've filled out many job applications with new employers in my lifetime. No company ever treated prospective employees so badly. The company or corporation would never survive. They would go out of business treating people like this.

The Sergeant has a somber moment. He confides that he wants to confer upon us some important advice. I wonder what gems of wisdom he has to share? Take care of yourselves? Well wishes? Hell no! Instead he explains, in a grave tone, that every platoon (he repeats *every platoon*, just for emphasis) has a thief. We must, he implores, watch our things. Or someone in our group will steal them. Now the recruits look at each other suspiciously.

We emerge back outside in the hot humid Missouri weather. Our drab Army bus is gone. In front of us now is a cattle trailer, like farmers back home use to transport their livestock.

New sergeants scream at us to get in the cattle car. People trip and get trampled. It is jam-packed to get everyone in. If there were an accident, many recruits would be injured or die. The truck jerks the hitch and off we go with nothing to hang onto unless you are by the exterior slats. Guys standing in the middle tumble and fall down.

We pull up in front of the dingy, corrugated metal reception area barracks. Sergeants scream because we are not getting out of the cattle car fast enough. People trip and fall. It is chaos. The drill instructors make anyone who falls assume humiliating stress positions on the ground with their legs spread apart. Recruits moan with pain.

The reception barracks are stark. Just bare metal walls with two lines of bunk beds. We are told to pick a place. I know from the frat I have trouble sleeping in a top bunk. I want a bottom bed but others rush and grab them. In the end it doesn't matter. At night we try, but it is nearly impossible for anyone to sleep. Forty young men lie awake wondering what the hell they got themselves into.

The next day at 4AM begins a process called hurry up and wait. Sergeants scream at us to get up, scream at us to get ready and scream at us to march faster. But once we get to our destination, we stand in line for hours.

Our first stop is a sort of barbershop where gruff people use some sort of sheep shears to cut off all our hair. Guys with long hair undergo quite a transformation. Even the fellows who anticipated this moment and got buzz jobs before coming to boot get sheared. The razors leave nicks and gouges in their heads.

You would think they would wait to cut off your hair until they have issued you a hat. Instead we march around and stand in the sun. Half the guys are white dudes and our now bald heads sunburn. The other half are black, Hispanic and Asian dudes. After a while even the darker skin on their heads sunburns. I never knew a black person could get a sunburn before this.

We march everywhere in the hot sun. The next stop is an outdoor medical tent much like the ones I helped set up back home in the national guard. Army medical specialists form two lines and we roll up our sleeves, then we walk the gauntlet between them. It is an anti-vaxxer's worst nightmare. The medics have high pressure air guns that inject a plethora of vaccinations and experimental injections into each arm.

We remain in our civvies for a few days until issued our BDUs, battle dress uniforms. The army system is designed to outfit soldiers as rapidly as possible in the event of a war. There are stations set up to swiftly measure your waist, inseam, shoe size, head size, etc. Then you proceed down the line with people throwing shirts, pants, coats and the rest of your kit right in your face and screaming at you to move on.

The heat, humidity and blistering sun are incredibly intense here in southern Missouri. At least we have hats now. We also have a whole bunch of other stuff that we don't need here, like winter coats and chemical/biological warfare gear. Everything goes into a big green duffel bag.

Your BDU clothes have a nameplate with your surname sewn on them. People here refer to you by your last name only. Except for your dog tags, which have your full name, military ID number, blood type and religious preference.

Most of the other guys have Catholic or Protestant on their tags. A couple have no preference. In my case, I couldn't get out of my mind the way the U.S. Army treated the Native Americans, killing their people and driving them off the land.

So, when I go through the dog tag line and they ask me my religious preference, I tell them Oglala Sioux in memory of the medicine man Black Elk and the Indians massacred at Wounded Knee. When I get my own tags, they have "Other than" in the place where religion should go. It was the only dog tag I have ever seen issued like that.

CHAPTER TWENTY-SEVEN

In the evening we post fireguards to watch over the barracks while everyone sleeps. There is a rotation with each recruit taking a turn at guard duty. Occasionally a sergeant will show up. If they catch the guard sleeping he has hell to pay. Other times a sergeant will sneak into the barracks in the middle of the night and scream, "Attention!"

At the sound of this cry everyone must immediately leap out of their bunks and line up standing at attention. After a few days of this, some comedians in our platoon start yelling attention as a joke.

In the darkness we have no way of knowing who yelled the order so, of course, we all leap out of bed and form a line, only to find it's a false alarm. The days are grueling, we aren't getting enough sleep and this crying wolf prank becomes increasingly more annoying.

This continues until an incident in the wee hours of the morning when we hear the order barked, "Attention!" By now everyone is sick of being punked. So, no one gets out of bed. An aggravated recruit yells, "Shut the fuck up and go back to sleep!"

Unfortunately this time it really is a sergeant and he is mad as a hornet's nest. We all get marched out to a ditch for endless push-ups in the mud until we are completely exhausted. Of course, every detail of our uniforms is supposed to be perfect, so when we get back to the barracks the recruits are all in a panic to use the washer and dryer to clean up.

Since we're also always supposed to have our boots shined to a mirror finish, we use rags to buff the black leather. The recruits screw up putting used rags in the washer. The uniforms come out mud free but with black shoe polish streaks all over them. The sergeant goes berserk and orders more push-ups in the muddy ditch, which only makes matters worse.

Life here in the reception battalion is a downward spiral. Nerves are frayed. We recruits are stressed out to the max. We know our time in processing is coming to an end. Rumor has it that reception is like the cub scouts compared to real boot camp, where we're soon headed.

But I figure this line about how horrible boot camp is has to be an exaggeration. I mean, some people make it sound like the drill sergeants in basic training are eight-foot tall with fangs. It can't be as bad as they say. But the rumors persist and I have to admit, I'm nervous and worried.

Today we meet a forlorn soldier who is being recycled from boot camp. We pump him for information. What is it really like? We figure he has been there and knows—sort of like a soul returning from hell.

The soldier starts telling horror stories of torture and violence, of sadistic drill instructors kicking and punching recruits. I figure this can't be true. Society would never allow it. He has to be embellishing his story. I can't stand the pressure any more. At the top of my lung capacity I scream at him, "No way! Shut up!"

Normally I'm a pretty laid-back dude. I can't believe I just completely lost it. I feel terrible. I regret yelling at the young man. But I'm conflicted and don't know who to believe. I shouldn't have treated him like that. What's happening to me?

The young soldier cowers and walks away. "You'll see," he snickers. "You'll see!"

Fortunately, we get a new sergeant in the reception center. He's a southern good ol' boy type, macho and arrogant, but not inhumane.

His job is to polish up our marching skills. The redneck teaches us cadences to shout out. We are supposed to repeat everything he says:

Him, "Hey, hey, Captain Jack."

Us, "Hey, hey, Captain Jack."

Him, "Meet me down by the railroad track."

Us, "Meet me down by the railroad track."

Him, "With that weapon in your hand."

Us, "With that weapon in your hand."

Him, "I wanna be a killing man."

Us, "I wanna be a killing man."

Now Sgt. Redneck becomes angry. He does not feel that we are yelling loud enough. We must do push-ups as a punishment. Lots of push-ups! Then we do more marching.

Him, "Get it right this time you faggots! Repeat after me! Louder! Hey, hey, Captain Jack."

Us, "Hey, hey, Captain Jack."

Him, "Meet me down by the railroad track."

Us, "Meet me down by the railroad track."

(After pausing and sounding exasperated)

Him, "You people sound like shit!"

Just me, "You people sound like shit!"

Of course we were not supposed to repeat that last line. He was admonishing us. But I couldn't help myself. Everyone bursts out laughing. Then all eyes are on the sergeant's face to see how he will react to my insubordination. I await my death sentence.

But the good 'ol boy cracks a smile. Unbelievably this sergeant is human. He even has a sense of humor.

"Y'all mother fuckers gunna die when you get to boot!"

The next morning at 4AM our brief reprieve in purgatory is over. New sergeants scream at us to get out of bed, then scream at us to grab our duffels and hurry outside. The cattle car to hell awaits. How they expect to get 40 guys, now with bulky equipment, crammed in there is beyond me.

The feeling is claustrophobic and suffocating. We are stacked like cord wood. I'm in the middle of the pack. People keep shoving even though there is no room. Finally the metal door slams shut. I feel crushed and can hardly breath. Every second is misery. But at least we don't have to worry about falling down. There is no room for that.

The cattle car finally arrives at its destination, a group of nondescript cement block buildings. We aren't in reception anymore. The real, official boot camp drill sergeants in their smokey bear hats greet us with all the subtlety and hospitality of a shark attack. They scream, they yell, recruits litter the sidewalk in stress positions on their backs with their legs in the air moaning.

Nothing we do is right. Everyone is confused about what they want. I think it is all a game that the drills purposely play to make compliance impossible. We run to our new barracks with our heavy duffels. I lunge and pounce on a bottom bunk. At least now I might be able to get a little sleep. But a giant of a drill storms into the room and demands that we vacate and run to a different barracks across the street. All the bottom bunks are taken when I get there.

This portion of boot camp is known as total control. Every move you make is monitored. No communication with the outside world is allowed—no phones, radios, music, cameras, computers, no nothing. The drills never speak in a normal tone of voice, they always scream. I spot a bag of mail addressed to us soldiers from home in the sergeants' quarters but it is withheld from us for days. Boxes with cookies and other treats arrive, sent by lonesome mothers. The drill sergeants laugh as they rip open the packages and throw the contents in the garbage.

The conditions here really are much worse than processing in the reception center. But I hear there is variation in the experience. Some sergeants are a bit more like boy scout leaders on steroids. You get one of those drills, you lucked out. Instead we get a maniac who is arguably mentally deranged.

Our insane drill, Sgt. Drock, reminds me of a Kodiak bear, standing about 6'8" and weighing about 250 pounds. He is a humorless man full of hate. Even the other drill sergeants dislike him. Officially the drills are not supposed to hit or abuse recruits. But our Sgt. Drock pushes us, shoves us, and goes overboard with stress positions forcing recruits into all sorts of bizarre contortions. The madman makes soldiers hold out heavy objects at arm's length until they scream with pain.

I observe our crazy Sgt. Drock and note his modus operandi. He avoids physically attacking recruits when the other drill sergeants are around and especially if there is an officer near. Then he acts orderly and mild. He's even friendly with some of the recruits in front of the captain.

This fellow Drock is going to be hard to deal with. He's a tough nut to crack because he's clever, in addition to abusive. His tricks are many and well-rehearsed. He can turn even the simplest chore into a torture session. We are marching now in a remote section of the base. Sgt. Drock gives the order, "Front lean and rest position—move!" Which in military jargon means get ready to do push-ups.

I understand that it is necessary for soldiers to be in top physical condition. I have no problem with push-ups. I've done thousands of them preparing for boot camp. But Drock has something up his sleeve. You see, we are marching on an asphalt road and the temperature on this hot, humid Missouri day is well over 100 degrees. In the scorching sun the black top is soft, like spongy lava, and as hot as a stove top.

If you have never heard 40 men screaming in pain, I can tell you it is an eerie sound. Our palms are burning and sticking to the pavement. Amidst the tortured cries of anguish, I hear Sgt. Drock's husky voice call out advice, "When you're in hell, you need to find a hot ladder and climb out!"

The advice is no help at the moment, but it sticks in my mind as tightly as my hands are now sticking to the hot asphalt. When Sgt. Drock orders us to recover, I leave skin from several of my fingers and palm behind on the road. But the cleverness of the sergeant's scheme is not lost on me. Because, you see, if any of the recruits complain about doing push-ups, most anyone who wasn't there would disregard it. I mean really, complain about having to do push-ups? This is the army after all. Man up, you wuss!

A sort of routine takes shape in this hellish madhouse. We are up at 4AM. Which I'm not unfamiliar with, having driven the school bus.

Next is PT which officially stands for physical training but unofficially the recruits dub it physical torture. Lots of pushups, sit ups, leg lifts, lunges and crunches.

I'm glad I worked out so hard before coming here. Some of the roly-poly guys are having a hard time. The leg raises are especially horrific, even for those of us who are in top condition. The lifts go on forever and, at the same time our stomachs muscles are screaming in pain, we must keep reciting, as loud as we can:

"We like it, we love it, we want more of it. More PT drill sergeant, more PT!"

If we are not loud enough, then they add more time with our legs in the air. Another tactic is to catch one guy loafing a little. Then they call out his name and the whole platoon is subjected to group punishment. Everyone focuses their discomfort and anger on that one poor soul.

After PT we do some barracks cleaning before lining up in an orderly formation where they can quickly account for anyone gone missing or AWOL. Then we march off to breakfast in a cafeteria. The food here is actually pretty good, but the atmosphere is terrible. Imagine being screamed at the entire time you are trying to eat. At the end of the breakfast line are bowls of cheese or prunes, we can choose which we want depending on the condition of our bowels.

The days are long, composed primarily of lessons on how to use various weapons. There are grenades, claymore mines and the LAW (Light Antitank Weapon). We flip up the sight on the tubular rocket and yell "back blast area clear" so no one will get toasted when the thing goes off. I don't get to try firing one because the sergeants took our training models out into the woods to shoot at the deer. I hear the gentle creatures get blown to pieces when they hit one.

Marching from one training area to another we yell out cadences to help keep in step:

Left, left, left, keep in step.
I don't know why I left,
But I know I gotta be strong,
And it won't be long,

Before I get back home.

Our voices become low and raspy from all the yelling. We're starting to feel pretty macho, like tough guys. But there is very little talk about sex and I don't think anyone is getting any, including jerking off, which would be nearly impossible since you are with people all the time. The recruits gossip about the cooks putting salt peter in our food to keep us from getting hard-ons. It sounds like an urban legend to me, but you never know around here.

Today they march us out for CBRN (Chemical Biological Radiological Nuclear) defense training. The carbon-lined suits are bulky and hot, like an oven in the sweltering heat, so they fill with sweat. The trainer explains that if we see a nuclear mushroom cloud on the battlefield, we should yell out what direction the explosion is and then everyone should fall face down on the ground with their feet toward the blast.

I'm skeptical of how well that procedure would go in a real nuclear war, but whatever. The trainer continues that we should make sure our M-16 is protected under our body, along with our hands. The purpose here is that we can get back up after the blast wave passes and debris stops falling and still be able to shoot. As an added bonus, if we are killed in the nuclear blast, which seems to me very likely, then our dead body will hopefully protect the gun from being damaged so another soldier can use it later on. Got to protect government property, you know.

As a culminating activity we arrive at a small brick building known affectionately as the gas chamber. Inside are some skulls and other Halloweenish paraphernalia placed there to scare us. The sergeant releases some CS (tear) gas and tells us to break the seal on our masks. I try to be coy, closing my eyes and holding my breath, but of course the sergeant punches anyone who doesn't open their eyes and inhale.

Outside the recruits wander around blinded by the acrid, toxic fumes while waving their arms, as directed. I have no idea why they tell us to wave our arms, how does that help? We look like poisoned chickens flapping our wings with long lines of drool and snot running from our noses and mouths.

Having been tipped off by a suave recruit that we were getting gassed today I skipped eating breakfast so I wouldn't have anything in my stomach to puke up. Now after miles of marching back from the gas chamber I'm famished. We get in the chow line for lunch with the sergeants screaming at us to hurry up. I manage to fill my tray with delicious-looking fried chicken, mashed potatoes and numerous other delectable goodies. But before I can sit down to eat the sergeant screams that we have taken too long. As ordered, I throw all that good food in the garbage can without getting a single bite.

I understand that in order to have a competent fighting force to defend the country soldiers must be in top physical shape, disciplined and well trained. I get that. But I don't understand the need to humiliate and mistreat people. The effect of our pain and suffering and degradation is that we become hard and mean. They are using psychological techniques developed over thousands of years of human martial history to turn us into killing machines that obey any order without hesitation.

The military gets away with a lot because most of its action takes place out of the public's eye. The recruits are hazed and mistreated. In the rare instances that we see female recruits, they complain of sexual harassment. Any time you have an institutionalized power differential dynamic, there is an opportunity for abuse—whether it is the police, a business type corporation or a school. In the military, the imbalance of power is on steroids. Your superiors have absolute, complete and total control over your life and destiny. The potential for abuse is enormous.

Being in the army now much of our time is spent with our main weapon, the M-16 rifle. We take these rifles apart and put them back together so many times we can do it blindfolded. My M-16 is an older model with a forward assist which was added during the Vietnam War because the guns were jamming under jungle conditions. On the side is a lever with three settings—single shot, three shot burst and full auto.

In order to get our M-16 and ammunition for the day's training we stand in line at the armory. The sun is beating down and we are suffering in the heat. I pull my canteen off of my LBD (Load Bearing Device) shoulder harness and take a swallow of warm water. The soldier behind me groans in a southern drawl that he has forgotten his canteen today. I hand him mine. He looks surprised as he shakes it to see how much liquid is left inside, then questions me, "Can I kill it?" I've never heard that expression before, but figure he means swig down all the remaining water. I nod silently in reply that he can. He should be more careful. Talking in line is forbidden.

Inside the armory is a counter behind which resides a crazy son of a bitch who yells mostly incoherent stuff. We have been issued a rifle card that we must present to him and God help you if you forget it. I pull mine from my chest pocket and he screams and shoves the weapon and a couple of clips of ammo across the sheet metal divider to me. All around on the floor are recruits in various stress positions moaning and wailing, the consequence for having forgotten their rifle card.

When I was young my dad gave me a 410/22 over-under to hunt rabbits and squirrels. I have had all sorts of shotguns, rifles and pistols before. It was just part of my life growing up. But here in boot they want us to forget about any other experience we have ever had with a gun. In fact, you cannot call your M-16 a gun. That will land you in big trouble. They even have a saying we must recite over and over:

> *This is my weapon* (hold up M-16)
> *This is my gun* (point index finger at crotch)
> *This is for killing* (hold up M-16)
> *This is for fun* (again you point finger at penis)

This nomenclature is all developed by psychologists. They don't want some country kid who grew up hunting rabbits associating their M-16 with the gun they used safely back home. The M-16 is a weapon used by soldiers to kill other people. They want you to internalize that and to be able to carry out the act of killing another person when ordered to do so.

There are all sorts of name games like that here in boot camp. For instance, we are never allowed to refer to any female as anything other than Suzy Rotten Crotch. It doesn't matter who you are referring to, could be your mother, your sister, your wife, your girlfriend, your daughter, whoever. If it is a she, we must use the term Suzy Rotten Crotch.

One day I try to get by with referring to one of the female workers as Suzy for short. I hate the rotten crotch expression. I hear a sergeant scream, "Drop and give me fifty." My punishment, inflicted to remind me I must say the whole thing.

CHAPTER TWENTY-EIGHT

We finally get back to the barracks after a rough day of training. We are ready to let down a little and relax but find that our mattresses, bedding and the entire contents of our lockers has been thrown, helter-skelter, all over the place. Sgt. Drock storms in and accuses one soldier, Mike Hidersheit, of some minor thing, like not folding the corner of his blanket tight enough. All the mess we are told is this kid's fault.

Hidersheit is a little slow on the uptake. But he is a nice farm kid from Iowa. He has some extra pounds of fat, probably due to his mother's cooking back home. He also has a bad case of acne. He is frequently singled out at PT for not keeping up and the reason the entire platoon must do more painful exercises. Now everyone blames him for the mess in the barracks and they start calling him Hydro-shit.

I don't join the mob. I just sort out my stuff from the mess and then help Hidersheit find his things. The barracks is supposed to be in perfect condition for inspection tomorrow. Everything must be clean and orderly, down to the most minute detail like how your razor and other toiletries need to be lined up on your locker shelf.

Sgt. Drock hovers over us as we try to clean up the mess, occasionally screaming at people. That fact that I helped Hidersheit has not escaped the insane sergeant's evil eye. He walks up to me putting the brim of his hat against my face. He is standing here, staring at me, not saying a word. But the message is clearly delivered and I know I'm in trouble. Your best defense in boot camp is to go unnoticed. I've been noticed.

The next day is a nightmare. All manner of punishment is meted out on the platoon because we failed the inspection we worked so hard to pass. We are physically and mentally reduced to nothing by the time we are finally called to line up at attention inside the barracks. Now we will find out why we failed. And who is to blame. All that group punishment, and one poor soul will be singled out now as the cause for everyone's misery. Who will be the scapegoat, the sacrificial lamb, this time?

Sgt. Drock strides in. He is holding some sort of checklist. Several recruits mumble, "Hydro-shit" under their breath. Someone elbows the forlorn farm boy in the side, and he groans out loud. Ordinarily this outburst would elicit an immediate and devastating response from Sgt. Drock. But the torturer has other plans.

He turns and stares at me. My heart sinks. It's payback time. In a cold voice with a crooked grin he explains that one soldier in our platoon did not have their boots polished properly. He walks up directly in front of me and stares. A couple of recruits mumble my name with disgust.

The thing is, I stayed up later than anyone else making sure all my stuff, and Hidersheit's, was in perfect order. That includes my boots, which I had carefully shined to perfection. I glance over and my glistening boots are sitting there, exactly how they are supposed to be, at the foot of my perfectly folded bed. We are trained to always stand looking straight forward but the other recruits can't help it. All eyes drift over to my bunk, checking out the boots. It is obvious they're fine.

Sgt. Drock walks over and picks up one of my trooper stompers. I have big feet and wear size 14. Because of the length of my foot, a small crease has formed in the leather at the back of the toes. There is absolutely nothing I can do to prevent that. Drock points to the crease and then heaves the boot as hard as he can against a locker, badly marring the leather. Now there is no way the boot will ever pass inspection again, by any sergeant or officer. I'm screwed.

I don't sleep all night. I have to force myself out of bed the next day. It is Sunday so there is a roll call for those who want to attend church services. When I was kid my mother demanded that I always go to Catholic church services and religious education classes. After I grew up, I stopped going to church altogether. I'm still a religious and spiritual person—but in my own way, combining elements of many different perspectives including Christianity, Judaism, Buddhism and Native American beliefs.

Here in boot camp, I go to church every Sunday without fail. This military base often reminds me of hell with all the suffering and pain and the way people mistreat each other. So church is a small reprieve, a little ray of light shining down here in the darkness from above.

I tried the Catholic service but the priest here is a fascist. I know most priests are decent people, not like this guy, who preaches that we are the army of God and must destroy the enemy without mercy. I line up and decide to hang with the protestants today. Their minister seems to have a clue as to what we are going through and his sermons are not political or nationalistic, but more about love and kindness.

Afterwards, back at the barracks, Sgt. Drock has a black list. Soldiers are called out one by one, my name included. We know we're in deep shit for something, but the crafty sergeant is slick and doesn't explain. The others are allowed a break to write letters or rest in their bunks. The doomed squad is taken outside for severe punishment, grueling exercises and stress positions. I think it over and finally get it. The black list is everyone who attended church services. The retribution continues every Sunday Sgt. Drock is in charge of our platoon.

More of our training is shifting to the field. The woods and meadows of the base give me some solace. Having taken botany classes I can identify many of the plants that grow here. It helps me cope with stress to see some flowers I recognize from back home. The plants are the same inside this horrible place as they are on the outside. Even on this sinister alien planet, nature is dependable.

On bivouac I have more time to talk with other soldiers. One young man with rotten teeth tells me he joined the army to get dental work done. Others tell stories of poverty and desires to help their disadvantaged family members. One tells me he just wants money to buy a Camaro.

I ask the other soldiers about their MOS, Military Occupational Specialty. Many are 11B10 light infantry, otherwise known as bullet stoppers. In the event of a war they'll be fed directly into the meat grinder.

I tell them I'm on the medical track. I'll be going to AIT, Advanced Individual Training, next summer. They stare at me inquisitively. So, I explain that I'm a college student signed up for the STO, Split Training Option. So I do boot camp this summer and AIT at Ft. Sam Houston the next. The college part elicits some oohs and ahs. Most of these kids never considered going to college, but I try to encourage them to do so someday with their GI benefits.

The diverse recruits have come from all over the country. So there are many cultural differences. But the soldiers have a saying that everybody bleeds red no matter where they are from or what color their skin is. At least within the platoon there is a feeling that we are all in this together. I'm sure racism is a problem in the military, but at least at this low level, there seems to be less prejudice.

One fellow soldier I get to know is Washington. He is a young black man from the inner city. Whenever things get impossible and we are suffering badly, Washington states blankly, "Life ain't all peaches and cream." Some of his other sayings I just don't get. Often, when we are in the middle of some exhausting field exercise, Washington yells, "Pancakes!" I finally ask him for some context. After weeks of nodding in agreement to "pancakes" without having any clue what he is talking about, today he explains to me, "my mama used to make me pancakes every morning for breakfast."

Washington will get no fresh pancakes here in the field. Since we are far away from the mess hall, we survive on MRE's, Meals Ready to Eat. The food inside the pouches isn't terrible. But I wouldn't want to live on this stuff more than a week or so because it causes constipation. Some of the guys start jokingly referring to the rations as Meals Refusing to Exit. Maybe this is done on purpose since the toilet facilities out here in the field are minimal. I'm amazed and wonder how it can be explained medically, that we eat three meals a day, practically never take a dump and still lose weight.

Maple sausage is breakfast, chili mac is lunch and beef ravioli composes dinner today. Along with the main course the MRE package includes some crackers, peanut butter, drink mix, a can of Sterno so we can heat food up in our canteen cup, condiments, toilet paper, cigarettes and matches.

The sergeants encourage the young soldiers to smoke and many of them have taken up the habit. In the civilian world when it is time for a rest, your supervisor will say, "Time for a break." Instead, here in the army, whenever it is time for a rest, the sergeants yell, "Light 'em up."

On a visit to the PX, a sort of base convenience store, many of the recruits buy butane lighters. In addition to lighting their cancer sticks they use the Zippos to burn loose threads off their uniforms. At inspection a loose thread can result in punishment. I trade the cigarettes in my MRE's for more peanut butter. It seems no matter how much I eat here I lose more weight. My stomach is flat and I have to cinch my belt to keep my pants up.

One of the recruits I recognize from protestant church service has gotten caught with a candy bar he bought at the PX. Sergeant Barns, a short, hot-headed drill is dressing him down about the "Goddamned Snickers." Every sentence I have ever heard Sgt. Barns utter includes taking the name of the lord in vain: the Goddamned weather, the Goddamned flies, the Goddamned lazy recruits, on to infinity.

After having the forbidden candy bar ripped out of his hands and lots of push-ups inflicted upon his slight frame the recruit returns to our huddle. Sgt. Barns is going to write him up for "Goddamned insubordination." The recruit gets a disgusted look of contempt on his face and whispers defiantly, "God never damned anything." I figure he heard that in Sunday school back home. But I'm afraid it doesn't apply here. We march back toward the barracks in dusty BDUs yelling cadence to keep in step:

Mama, Mama can't you see
What the Army done to me.
They took away my faded jeans
Now I'm wearing Army greens.
Used to date a beauty queen
Now I hug my M-16.
Used to drive a Cadillac
Now I hump an ALICE pack.

The troops are worn out, dirty and soaked with sweat. But it is too early to hit the barracks and clean up so Sgt. Drock orders us over to the training room. We pack in close together on folding chairs and await instruction. I hate this place. I don't mind the legitimate training on various military matters. It's what's attached to the wall in the front of the room that gives me the creeps. Our Charlie Company mascot is a giant, bright red devil's head approximately six feet tall complete with horns and a pointy beard.

The boorish drill sergeant enters. At this point we must begin chanting as loud as we can, "Charlie, Charlie, Charlie 13, drive on drill sergeant, drive on."

The hair on the back of my neck stands on end repeating various chants over and over in front of the devil. I feel like I'm stuck in a satanic cult ceremony. Sgt. Drock's eyes roll, he appears to be in a trance. Occasionally he screams at us to yell louder. The whole ritual is bizarre. Doing this we aren't learning anything that would help defend or protect our country. What's the point?

We are finally ordered to get up from our chairs and file out the door. It is a rare sight to see a female drill instructor here. They are usually occupied with training the young women far away in a different part of the base. But now, I spot a short, chubby female drill wearing an Australian style bush hat pinned up on one side. She looks incredibly ugly, wrinkling up her face with scorn, and screaming, "You stink" as each of us pass by her.

You know, in the civilian world this little troll wouldn't be worth getting annoyed with. Someone like her could never get away with treating people like that. I'd laugh at her and tell her to go away. But here we are powerless. We must suffer continued verbal and physical abuse with no recourse.

In addition to questioning what kind of mental disorder these drill sergeants have that they treat other human beings this way, I also wonder what kind of people we recruits are that we allow ourselves to be humiliated and mistreated over and over here in boot camp? Or what kind of people see other people being mistreated and do nothing to intervene? Isn't it rather cowardly to submit to this kind of degradation?

Does the United States, as a nation, really want an armed force composed of people who allowed themselves to be humiliated and mistreated this way? What are the consequences? In war time do abused soldiers behave humanely and honorably? Or do they act like animals and retaliate against and mistreat others, including innocent civilians?

As I learned in the fraternity system, when pledges are hazed and mistreated, then when these pledges get to be upperclassmen, it becomes their turn. They often enthusiastically pass on the maltreatment by heaping punishment on the next, incoming generation of freshmen. I've heard that people who are abused as children sometimes struggle with abusing others when they grow up. The sergeants who abuse and torture us were once mistreated this way themselves. How can this chain of abuse be broken? In order to have an adequate national defense is it really necessary to treat people like crap?

Personally, I have come to the conclusion that the entire military system in this country needs to be revamped and run more professionally, like a business. People should be hired and fired, apply, volunteer or quit their job like in any other organization. There is no need to make people like me give up their personhood and freedom signing away 8 years of their life. Soldiers should be treated with dignity and respect. And maybe, just maybe, if the Defense Department had to adapt accounting practices like every other business, then they wouldn't be losing, and unable to account for, trillions in spending that is routinely lost or wasted.

I understand the need for a physically fit, well-trained and well-disciplined military. Our country needs a strong defense and we should be willing to do whatever it takes, as far as spending and manpower, to achieve that goal. There are training and instructional how-to activities here in boot camp that I consider useful and appropriate. But a lot of the sadistic, degrading and humiliating treatment I see as pointless and actually counter-productive. For one thing, a lot of really competent, intelligent people simply do not want to go through this, so they don't join up.

The regimen of boot camp is overseen by TRADOC, which stands for Training and Indoctrination. The system has been developed by psychologists and military strategists over hundreds of years with the goal being to completely break down new recruits so that the military can rebuild or recreate them into soldiers who will kill and follow orders like robots. So, they intentionally aim to break the will and spirit of recruits. But then what happens to the strong-willed spirit that won't be broken?

Most people are simply too cowardly to resist. They just submit to the humiliation thinking they'll go along with it until it is over and then things will be fine, or at least better. They figure they'll put up with the abuse and eventually get their dress uniform and their family will be proud of them marching around in it at graduation like the Wicked Witch of the West's flying monkeys and Winkie Guards chanting, "O-Ee-Yah! Eoh-Ah!"

But what impact does this submission, this breaking down of the will and personality, have on the human psyche and spirit? The suicide, homelessness and mental illness rate for veterans is sky high. Couldn't at least part of PTSD, Post Traumatic Stress Disorder, be attributed to the unseen spiritual and psychological damage inflicted when a person totally submits their will to another and allows themselves to be controlled and humiliated?

I confide my inner feelings with some of the other soldiers. Some agree with me in principle. They hate the maltreatment. It makes them sick. But they tell me they have nowhere else to go. They are penniless with no job prospects back in the hood and are desperate to help their families who are struggling for even the most basic necessities of life, like food and shelter.

Other soldiers just smile when I relate my views on the subject.

They seem okay with the humiliation and degradation figuring that's just the way things are. They say their parents or relatives went through the same indignities, so they can too. Some figure they'll put up with it for now and then someday, they'll get the chance to enjoy humiliating other people, the way they are being treated now. Their attitude makes me sick.

CHAPTER TWENTY-NINE

---

*I*t's 0200 and an unknown soldier is shaking me awake. It seems we never get enough sleep, and tonight I pulled fireguard. They say you work 12-hour days in boot, but I can tell you it is really more like 24/7. Even sleeping is fitful and disturbing. So, I get up and walk among the bunks making sure everyone is accounted for.

I feel like propping my eyelids open with toothpicks. I can barely stay awake. Out in the hallway I plug in the buffer and carefully wax the floor so it will be ready for the next inspection. The noise and motion of the swirling brushes keeps me conscious. One thing you do not want to do here in boot is fall asleep on fireguard. After the floor is shined to perfection, I just hang out for a while, listening to the guys snore. All of a sudden, I see a dark shape approaching.

"State your business!" I bark in my gruffest voice.

The menacing figure emerges into the dim light. Sgt. Drock's six-foot-eight-inch frame is unmistakable. I thank God I'm awake and paying attention. The seconds tick by. The tormentor does nothing but stare at me. Finally, he guffaws, "State my business? You my business!" Then he fades back into the darkness.

This was a terrible night to pull guard duty. Tomorrow we have our two-mile run. I need all the sleep I can get. But the next soldier on the guard list pulls a pillow over his head and refuses to awaken. Damn! I have no choice but to cover his watch. I can't leave the barracks unguarded. So, I sit and thumb through my SMART book, a manual of basic army information we need to know. I've always been a good book learner. I've already memorized the whole manual, but there's nothing else to do around here so I reread it.

Thankfully after two hours of struggling to keep from dozing off, the next soldier in line awakens and takes position on guard. I lay my head down and it seems like only seconds later I hear Sgt. Drock screaming for us to get the hell up. Those in command have made a wise decision. For our two-mile run they will let us wear tennis shoes instead of our army boots. Out of a locked closet we retrieve our shoes from the civvies we have not seen since the reception area when we were issued our BDUs.

The soldiers have all sorts of colored tennis shoes and it looks out of place from the usual, uniform drab colors. I'm lucky. I splurged on a pair of top-of-the-line Nike Air running shoes before coming to boot. I'll take any advantage I can get around here. We are herded onto a bus and driven to an outdoor cinder track. There are several other buses, as different platoons are here for the timed run.

Letting us wear our tennies was a good move, but now the commanders make a bad decision. It's incredibly hot and the humidity must be 100%. Sweat pours off our foreheads and into our eyes just standing here. But we cannot risk wiping our brow, we are at attention and must not move, even though our eyes sting terribly. This is not a good day for a run.

We begin the timed race in a humid furnace. Thanks to the Nikes, and a lot of conditioning before boot, I break out toward the front of the pack. The heavy cotton camo BDUs soak up sweat and add pounds of weight. I'm told the fabric is coated with some substance that helps soldiers avoid satellite detection, but that reduces breathability. The blistering sun, and oppressive heat, are nearly unbearable. I finish the two miles totally exhausted and lay on my back panting. Thankfully my time was well under the requirement to pass PT.

Finally, I'm able to sit up. Some of the soldiers are still running on the track. Hidersheit is way behind, bringing up a distant last.

Members of another platoon are making fun of the farm boy, yelling insults. I walk over and tell them to shut up. They refuse at first, but then I tell them I'm a E-3 PFC, the advanced grade I got from the army thanks to having completed 3 years of college before I signed up. The hecklers grumble, but eventually stop. I start cheering Hidersheit, "Come on, you can do it!"

But the crushing heat is relentless and eventually wins. Hidersheit quits running and starts to walk. Several other soldiers are also falling out, walking, or simply stopping altogether. The sergeants go nuts. They round up all the dropouts and have them stand at attention in the scorching sun. The rest of us are allowed to hang out in the shade while the individual times are recorded.

It's time to go. We line up for the bus. But there is some commotion back by the track where the soldiers were standing in the sun. I can't make out exactly what's happening but something isn't right. It looks like one of the soldiers is lying on the ground. We sit looking out the windows of the bus trying to figure out what's going on, while waiting for some members of our platoon who were in the dropout line.

When everyone arrives, the door of the bus closes and we head out. In the rear seats we pump the last recruits on board for information. They sit wide-eyed and appear shocked. Finally, one shakes his head and states excitedly, "It was so hot in the sun. We could hardly take it standing there. One of the soldiers from the other platoon fell down. He was limp and not moving at all. A sergeant came and told us to leave. I heard him, he said, 'Damn, he died on me. Now I have to fill out the paperwork.'"

Back at the barracks we all just want to take a shower and rest. But Sgt. Drock is up to his usual antics acting like an insane gorilla. He walks down the line of bunks pulling the neatly folded blankets off and tossing them through the air. It will be interesting trying to pass our next inspection with him tearing everything apart again. All the while the crazy sergeant is destroying our barracks he rants and raves about Hidersheit and how all our misery is because he failed the PT test.

Before coming to boot I read a lot about what it would be like. At this point in the training the drill sergeants are actually supposed to be backing off the total control mode and developing better rapport with the troops. But Sgt. Drock isn't with the program. If anything, he gets crazier and more violent every day. The army is all about uniformity and standardization. But something tells me I'm not having the usual boot camp experience here.

I pick up my stuff after Sgt. Drock's tantrum, take a long shower, then collapse onto my bunk after carefully remaking it. We actually sleep in our uniforms on the fully made beds without getting under the covers. There just isn't enough time in the morning to get dressed and fold beds. Soon I have fallen into a very deep slumber. I'm partially awakened by a commotion in the showers. Sgt. Drock is yelling, soldiers are yelling, I figure someone has committed some insignificant infraction, like leaving the soap out or something. Or, who knows, maybe no one has done anything wrong at all. Maybe Sgt. Drock is just acting crazy again. Anyway, I'm sleep deprived so I ignore the racket and drift out of consciousness.

But someone bumps into the bunk jarring me awake again. I finally get up to see what the heck the ruckus is all about. I stop the soldier on fireguard and ask, "What's going on, anyway?"

"It's Hyro-shit. He tried to commit suicide. Cut his wrists in the shower."

"Oh no," I mutter, running to the showers. But all there is to see are a couple of soldiers mopping up blood on the floor. They have already taken Hidersheit to the hospital. I keep asking others about the incident. The fireguard found him. He lost a lot of blood but they think he'll be alright. That's all the information I can get. I don't sleep the rest of the night.

In the morning we get into formation. We stick our arms out to make sure we are spaced properly with the soldiers next to us. An old staff sergeant walks by and calls our platoon to attention. This is unusual and we don't know what to make of it. We are Sgt. Drock's platoon and it is Drock's responsibility to call us to attention. I have noticed during my time here that Sgt. Drock and this staff sergeant do not get along. You can practically feel the seething hatred between the two. The staff sergeant knows something about Sgt. Drock. I'm sure of that. The two have words, but I cannot make out what is said.

Since I have E-3 status I'm told to lead a small group of soldiers over to headquarters. Apparently, there is some issue with their paperwork or something. As we march along, I lead cadence as best I can. I'm really not into this stuff.

> *Left, left, left,*
> *I left my wife and 49 kids,*
> *Home in the kitchen without any gingerbread left.*

The others burst out laughing. But, regrettably, the brief reprieve and laughter are short lived. Before long I notice that a long, green Ford LTD drives past. Too late I spot a red license plate with stars on it. The chauffeur slams on the brakes and the big land yacht screeches to a stop. Then the tires squeal in reverse backing up right next to us. Out of the back seat flies a general who is mad as hell.

Whenever a vehicle tagged with one of those red plates passes by, you're supposed to stop what you're doing, come to attention and salute. We've screwed up badly. The general is a mean-looking hot head. He screams, he yells, foam and spit fly from his mouth. His cheery red face is contorted.

"Give me fifty," he demands.

We all drop and do fifty push-ups. I can't see the general's eyes behind his G-15 sunglasses. But I imagine they must be pure white, like a zombie. This guy is just plain scary. He continues to scream like a madman in an asylum. We do more push-ups until our arms give out. All of this, I figure, is part of a big power trip these people are on. What are us trainees supposed to do when those in authority here are acting like bullies and immature narcissists?

I guess we'll just have to act like the adults in the room. After the spooky skeleton man in the big fancy hat peels away in his obese cruiser I have the soldiers line up. As instructed, we'll continue on over to headquarters. Keeping a wary eye out for red plates I lead the cadence:

> *I don't know why I left,*
> *But I know I gotta be strong,*

> *And it won't be long,*
> *Before I get back home.*

Because we're away from our platoon at noon, we get to eat in a different mess hall at headquarters. They serve steak and shrimp, all you can eat, and no one screams or yells at us. We can take our time. What a treat! Then we arrive back at the barracks for afternoon training which covers CPR and field medicine, like treating wounds. The instruction is appropriate and useful. When we study heat stroke, I'm reminded of the soldier who collapsed yesterday at the track. I figure I'll never know what happened to him, or Mike Hidersheit.

I finally had a tolerable day here. Except for the madness of the ring wraith general, things went okay. I even get a decent night's sleep, in bed at 9PM, no fireguard duty, and up at 4AM. But had I known what was in store this day, I think I would have stayed in bed, or reported to sick bay, or gone AWOL or anything else to escape.

When you're in reception, if you have vision problems, they won't let you wear your glasses from home. Instead they issue you these big ugly black things, that make half the guys in the platoon look like Buddy Holly. They pull the prescription off your civilian glasses and I swear the army lenses are sort of a rough guess. Back home my friend Sue at the optometry shop always gets my frames and lenses perfect. But not here in the Army. I hate the black goggles they issue and I only wear them when we fire our M-16s. Which is not supposed to be today, so I leave them in my locker.

Something happening at formation now tips me off that this is no ordinary, routine day. The staff sergeant shows up first. The short, stocky man is standing in front of the whole company now, not just our platoon. Instead of calling us to attention, he paces back and forth as he addresses us.

"When Sgt. Drock show up, and he call you to attention, I want every one of you mother-fuckers to yell as loud as you can, 'shut the fuck up!' I not joking. Every one of you, yell it, loud as you can. That's an order! You got it?"

The soldiers of Charlie Company look at each other in disbelief, not knowing what the heck is going on. But we can't delay too long, we have been given an order. Over 100 men scream, "Yes, Sergeant!"

We mill around at ease for a while, waiting. Then down the sidewalk strides Sgt. Drock, an imposing figure as always. He takes one look at the company, disgusted at the lack of order, and screams, "Attention!"

At that command, every member of Charlie Company yells enthusiastically, and with maximum decibels, "Shut the fuck up!"

I'm no psychiatrist, but I think that about any sane person would classify Sgt. Drock as mentally ill. The evil giant just stands there, for once shell shocked and unable to respond. Finally, he grabs the Smokey Bear hat off his head, throws it onto the ground, stomps on it with his army boot, and walks away.

The staff sergeant returns, calls us to attention and then marches us over to the armory. We are told to get our M-16's, ammo and full CBRN protective equipment. Three other drill sergeants lead their platoons off to the field. But Sgt. Drock is nowhere to be seen. Finally the staff sergeant tells us to just go back to our barracks and wait.

We hang out with all our gear, sitting on our bunks, waiting, like convicts on death row, knowing the end is near for us. Then, with an extraordinary amount of screaming, even for Sgt. Drock, the crazy drill shows up and orders us to run, not walk, outside. As I exit the barracks sprinting into the bright sunlight of the day, I have an eerie experience. I look down and sense immediate danger, seeing the looming shadow of a man, obviously a soldier. The outline of the steel pot helmet, rifle and ALICE pack is unmistakable.

I often live life as if I were an actor in a theatre play. I have had many roles in my short life. But never have I experienced such shock as when I realize the dangerous shadow I recoil from, is mine. Every military movie, every war story, every book about historical battles I've ever absorbed, now comes flooding into my mind. The good deeds and every horrible act, that any combatant has ever committed, I now own. I'm a soldier. That is who I am now. Like it or not, through all the ages, people like me have assumed the role, worn a uniform, forced by conscription or volunteered, we are all the same: Roman Legions,

Knights Templar, Spanish conquistadors, or WWII GI's, we are soldiers.

Sgt. Drock marches us out into the field, far away to a remote location on the base. It is dusty and hot as hell. I have a bad feeling. But I'm a soldier now. I do not question. I feel rugged and strong. My voice is hoarse. I look at the faces of the other men. We all look tough as nails. Sgt. Drock yells, "Stand tall fourth!"

We stop marching. Sgt. Drock orders us to lock and load our rifles. What the hell is he up to? We're ordered onto our bellies into the prone firing position. Take aim! Take aim at what? In front of us is nothing but a field, beyond that the rolling deciduous forest of the Ozarks. "Fire!" Sgt. Drock blares the command.

Normally in boot camp trainees practice at the rifle range, spaced out, with safety procedures and a backstop so the bullets don't fly randomly off for miles. What the hell we are doing out here in the wilds of Missouri firing rounds off into the distance? I have no idea. I was worried because I didn't bring my army issue glasses, but it doesn't even matter. There are no targets to aim at or score. Sgt. Drock laughs like a crazy man, delighted that we are following his commands.

We spend the afternoon marching, running and setting up ambushes in the heat. Burdened with the weight of the bulky CBRN gear, even the smallest task becomes unbearable. But Drock never lets up. We are suffering. Our bodies scream with anguish. But we must ignore the pain, and observe Sgt. Drock's demands to press on.

Afternoon training over, we are marching back to the barracks now. My boots feel like ninety-pound bags of cement. But Sgt. Drock is not finished with us. Out of nowhere he keeps randomly screaming, "Hit it."

The "hit it" command in infantry is used as a warning of incoming fire or other danger. At this command we are to immediately dive spread eagle directly onto our bellies and stay down on the ground. It is far easier on the body to drop to a knee first or put your hand out to cushion the fall. But if Sgt. Drock sees anyone trying to avoid landing directly on their belly, he gives them a swift kick.

We are getting bruised up badly by this regimen. All the cumbersome, heavy CBRN equipment on our backs makes matters worse. At the next command of "hit it" I follow instructions exactly, leaping outward spread eagle to impact the ground on my stomach, the weight of the pack driving me into the ground. But this time my gas mask, and its case, jam sharply up under my left rib cage. I feel a jolt of incredibly intense pain, as if an internal organ has been torn or ruptured.

My mind is in a panic now. I know I've been hurt badly. I clutch my side and moan. But everyone else is getting back up, so I must too. I fear Sgt. Drock and know if I report the injury, he may intentionally force me to do something that will make matters worse. I march along now in extreme pain, slightly bent over and clutching my side. Fortunately, I'm on the far side of the platoon so the sergeant doesn't notice until we are nearly back at the barracks. When Sgt. Drock finally observes my condition, the monster approaches me, then punches me hard in the sternum. I fall backward, but some fellow soldiers break my fall.

I lie on my bunk now in a fetal position, trying to relieve the sharp pain in my side. It feels like a side ache on steroids. I'm sweating and nervous, but what can I do? Finally, we are called outside to line up for dinner. I'm the last one out of the barracks. Several soldiers are in a compromising position, bent over at the waist holding their ankles. Sgt. Drock occasionally orders trainees to assume this position in order to degrade and humiliate them.

When I arrive, the crazed sergeant walks up to me holding an M-16 barrel to my nose. He stares at me, then barks, "Bend over, I'm going to fuck you in the ass!"

You know some people can submit to this kind of humiliation, allowing themselves to be mistreated, but some of us can't. At this point, I really don't care whether my father, or uncles, or cousins, or presidents or famous persons or movie stars or anyone else allowed themselves to be treated this way. They can take the recognition and military bragging rights that come after sacrificing your soul. I'm done with it.

I limp away. Sgt. Drock screams, "Where the hell you think you going?"

But I don't stop walking until I come to the door of our captain's office. "Private First Class Miller requests permission to speak," I state, trying to remain calm. Our captain is a young, college educated, black man. He listens intently as I relate my injury, then he fills out a form so that I can report to sick bay. But I'm not finished. I continue, identifying the many abuses Sgt. Drock has heaped on our platoon. Captain Price does not seem to want to hear about what I'm saying. But he listens quietly, and then sends me back to the barracks.

CHAPTER THIRTY

At the morning formation a group of soldiers from the company is pulled out to report for sick call. I'm overjoyed to hear my name. I'm experiencing excruciating pain, like a razor sharp spear is jabbing me in the side, up under my ribs. We are driven over to the hospital in the back of a truck.

I fill out some forms in the waiting room, then sit for hours. Finally, my name is called and I get to see a military doctor who seems hurried and unhappy that I'm even here. I try to explain my injury, then lay on a table while he probes my side. The doc keeps asking me, over and over, "Do you want to get out of the army?"

I'm not sure what to say. The answer is, yes, I do now, but so many people you run into here on the base seem motivated to give you the exact opposite of whatever you want, so I'm unsure what to say. Plus, I know I have a serious injury and my primary concern, for now anyway, is diagnosis and treatment. Finally, since a reply is all this doctor seems to care about, I say, "Yes."

Well, that was the wrong answer. The doctor scoffs and immediately dismisses me. He no doubt figures I'm just faking an injury to get discharged. Before he leaves, I make a desperate attempt to quickly relate several of the medical conditions the civilian doctor at my MEPS physical told me would keep me out of the military if I wanted.

"My lungs are damaged with silicone and cement dust from working at my father's shop. I have severe hearing loss and tinnitus. I broke my neck once and fractured my skull in a work-related farm accident. I...." But it's no use, the military doctor snickers and walks away.

I pile into the truck for the ride back to the barracks. The rest of the company is gone, off to the field for some training exercise. It seems weird to be in the barracks with only a handful of other soldiers from sick call and no sergeant to yell at us. I get everyone who can help busy cleaning the fixtures with Brasso, waxing the floors, making sure the beds are tight, policing the grounds for litter, even washing some dirty BDU laundry for other soldiers.

We end up missing the whole day of whatever the rest of the platoon is doing. A soldier I've never seen before stops by with some MREs for us to eat for lunch and dinner. I'm just glad I didn't have to do PT. With my medical condition I'm not sure I could have stood the pain. Eventually we hear the others marching back. They burst into the barracks, covered in mud, several are bleeding from cuts and scratches. Sgt. Drock is screaming and flipping over the bunks we had just neatened up.

Between my piercing side ache, and worrying how I can get through PT tomorrow, I get little sleep all night. In the morning I get dressed and report for formation. Sergeant Goddamned Barnes is standing out front. He holds a pharmacy bag in his hands, out of which he pulls Goddamned medicine for the Goddamned slackers. Each time he thrusts his claw-like hand into the bag he pulls out a prescription, makes a mocking face and then throws the bottle off into the field.

Each one of the soldiers who had reported to sick call the day before is expected to crawl out into the field on our hands and knees and search for our prescription while Sgt. Barnes makes fun of us and derides us as losers. Later I check the labels on our medicine bottles. I'm no pharmacist but it appears to me that all of us have been prescribed the same thing, which is some sort of anxiety pills. I throw mine in the trash.

The dreaded time has arrived for PT. My innards are on fire. How the hell am I going to manage sit-ups? A drill sergeant named Hulbert stands on a large box in front of the company, like a hormone-saturated bull screaming orders. We start with push-ups, which I can fortunately manage in my wounded condition. After we knock out fifty, Sgt. Hulbert has us hold ourselves in the air, in the push-up position, for what seems an eternity. Through the pain, the soldiers are screaming, "We like it, we love it, we want more of it, more PT drill sergeant, more PT!"

A couple of the soldiers who were at sick call yesterday are unable to continue holding themselves all the way up in the air. They are in push up position but their exhausted arms bend and they hover near the ground. From the corner of my eye I notice Sgt. Drock descending rapidly upon the formation. He pulls back his long thick leg and then forcefully swings it forward like a giant pendulum, drop kicking each exhausted recruit in the stomach or chest. The blows make an awful thud I'll never forget, like thumping a watermelon, but amplified.

"Oh God," I think to myself. "Those soldiers are getting seriously hurt." It gives me a sick feeling in my stomach. Like coming upon a traffic accident with terribly injured victims. Any decent human being dislikes seeing, or hearing, other human beings' bodies being damaged. But then, in the midst of the carnage, a loud confident voice cries out with authority, "Stop that!"

Sgt. Drock swings around to identify where the voice came from and gets a panicked look on his face. Holy shit, it's the captain. The conniving sergeant wasn't careful enough to conceal his abuse of the soldiers this time. Sgt. Drock is busted! I know there's no longer any way the captain can ignore the maltreatment. He has heard complaints, and now he has seen it with his own eyes.

I feel like cheering when the staff sergeant arrives. The captain calls Sgt. Drock to attention, then along with the staff sergeant, they lead the mad man off to a distance and begin dressing him down. I can't hear what they say, but I figure it's a clean deal. By that I mean the staff sergeant, the captain and Sgt. Drock are all three black men.

There is no way anyone can say that Sgt. Drock's troubles are racially motivated or the result of discrimination. Our tormentor is, as we soldiers say, booked for a hurt dance.

The world is a strange place. I lay in bed last night searching my mind trying desperately to figure out some way to survive PT today, and I came up with nothing. There was just no way to avoid the strenuous exercises and whatever further harm they would do to my injured body. But here we are, Sgt. Drock is gone, PT has been called off and we're ordered back to our barracks. The mathematical numbers and physics laws that order the universe have a strange way of balancing everything out. That, or there really is a God who was looking out for me today.

Our platoon has a new drill, Sergeant Bailey. I'm familiar with this fellow already as he has led some of our training sessions. He is a hard man, with sharp chiseled facial features that make him always look cross. But Bailey is a fairly decent person, concerned mostly with getting the soldiers boned up on skills and requirements to make it through boot camp. He can be cold and mean and is obviously battling demons from the past. But at least Sgt. Bailey is battling his demons, in Sgt. Drock's case, the demons had already won.

Sgt. Bailey pulls me aside. The tall sinewy man digs a cigarette out of his chest pocket and offers it to me with the following advice, "Unfiltered Camels! Best damn smokes! Forget all those other candy ass cigs. Marlboro Reds? Hell, I'd rather roll horse shit!"

The sergeant is obviously unimpressed when I tell him I don't smoke. No, not even unfiltered Camels. He looks at me a long time, sort of cross eyed, like he's trying to figure out what the heck is wrong with me. He takes a long drag on his beloved Camel cigarette, slowly blows out a cloud of smoke, and sighs, "Round up that band-aid brigade of yours and report back here at 1400 with your go-fasters on."

I spend half my time in the army trying to figure out acronyms and military slang for various things. I imagine over the years a few people have even been killed due to miscommunication, but that's the way it rolls around here. They have their own official nomenclature and ways of doing things on this alien planet, and like any foreign place, they also have their own slang terms and jargon.

In the lingo of California surfers the phrase "white pointers" refers to dangerous Great White sharks that can rip a fiberglass board, or a leg, apart in one bite. While in Australia the same slang term, white pointers, refers to nude female sunbathers. A surfer from down under comes to the golden state and is alerted to the presence of white pointers at Surf Beach near Vandenberg AFB. The Aussie decides to hang eleven at Van so he can check out the caligirls' hooters and instead he gets bit in two by a man in a grey suit.

I find all the soldiers who reported to sick call yesterday and then ask around until I discover that go-fasters refers to our civilian running shoes.

As I feared, it's 1400 and Sgt. Bailey is going to administer a PT test. I just explain, outright and honestly, that I'm in no condition to test. He counters that any soldier who can't pass the PT test, will get recycled in boot camp. That sounds like hell to me. To have to go back to the reception area and start this whole nightmare scenario all over again. But what am I supposed to do? The internal organs on my left side hurt like hell, I feel light-headed and nauseous. I think I may have ruptured my spleen or something.

Sgt. Bailey has us do push-ups. Even in my weakened condition I can knock out fifty, which is passing. Next are sit-ups. This is going to be impossible. I already know that. But the sergeant insists I try, so I get down with another soldier holding my go-fasters and attempt to sit-up. I try not to scream. The stitch in my side is overwhelming. Eventually I have to stop. Sgt. Bailey and the others encourage me to keep going. I try to work through the discomfort, but it's no use. I can't stand the pain, and anyway, I fear I may make the injury worse if I continue.

Afterwards the sergeant informs me that he is filling out an official report, stating that I have failed to complete the required PT test. He tells me to report for sick call in the morning. *I pray, dear God, get me a different doctor than last time, one who knows what they're doing. I don't want to die in this hell hole.*

Morning comes. I stand milling around with a small group of

soldiers on sick call, waiting for the truck to the hospital. One has broken ribs. He was drop kicked like a human football by Sgt. Drock. Another has a bad infection oozing pus from the side of his face. Others are clearing their sore throats and spitting massive lubes, the concrete street is dotted with the yellow-green wads.

I have so much hope riding on this sick call. I'm determined to get myself out of this awful place alive. After waiting forever at the hospital, it's finally my turn. My heart sinks when the same doctor as last time appears. He looks around the waiting room at everyone and sneers, "What are you oxygen thieves doing here again?"

This scene is especially hard for me as my whole goal in joining the army was to go to medical school and become a doctor. I know I'd never treat patients this way. The military doc spends all of about two minutes listening to me describe my injury and then cuts me off. He demands to know if I want out of the army. I figure I'll handle it differently this time and explain, "No, I do not want out of the army! But I do have a severe pain in my abdomen and I need medical attention."

I have never dealt with people quite like this before. Most doctors and nurses have always been kind and compassionate to me. Not this military doc. He is pompous and could care less about us. I feel so hopeless when he scoffs and tells me to get out.

While I'm leaving the hospital, I encounter numerous civilians. If you have never been in the military before I can tell you it is very odd the way people treat you when you wear a uniform. A few will reject you. Perhaps they've had a bad experience with a soldier or they oppose war. I want to tell them, "Hey, I consider myself a peace activist." Just because you wear a uniform doesn't necessarily mean you are pro-war.

But mostly people kind of grovel at your feet. I guess they are so enamored at the sight of a uniform they think everyone who wears one is a good person or something. They assume a lot. From my experience, I have never met so many bad people concentrated in one place as this military base. I mean, many of the worst serial killers in history were once soldiers. Lee Harvey Oswald, the assassin who murdered John F. Kennedy, was a decorated marine.

This has been a depressing, discouraging day. I had hoped to get some medical attention and instead I was treated shabbily again. The life of a soldier is often miserable. There are many discomforts and worries here that one does not encounter in civilian life. All the pain and suffering have the effect of making a person hard and coarse and aggressive. These are the conditions and regimen necessary to turn an ordinary person into a killer. It is really impossible to understand what it is like, unless you experience it personally.

It is frustrating to me that, while I'm going through so much turmoil and torment, these civilians at the hospital keep coming up to me and saying, "Thank you for your service." I know they mean well. But I get the feeling they're just appreciative to have someone else fighting their battles for them. I want to tell them that the military is like a mirage, they don't realize what's really going on. Look behind the curtain I'd say, there is no Wizard.

Seriously, I would wager 99% of the wars fought are completely unnecessary. Conceited, power hungry politicians throwing their weight around and not doing the hard work of peace-making. Other people suffer because of their arrogant swagger. Bullets are left to do what words, rightly used, could have avoided.

As I leave the hospital to board the truck, another civilian couple approaches me. They thank me for defending their freedom. I try to keep my mouth shut. They search my face, eliciting a reply. They repeat again, "Thank you for your service." I can't hold back any longer.

"If you think it's so great, why don't you join up?" I reply grudgingly. They retreat, acting shocked and offended.

The thing is, I like freedom too. In fact, I like it a lot. But I have never had less freedom in my life than I do right now in the army. In the past I've felt guilty, or even cowardly, because I hadn't served in the armed forces, and someone else had to "defend freedom" for me. It was one reason I joined the military. To defend freedom. But I don't feel guilty anymore. Not after what I've experienced here. In fact, I'm not even sure that military establishments and war result in freedom at all.

According to America's founders, liberty is endowed by the creator, it does not emanate from the smoking barrel of a gun.

Freedom is not the absence of law, but the presence of a minimum set of good laws, a balanced condition, not anarchy and not tyranny. Good laws free people. An example of a good law would be a homicide law. True, the law restricts murderers' freedom to kill people, but for the vast majority, homicide laws act as a deterrent and framework to "free" people from the likelihood and danger of being murdered. I think the best way to "defend freedom" is to get involved in the political system and work for good laws, and honest, reliable government representatives.

Back at the barracks the platoon is hanging out. I know I can't take any grueling maneuvers. Fortunately, it will be a slack day. The photographers are here taking pictures for some sort of boot camp yearbook-type publication. We line up at attention on some tiered bleachers so that everyone's mug can be seen in the group shot.

Then, one by one, we are quickly processed through a small dark mobile studio for a formal portrait. We sit in a chair with a dress uniform neatly fitted to the front of a headless mannequin. They plop one of those banana hats on your head and then move the dressed-up dummy in front of each one of us so it looks like we have on the dress uniform. Like so many things in the military, the photos are just a facade.

Sgt. Bailey calls me in at the end of the day. The report from the hospital states that I am trainable. I explain that I have been injured. He replies that if the medical facility says I am trainable, then he will train me. I tell the hardened sergeant I want a discharge. He goes into a rambling recitation of the nature and consequences of a trainee discharge. I repeat that I want out. The sergeant claims that it will take months because I'll probably end up being recycled and as a consequence, I'd miss the start of college classes. I say I can't miss the start of the semester. The sergeant recommends I give "maximum effort" in order to graduate.

Telling me, in my current condition, to give maximum effort to graduate, is a little like telling a blind person to give their maximum effort to read the letters on an optician's eye chart or telling a quadriplegic to give their maximum effort to get up and dance.

CHAPTER THIRTY-ONE

I pulled KP duty in the mess hall today. Most soldiers hate the menial chores of kitchen patrol. But I'm actually relieved because nothing that I could encounter in the cafeteria galley would be as strenuous as PT or the trauma I might experience training in the field. Believe it or not, my only complaint about KP duty is the noise. I stand in front of a giant, stainless-steel sink while cooks noisily sling clanking, banging metal pots and pans for me to scrub.

One thing about boot camp, there is no escaping loud noise. The decibel levels can be deafening. Conversation is not the same as the civilian world. The sergeants scream, and then make us scream back. There is the pop, pop, pop of our M-16s and the concussion of grenades and claymore mines will rattle your innards. The trucks are loud, the construction machinery is loud, the mock bombs during firefight simulations are loud. Everything is very, very loud.

When I was fourteen, I fractured my skull in a farm accident while detasseling corn. My inner ear bones were dislocated and my tympanic membranes torn. The operation to repair the damage was unsuccessful. I don't hear well under normal conditions, let alone in noisy environments like this army base. Loud noise exacerbates my tinnitus, which is a terrible ringing in my ears.

I finally get dismissed from KP after everyone has been fed and the kitchen is cleaned. I take off the filthy apron, toss it in the laundry hamper and walk toward the doors of the mess hall. Inside my aching head is a crescendo of random percussion instruments banging out annoying tinnitus noise. I haven't had a drink all day and I'm dying of thirst, so I stop at the water fountain. The cold water tastes heavenly going down my parched throat.

Out of nowhere I feel a muscled hand grab my arm and pin me against the wall. Startled, I see Sgt. Hulbert and he's mad as hell. Hulbert is one of those guys, built like an Olympic weightlifter, full of hormonal energy, but with glasses so thick it is difficult to see his eyes. He carries a long flat stick everywhere he goes that he randomly slams against flat surfaces like tables and walls. His idea is that soldiers will get conditioned to the unexpected sharp crack this produces, and it will help us overcome our startle reflex.

I have no idea what I've done to set off the hyper sergeant. I'm not resisting, just trying to breath, as he crushes me against the cement block wall.

"Are you refusing to obey my order?" he barks out.

"What order?" I reply meekly.

"I told you twice to move away from that damn water fountain. Why the hell did you stay there, drinking all that time?"

"I didn't hear you. I was just thirsty, that's why I drank so much."

"Bull shit!" the enraged sergeant screams. "I yelled at you twice, there's no way you didn't hear me!"

"I have a hearing problem, sergeant."

"What the fuck are you talking about? Report to my office. I'm writing you up!"

When a sergeant, or officer, says they are "writing you up" that basically means that according to them you have violated the Uniform Code of Military Justice, a serious infraction that will go in your official file. I just cannot believe this is happening to me. My life has descended into a complete and total Charlie Foxtrot. Just a month ago I was a free man, a student working my way through college, getting good grades and pursuing happiness. Now my dream of going to medical school has been ruined, I'm miserable and my life is falling apart.

I knock once, just once, on the door to Hulbert's office and state, "Private First Class Miller reports as ordered, sergeant." I wait until given the order to enter, open the door, march in a smart military fashion to within three, exactly three, paces in front of Hulbert's desk and stand at attention. I must get every detail correct, I'm in enough trouble already.

The bulked-up sergeant sits, reclining in an office chair, with his boots propped up on the metal desk. He looks me over, or at least I think he is looking at me, it's hard to tell what his eyes are doing behind those opaque lenses. He grudgingly gives the next order, "At ease."

I assume the position of parade rest, precisely correct, and then for some unknown reason, perhaps a case of the nerves, I utter, "Yes, sir." A dumb move.

Hulbert grabs his stick and slams the desk hard producing a loud crack. "Do not call me sir!" he bellows. "I work for a living!"

"Yes, sergeant!" I scream.

Hulbert relaxes a bit in his chair, grabs a triplicate form from the desk and cuts to the bone, "I'm charging you with failure to obey a lawful order." The sergeant stops to gauge my reaction, then continues his description of the incident. "You were drinking at the water fountain in the mess hall. I had to tell you twice to leave it alone. In the army, reaction time must be immediate and correct. Do you understand?"

"Yes, sergeant," I reply respectfully. Then, at great risk, because all you are supposed to say at this point is 'yes sergeant' and then shut up, after which he will say 'dismissed' and it will all be over, whether or not you had anything else to say, but instead, I break with established procedure and, humbly add, "Sergeant, I regret this incident, but I was not disobeying your order, sergeant. I have a hearing problem, sergeant."

I expect to get clobbered for not following standard protocol, but the boorish sergeant removes his thick glasses and sits up in his desk. I can actually see his eyes, which surprisingly, are not full of hate.

Hulbert asks me to explain myself and I spend several minutes relating medical issues, including my hearing loss.

Sgt. Hulbert asks for clarification, then pulls another official triplicate form from his desk and states, "I'm recommending, for your own good, and the good of the U.S. Army, that you be granted a discharge. Dismissed!"

I snap to attention, about face, and march sharply out the door. I have just been given a ray of hope. An infinitesimally small ray of hope, granted, but still a possibility that I may escape from this hell hole.

After a listless night's sleep, I roll out of my bunk in the morning and prepare for doom. My side still aches and PT will be hell. I'm not sure I can make it through the day. I actually wish I could do KP duty again. Only with ear plugs this time. And remembering my canteen, so I can keep hydrated in that hot kitchen.

I exit the door to the barracks and head outside for formation. But Sgt. Bailey pulls me aside. Oh God, now what? I stand tall, determined to take my punishment like a soldier. I search Bailey's face for a clue, but he is hard as steel. We stare at each other for a long time. It is the sergeant who finally flinches. A flicker of humanity. He clears his throat. He has something to say, but doesn't want to say it.

"An NCO reviewing the charges, that you disobeyed a direct order by Sgt. Hulbert, has recommended that you be sent to the brig." Bailey grimaces. "That's the military prison on base."

"Whatttt...." I blurt out, incredulously. "I can't believe this is happening."

"Your military bearing!" Bailey reminds me. Sgt. Bailey is big on ALWAYS maintaining military bearing. I reposition myself at attention, silent and staring straight forward.

"The MPs will be here shortly to escort you to prison."

"Yes, Sergeant!"

I'm shell shocked. I thought things couldn't get worse, and they just did. The military prison is a notoriously terrible place to be locked up. Like a medieval dungeon. How can this be happening? The army sure has a way of making you think you have an opening to escape, and then slamming the door in your face. I'm devastated.

Bailey reluctantly starts to walk away toward the platoon, then stops. Turning back towards me he questions, "What order did you refuse to obey?"

"I did not hear Sgt. Hulbert tell me to move away from the drinking fountain because I have a medical problem with my hearing, sergeant."

"So, this is about a drinking fountain? And you didn't hear him because of a medical problem?"

"Yes, sergeant!"

"Report to my office. I'll be back after I run this foxtrot uniform platoon over to PT."

I'm standing outside Sgt. Bailey's office when he arrives. He doesn't say a word, just pulls a triplicate form from his desk and begins to write earnestly. When finished he slides the form over the desk for me to read and sign.

Basically, the form states that the sergeant has observed me carefully and is convinced that I'm sincere about my medical complaints, that I'm putting forth 100% but unable to perform due to injury. For my own good, and the good of the U.S. Army, he recommends that I be discharged.

"Report to the armory. Stay there all day. Try to help that crazy mo fo in charge over there. And for God's sakes, stay out of trouble!"

"Sergeant. What about the brig? What should I tell the MPs?"

"I'll take care of that. Get outta here."

The corporal in charge of the armory is a raving lunatic. I report and explain that I'm there to assist him all day. He yells all kinds of incoherent crazy stuff. Hey, all I care about is staying out of trouble. The first work assignment he gives me is to break M-16 stocks. I look at him incredulously. He yells something about the damn army inventory system and how he can only get new parts if he turns in broken ones. He hands me a hammer and a pile of the hard, plastic rifle stocks.

I may just be an E-3 in training but I'm not clueless enough to be the one held responsible for damaging government property. No, I'm not going to spend the day busting stuff up so he can request new replacements. I refuse. He gets a crooked grin on his face and hands me a broom to clean the floor.

* * *

It's been a few days now and I've been assigned to a new platoon. We are officially in limbo, as the army chain of command figures out what to do with us. Our group includes misfits, mental cases, medical problems, criminals, loafers and a whole group of sane, decent people, including religious objectors, who just want the hell out of here.

Mostly we pass the day sitting on benches in front of the barracks waiting for our orders to come through. It is hot as hell and the army has provided us with a giant lister bag so we'll at least keep hydrated and not "die on them." I have never seen time pass so slowly as it does now. We are stressed out, not knowing what our fate will be. Answers and paper work trickle in rarely and sporadically. The young man sitting next to me is shaking uncontrollably. He is obviously having a mental breakdown. I try to talk to him, but I'm not sure he understands.

The days of idle time have allowed my side to recover, at least partially, so I'm no longer in constant pain and can move and perform some light, manual tasks. Personally, I'd rather be busy doing something to help pass the time. So, I volunteer for every work detail I can handle in my current condition. The attitude of some of these guys here in limbo bugs me. One soldier from the Bronx named Rivera keeps referring to our group as the "goon platoon." He thinks it's funny, but I don't. I tell him to knock it off. No matter how difficult and humiliating your situation is, a person ought to maintain their self-respect and dignity.

I'm not a goon. I haven't done anything wrong. I joined the army for noble reasons: to become a doctor, to defend freedom and my country, to help others in time of need. The military system has serious problems. That's not my fault. I just want out of here now. I want to go back home and try to piece my life back together, to come up with some new path forward.

At E-3 I have the highest rank in the group. I try to get this disorganized bunch of misfits to march appropriately when we need to. I tell them to hold their heads high. When we encounter members of the old platoon, who are still in training, they often jeer at us and hurl insults. The sergeants encourage this. I think they want us to look bad, like losers, perhaps to discourage others from dropping out and joining our ranks. But I'm not buying it. I tell the misfits to be strong, not afraid, that things will work out.

The soldiers here in limbo are bored to death. They are nervous as hell about their fate. I volunteer the group for various tasks and we spend hours cutting the tall grass in overgrown fields with hand scythes or picking up litter along roadways. The work is menial but I know we're better off keeping occupied doing something constructive, to help pass the time, to stay in shape physically and to maintain spiritual and mental health.

A grizzled old Sgt. Hughes, in particular, dislikes our group. And within our group, he especially hates me for some reason. He will nitpick the slightest thing he can find. Like calling me out for shaving the hair on the back of my neck, which I guess is against regulation. But, fortunately for me, he has jumped on the bandwagon with the other sergeants and filled out a recommendation that I be discharged.

The problem holding up my exit from the military is that there is disagreement among the officers and enlisted personnel as to how I should be processed out. A representative on base from the national guard named Kopp insists that I be granted a medical separation and receive an honorable discharge from the regular army with full military benefits, including VA and the GI Bill for college. The sergeants are pushing for a trainee discharge where I would get an honorable discharge from the national guard, but not be eligible for most veteran's benefits.

After days of feeling like a human ping pong ball Captain Price calls me in. I'm thankful that he got Sgt. Drock transferred. In fact, I have heard rumors that Drock got transferred out of the country, all the way to Germany. But I don't know what to expect now. The captain explains that the medical separation will take a long time. The trainee discharge will be faster and get me back to college in time for the fall semester, but I won't have benefits like the GI Bill. He looks at me for my reaction.

I really don't want anything from the Pentagon or U.S. military. They can keep any and all of their benefits. At this point, I just want my freedom back and to get out of here. I have a college scholarship for good grades and if I get back in time for classes, I figure I'll work hard to keep it. But I'm careful what I say. I simply tell the captain that I request the trainee discharge. He concurs and starts filling out the paperwork.

I return to the circle of soldiers in limbo surrounding the lister bag. We sip lukewarm water from our canteen cups. It is deathly hot and they beg me not to volunteer the group for any more work details. I can't blame them, so we all just sit, waiting and waiting, for someone's paperwork to come through. Sgt. Hughes approaches. This could be it. Who will it be?

Hughes is angry, as always. He calls my name. Did my discharge come through? I try not to hope. I don't want to get let down again. He leads me over behind the armory where no one can see us. The red-faced sergeant begins a long disparaging harangue about the uselessness of a college education and how diplomas are worthless paper. As the fiery speech goes on and on, the sergeant becomes angrier and more belligerent.

I don't know what to expect. The sergeant shoves me hard and my back makes a loud metallic bang as it impacts the corrugated metal of the armory. I look into his glaring eyes and see pure hatred. Like a volcanic eruption the angry words, mixed with foamy spit, explode from his contorted mouth, "What do you think is the purpose of the United States Army?"

I consider an answer to his demand carefully. The aggrieved sergeant is obviously losing it. I fear he may become violent and I'm not sure exactly what to say. I try to state calmly, "The purpose of the United States Army is to defend our country." It is the best answer I can think of.

This reply does not please the agitated sergeant. In fact, it enrages him. Again, he hammers my chest with the heels of his hands, shoving me hard against the metal wall as he repeats his interrogation, "What is the purpose of the United States Army?"

I desperately search my mind, racking my brain for a better answer. But I can't think of any. This madman is so angry I fear leaving him to wait any longer for a reply. So, I repeat my original answer, "The purpose of the United States Army is to defend our country."

Well, now I've done it. That is definitely NOT the answer the fuming sergeant is looking for. The hardened war survivor goes berserk and begins repeatedly shoving me, harder and harder, into the metal wall. By now a small crowd has gathered around at a distance watching the display. The crazy corporal in charge of armory is there, as well as the members of my new limbo platoon. They have heard the ruckus and are wondering what is going on? What the heck I have done to elicit the sergeant's wild, over the top behavior?

The scenario continues with the sergeant demanding an answer to his question, "What is the purpose of the United States Army?"

For my part, as hard as I try, I cannot think of a better answer. Lacking any other response, and fearing the consequences of not answering at all, I continue to repeat, "The purpose of the United States Army is to defend our country." This, of course, adds fuel to the fire in the sergeant's hot head and only escalates the situation, resulting in me being shoved, again and again, harder and harder, into a metal wall that booms in response to the impact.

Finally, at the point where I don't think my spine can take the punishment anymore, Sgt. Hughes just stops cold. He stares at me like I'm naïve and unknowing. This stare down is lasting a long time and I'm very uncomfortable. Finally, he comes out with it. His perfect answer to the big question. He states it flatly, "The purpose of the United States Army is to kill people and destroy things."

I suppose, in the final analysis, he is right, and I am wrong. Maybe I'm too idealistic. Possibly my standards are too high, too unrealistic and detached from the reality of what my country has become under people like the fascist occupying the White House. Perhaps the United States has just become little more than a brutal bouncer for the multinational corporations.

In the words of Major General Smedley D. Butler, the highest-ranking marine of his time and twice recipient of the medal of honor:

I spent 33 years and four months in active military service and during that period I spent most of my time as a high class muscle man for Big Business, for Wall Street and the bankers. In short, I was a racketeer; a gangster for capitalism. I helped make Mexico and especially Tampico safe for American oil interests in 1914. I helped make Haiti and Cuba a decent place for the National City Bank boys to collect revenues in. I helped in the raping of half a dozen Central American republics for the benefit of Wall Street. I helped purify Nicaragua for the International Banking House of Brown Brothers in 1902–1912. I brought light to the Dominican Republic for the American sugar interests in 1916. I helped make Honduras right for the American fruit companies in 1903. In China in 1927 I helped see to it that Standard Oil went on its way unmolested. Looking back on it, I might have given Al Capone a few hints. The best he could do was to operate his racket in three districts. I operated on three continents.

I suppose I could stick it out. I could stay here in the army and finish boot camp. I could continue to submit to humiliation and abuse on a daily basis, so that someday, people would think more of me, based on their lack of experience in such matters. I signed up, volunteered honestly for 8 years of my life, fully intending to work 100% to fulfill that obligation. I have done nothing dishonorable. I have, however, been treated dishonorably. Leaving this place, I will give up my chance to study in the army medical program. I will give up any and all military benefits. And people, not knowing the situation, will judge me based on their own lack of knowledge, of history and of the events I have experienced.

But I will gladly give up any right to brag about being a macho warrior. I will suffer the disrespect of relatives and acquaintances and all the others who think they know more than they do. I will give it all up, to retain my self-respect, to harbor that last grain of human dignity that no one can take away from you *without your consent*. To me, honor and integrity and truth and fairness and justice and chivalry and peace and love and courage and courtesy and kindness and yes, just plain common decency, are more valuable than accolades and money and careers and positions and titles and ranks and medals and privileges and lines on a resume.

The military system is rotten. War, as General Sherman pointed out, is hell. I would add that anything associated with war is hell. The psychological indoctrination of soldiers is an evil art, based on ancient and well-established procedures and conditioning, essentially black magic that is morally wrong and dishonest. Such immoral practices only serve those in power, to control humanity economically and politically. In the words of the notorious NAZI commander Herman Goering:

> *Why, of course, the people don't want war. Why would some poor slob on a farm want to risk his life in a war when the best that he can get out of it is to come back to his farm in one piece. Naturally, the common people don't want war; neither in Russia nor in England nor in America, nor for that matter in Germany. That is understood. But, after all, it is the leaders of the country who determine the policy and it is always a simple matter to drag the people along, whether it is a democracy or a fascist dictatorship or a Parliament or a Communist dictatorship ... voice or no voice, the people can always be brought to the bidding of the leaders. That is easy. All you have to do is tell them they are being attacked and denounce the pacifists for lack of patriotism and exposing the country to danger. It works the same way in any country.*

I don't know if there is another way to prepare for national defense. I'd like to think that there is a better method, a more dignified, fair and decent way to train people to keep the peace. I'm no expert. I hope that there is a better way. But, for my part, I want no further involvement in this rotten dark enterprise on this army base. I have made the decision that I want out of here, out of this torment and hell I find myself in. One thing sticks in my mind, perhaps because the skin of my fingers was sticking to the asphalt when I heard Sgt. Drock bellow it: "When you find yourself in hell, you must climb a hot ladder out." That's exactly what I intend to do now.

"What the heck happened? Why was Hughes shoving you against the armory like that? What the hell did you do wrong? Man, you must be in big trouble now." My fellow soldiers in limbo pump me for information. They seem amazed and confused as to what took place. But I don't feel like talking about it.

"We had a disagreement about the purpose of the army. That's all," I reply, deflecting any further discussion.

CHAPTER THIRTY-TWO

It's late afternoon. The regular platoon is returning from the field where they have been training in hand to hand combat. Basically, for hours in the sun, they have been beating on each other with pugil sticks. The soldiers are hot and sore and in an aggravated mood. They yell at us, as we sit on benches in a circle around the lister bag, to stay out of the barracks because they get to shower first. No one here in limbo had any intention of showering before them, so they can save their breath.

They emerge later in the evening, cleaned up and in fresh uniforms. As a reward for smacking each other on the head with pugil sticks enough times to pass the self-defense test, a beer truck has arrived. Once again, they shout angrily at us to stay away. We don't deserve any beer they say, hurling insults. Sgt. Bailey joins them for a brew, puffing on his unfiltered Camel. He has eased up on the regulars, as is the custom at this point in boot camp.

So now, after tormenting and insulting trainees for weeks calling them maggots, knuckleheads, mo fos, pukes and so on the sergeants are going to let up a bit and supposedly create a bond with the young men. I have to admit it seems to work for many, but personally, I don't buy it. The soldiers around me lament that they don't get to join the party and drink beer or have a cigarette. But I don't want any of that swill or stinking tobacco smoke. Having had enough bad experiences with substances in my life, I've sworn off alcohol and drugs for good.

It is hard to explain just how badly a person wants out of the army, when they've decided they've had it. It is like a switch flips in your brain and you know there is no turning back. All of the soldiers in limbo are on pins and needles, hoping desperately for their discharge papers to come through. One young black soldier who wants out, is getting recycled instead. He tells me a white officer is against him and wouldn't let him out. I don't doubt his story. I have empathy for him.

We sit around our circle, waiting endlessly in the heat, for any ray of hope. You can barely imagine how emotional we become when a couple of sergeants arrive smiling. We've never seen these sergeants before, but they have good news. All of us have been approved for discharge. We just need to go over to headquarters to finish our paperwork. This is a deviation from the past, when discharges trickled in one, or a few, at a time.

The sergeants are driving a heavy duty, four-wheel-drive troop transport that looks like a transformer monster. It sits high off the ground for clearance on giant all-terrain wheels making it difficult to board. After we're all inside, the sergeants slam the back doors shut and lock them. We are overwhelmed with emotion, thrilled to finally be leaving this awful place.

Among other things, Fort Leonard Wood is a training ground for heavy equipment operators. There are vast landscapes covered with mountains and valleys of dirt so that construction engineers can train on bulldozers and graders. We cannot see out of the truck we're in. But suddenly the ride becomes jarring and erratic. I harbored some doubts, but now I know for sure, we aren't going to headquarters to get discharge papers.

Before the whine of the diesel engine drowns them out, the recruits hear the sergeants laughing up in the cab. Then all hell breaks loose as the vehicle starts flying over obstacles. Trainees in the back with me are literally going airborne as the massive truck jerks high in the air and then slams back into the ground. We bounce off each other, the floor, the ceiling and benches.

In movies, the 007 spy James Bond orders his martinis shaken, not stirred. I would describe the soldiers in our group as bruised, not broken. After a wild ride that seems to go on forever, we are left in a tangled pile of bodies. I take a quick inventory: a bloody nose, some deep scratches and lots of bad bruises—but no broken bones.

Back at the barracks the sneering sergeants tell us *worthless POS* (Pieces Of Shit) to get the *fuck* out of their vehicle. Nice, real nice. I help our mentally ill comrade down from the truck. He is terrified and shaking uncontrollably. He doesn't understand what just happened or why—that the sergeants who did this to us are just assholes.

Another week creeps by. The waiting, and not knowing, is driving us crazy. Occasionally, out of nowhere, one of our group will receive orders to report to the captain. I'm starting to discern a pattern to the madness: after seeing the captain for separation papers the trainee is ordered to gather all their army issued clothing and equipment for inventory. Then the trainee disappears, jerked out of our lives like a marionette on strings and lost in a regulation black hole, never to be seen on the base again.

I actually think my time has finally come. Two sergeants approach our group. Everyone waits expectantly, wide-eyed and engrossed in apt attention, to see who they've come for.

"Which one of you is PFC Miller?"

I immediately snap to attention and shout out my name. I try to hold back the emotion and keep an iron face. But inside my heart skips a beat. I can't believe it is finally happening. The sergeants tell me gather all my things for inventory, have them packed in my duffel and be at the intersection of two streets at 14:00. They emphasize not to be late, that I'm being processed out. Be there and wait, they say. Do not leave or you'll miss your ride.

This sounds genuine, for real this time. The part about packing everything up in my duffel fits the pattern. The captain must have already put in for my discharge. I rush into the barracks, clear out my locker and make sure I have everything. I'm nervous as hell. I don't know the streets of the base very well. I wish I had a buddy along, so we could go through this together. But I'm going to have to walk this walk alone.

The sun is hot. The duffel is heavy. I set out early, walking the streets searching to find my destination. I have no phone, no GPS, no map, no directions and no one to ask. I see a long passenger car with red plates and snap to attention. I'm not making the "failure to salute an officer" mistake again. I'm worried sick I won't find the right intersection and blow my chance to get out of this hell hole.

I finally locate one of the streets and walk along it all the way to its terminus, without seeing the right intersection. Now I'll have to back track the other way. I'm sweating profusely and totally stressed out. This is a giant base. I've never been to this part before, everything looks strange. Why did they pick a rendezvous location so far away?

I'm checking every street sign as I trudge along. Each time I read one, and it's not the one I need, my heart sinks. Time is running out. I thought I'd be overjoyed during the processing out, instead my nerves are shot and my back is screaming in pain under the duffel's heavy load. I feel like stopping and throwing out the CBRN gear, but the sergeants warned me I would need everything that had been issued to pass the inventory.

Finally, I find the designated intersection. They could not have picked a more inconvenient location. I have been walking for miles. I only have 15 minutes to spare. But, hey, I'm here, and I'm not late. I stand now on the sidewalk in the hot Missouri sun waiting. Each time a car passes I hope it will be my ride out. But none stop. I wait for hours. I missed lunch. Now I'll miss dinner too.

The sun finally slips below the horizon, a merciful release from the heat. But where is my ride? It will soon be dark. I continue to stand here, afraid to sit on my duffel. An officer may drive by and I need to be able to snap to attention at a moment's notice. But my knees are starting to buckle. I'm hungry and confused. Did I get the address wrong?

It's dark now. I stand here on the sidewalk at the correct intersection but there is still no ride. I keep asking myself if I should leave and go back to the barracks. It will be hard to find the way in total darkness. But what if the ride comes and I'm not here? I don't know what to do. A jeep approaches. I watch carefully. One of the sergeants who told me to be here is driving, but erratically. A couple of other sergeants are in the vehicle laughing and yelling.

The jeep doesn't stop. I feel something light and metallic bounce off my uniform. They have thrown beer cans at me which now roll lazily down the street. One of the sergeants yells, "Get the fuck back to your barracks. You ain't never gettin' outta the army!"

The experience changes me. I was always trying to remain hopeful and upbeat, despite everything, to be there for the other guys in limbo, to keep their spirits up. But now I spend a lot of time just staring blankly off into space. There is nothing I can do to affect my outcome, to control my future now. We are at the mercy of these crazy dictators, their angry outbursts and mean, childish head games.

I don't volunteer for any more work details. I only do what I'm ordered to do. Nothing more. I just take a place on the bench and sit all day occasionally sipping lister water. The other guys talk sometimes, speculating about when their discharge may come through, or what they'll do when they get out. But not me. What's the use? I rarely talk anymore.

"You ok?" they say.

I don't reply, just nod my head.

Sergeant Bailey comes over with work assignments for the day. I pull armory duty. I walk over by myself. I'm not looking forward to working with the lunatic who oversees this place. And no, I'm not breaking any parts so he can get new ones. In the army you have to follow *lawful* orders. He knows damn well that it is not a lawful order to destroy government property, and so do I.

I clean, inventory and sort CBRN gear all day. I'm working on gas masks right now. When they are processed, I stick them in a cubby hole corresponding to the correct number. The corporal is in the other room, ranting and raving. Mentally, I'm about as low down as a human can sink. I have no joy left in my life. I experience no happiness. I'm completely depressed with no way out. Thoughts of suicide flash into my mind. I feel like crying, but you can never, ever, do that in the army. You cannot show any sign of weakness here. Human predators are everywhere waiting to pounce. Man is wolf to man.

Once you sign up, or are drafted, the army will do about anything to keep you in. It is like a giant prison. They know all sorts of tricks. They've had thousands of years to learn the evil arts. But then, if you do somehow get on a track out, a chance to escape, they demand a pound of flesh. They are not going to let you go easily. I'm not sure if they're jealous that you are getting out, and they are stuck here in this hellish place, or what. Perhaps a psychologist (not an army one) could explain.

This is the lowest I've ever felt in my life. Too many times I've gotten my hopes up, only to have them dashed. I grit my teeth and clean another field protective mask. There's no one here to talk to. In the distance I can hear the corporal jabbering but he makes no sense. It's no use. I can't go on like this. I'm losing it, and I know it, but have no strength left to resist the darkness. I'll have a mental breakdown. Maybe kill myself. Or I'll go AWOL or pass out and die here. *Oh no! Please God, help me!*

A strange noise tingles my ears. What is this? An angel's harp? Have I died and gone to heaven? No. Against orders, the renegade corporal has turned on a radio. I haven't heard any music for so long I'd forgotten it existed. The beautiful, high-pitched tones are other worldly. Something is happening. The musical notes are penetrating deep into my brain. I haven't spoken for so long, but now my lips utter two words, "Stevie Nicks."

A memory returns. I'm transported back to the auditorium on the college campus. I'm holding a flashlight. I feel fine. I'm happy and content, a jovial frat boy making teamsters wages working at a rock concert. The elfish waif on stage is spinning around in flowing silk veils. She begins to crone out *Leather and Lace*. Hundreds of young men surround her screaming, "We love you Stevie!"

I can't help it now. I'm standing here sorting gas masks in an armory and I'm laughing out loud. The corporal shows up. He wants to know what the hell is so funny. I can't explain. In my life music has always had the power to lift me up. I have been saved!

Things are different now. I'm a different person. I'm cold and hard. I rarely smile. I talk very little. But deep inside, I'm okay. My heart is okay. I hang out with the limbo platoon, sitting on wooden benches, waiting. We kid around sometimes. I have a huge repertoire of jokes.

When they implore enough, I tell one, pull a comic gem from my treasure chest. I have to admit, it is great to see these suffering souls smile and laugh.

Then one day it happens. Sgt. Bailey arrives. Rivera and I are called out to report to the captain. In his office, Capt. Price says little, just hands us an envelope and tells us to pack up all our gear. I can hardly believe this may be it. I study the printing on the front of the white paper package suspiciously:

Dept. of the Army
Headquarters
USTAC Engineer
Fort Leonard Wood, Missouri 65473
ATZT-AGPS

Official Business
PENALTY FOR PRIVATE USE $300
For: Bert J. Miller
This envelope contains official separation papers.
If found drop in mail box. No postage required.
DD Form 473 1 Jan 70
Previous edition will be used.

This paperwork looks too real to be a fake. If it's a ruse, it's awfully well done. I'm not sure even the army would go to this length to put someone down. I'm giving myself room to let in a tiny bit of hope. Wow, can this be real? Is this actually happening?

Rivera is having a discussion with the captain. He explains that he's misplaced his army issue, heavy winter coat. I'm incredulous. For one thing, how the hell did he lose the coat? For another, I could swear I saw him put it in his duffel when we packed at the barracks. I kind of want to wring his neck. I'm happy to have someone to go through this process with, but I'm anxious to have everything go smoothly. I don't want to blow it, have some minor detail cause a problem or delay.

The captain seems annoyed. He pulls a triplicate form out of his desk drawer and starts typing. Rivera will have to compensate for the coat out of his army pay. Then, unceremoniously, we are dismissed. We wait outside for further orders. I grill Rivera, "What the hell is the deal with your coat?"

He explains sheepishly, "I want to have an army coat with my name on it to wear back in the hood."

I get it now. Rivera wants to pass as a badass army vet back in his borough. I would have never thought of doing that. Personally, I don't want any souvenirs from this awful place. I just want the hell out of here. This has been a terrible experience and I don't want to claim it was anything else. But I suppose the heavy coat will keep him warm during the winter back in the big apple.

We receive vouchers for a meal and a Greyhound bus ticket home. Then we're sent to accounting to receive our pay. I stand in line. At the window the lady hands me a W-2 form and counts out $647 in cash. That's weird. I have no idea why they pay us in cash. It seems like a way for soldiers to lose their money or get robbed. I take the clean, crisp new bills and stuff them in my pocket.

I wonder what the guys sitting around the lister bag are thinking about Rivera and I leaving. We have disappeared from their world. Will we ever see them again? I doubt it. They have no idea what being processed out will be like. Rivera and I are finally experiencing it now for real. I wish I could communicate with the other guys, to tell them it's okay. But there is no way to message them. They must sit and wait, doing their time in limbo.

CHAPTER THIRTY-THREE

*B*efore I change into my civvies and head over to the bus station I'm told there is one more task for me to accomplish in uniform. Apparently, this involves an interview with a high-ranking commander of some sort. The sergeants seem nervous, rehearsing with me the procedure on how to properly report to an officer. They repeatedly warn me, "be careful what you say."

I don't get what the fuss is all about. I have no idea what's going on. I figure, possibly, I'm in for one last, royal Alpha Charlie before they let me go. So, I very carefully follow all the protocols. A deep voice inside the office beacons me to enter. Inside, at a large desk, sits a startlingly handsome officer who looks like an actor I once saw play Davy Crockett in the movies. Judging by all the fruit salad on his uniform and shoulders, this guy is heavy, the real deal.

The top brass tells me, "You can have a seat." That is different from the usual "sit down" I get from officers or "sit down and shut up" I hear from sergeants.

I'm fully engaged, with all my antennae up, trying to figure this situation out. But this fellow is disarming. His conversation is articulate, just small talk so far, but he uses proper grammar, not the unschooled mish-mash of slang and gutter profanity you mostly hear around this place. To the sergeants and other enlisted personnel, it's almost a badge of honor to use words like "ain't" and the f-bomb.

I've made up my mind to speak as little as possible, just "yes, sir" and "no, sir" if I can get away with it. The reason I'm tight-lipped is that I harbor doubts, thinking this whole discussion may be an elaborate set up, a trick where, if I bad-mouth the army, they cancel my discharge. I don't trust anyone anymore.

The officer finally relents, recognizing that I'm not communicating for a reason. He feigns understanding of where I'm coming from and wants me to let down my guard. To put me at ease he opens a file on his desk, pulls out a college transcript, and starts talking about the college classes I've taken. He mentions that his brother is a scientist and congratulates me for being on the Dean's List for good grades.

I'm a little freaked out about what they have in that file besides my grades. But I let up a bit and talk about some of my college courses. There's something strange and unfamiliar about this officer. I can't put my finger on it. He's intelligent, well-educated, level-headed, considerate and not rude—but that's not it. There is no snarky or mean air about him. But it's something else. I finally solve the enigma. This guy is mentally healthy. I know it sounds weird, but mental illness hangs like a dark cloud over this military base. Never in my life have I encountered so many psychologically impaired and disturbed people. It is actually refreshing to be in his presence.

The officer asks me about my experience in boot camp. I hesitate and decide not to be forthright. I like this guy, but it's too much of a risk. I want to level with him, but I also want to get out of here. I'm not going to say anything negative. He awaits my reply. I finally acknowledge, "Well, I learned a lot, sir." An ambiguous reply that is subject to interpretation.

Officer Davy Crockett pauses and sits back in his desk, conceding that I'm not going to talk openly, and he has no intention to force me to do so. That's just not going to happen. So, he now launches into a long mea culpa for the army, and explanation of his intentions.

"At present," he explains. "The army has too many drop-outs and juvenile delinquents that society pawns off on the military to 'straighten out'."

He states his desire for higher standards, for recruits with more education. He laments that our country's best and brightest are choosing academia or the corporate world and shunning military service. This must change, he stresses. He complains that he spends half his time dealing with reports of sexual abuse. Boot camp should produce fluid thinkers with a moral compass he exalts, not pathological robots that methodically kill when ordered.

His goal is that someday the trainees learn to support each other, to work in teams, buddy pairs he calls them.

"How can we effectively fight the enemy when we are busy fighting each other?" he asks. There should be unit cohesion and no more harassment, no hazing or humiliating insults and no name-calling by drill sergeants.

There should be more women in the armed forces and, along with that, a zero-tolerance policy for sexual harassment. His idea is that someday male and female recruits would train together in a coed environment. I can't help but raise my eye-brow to that. This guy's a dreamer, a real crusader. But he's also got some power to make things happen. He's not just shooting off his mouth, so I listen intently.

He finally ends with a philosophical treatise on the intent of America's founding fathers, how they warned against an overgrown military establishment and desired for the country to have a citizen-soldier militia. I sit here listening quietly. I basically agree with everything he says about the army. But I can scarcely believe I'm actually hearing it out of one of their own mouths. When finished he awaits my response. I reply simply, "Good luck, sir."

My "good luck" has a double meaning. By that, I do honestly hope his plans and ideas come to fruition. I would hope that no future recruits ever have to suffer what I've gone through. But I have to say that my "good luck" is also my evaluation of his chances of success. The armed forces of the United States are like a giant battleship, and it takes a long time, and a lot of energy, to change the inertia and direction of such a massive entity.

I'm boarding the greyhound bus now in my civvies. My military BDUs and equipment are in my duffel bag packed away in the luggage compartment. At least my tennis shoes fit. My shorts and t-shirt are too baggy now. I've lost so much weight, I'm thin as a fence rail. That's one thing boot camp will do for you. I like the anonymity of wearing civilian attire though, people don't make as many assumptions about you and you don't have to put up with the conservative types groveling at your feet because you have on a uniform.

I'm not an overtly religious guy. But I do feel a strange spiritual aura, or other-worldly presence, as the huge, silver ark of a bus approaches the entrance to FLW. It's as if the check point represents the gates of hell and I'm exiting through. The concertina wire above the walls and sentries armed with M-16 rifles provide a daunting barrier, impenetrable to me, except for the key paperwork handed over by our driver. The boom bar is raised, the bus engine roars to life and I leave the base behind. I feel a sense of physical and spiritual liberation. I'm free! I have not felt this way since the day I crossed the imaginary line in the recruiter's office, officially inducting me into the army.

I'm elated! This is the best day of my life so far, I think to myself, as the bus twists and weaves through the forested hills of the Ozarks. We make stops in many small towns where I delight in seeing the brightly colored civilian clothes, cars and buildings. I didn't realize how sick I was of drab army green.

When I get back to my hometown, I report to the local national guard center. I chuck my duffel bag up onto the counter where a woman in uniform inventories all the gear.

"Do you want to keep anything?" she asks. "How about your field coat, or your canteen or some BDU pants?"

"No thanks," I reply. I don't want anything from the army except to never hear from them again.

"Well, we can't reuse your boots," she explains. "That's against regulations."

"Just throw them away then," I state plainly, as I leave through the door.

I can't move back into the rental house, because the summer sublet is still living there. So, I take off, walking home. I hate to boomerang back to living with my parents for a couple of weeks, but I don't have a lot of options. Renting a motel room seems foolish. I need to conserve what little money I have. There's $647 in cash in my pocket from the army, instead of a few thousand I would have had in my bank account if I had worked pouring cement foundations for Leroy all summer.

In addition to the cash, I have only two other mementos from my time in the service. The dog tags around my neck and a large envelope of official discharge papers. I looked through the paperwork during the bus ride home. Included is a DD-214, an important document that certifies my discharge from the army.

The document records that I served exactly 100 days in the military, from the time I was sworn in, until the day I was discharged and left the base. I know that in the future some people will poke fun at me for only serving 100 days. But I know that I would have served longer had I not been injured and had I been treated decently and honorably by the military.

What makes me mad is that there are so many people, famous movie stars and entertainers and politicians, who support war and engage in propaganda glorifying the military but who never served one single second in the service. They are chicken hawks like John Wayne (too busy making Hollywood movies to serve), or Sylvester "Rambo" Stallone (who fled to Switzerland and worked as a girl's gymnastics coach to avoid Vietnam) or rock star Ted Nugent (who crapped his own pants to flunk his MEPS physical) or Rush Limbaugh (had a bad pimple on his butt) or Donald Trump (sore heel but could still play golf, soccer, tennis, etc.). If they had been in the military one single day, then I served 100 times longer.

The biggest regret I have about my time in uniform is when I yelled at that young boy in the reception center, who was trying to warn us what it was like in boot camp. He was just telling the truth, but I couldn't believe it. It seemed like an exaggeration at the time. But in retrospect, he was right and I was wrong. I was wrong about the violence and abuse we would encounter in training, and I was wrong to scream at him and make him cower away. You have to be careful how you treat people. If you are mean or hurt them, you will carry that stain with you forever. Don't let anyone, a boss, the army, a professor, a lover, not anyone, turn you into something you're not, or do something you know is not right.

I'm walking to my parents place now. I recognize everything: which families live in which houses, trees I've climbed, restaurants where I know the whole menu, creeks I've waded and canoed, rolling farms I hiked and hunted a thousand times. I feel myself letting down my guard, a little at a time. Everything is so familiar I feel more secure and relaxed. The birds chirp their songs, the squirrels chatter excitedly, and tree limbs wave hello. All welcoming me back home with open arms.

I'm rehearsing in my head what I'll say to my folks when I get to their place. But I'm on their front porch before I've got a plan. So, I knock, figuring I'll play it by ear. My mom answers the door, throws her arms around me and gets all teary eyed. Leroy is next, patting me on the back. It feels strange to reunite at this moment, because they don't know what has transpired.

Maybe at some future date I'll reveal more. But for now, I keep my explanation simple. No, I'm not going to be going to medical school in the army. No, I didn't finish boot camp, I got injured and was discharged early. I just need a place to stay for a couple of weeks, then I'll move into the rental house with my old roommates and start classes in the Fall.

The questions come fast and furious. I try to explain. I don't know what career path I'll take now. I need time to rethink that. I'm okay. I was hindered by old injuries and also new one, I hurt something internally, but I don't know what. My mom immediately goes to the phone. There is still time to call, she'll get me in with our family doctor tomorrow. Actually, I figure that's not a bad idea. I still have a side ache.

I finally break away and retrieve my backpacking pack from their attic. I get some different clothes out, the civvies I have on are the same ones I wore the day I left here for boot. They desperately need to be washed. I take a long shower and then crash in my parent's extra bedroom.

I've had the same family doctor my entire life. I study the same sentimental prayer, framed on Doc Tegler's office wall, that I have read every time I've had an appointment, since I learned to read. And before that, my mom read it to me:

"God, grant me the serenity to accept the things I cannot change..."

The doctor listens quietly to my story. This man is basically the opposite of the army doctor I dealt with in boot camp. He is genuinely concerned. I lie here on the table as he gently probes my side. It's impossible, he explains, to know for sure without operating, but he believes I may have ruptured or lacerated my spleen when I dived onto the gas mask.

"You're lucky," he says. "You could have bleed to death."

I decline exploratory surgery. I'll live with it for a while and see if it gets better. Yes, I'll let him know and come back if it doesn't improve. Now comes the doctor's respectful, but firm, lecture: human beings are not made of steel, and even if they were, steel parts wear out and get broken, just as they do on your car. I need to take better care of my body. I've had some serious injuries in the past. I need to acknowledge my limitations. Joining the army was a mistake. I can't go on working with Leroy either, pouring cement and sandblasting, for the rest of my life. My lungs and back are compromised. I must find a new career, one without the strenuous physical labor, and one where the work environment is quiet, to preserve what little hearing I have left and to calm my tinnitus, the ringing in my ears.

I sincerely thank the good doc. I admire doctors and dentists and nurses and all the medical workers who dedicate their lives to helping others. I admire them. That is the main reason I wanted to be a doctor, to be like them. That dream has blown up in my face. But I'll figure out something else, maybe an associated medical field. I'll talk to a career counselor at the college. That will give me a better idea about what classes to take before registering for the fall semester.

I swing by to pick up my mail. My post office box is empty, save for a note: *mail in excess of box.* So, I stand in line and then collect an arm full of paper, which I stuff into my day pack, before heading over to the college. I just absolutely love the atmosphere on campus. I can't wait to get back in school again. The vibe is always so energetic, youthful and positive. A few students are milling about on the lawn, playing frisbee, reciting poetry, tight-roping between trees. To some people, their activities may seem trivial, silly or inconsequential. To me, it is the opposite of military training or war. What goes on here, are the trappings of civilization. What I want, and need, more than anything else, right now, is civility.

I go to the student *Free the Environment* activity center in the union and sit sorting through my mail. Everything I don't keep goes in the recycling boxes. I pause, remembering something, and remove the dog tags from around my neck. I take one last look at the information stamped on them: my name, DOD ID number, O-Negative blood type and for religion, *Other than*. They have a contraption for crushing aluminum cans here and I put it to good use, smashing the tags and then chucking them into metal recycling. *Other than* my ass.

An official government envelope contains an honorable discharge from the national guard. I appreciate that they sent that, but I still consider recycling it, along with the other papers I received when I was discharged. That way I'd have nothing left from that awful place. But I change my mind. Before I left the base, they warned me to keep the DD-214 and other official paperwork, as I might need it someday.

I recycle some catalogs and other unimportant papers. These advertising firms must clear cut entire forests to make all this glossy paper. Then I open a forwarded letter from the university. I saved it for last. Anything concerning school is of utmost importance to me now. I'm really looking forward to the fall semester. I can't wait. Inside, typed on official letterhead, is correspondence explaining that my scholarship has been canceled and any other student aid revoked, due to my missing the deadline to sign up for registration.

My heart actually skips a beat. I can feel it drop in my chest. It's a good thing I'm sitting down. I feel light-headed, like I might pass out. Putting my head between my legs I try to center and calm myself. How can this be? How could this have happened? I've been gone in the army. There was no way for me to sign up for registration. I couldn't get mail or phone calls in boot camp if they tried to reach me. I feel devastated, psychologically obliterated.

There must be some mistake. I run, not walk, over to the registration building. The secretary says I need an appointment. I tell her I just got back from the army and have a problem with my scholarship and registration. She demurs, but I insist. I must see someone immediately. She searches her computer for the administrative assistant who reviewed my case. I'm in his office now.

This fellow is middle-aged. An affable bureaucrat in a suit. I explain my situation. He checks the file. We tried to call you several times. We wrote a letter. Well, they called the rental house and sent the letter there. I was away at boot camp, I explain. I never received anything. Yes, that's right, he remembers, since I was in the army, he thought I'd receive GI benefits and not need the scholarship. He's sorry, but there's simply nothing he can do.

I'm screwed. My college education has run into a brick wall. Without work-study status my employment at the information center is over. I have no job! I have $647 in crisp new bills that won't even cover rent for a semester. I don't want to take out a loan, and it's too late to apply for a loan anyway. How can this be happening? Why me? It meant everything to me to get back in the swing of college. My life has gone down in flames.

CHAPTER THIRTY-FOUR

Morning comes and the initial shock of losing my college scholarship is fading. I have to face reality. The writing is on the wall. I could go to work for Leroy now, but pouring concrete will end with the fall frost. I need to think long term instead. The doctor was adamant, I need to find a new career. But what field can I break into with a decade of experience doing cement work, a high school diploma and three years of college but no degree? To make matters worse, the country is in a deep recession. The fascist is still in the White House and, as always happens when any country is led by an extreme element of either the far right or far left, the economy has crashed.

It seems everywhere I go businesses and government agencies are laying off. Unemployment is at record highs. No one is hiring. I send out a stack of resumes every morning, then get dressed in my best threads and wear out my good shoes walking the business district inquiring about employment. But there are no leads, nothing.

I finally get an offer from a real estate company. I can work there on commission. I won't get paid unless I sell something. But at least I would have a position. And, I am told, it is an up and coming agency.

Life sure takes crazy twists and turns. I never thought I'd have a life career in real estate.

The agency gives me materials to prep for the license exam. It's nothing complex, some basic real estate concepts and property laws, a little simple math. I use some of my army cash to purchase a couple of white shirts and colored ties at the men's clothing store. I'm ready for my first day, shadowing a real go-getter agent. But before I leave home to meet him, there's a phone call. It's the registrars' office at the college. They have reviewed my case, reinstated my scholarship and I'm approved for the work-study program. I need to select my classes for the fall semester. Wow. I'm getting jerked around like a human yo-yo. My life is a roller coaster ride.

The real estate agent's name is Jerry Ambrose. Jerry is a hyper-active, type A personality. I'll bet he sells lots of houses. He isn't all that pissed off when I cancel. But he lets me know, in no uncertain terms, that I'm missing out on a great opportunity, at a growing agency! The fact that I'm a native of this city, he explains, means that a lot of people know me, and therefore I could have made it big in real estate, probably retired in 25 years as a millionaire. Well, thanks anyway, Jerry.

At registration most of the classes are filled. I have no inside connection like I did when I drove the school bus. I don't even know what my career goal is anymore. Maybe a medical field? I'll try to get some science classes. I take what's left:

Anatomy, Statistics, Physics and Astronomy, Fitness Jogging and a Ballroom Dance class. Hey, I need PE credits.

I'm gathering my things and moving back to the rental. But before I leave my parents' place, my uncle shows up. I've been dreading this day ever since I got discharged. You see, my uncle is a WWII vet. One of those guys who is a member in all the veterans' clubs, who has a veteran's license plate, a veteran's hat and so forth. He is a member of the "greatest generation" having served during "the good war."

I'll be the first to say opposing Hitler and the Nazi's was straight-up a good thing to do. No argument there. But the United States is not fighting Hitler anymore. Now it's my generation's time to serve and the U.S. armed forces are being used like an international bouncer service so multinational corporations can bully and exploit smaller nation's workers and resources. Kind of hard for me to feel the cause is just and righteous under these conditions.

Anyway, the WWII story is not quite as clean and neat as some people make it sound. I mean, if they really wanted to end WWII quickly instead of invading Normandy, they could have invaded Wall Street since the big banks and corporations financed Hitler's rise to power and provided the Nazis with money and materials all through the war, even used slave labor in concentration camps to build their products.

The U.S. sent a boat load of Jewish refugees stranded off the Florida coast back to Europe to be killed in the Holocaust and the U.S. even refused requests to bomb the railroad tracks to Auschwitz and other death camps—maybe they were afraid of damaging corporate property or diminishing the slave labor supply since that would reduce corporate profits. Then there's the whole matter of fire-bombing civilian refugee populations in Dresden and Hamburg and nuking a bunch of Japanese civilians and American POWs held in Hiroshima and Nagasaki, when that was not necessary to end the war.

> *The use of this barbarous weapon at Hiroshima and Nagasaki was of no material assistance in our war against Japan. The Japanese were already defeated and ready to surrender. In being the first to use it, we adopted an ethical standard common to the barbarians of the Dark Ages. I was not taught to make war in that fashion, and wars cannot be won by destroying women and children.*
>
> —Admiral William E. Leahy, U.S. Navy,
> Senior-most United States military officer
> on active duty during World War II.

My uncle brags about his military service a lot and today is no exception. I just keep my mouth shut. I figure no generation is any greater than any other, and every generation has its rogues and heroes. Unfortunately my recent stint in the army comes up in the conversation. My uncle flat out asks me why I got discharged early. I tell him I got injured. He doesn't acknowledge that, just starts in again about how great the army is.

I want to say something, but how can I relate my experience, that contradicts his, in a few sentences? I tell just one story, about the young man who collapsed after being ordered to stand at attention in the hot sun after the two-mile run, and how the sergeant there complained that the boy had died on him and now "he has to fill out paperwork."

My uncle dismisses the story saying that sergeants have to be tough. But Leroy seems deeply affected by it. My dad doesn't think its right to mistreat young recruits like that and he asks my uncle how he ever got through boot camp. My uncle replies that he, "just got in line like everyone else."

Everyone's life experience is different. I have no idea what my uncle went through in boot camp. Was boot camp different then? Or, was it similar, and he just acted submissive and let the sergeants and others in authority abuse and humiliate him? I have no idea. I don't want to denigrate his experience but he shouldn't denigrate mine either.

A thought comes into my head. Maybe I should ask my uncle, "If a sergeant came up to you and told you to bend over, he was going to fuck you in the ass, would you just get in line for it?" I mean, that's what a sergeant told me to do and I caught holy hell for resisting that kind of abuse and refusing to go along with it. But, again, I just let it go. I figure it's wiser and better judgement to just drop the whole thing. He has his truth and I have mine. His generation has their truths and my generation, we have our truths.

My uncle may have been able to blow off what happened to that young recruit, forced to stand at attention in the hot Missouri sun until he collapsed, but Leroy can't stop thinking about it. He asks me if there were any other bad things that happened while I was in boot camp. I'm really not ready to talk about everything that took place, but I do relate the story about Mike Hidersheit, how he was bullied and picked on incessantly, and ended up trying to commit suicide.

Leroy has his faults, but he also has a core sense of right and wrong, of common decency. He expresses heartfelt empathy for the farm boy's plight. But, I think, deep down, too, Leroy also harbors some skepticism about my story. Doubting Leroy asks me where Hidersheit was from. One thing you do remember pretty well from the army is where people were from. I tell Leroy that Mike mentioned he lived near Cedar Rapids, Iowa. Leroy is a pretty direct kind of guy, not well educated, but street smart. He calls directory assistance and, with a name like Hidersheit, it is not hard for the operator to find a phone number. Leroy has me make the call. The phone belongs to Mike Hidersheit's parents. It turns out that Mike is living at home. I ask to speak to him.

Hidersheit can't believe it's me. He's happy to hear my voice again. A blast from the past! I make arrangements. Leroy and I drive all the way to Cedar Rapids and meet Mike at the Red Lobster restaurant for dinner. It's kind of crazy seeing the smiling, pudgy kid waltz in and sit down at our booth. Sort of like seeing a character who appeared in your worst nightmare, but now alive and in the flesh. It's a heartfelt reunion. Leroy pays for dinner. We don't discuss the suicide attempt. Leroy looks at the scars on Hidersheit's wrists, and doesn't say a word. Leroy isn't book smart, it's physical evidence he believes in.

I don't have much in this world now. Just the contents of my backpacking pack. Some polo shirts, jeans, a leather jacket. So, it's not hard to move back into the rental. An Electrolux vacuum cleaner salesperson comes to the door and I take her up on an offer to demonstrate the heavy machine by cleaning the carpet in my room. I remember watching my old roommate Jay trim his nails and casually drop all the clippings on the floor. Ever since then, I always deep clean a rented room before moving in.

All the positions at the Information Center are, of course, filled. In fact, all the choice work-study jobs have already been taken by now. I search for something, anything, and finally land a job slinging espresso and cappuccino at the coffee shop in the student union. Being on campus, the workplace will be a close walk to all my classes and I won't have to commute.

I buy one of those Indiana Jones style swashbuckler hats. I hate the buzz job I'm still sporting from the army. Signing up for every shift available, I become a regular fixture at the counter with customers requesting my caffeine concoctions. I luck out and get my old usher job back at the Center for Performing Arts and, of course, as always, I post magazine subscription blanks and other offers on bulletin boards around the campus. So now I've got some cash coming in, my tuition is covered by the renewed scholarship and I'm starting to get back into the swing of college.

I will say it takes some time to readjust to civilian life. I've been through a pretty traumatic experience and I still wake up some nights in a sweat after nightmares about boot camp. In one version I spend eternity in limbo, never getting out. It helps that two of my roommates at the rental had bad experiences in the military. They can relate to where I'm at, and understand if I seem edgy or mistrustful.

I wish I had a girlfriend. I thought maybe I might meet someone in my ballroom dance class. I do enjoy my dancing partner, Marge, and we get pretty good at the Foxtrot, Waltz, Rumba, Cha Cha, and Swing. But it turns out my gaydar failed again and I find out that Marge is a lesbian. So, although I enjoy our time together in class, I can't exactly ask her out.

I like studying all the minute details of the human body in my Anatomy class, I'm persevering through another statistics course, I stay in shape dancing and jogging but I'm having trouble keeping my head above water in one section of physics.

The professor is a NASA scientist who calculates the trajectory of space probes. I'm sitting in the lecture hall today focusing like a laser, trying to keep up with him. In a white lab coat, the scientist begins an equation at one end of the giant chalk board, which is about a quarter of a block long. I rejoice when I am still following his thought process as he reaches the end of the board. Whew! I think I can cut it in here.

But now the stately astrophysicist walks back to the beginning of the board and continues. The equation was not over! He does this several times until the entire chalk board is covered with a maze of mathematical symbols. I'm completely lost. I cannot handle this level of complexity in my current state of mind. I gather my papers, stand up in the lecture hall, and walk out. At the registration center, I request to drop the class.

After suffering through a week straight of horrible nightmares I'm exhausted. The temptation of using alcohol or pot or some other drug to escape the mental pain is growing. My roommates, and most of the other students on campus, imbibe a lot. Much of the social life in college revolves around bars and drinking. It seems like everyone is doing it. Except me. I'm lonely. I desperately want to make friends, and especially a girlfriend.

But, deep down in my soul, I know, I have to resist the alcohol trap. Something about my constitution, and psyche, just don't mix well with mind altering substances. Still, I'm deeply troubled. On the worst night, I wake up in a delirium, soaked in sweat. Like some lunatic I wander out to the garage and grab a can of spray paint. Students have been painting graffiti all over the sidewalks on campus, everything from anarchy symbols to gang messages and swear words.

It is three in the morning and I'm standing in the sweat-soaked hospital pants and t-shirt I wore to bed. I try to sum up my bad experiences in the army and all my pain and suffering over failures in my life, in a few words. There is so much about the world I don't like, so many things that happen are just plain AFU and wrong. I pick a prominent street corner, near a bus stop, a clean slate with no graffiti. With the spray paint I spell out my gut feeling in giant letters on the cement sidewalk, *SATAN SUCKS*.

I feel a catharsis. Now I need to let go and loosen up. I'm not going to quit, not going to drown out the pain with drugs or alcohol. There is a group of veterans on campus working against reinstatement of the military draft. I join up. So, there are two groups in the student activity center I'm involved with now, *Students Against the Draft* and *Free the Environment*.

I get to know some of my coworkers at the coffee shop. Perry is a republican business major. We get along fine as long as we don't talk politics. Caroline is a divorced nursing student. She talks about joining the army to get financial aid. I tell her about my own experience. She seems skeptical of my stories. I think she'll end up joining. She's having trouble paying her bills. Ray is a Muslim from Indonesia. He is easy going and funny. Just don't mention jihad. One day the topic comes up and he gets an uncharacteristic, mean look on his face. I think he really believes in that.

Together we play pranks on the students working at the ticket office across the hall. They have a popcorn machine there for the Bijou Theatre movies. One night I call, pretending to be a customer. A coed with long brown hair named Sarah answers. I can see her pick up the phone. I tell her I'm having a party and need to order a very large amount of popcorn. She inquires how much. I tell her 10 buckets. But I keep calling back every few minutes to say more people are coming to the party than I thought, and I need more. She says she'll do her best. We watch her frantically popping away for over an hour. Finally, when I get up to a pickup truck-load, she realizes she's been punked. We wave at her from across the hall as she puts up a sign saying, *free popcorn.*

The semester flies by so fast, before I know it, finals are over. I've aced all my classes and with that 4.0 GPA my scholarship is secure. I've served thousands of steaming cups of coffee and watched dozens of student recitals at the Center for Performing Arts. Money is tight, but at least I'm not a starving student. Working for food service in the union has some advantages: left-over popcorn and stale sandwiches are free. I splurge on a couple of tickets to the big holiday celebration *Cocoa and Carols* and ask Caroline to go out with me.

Life is not bad now. I'm having some fun. But something weighs heavily on my mind. I'm halfway through my senior year and there are some classic college experiences I never got to try. I always wanted to live in the dorms, like most normies do, but that was always out of my price range. Another college bucket list item for me is studying abroad. My parents paid for my sister to study in Spain and now she lives in Germany with a refrigeration executive. I feel like I've missed out on the opportunity for international culture and travel.

Of course, I haven't got enough money to fly overseas, let alone spend a semester studying in another country. But, strangely enough, I get a new ad blank to post on campus bulletins boards, along with the usual magazine subscriptions and GRE study materials. The post is from a tour company called Club Europa that offers low cost student tours of Europe. The incentive for posting is that if 8 students sign up for the tour using my ad blanks, I'll get to go on the tour for free. I plaster the entire campus and town, bulletin boards, walls, lampposts, every surface I can staple or tape a flyer to within miles of the campus. We'll see what happens.

I register for second semester, some science classes along with Latin and medical terminology. I strongly recommend Latin for anyone thinking of going into a scientific or medical field. It makes understanding the vocab so much easier. I mean *otitis media* is really just inflammation of the middle ear and an *Ursus horribilis* is ultimately just a horrible (grizzly) bear.

I usually train the new hires at the coffee shop. Today I'm explaining how to make mocha java and other blends to a cute young coed with short curly hair named Cindy. After work I tell her to hop in the pastry cart, I'll give her a ride to the time clock. She naively climbs in and I lock the door. But instead of clocking out I take the cart over into the elevator and push the button for third floor. They're having a serious business conference up there today. It will be interesting hearing what the stoic executives in their three-piece suits do when the elevator opens revealing a girl locked in a bakery cart. It's a pretty good initiation we have for new employees. Cindy gives me a kind of panicked *what the hell* look as the elevator door closes.

After class I head over to the campus lawn for a demonstration with some friends from the *Students Against the Draft* group. We are protesting against the fascist president because he has been arming the radical jihadist terrorists in Afghanistan with stinger missiles and other weapons. So far, he has given them over $5 billion in aid. He even called them "freedom fighters" and invited them for lunch at the White House. I'm doubtful that he cares one bit about our protest, but at least we tried.

I really enjoy the social aspect of college, meeting new people and hanging out. I suppose maybe Jerry Ambrose was right, maybe in 25 years I could have become a millionaire selling real estate. But, honestly, the people I have met here at this great school, I wouldn't trade those experiences for anything. I do truly love the college life and I think more should be done to ensure that every young person has the opportunity for higher education after high school, either at a university or a trade school. My advice: get an education, wherever and whenever you can. If you can't swing it the traditional way, do it however you can.

I've known students who have gotten a free ride because they were an athlete or they were a member of a minority or they had rich parents. I got a tuition scholarship for good grades. But what about the rest of the students who have no financial support? I personally prefer the work study route. I think students who work their way through school appreciate it more. The problem is, prices have gone way up and wages have not. It's getting nearly impossible these days to work your way through school without taking out loans. That to me is a shame. It's just not right and not good for the country either. We need an educated workforce to compete in the global economy.

I stop by the library lost and found to see if anyone has turned in my umbrella. I had a nice one, tough cotton fabric and a wooden handle. But I accidentally left it on one of the tables after I got done studying. No one has turned it in. I know it doesn't seem like a big deal. But since I have no car, and walk everywhere, an umbrella is a crucial part of my college kit.

Money is tight and that kind of a loss hurts. Now I'll have to buy another umbrella and I hadn't budgeted for that expense. A big part of life is learning to deal with losses, big and small. You don't really get to know much about a person by observing them when they win or gain something, but you can really tell a lot about someone by how they deal with loss. I try to be positive, but the loss does darken my mood.

As much as I enjoy the other students and professors, there are times when I feel like being alone. This is one of those times. I have a wooden boomerang I've fooled around with for years. When I need time to think I take the boomer out to a large vacant field by the rental house. This is one of the last large expanses of grass left on campus. I'm sure they'll build something on it someday. But I really wish they'd leave more open green space. I judge the wealth of a society not just by how well the human population is living and how much stuff they have, but also by how much nature they can afford to leave alone.

I take the boomer out to the center of the field. I've gotten really good at this. I can make the aboriginal weapon return close enough for me to grab it in my gloved hand. I have a little pranky ritual I partake in here. There's a street along the south side of the field. I lean back and throw the boomer hard at cars as they drive by. Often, they slow way down, or slam on their brakes, seeing the weapon swinging around in circles and coming right at them. Of course, I have it timed so the boomer changes directions at the last minute, stopping short of the vehicle, and returning to me. It's not something I should be doing. I know that. I kind of hate even telling you about it actually. But I have to be honest with you. I'm not exactly normal, not a bad person overall, but I do have a dark side.

I've been going out with Caroline from the coffee shop this semester. I like her. She's a decent person. I'm not sure how far the relationship will progress though. Caroline has a very jaded, somewhat pessimistic outlook. I think her first marriage must not have been good. It ended in divorce anyway. She talks about joining the army to help pay for nursing school. I just don't think I could ever be married to someone in the military now. Not after the negative experience I had.

We go to a movie and then take a long walk around the campus afterwards. Caroline is pretty, but older than other women than I have dated before. She has long black hair, big blue eyes and a shapely, full figure. It has been such a long time since I have been with anyone. Of course, there was no chance for socializing while I was in boot camp and, besides that, I'm kind of shy sometimes. It took me a while to get up the nerve to ask her out. I wish there was a better way to tell who was already going steady, or who would be interested in going out with me. I don't have good intuition for these things.

We end up back in my room. I'm usually pretty laid back about sex, letting my partner take the lead. But it's been a long time, and I desperately need to feel a human touch. I was around so many cruel and violent jerks in the army for so long, I just crave love and kindness. The sex is completely consensual, but I'm more assertive than usual. She has one demand: I must use a condom. I was going to anyway.

"Don't get me pregnant!" she implores. I figure it's for sure now that she's joining the army. There's no way can you get in, if you're preggers. That's why she's so adamant.

We kiss for a while and then start making love. Caroline takes off her clothes. I notice her body is more mature than the girls I've been with before. She has some scars and her bust droops but the experience is heavenly. After we finish, I feel completely at peace and fall into a deep sleep. Caroline walks back to her apartment alone. When I wake up in the morning I feel terrible that I didn't stay awake and accompany her home.

I think it is great the way some people find their true love, get married as virgins and are only ever with that one right person their whole lives. I've met people who experienced that. They seem very satisfied and joyful together. I salute them, and I'm happy for them. That scenario well may be the preferable, best way to live your life. But, for better or for worse, it hasn't been my experience. I'd love to meet someone special, get married and have a family someday. It just doesn't seem to be happening for me.

CHAPTER THIRTY-FIVE

*S*pring has sprung, the second semester of my senior year is ending and I have no idea what I want to do with my life. I have enough credits to graduate with a pre-medicine, general science degree. But my dream of going to medical school has gone down in flames. I simply don't have the money. I go now to see a career counselor. She suggests I go ahead and borrow a quarter of a million and become a doctor.

"You'll eventually make good money and you can pay it all back," she advises.

I ask about other options. She suggests a slew of related fields: physical and occupational therapy, med tech, physician's assistant, radiologic technologist, respiratory therapy, nursing, pharmacy, optometrist, dietician, psychiatric aide, dental hygienist, phlebotomist, ad infinitum. My head is spinning with all these options. Which one should I choose? How could I pay for grad school? I can't decide. She takes another look at my transcripts.

"You really should take one more chemistry class," she relates. "It would help you get in somewhere."

I'm lying on the couch at the rental racking my brain. What the heck should I do? I have to make some decisions. I need a change. I need to pick a career, but I can't decide on which one. I like my roommates, but I want to try living somewhere new. I need money to do anything, and I have very little. The counselor suggested I take one more chemistry class. I just don't know.

I take a mental break to get the mail. There is a letter from the posting company. Two students have signed up for the Europa Trip. That's another quandary. I want to travel but I need 8 students signed up to qualify for a free Europe tour. I grab my backpack full of flyers, tape and a stapler, then walk the town posting ads everywhere. At least it is good exercise and gives me time to think.

I'm up early. Today I take action! First, I hit the registration office and sign up for a chemistry class. It's a tough class, and it will be even more challenging condensed into a short eight week summer session, but I'm psyched and motivated. Taking just the one class, I can focus all my brain cells on one single subject. If I can nail down this last chem class, I'll have a better chance getting into a grad program next year.

Next I talk to Leroy and Hondo. They need help at the shop. I know the sandblasting, stone cutting and cement work will be brutally hard, and bad for my health, but I need cash badly. I tell them I'll work as many hours as possible. But I'm also keeping the coffee shop job. Back on campus, I talk to the supervisor and sign up to pour brew weekends and every night except Tuesday and Thursday, when I have chem class and lab. Finally, I stop by student housing and get a room and board contract in the dorms, which is discounted for the summer. I have crunched the numbers and I'm cutting my finances to bone. I don't know if I can pull it off, but, hey, I'll give it my best shot, and at least with room and board I'll have a place to stay and be well fed.

I say my goodbyes to my old roomies at the rental and move out. The dorm room is small, but for the summer I'll have it all to myself. Usually they cram up to four students in here. There is a small porcelain sink, a closet, a shabby veneer desk and two double bunk beds. On the wall I put up a promotional kayaking poster and a nature calendar I got for free. This is home now.

I recover a kite from the branches of a tree, one of those colorful Chinese ones with the long tail. I get a huge ball of string and fly it out the eighth-floor window of my dorm room. You can see that kite zigzagging across the sky from all over town. When I walk to work, when I walk home, when I go to chem class, anytime I'm out and about, I look up there and I'm happy, remembering that I always wanted to live in the dorms, and now I am. I know it's not the normal way you're supposed to do it, as a freshman, during the regular semester, I mean. But, hey, at least I got my chance.

This summer is crazy. On a typical day, I'm up by 5AM, get dressed in old work clothes and then head down to the cafeteria to be at the front of the line when they open at 6AM. The food is great. I'm friends with all the cooks. I normally eat a couple of heaping trays for breakfast. After breakers it's a two-mile hike to Leroy's shop on Riverside Drive where I start loading up the trucks.

I ride out to a work site with Phildo and Hatchet Jack. These guys are 6'5", 240-pound, steroid-enhanced, Gold's Gym muscle men. In comparison I'm 5'11" and 185 pounds. I give everything I have physically to keep up all morning, then we head to the nearest all-you-can-eat buffet to stuff ourselves for lunch. The work is incredibly hard, down in the dirt, carrying super heavy loads in hot and humid weather, served up with a sunburn and bug bites.

If it rains, and we can't pour cement, we'll be inside the shop all day sandblasting and stone cutting. The noise level shakes my innards, my head buzzes with tinnitus, thick dust chokes my lungs and occasionally a toe or finger gets cut or crushed. We wear thick leather weightlifting belts, but the heavy rock we must move is way more poundage than a person ought to lift and our backs ache with pain. I can relate to the slaves who built the pyramids, we have a similar routine. But the pay is good, and that's what I need right now.

After we sweep up the silicone abrasive on the shop floor and clean out the cement mixer it's time to walk home. I try to make it back to the dorm and get cleaned up before the cafeteria closes at 7PM. It's a coed floor and very different from living in the all-male frat or rental. I pass by young women wrapped in bath towels in the hallway on the way to the shower. At dinner I find a seat with new friends and eat several heaping trays of food. Amazingly, devouring all this food, I never gain a single ounce. All the calories get burned up at work.

After dinner I run down to the student union, pull on an apron and start making coffee. I take along my chemistry book to study when there's a lull. Two nights a week I have either class or laboratory. Chemistry can be complex. This isn't a blow-off class and the pace to get through all the material during a short summer session is mind boggling. My lab partner is an older woman, who is already working as a nurse. She needs the course to complete an advanced degree. I'm lucky, she's smart and nice. In some ways, she reminds me of Caroline who is off to boot camp for the summer.

Class in the Chemistry Building runs from 7-10PM. The coffee shop closes at 10PM but it's usually at least 11PM by the time I get everything cleaned and put away. I'm always completely exhausted as I trudge back to the dorm. Sometimes students have parties in their rooms but I can't join them. I'm simply too worn out. I set an alarm and then try to study in bed each night, drifting into slumber with atoms, molecules and ions dancing in my head. Saturday and Sunday, I work at the union all day serving pastries and pouring tea. The only time I'm not in class, studying or at work, is late Saturday night when I head downtown to the popular *Field House Bar* where Hatchet Jack works as a bouncer. We shoot the breeze for a while and I skate in without paying cover.

Another night and I'm walking home late from the bar now, completely sober. I've learned my lesson. I never touch booze any more, not even a drop. The street lights cast a dusty grey glow as I amble down the dark sidewalk. Suddenly a scooter jumps the curb and nearly runs me over. A frantic young woman explains that someone has been following her. She's frightened and asks if she can walk with me back to the dorm. Of course, I agree.

She parks her motorbike in the rack and we walk into the dorm's bright lobby. I recognize her now, a student I've seen working as an usher at the arts center. We've never met before so she introduces herself as Tracey and thanks me for chaperoning her home. We stand talking for a while, then I walk her back to her dorm room.

Now whenever I eat in the cafeteria I sit with Tracey and Greg, an engineering student I've known since high school. I finally get up the nerve and ask Tracey out. She agrees, so I request a night off at the coffee shop and use my student discount to purchase a couple of tickets to Tennessee Williams's *Cat on a Hot Tin Roof* at the University Theatre.

After the play we walk back to my dorm room. We play a card game. Then Tracey asks if I would like a back rub. My back is sore from work and her hands feel good rubbing out the knots. She comments on my hard muscles. One of the perks of pouring cement is you get pretty buff. Afterward I ask if she would like me to rub her back. Since I took off my shirt she asks if she should take off hers. I say back rubs work better without a shirt or bra on.

Tracey has a nice body with shapely curves and snow- white skin. One thing leads to another and soon we are making love on a bunk bed that, no doubt, has seen plenty of action in this dorm room. So, now I have a girlfriend. During my life there have been so many long dry spells when I wanted to be with someone, but couldn't quite pull it off. I'm determined to enjoy the intimacy of this new relationship to the max.

Both Tracey and I have class and work so there isn't a lot of time. But late at night we occasionally get together and share a bed in my room. It is the longest I have dated anyone and we experiment in bed with lots of different things I've never tried before. Tracey is attractive, and a good partner but she has some idiosyncrasies that annoy me. For instance, I always take a shower when I get home from work and she doesn't. When this happens, and we are together, well, frankly, sometimes she smells bad. But she's a nice person, and sexy, so I don't mention it. I don't know how I would broach that topic anyway.

Another area where we don't mesh well is marijuana use. It seems Tracey is always trying to stone me. Frequently she brings me pot brownies. I find these in my room, in my lunch bucket, in my backpack, she even has a friend at the front desk who lets her sneak these into my dorm mailbox. Yes, Tracey is always trying to get me high. But two things I'm careful to avoid are mind altering substances and unsafe sex. I throw the brownies away and always use a condom.

Today, besides a pot brownie, I find a letter from Club Europa in my mailbox. Four students have now signed up for the tour. Do I dare allow myself to hope I might earn a free trip? I continue to post the flyers on bulletin boards while walking to work, in the dorm, in the student union, at the coffee shop, all over the place. I have a bundle in my backpack and slap them up everywhere I go.

It is July 4th weekend. The first time this summer I have no work and no class. I made arrangements with Greg to take a canoe trip. He's interesting, a marine who is finishing an engineering degree. I knew him in high school when he was a motorcycle head. There has been a lot of rain this week. The river is running high and the current is swift.

Ordinarily I would not attempt this feat. But Greg is a competent fellow who I trust. We put the canoe in below the dam on Burlington Street. There are no other obstructions all the way to the Mississippi. The swift water catches the little craft and off we go. The only other living things we see all day are beavers, herons and muskrats.

Some fishermen have left lines out, suspended on ditty poles stuck into the mud bank. I maneuver the canoe in close. Greg steals a couple of large catfish. At dusk we pull the boat up a steep grassy bank and build a campfire. Fresh fish roasted on a stick is for dinner. Then we roll out our sleeping bags and climb inside to avoid the bugs.

Up with the sun, the next day is similar. We watch a mink scurry along the bank and deer grazing in a field. Under normal conditions we never would have made the big muddy Mississippi in two days, but with the swift water, here we are at the river's mouth. I suggest we try paddling out into the intimidating Ol' Man River. Whoa! The powerful current is a whole different level. We struggle to get the tiny canoe back to shore.

Greg calls his father who arrives hours later in a pickup truck. He made us a deal that he would come fetch us if we treated him to dinner at the famous *Tomahawk Café* on the way home. We sit in a booth, Greg and I recounting our adventure. The waitress comes. Greg's father orders the catfish. I look at Greg and smile. We order hamburgers.

"But the catfish is good here!" his dad exclaims.

"Had some yesterday," we reply.

It's Monday. I'm at work early. Phildo and Jack are late. I load the trucks by myself. They finally arrive hungover from a weekend of partying. I feel fine. They tell me about their exploits as we ride on the way to the job. Straight shots, strippers, a skirmish outside the bar, Jack punched someone, Phildo bailed him out. How about me? Well, I went canoeing and caught two catfish. How exciting they say. Yeah, well, I feel a whole lot better than you guys do this morning and I don't have to make a court appearance next week either.

The summer session comes to an end. I squeak out a C in chemistry. Too much cement work, too much coffee served and not enough time to study. That grade won't look great on my transcript, but at least I got credit. I have a couple of nights off a week now. So I work on writing an editorial letter slamming the fascist in the White House for overspending on the military and giving tax breaks for the rich. The country's annual federal budget deficit is exploding. Hey, I have to balance my checkbook, why doesn't the government? The editor of the student newspaper likes my edit and prints it. Would I consider working as a staff writer for the paper she asks? Hell yes!

Every spare moment I have now I'm either posting flyers or writing copy for the newspaper. A letter arrives from the tour company. Six students have signed up. So close, and yet, Europe is still so far away. Working as a staff writer for the student newspaper it has been rewarding to see my articles in print. I slam the fascist on his environmental record, on funding for family planning and women's rights, on his unnecessary military attacks and on the terrible economy. It feels good to release my pent-up frustration. The jerk in the White House has trashed everything I believe in. That hurts. But I no longer feel helpless. In some small way, I feel like I'm fighting back now. Like a mosquito biting a charging elephant on the ass.

The deadline for the last student tour of Europe this summer is coming up. I have seven travelers enrolled, but not the required eight. *Oh please, I've come too far to fail now.* But, the magical eighth tourist doesn't come through. I wanted this so badly. I call the tour company. They can still get me on the last tour, but since I'm one traveler short, I would have to pay $500. The dorm stay has been expensive and I only have $547 saved up in my bank account from this summer's work. It would be totally irresponsible to blow the whole wad on a trip.

What would I do when I got back? The dorm contract would have expired. Where would I stay? I'd have nothing for a damage deposit for a room, nothing towards grad school and nothing for food or anything else.

I'm usually pretty level headed with money. I've had to be to survive. What should I do? I want this experience so badly. What the hell. I write out a check for $500 and send it off to Club Europa. Is this really happening? Am I going to see those faraway places I've read and heard about? I tell Hondo I need two weeks off. It's unpaid vacation. The opportunity cost is severe. What will I do when I get home? Guess I'll worry about that when I get back.

Actually, the biggest regret I have now in signing off on the tour is the damage it will do to my carbon footprint. I've been walking everywhere and recycling faithfully. This one flight in an airliner sporting gigantic jet engines will blow through more carbon than I have the entire year.

People tell me not to worry, that the airplane will fly whether I'm on it or not. That's BS. Just a way to rationalize something you want to do and not admit the consequences. I understand completely the damage this trip will do to the environment and global climate. And I'm going ahead and doing it anyway. To all future generations, I apologize. Other people, my family, my friends, are taking trips. I don't want to feel jealous. It will be exciting and fun. I can't resist. If the earth perishes from pollution someday the reason will be that so many of us humans simply could not resist the perks of the modern industrial lifestyle.

I meet up with a girl named Sandy from Wisconsin at the airport. The tour company has provided us with backpacks and suitcase tags emboldened with the Club Europa brand so we can easily spot fellow travelers. Sandy is short, sweet, cute and totally thrilled to begin our voyage over the sea. We finally board the giant airliner bound for Europe. It's a long jaunt, but not so boring sitting next to a pretty girl like Sandy. The plane encounters some turbulence, it feels like an elevator gone haywire. My ears are so screwed up I get dizzy easily. *Dear God I don't want to throw up in front of my new friend.* Fortunately, the triple dose of Dramamine I've taken gets me through.

The anti-nausea meds make me drowsy and I fall asleep. We are landing at Heathrow in the UK before I awake. Sandy's head is on my shoulder. My face resting in her hair. Kind of familiar posture since we just met hours ago. When we exit security our tour guide meets us with a sign labeled, *Europa Tours*. He's a short, friendly Austrian named Hans who will accompany us throughout our journey.

CHAPTER THIRTY-SIX

The lock on Sandy's suitcase breaks while climbing the stairs to the London hostel. There's no way for her to keep the two halves together with a broken lock, so I take off my belt and use it to secure the suitcase. Sandy thanks me and together we're off to explore Buckingham Palace, the Crown Jewels and Hyde Park. But without my belt, I have to keep pulling on my pants to keep them up. There's no way to repair the suitcase and I only have $47 dollars so I don't want to buy a new belt. Looks like I will be touring Europe holding my trousers up.

Our student group travels in a large bus, which is gangly and embarrassing. I feel like a tourist. But this is necessary to keep the price of the tour down. I sit with Sandy and watch the novel sights out the window. I've also made friends with Tim, a typical college prepster who is carrying with him a valuable oil painting rolled up in a tube that he intends to deliver to his mentor, a violin maestro in Italy.

Another young woman on the tour has caught my eye. Her name is Nedra Obradovich from West Palm Beach. It is hard NOT to notice Nedra. She's one of those genetic rarities that pops out at you like a flash bulb, a near supermodel beauty. I've only talked to her once so far. She tells me that her uncle Ed played football for the Chicago

Bears and she is Serbian. Remembering my old roommate Jay, I joke with her that I'm Croatian. She gives me an odd look. I guess I have a warped sense of humor.

Some of the students on the tour decide to go to a theatre play while in London. The tour guide takes requests for tickets. No thanks, I say. I don't have money to spend on any extras. The only food I eat are the two meals, breakfast and dinner, provided by the tour company. Sometimes at breakfast I scarf an apple or croissant and hide it in my pocket so I have something for lunch. I'm not used to this scant diet. My stomach aches. Also, my eyes have been scratchy, I think from jet lag. A pharmacist suggests I purchase drops. Now I only have $42 left in the world.

We cross the English Channel on a ferry boat. I take lots of Dramamine. It will be nice when they complete the Chunnel someday. I'd rather ride under the ocean in a vehicle than ride on top the waves in a boat. Eventually we reach France, such a wonderful country. I greet people with, *"Bonjour!"* We see the Louvre and check out the Mona Lisa, then we're off to the Eiffel Tower, the fancy walls of the Versailles Palace and Notre-Dame Cathedral. Everyone goes for lunch at street cafés on the Champs-Élysées. I have no money for that, so I excuse myself and look at the store windows.

Occasionally I spot Nedra shopping or wandering around by herself. She is the most independent person I've ever encountered. She doesn't mind being alone. I'm a bit insecure, pairing up with other travelers and always being careful to catch the tour bus on time for the next stop. Half the time Nedra misses the deadlines without a care in the world. Then she magically rejoins the group later at another stop. Is she taking cabs? The Metro? I have no idea how she does this. She's a mystery to me.

Tonight, everyone is going to the Moulin Rouge to see the famous dancing girls memorialized by Toulouse-Lautrec. It sounds like fun, but expensive. I bow out and am surprised that Tim is also free. We cruise the cheerfully lighted streets, enjoying the Parisian nightlife. In a little bar called the Silver Moon we meet a couple of French girls. I've heard some negative myths about French girls being easy. But these two are really nice and so much fun. They tell us they want to take us somewhere, a surprise. I look at Tim. He shrugs his shoulders. We get in the taxi. The girls lock the doors. We speed off to a round-about that circles the Arc de Triomphe. Little do Tim and I know the girls have bribed the driver, and we go faster and faster around the stately monument until we are plastered to the sides of the taxi by centrifugal force, yelling for our lives.

The next day we arrive in Belgium. We see a statue of a young boy taking a leak. Sandy and I wander the granite cobblestone streets together. Nedra is MIA since our scant breakfast. When the beauty finally arrives at dinner time the tour guide tells her she must check in more often. He was worried about her. I had no lunch and I'm half starved. We sit at long wooden tables and the waitress brings us cheese pizza. That's it, just cheese pizza. I figure what heck, I'm famished, so I wolf down slice after slice until I am full. Then the waitress has us all get up and she takes us to another dining room with a luscious smor-gasbord filled with fruit and veggies and meats and wonderful desserts. What a diabolical, cheap trick! I finally have the opportunity to enjoy a delicious meal and I'm already full. Why did they do that?

Next on our schedule is Germany, such a neat and orderly country. Our big bus plows down the autobahn faster than it probably should, but I can't blame the driver. The road is so well engineered and there's no speed limit. I wish I had the Shelby Mustang muscle car I drove in high school. It would be a blast on this smooth, wide open road. It's a weekend so no trucks are allowed.

We reach our destination, Heidelberg, in record time and tour the beautiful ruins of the Schloss Heidelberg Fortress. Everyone wants to go out for lunch in the old town, Altstadt. Being low on funds, instead I go for a hike on a trail along the high bank of the Neckar River. Into an enchanted, dark forest I wander for hours with the feeling I'm in the middle of nowhere. Then skipping down the trail comes Nedra. Who is this chick? How did she get here? She seems to appear and disappear out of thin air.

Crossing the border on the bus we are now entering into Austria, our tour guide's home turf. The mountainous terrain of the Alps is a mountain climber's dream. I'd love to try out some of the climbing skills I learned at Devil's Lake but there's no time in our tight agenda.

In Salzburg the driver plays the soundtrack from the *Sound of Music* as we pass by scenes where the movie was filmed. I loved that flick.

It is evening and some of the guys want to go for a drink at a Bavarian bar. I tag along but have no intention of actually imbibing. We sit at a large wooden table across the room from another table filled with locals. Everyone but me is chugging down steins of fine brew. I notice that the Bavarians keep glancing our way with disgust. They seem to be talking about us and are not happy we're here.

The evening progresses. The Bavarians become angrier with each new round. They hurl what sound like insults our way but no one in our group speaks German. It's my turn to buy a pitcher. To be social, I agree, even though I'm only pretending to sip beer from my stein. As I head to the bar for a $10 pitcher one of the Bavarians arrives at the same time. He budges in front of me. I acquiescence, not wanting any trouble. After being served, the irate man in the Tyrolean hat turns and barks in my face, what sounds like, *"Ihr Präsident ist ein Schwein."*

"Excuse me?" I reply in my most polite voice.

"Ihr Präsident ist ein Schwein," he screams so loud everyone in the bar stops talking and watches us to see what will transpire.

"Präsident?" I inquire. "You mean the president? The president of the United States?"

The Bavarian assumes a wide stance, bracing himself for a fight and yells, *"Ja, dein Präsident ist ein Schwein!"*

"Oh," I sigh, finally getting it. He and his buddies hate the fascist in the White House. "Yes!" I agree. "I don't like him either. The president is very bad."

The man's fists uncurl and he relaxes. With a curious look, he asks, *"Du magst den presdient nicht?"*

"No!" I reply emphatically, giving a repeated thumbs down gesture, I'm sure must be international. "He is no good!"

The Bavarian smiles and hands me his pitcher. *"Das ist für dich,"* he yells happily.

I indicate, is this mine? He slaps me heartily on the back, sending me back to my table with both pitchers. The Bavarians begin singing the U.S. national anthem. Afterwards we join them in singing theirs. We slide our tables together. The conversation is imperfect, but thankfully most of them speak some English. We party together the rest of the night.

I wonder to myself, on the way back to the hotel, how important communication is. The evening could have ended badly, in a big angry disagreement, or even a terrible fight. Someone could have gotten seriously hurt. All over a simple misunderstanding. Apparently, they assumed, because we were Americans, that we all supported the president, which was definitely not the case. I only have $32 left now, but the pitcher of beer was worth it, for, I make a mental note, improvement of international relations.

Regrettably this is a low-cost student tour and we only have a couple of days to visit each country. But at least I'm getting a small taste of new cultures and places. We leave Austria and stop in Lichtenstein to see an old, white castle that looks like Tolkien's Minas Tirith. Then we're off again, finally pulling into Lucerne, Switzerland. I depart the bus and my jaw drops. The scene is so magnificent it looks like it could only exist in a fairy tale. Craggy, snow-capped mountain peaks surround a lake the color of a blue jewel. We visit a park with a lion statue carved into the rock wall. Then everyone wants to take a gondola ride up to Mt. Pilatus. Lacking the funds, I demur, taking a stroll by myself.

I come to the long Chapel Bridge across the lake. Who should appear but the mysterious Nedra, her long golden locks flowing in the brisk alpine breeze. We walk together across the covered pathway lined with colorful flowers. Murals highlighting events in Swiss history decorate the ceiling panels. It's an intoxicatingly romantic setting. I'm thrilled that she seems to enjoy my company. I can tell she likes me, but in what way? I must resist falling for her. I'm not getting my hopes up. She's way out of my league. We roam the little shops of the old town, which appears not to have changed much for thousands of years, laughing and chatting jovially.

There is an older 30-something dude on the tour who tells me he's an undertaker. He must be rich because every town we visit he talks about buying real estate. Now he's going to look at a spectacular Swiss chalet with several of the girls tagging along like groupies. But not Nedra. She frowns and whispers to me that she suspects this fellow is a poser. In the evening I'm assigned to room with him and inquire about his financial situation. He laughs explaining he has no great fortune. Pretending to be a buyer of luxurious things is his method of attracting women. I have to admit the subterfuge seems to work. He's always surrounded by ladies, but I figure it's not my place to blow his cover.

Today we say *buon giorno* in Italy. There are museums packed with incredible statuary and massive towering cathedrals. Taking an abundance of photos, the girls huddle around the statue of David with his junk clearly on display for all to see. Tim goes off to practice violin with the master and, as a gift, Tim presents him with an oil painting. Then we head out to our next destination, which is easy to find, because all roads lead to Rome.

Having been (forcefully) raised as a Catholic it is meaningful for me to see the Vatican. I crane my neck, taking in the artistry of Michelangelo covering the ceiling of the Sistine Chapel. Outside I marvel at the Colosseum and Forum, the ancient ruins are located literally in the midst of the modern city. I never pictured it would be like that.

The group gathers in St Peter's Square for an informational pep talk by our guide Hans. Someone asks what the temperature is. Of course, our Austrian guide recounts this in degrees centigrade. But all the Americans want to know the Fahrenheit reading. Having just taken advanced chemistry I quickly multiply by 1.8 and add 32. I figured I'd use that formula someday. Everyone departs for various paid tours and lunches in quaint restaurants. Those are not in my budget so I search until I find a small laundry where they wash and fold my dirty clothes for $2.

The last country on our trip is Spain. I took 4 years of Spanish in high school so I can fumble my way around Barcelona, locating streets and bathrooms. The endless beach is fantastic and the Sagrada Família looks like a giant sandcastle. We stop at some small towns on the way to Madrid. The tour guide always gives us a strict time that we must meet back at the bus. It's evening now and we're all here, except Nedra. I can tell the short Austrian is pissed. Over an hour late Miss

Universe finally saunters in, a bit sweaty and disheveled, but gorgeous all the same.

This time the angry tour guide lets her have it, a stern reprimand about the need to be on time and not make everyone wait. Nedra listens stoically, like the Venus de Milo statue I saw in the Paris Louvre. Afterwards she gets on the bus and asks if she can sit next to me. Of course, I'm delighted. I ask her what happened. She recounts how she lost track of time browsing some jewelry displayed by a street vendor. When she realized she might be late, instead of using the walkway, she took a shortcut cross country and got lost in a goat pasture. I've never met anyone like her before. She is so confident and seems to have no fear of anything. I admire her keen sense of adventure, but doubt I could ever keep up with her.

I like Spain a lot. The people here are so friendly. The waiters in the hotel lounge give us free appetizers and wine. I stick with bottled water. I look out over the city and see quite a bit of poverty, something I did not expect in Europe. The beaches and pools here are top-free. In fact, if you like, you don't have to wear anything at all. I hang out at the hotel pool waiting to see if any of the girls on our student tour will shed their clothing. A couple of them go topless, which the guys enjoy seeing immensely. But most stick with the social norms from back in the states and wear bathing suits.

Everyone is buying last minute keepsakes before we depart for home. I get caught up in the herd mentality and purchase a nice wool sweater for $23. It will keep me warm next winter. Airports are not stress free anywhere. A southern good old boy from our group forgets his passport back at the hotel and the tour guide flags down a taxi for a mad rush back to find it. Somehow, we all manage to get on the airliner in Madrid and head back over the big pond to Chicago.

I take copious amounts of Dramamine and sleep most of the way. I awake to find our arrival has been delayed. I'm worried sick I may miss my connection in O'Hare. I need to catch a little puddle jumper plane back home. I flag down the stewardess and she tells me she'll do whatever she can to help. Sandy asks about returning my belt. I tell her not to worry. I can't wait for her to get her luggage. I only have $7 in my pocket. I have to catch my connecting flight or I'll be stranded. I do regret that I won't get to say goodbye to everyone. Nedra said she was going to give me her address and phone number. Darn!

The giant airliner finally lands and taxis. The stewardess has me standing by the exit door with my pack. Because of my predicament, I get to be the first off. The plane stops, the stewardess opens the hatch, I take a step out and nearly fall into thin air. The exit ramp was not in place yet. The stewardess looks shocked. It was an honest screw up. I catch my breath, wait, and when it's finally ready, I dash at top speed through the gates looking for Mississippi Valley Airlines. There it is. But seating has ended. I beg the fellow at the counter to let me on the plane. Thankfully it's a small airline. An attendant escorts me out onto the airstrip, they reattach the stairs, and I'm on board!

Well, here I am. I've been across the wide Atlantic Ocean, toured Europe, and come back again. I had $7 left in my pocket when the plane landed and I used it all for a taxi. Now I'm standing here in my hometown, with my backpack containing all my worldly possessions. I have no money, no place to live and no plan for the future. Was it worth it? Yeah, I really, really wanted to travel to far off places. I may be destitute and homeless, but like an education, travel experiences are something you can never lose, and no one can ever take away from you.

CHAPTER THIRTY-SEVEN

I call my brother Hondo. He lives in a trailer now with his wife and child. There isn't much room but he wants me to come stay with them until I can find another place. How great of a brother is that? I don't want to impose too long, so I begin searching for another place to live, but it's tough since I have no money for a damage deposit.

Before I left, I applied for another year of undergrad scholarship, which has been approved. I also got clearance for work-study status and got my old job back at the coffee shop. I already have enough credits to graduate, but I love the college life and decided to hang on for just one more year of undergrad. I can't decide on a career and don't have money for graduate school anyway. I love writing for the student newspaper and get hired there as a staff writer. I'm even thinking I might like to pursue a career in journalism.

Since I have no clear career plan, I'm free to register for whatever classes I want. So, I sign up for things I'm interested in, but never took before, since I needed science and math for medical school. I will be studying Civilizations of Asia, Archaeology, World Geography and Introduction to Law.

At the registration center I bump into Julia, my old lab partner from zoology, a blast from the past. We talk for a while. She seems more mature and sophisticated than the last time I saw her. She mentions that she ran into Danette on the other side of the river, which on this campus means the hospital or medical school. I try to inquire casually about that, but my radar is way up. Apparently, Danette is studying nuclear medicine. Remembering her bad grades, and inability to complete a science lab, I blurt out something about how the heck she managed to get into that. Julia smiles recounting how Danette made good use of her Greek connections, some sorority sisters pulled strings. If I see the west bank of the college go up in a mushroom cloud, now I'll know what happened.

The search for a new pad is going nowhere. But I continue looking everywhere I can think of, newspaper want-ads, the information center, and bulletin boards when I'm posting flyers. Classes are going to be starting soon and I'm still crashing with my brother. I heard about a communal living experiment called the River City Housing Co-op from my old dance partner Marge. The idea being that in this college town landlords rip everyone off with high rent so some students started a cooperative venture where they own houses and rent rooms for less.

Sounds like a good idea to me. I'm a little unsure about what the people living there will be like. I mean, is this a Woodstock crowd of burned out hippies from the sixties? I guess I'll find out. The Co-op requires new prospective members to attend a dinner. I make the arrangements and head over for an evening meal. They purchase groceries together and each member cooks a meal one night a week. This should be interesting.

Living out of a backpack I don't have a large wardrobe, just some old polo and button-down shirts and jeans left over from when I lived in the frat. The preppy clothes are probably not appropriate attire for this event, but I go with what I have. I'm looking for the right address and I'm impressed when I see three cute little houses in a row not far from the performing arts center. These people have something going here.

I'm invited in by a young man who looks like Jesus. I enter the dining room. There are four people already seated. One I already know, Marge from ballroom dance. Another boyish fellow wearing an Observation Club t-shirt that boldly proclaims, *See more, Be more.* There's a young woman who appears to be blind examining her food with her fingers. And, finally, the most attractive woman I have ever seen in my life, who states in a kind voice, "Hi, my name is Laura, welcome to the coop."

They say that when people meet for the first time they can tell within a few seconds if there is any possible chemistry between them. In this case, with Laura, it takes me less than a millisecond. She has a clean, wholesome look and an engaging, friendly demeanor that both intrigue and confuse me. I'm definitely interested, but never expected someone like her to be in a cooperative society. Jesus explains that he has cooked an African meal for us. I dip some flat bread into something that looks like fried peanut butter and hope I'm accepted to move in.

My classes have begun and they're okay, but I lack enthusiasm. Unlike my pre-med classes I don't feel like I have a lot at stake and don't study much. I actually spend most of my time in the newsroom of the student paper. We have an AP wire service and there are rows of computers with journalism students typing away. The place has an exciting, tuned-in vibe. My editor suggests stories which I complete. Then I concentrate on hard-hitting editorials blasting the fascist president. The next election is coming up in November and I'm hoping the moderate, centrist candidate is victorious. No way am I throwing my vote away this time on a third-party candidate who has no chance of winning.

I'm back slinging brew at the coffee shop. Caroline has returned from boot camp. She looks older and sort of sad and weary. Everyone asks her what it was like. She basically substantiates everything I said about abuse and mistreatment in the military. I feel bad that she had to go through that. No one should have to suffer that kind of mistreatment in order to get an education. I do feel exonerated by her stories though, since some of the workers here did not believe me. Caroline wants to go out with me, but I just can't wrap my head around that. She'll be in the armed forces for eight more years to pay for her nursing degree. I don't think it would work out between us.

Before leaving my brother's trailer I give him the sweater I bought in Europe. I don't have any money to compensate him and, frankly, the sweater is the only thing I own that is worth giving anyone. I'm so thankful for his generosity, I want to give him something.

I've been welcomed into the housing cooperative. I use my first coffee shop paycheck for the damage deposit. The rent here is so much cheaper than anywhere else in town. By eliminating the profit motive, the co-op can charge tenants less and still save money to buy more houses. There are some things here that I have trouble getting used to, like the communal meals. I go to the store and buy some of my own food so I'll have a stash when I get hungry.

On the way home from the New Pioneer grocery I bump into Laura, who lives in the co-op house next door. She has such a beautiful smile. We walk toward home together and then stop on a scenic bridge over the river to talk. I tell her a little about my experience in the army, and how I'm a peace activist now and work at the newspaper writing edits about the fascist president. She seems surprised, having thought maybe I was the conservative frat rat type because of the clothes I wear. That just shows, you can't judge a book by its cover.

Sandy from the student tour is in town visiting from Wisconsin. We meet at a local bar. She returns my belt and offers to share some pictures she took in Europe. I choose one of Tim and myself outside the *Silver Moon* in Paris with the two French girls we met. That's a good memory. I take one other, a picture of the whole tour group. Sometimes I look at it and Nedra's face pops out. I'll always wonder what would have happened, if I had time to say goodbye to her in Chicago and had gotten her phone number. Oh well.

We are having a big potluck with all the members of the co-op today. So many interesting people live here. There is tall lanky Kevin with granny glasses who is pre-med. And Betsy, who is sweet as pie, but falls into the burned-out, hippie chick mold. Everyone finishes eating and is sitting around conversing. I take my dirty plate into the kitchen to find that Laura is there doing all the dishes by herself. One problem with communal living is that it's difficult to divide labor and get everyone to pitch in sometimes. I roll up my sleeves and we talk while cleaning plates.

The newsroom is ecstatic. We've won a prestigious award, having been chosen as the best student newspaper in the country. All the writers are bearing down now trying to live up to our new reputation. I stay late most nights giving my maximum effort to bring interesting stories to the editor. My most recent work is a critique of military overspending. I'm watching for new material to come in over the wire and up pops a story, dateline, Cedar Rapids, IA. A Michael Hidersheit found dead today near a river. The body shows signs of severe beating and authorities are treating the death as a possible homicide. The possibilities race through my mind. Maybe it was a robbery or a drug deal gone bad.

R.I.P. Mike Hidersheit.

The weekend has come, and it is a spectacular one. The sun is shining and the temp is perfect. The kind of fall day when you just have to get outside and do something. I'm wandering down by the boathouse on the grassy river bank and who should I see but Laura from the co-op. I don't know her that well yet, so it's a bit presumptuous, but I ask her if she'd like to go for a canoe ride. She smiles in agreement.

I get in back of the old aluminum canoe to steer and Laura sits up front. The only problem is that I'm nearly deaf and typically rely on reading lips. But now I can't see Laura's face because I'm sitting behind her in the boat. The river is low and we paddle a long way upstream in the lazy current. Laura keeps asking me questions, and I try to guess what she is saying, but I can tell she thinks some of my responses are off the wall. Or I just don't answer at all.

We stop on land to examine some trees gnawed by beavers. When I'm facing her, I can converse just fine. Laura is not only perceptive, she's also studying speech pathology in college. She figures out that I have a hearing loss. I'm always a little embarrassed to admit that on a first date, but she's so kind and understanding I'm glad to have the hearing situation out there.

There is a career fair in the student union. All sorts of employers have set up booths. I wander around looking for any journalism jobs, but there are none. To be honest, I can see that if I was solely interested in finding quick, lucrative employment I should have just majored in business. Practically all of the employers are large corporations. I see a booth full of military recruiters and keep far away from that one. What am I going to do for a life's career? I have no idea now. I'm passionate about writing, and would love to land a job at a magazine or newspaper, but there are no jobs like that here. It doesn't help that almost all the classes I have taken are science or math, not English or journalism.

The members of the co-op are having a big Halloween costume party. None of us has much money so we'll have to be creative. I go to a political headquarters and get some re-election buttons for the right-wing president I despise. I put on one of the white shirts and a tie I bought when I thought I was going to be a real estate agent, then I deck my chest with the campaign buttons for the fascist and go to the party as a republican. There are all kinds of crazy costumes. I see Laura sitting on a couch with an Egyptian sphinx. She has on a white t-shirt with green stains and cotton balls all over it. Later I get a chance to ask her what she is supposed to be. She tells me she's mold.

I win the scariest costume award. Laura gets the nod for most creative. We go home together and sit talking on the couch. There's a strong attraction between us. One thing leads to another and we kiss. I'm pretty sure I'm falling in love. But I think we both need some time to digest what's happening. Our relationship has progressed so smoothly. This time it feels different for me, like it is right and going to last.

The next day rolls by. I finish writing a newspaper article on how bad the economy is doing under the fascist in the White House. Walking home in the evening light, I'm dreaming about how well everything went last night with Laura. I'm in an upbeat mood, happy and confident. So, I decide to drop in next door to see if Laura is home. I knock and proceed into the living room. There on the couch sits Laura with a handsome fellow. It's pretty obvious they've been on a date. I feel kind of dumb and startled, as I really thought maybe Laura was going to be "the one" for me. I really liked her a lot. But, obviously, we aren't going steady or anything. We haven't even known each other that long. I guess my feelings of affection got ahead of reality.

I excuse myself and head back over to my room. I put on my

flannel pajamas and crawl into bed. I'm lying on my back now, thinking about how clueless I am when it comes to dating and relationships. I'm unable to gauge how women feel about me. And I fall in love way too quickly. From my perspective, I thought my experiences with Laura were really something special. I could see where this time it might be a lasting relationship. I just didn't understand. She's dating different people, which is fine, that's what you should do in college, to gain experience and know what you want in a partner.

I'm in that semi-conscious state, just prior to falling into deep REM sleep, when I feel someone shaking me awake. It's Laura. I'm kind of confused. But she seems earnest, like she has good intentions and needs to talk. She tells me that she had agreed to the date with this other fellow some time back, before we had gotten together. And ... she assures me that she cares for me and wants to be with me. Wow, I must say I'm thrilled. It was a good thing too that she came over to let me know where things stand. I was feeling kind of clueless and might not have had the courage to ask her out again, figuring she was going out with the other guy.

Election day comes. I make sure to cast my vote. The incumbent fascist is leading in the polls. The moderate challenger has chosen a woman as his running mate, the first female candidate for vice-president in U.S. history. The fascist brags about his support for massive military spending, tax breaks for the wealthy and cuts in aid for the poor. The moderate supports a freeze on nuclear weapons and the Equal Rights Amendment for women. I'm sitting in the newsroom now with the other writers watching the results roll in from across the country. The fascist wins in a huge landslide, only Minnesota and D.C. go for the moderate. I'm crushed.

The semester ends. My grades are mediocre. The December weather turns nasty. The humiliating election defeat still stings. But I'm okay. Laura has moved out of the co-op and into an old apartment complex in the middle of downtown. The place is a historic building, with all kinds of interesting features, like built-in compartments for ice blocks necessary before refrigerators. Laura has asked me to come over for dinner. I bring her flowers. She's made falafel. I can tell we are both feeling it now. We're falling in love.

There is a reason the plot line of so many movies involves the early stages of romance. It is a truly magical experience. One of the highlights of life. I gather my things and move in with Laura. We don't have much money. The weather is snowy and cold. But in our little apartment we experience the warmth of pure joy. Laura dislikes the president as much as I do and it helps me get over the election to discuss it with her. Laura has a stereo and plays intriguing music that is new and different. We shop at the organic grocery and prepare tasty meals together.

Even our smallest outings are fresh and exciting. We walk in a snowstorm to a Chinese restaurant and are the only customers on this blustery evening. The fortune in my cookie reads, *An unexpected friendship will prove long lasting*. The next morning I borrow snowshoes from the Touch the Earth Outdoor Program and we trudge through the drifts in a hickory-filled park. I try out the ice-covered creek and break through soaking my feet. I laugh out loud without a care.

Laura leaves to visit her family in Kansas City. I busy myself installing a makeshift shower in the bathroom. The old apartment has only an antique, free-standing tub. My life consists of writing news stories, serving java at the coffee shop and watching old movies on a borrowed VCR late in the evenings. Even though I'm no longer living in the housing co-op I have signed a lease so I'm careful to always pay my rent on time. Shelly, a chubby football team groupie who lives in the co-op, has offered my room there to a homeless black woman since I wasn't using it.

I register for spring semester. My classes are Indians of North America, Social Work, American Sign Language and a physics seminar taught by the Dean of the College, Howard Laster, a brilliant astrophysicist. I absolutely love studying with Professor Laster. We spend hours in his office discussing current topics like global climate disruption. The threat of nuclear war is hanging heavy on everyone's mind these days as the fascist in the White House strains relations with America's adversaries to the breaking point. The professor and I delve deeply into possible war scenarios, calculating the circular error probable and megatonnage of various weapons systems and prospects for survival of the human species.

Most of our neighbors in the apartment complex are older. There is a Japanese writer who invites us for tea and describes the book he's working on. An elderly couple, Fred and Emma, live at the end of the hall. Fred invites us over to watch a video, which turns out to be *Playboy Playmates of the Year*. In a totally inappropriate conversation Fred explains that all of the young ladies pictured in the film are virgins. Laura and I just look at each other and try not to laugh.

Then there is the eccentric old lady across the hall. She's a mystery to us, but rumor has it she was a successful author of children's books in her younger days. Sometimes I smell smoke coming from her apartment. I get up the nerve to ask her and she insists she just sometimes forgets and leaves food on the stove. The Japanese author has started carrying his writings around with him in a backpack fearing she might burn the place down. Finally, one day, when the smoke is very thick, I call the fire department. The firemen enter her apartment to find a small bonfire on her living room floor. She claims she was trying to smoke out bugs. The fire chief is angry and threatens to evict her. I feel bad about that, but the historic building is a tinderbox and many elderly tenants could perish in a fire.

CHAPTER THIRTY-EIGHT

I love my life. Kind of strange, I have barely enough money to survive, my dream of becoming a doctor has gone down in flames, I have no career plan and the country is going to hell under fascism and yet, my life is filled with joy because of the wonderful partner I have found. It feels so good to say I love you to someone, and it is so affirming when that person tells you they love you too. All my life I've wanted a committed, caring relationship, and now that dream has come true. Laura and I even talk of getting married and having children someday.

I tell Laura, "I'm going to call you Etna."

Laura replies, "Why's that?"

I explain, "Because I'm glad I met ya."

In my sign language course, we have an assignment to learn a song and sign it to the class. Being a speech pathology major Laura is good at ASL and she helps me learn to sign the words to the *Jolly Swagman*. We have no car and walk everywhere, to class, to work and to the grocery, which makes me feel good that we're not contributing to global warming. My physics prof is a brilliant man who makes dire predictions of what will happen if fossil fuel burning continues. But it seems no one is listening to scientists.

My brother Hondo has gotten a divorce. He brings us a birdcage with a colorful parakeet that needs a new home. Laura and I name the little bird Perchy. We don't like confining Perchy to a cage so we leave the lid off and the parakeet can fly freely around the apartment. Perchy likes to land on our heads and will sit there for hours. It feels like we have a family now.

It is late at night. We have no money for a bed so Laura and I sleep on the floor with a single futon. We are awakened by Fred down the hall. The old guy has been out carousing around again and Emma has locked him out of their apartment. Fred alternates between trying to command, and then beg, Emma to let him in.

"Emma! Open up this door right now, dammit! I'm a man and if you let me in, I'll prove it!"

The door doesn't open.

"Please Emma, please. I'm so sorry. It's cold out here. Please let me in."

Laura and I just look at each other and laugh. Yes, it is funny, but it's also annoying getting woken up like this late at night. Stan's Barber Shop is across the street. When I go to get my haircut, they tell me stories about Fred's escapades. Once Fred told a customer that he had his own airplane. The fellow didn't realize the old man was kind of senile and arranged for Fred to fly him to Chicago. Of course, Fred never showed up. He has no airplane. He does however have a .45 magnum handgun like Dirty Harry, which Fred likes to brandish at people who disagree with him. I hope no one gets hurt.

I continue to pay rent at the co-op even though I no longer stay there. I really do like those people. The experiment in cooperative living is a good idea and it has played a crucial role in my life. Without the co-op, I never would have met my true love Laura. But I worry about the future of the enterprise. One problem with any communal venture is that some people do not pull their share of the load. Some members shirk the work of cleaning and maintaining the houses. Others go without paying rent. The people who live in the co-op don't have the heart to kick anyone out. So, this gets to be a problem.

One person who keeps the whole place afloat is Steve, the co-op treasurer. Steve is a brilliant accounting major, tall and lean, with a quick wit and great sense of humor. But there is only so much he can do when too many people are loafing along not paying rent. On top of this precarious situation an irresponsible member named Phoebe has misplaced the cash bag she was supposed to deposit at the bank. She says she left it in a desk drawer and it disappeared so someone must have stolen the money.

I'm not sure how Steve is going to work this one out. He's good with numbers but he can't spin straw into gold. I fear the co-op could lose some houses or eventually fold, which would be a tragedy in my view. The whole concept is such a noble venture. Students are at the mercy of landlords in this college town and many landlords are unscrupulous, never returning damage deposits and charging exorbitant rent. If anyone can salvage the co-op Steve can. He's a great guy who I'm sure will be very successful someday. He has a beautiful girlfriend, Mary, and a solid career in accounting. He is proof that good guys don't always finish last.

Spring break is here. Laura and I have signed up to go on a hiking trip to the Grand Canyon guided by the fellow who taught my rock-climbing course at Devil's Lake. With about 24 others we pile our backpacks into an old, half-sized school bus. The guide then lays some wrestling mats on top of the packs and we are expected to ride atop this lumpy base all the way to Arizona. He cheaped out and we had to share a motel on the canyon rim with a couple we have never met before. They have very noisy sex this evening, "sorry, sorry, ouch, sorry." This is awkward.

The next day begins at the top of the canyon in three-foot deep snow drifts but as we hike down the temperature warms. Each meter walked on the trail signifies one million years of geologic history. It takes most of the day to descend through colorful layers of limestone, sandstone and shale. By the time we reach the bottom of the canyon we have shed all our parkas, hats and gloves and are so warm we're now wearing jogging shorts and t-shirts.

Unfortunately, the guide has oversold the trip. Instead of accommodations with beds, showers and home-cooked meals at the Phantom Ranch, we will be sleeping in pop tents and eating freeze-dried food. At least the scenery is spectacular. Laura and I hike out to

Ribbon Falls via the North Kaibab Trail. The shimmering green algae is a striking sight against the backdrop of reddish stone. Too soon it's time to head home. The trip back is worrisome. The guide gets high while driving. He also had an affair with a young woman on the trip and she cries the whole way back, while a youngster on the trip sings 99 bottles of beer on the wall up to about a million.

Spring is in the air. The grass has greened and the magnolias are blooming pink. I'm finishing my last weeks as an undergrad. Walking across campus I hear some young men yelling my name from the steps of a stately pillared building. I investigate and discover some Kappa brothers from my days in the frat.

Having been thrown off campus they no longer have a house, but still observe many of the old traditions and rituals, one of which is to smoke a reefer on the steps of the old capitol in remembrance of the Kent State massacre. I'm not sure if the brothers really have any deep sentimental feelings about the massacre. But traditions persist. This ritual was established in 1970 and if you look at the Fraternity composites from the 70's everyone in the house had long hair. I take one, and only one, toke, to honor the victims.

R.I.P. Peace protesters massacred at Kent State.

The brothers ask what my career plans are and I reply, honestly, that I have none. They encourage me to apply at several large corporations that have lots of Kappa's in high level management positions. They assure me they can pull strings and get me a position. I'm sure they're probably right. Most Greek houses have affiliations with different corporations. But I could never go corporate. That just doesn't fit who I am. I know it's the path to go if you want to make the big bucks. I have relatives who've gone corporate, but it's not for me. I do agree to go bass fishing with one frat buddy at a big quarry outside of town. But when we get there with our poles and tackle boxes a boss hog county sheriff ruins our plans yelling, "You cocksuckers from the university think you can come out here in the country and catch all our fish. Get outta here!" Abusive law enforcement officers like that ought to be weeded out of the profession.

I can't believe I'm actually graduating. When I signed up for my very first class at this college, I remember thinking that the 120 semester hours required for a degree seemed intimidating and barely possible. But here I am with semester hours to spare and an honors GPA. The Dean of the College, who is my physics seminar instructor, nominates me for Phi Beta Kappa. The law school sends an invitation to apply. But I have no money for law school or medical school or any other sort of graduate education right now.

I skip the commencement and induction ceremonies. No cap and gown ritual stuff for me. Instead I go right to work pouring cement with Leroy, Hondo, Phildo and Hatchet Jack. In August Laura and I are planning a wedding. Looks like I will (literally) marry the girl who lived next door. I never really popped the question, we just sort of discussed it. I made it through my undergrad without borrowing a cent but Laura has some student loans and one year of grad school left. At this point, I need to earn money for our daily expenses and pouring cement foundations is the best option I have.

So, my life now consists of laboring at Leroy's shop all day, returning home, taking a shower and eating dinner with Laura, then working until late in the evening at the newspaper, a job I love and don't want to give up. Any spare time is spent with my future bride planning the wedding. We don't have much money but we don't need, or want, a big, elaborate affair. I use my connections at the student union to reserve a cute little chapel on campus. My friends at the coffee shop will cater the reception in the union ballroom. We select ferns for flowers, order wedding invitations on recycled paper and Laura asks a friend to play guitar and sing.

The big day has come. Laura and I get ready for the wedding ceremony, her in a simple white dress. She doesn't need anything fancy, she's so beautiful, she'd look good in a burlap sack. I wear a grey suit I purchase on sale at J.C. Penney. We have no car, so we walk to the chapel. People are already there, not many, the chapel is small, just our close family and friends. Hondo is my best man. Laura's sister Mary is her bridesmaid. Ed, the priest, has us sign the marriage certificate. The guests are amused by an oddball photographer we recruited from the local film developing shop who keeps sticking his camera in through the open windows for candid shots. We repeat our vows:

I promise to be true to you,
In good times and in bad,
In sickness and in health,
I will love you and honor you,
All the days of my life.

Wow! I'm a married man! I always dreamed of forming a stable, loving relationship. This is it, the best day of my life! Everyone is so happy for us. We walk through a shower of rice across the street to the union ballroom where my co-workers have assembled a tasty meal. Friends from the co-op arrive. This is so fun. Today I'm thankful to be alive.

Leroy owns a large Chevrolet Suburban which he generously loans us for a honeymoon. We throw the futon in back, grab a change of clothes and head out with no set plans. Just two drifters off to see the world. We drive to the university in Madison, WI and walk around the lake. We sleep in the back of Leroy's wagon and eat one big meal a day at dinner. Tonight it's vegetarian stroganoff at a counterculture restaurant. Renting a tandem bicycle, we tour Mackinac Island. I love it! No cars allowed! Across the border into Canada we cruise through Sudbury, a barren environmental sacrifice zone.

We re-cross the border at the misty Niagara Falls, a classic honeymoon destination. New York state is beautiful. We love the Adirondack Mountains. Dinner is at the *Hungry Trout Café*, in a window seat overlooking a clear mountain stream. Being a fan of Henry David Thoreau, we make the pilgrimage to Walden Pond outside of Concord, Massachusetts. I'm so thankful for Thoreau's prose, it has been a guiding light. Laura's smiling head pops up out of the mirror-like flat surface of the water in front of me while I'm swimming in the crystal clear pond. This is so much fun, it's almost surreal.

In Maine we purchase a giant lobster off a fisherman on the docks. But we have only a small wok we brought for cooking. We get the water boiling, then hold the lid down hard as the crustacean flaps around wildly. Our money nearly gone, we get on interstate and point the Suburban home. What a trip! Laura thinks we're crazy driving so far. But these are memories we'll never forget.

Laura's final year of speech training flies by. She lands a job working in a residential facility for special needs children in the capital city. She's so good at her work. I'm very proud of her. But now we must move. I'm a sentimental person, especially when it comes to places I've lived. We empty all our belongings out of our little apartment. While cleaning I find a single pearl bead that was missing from Laura's dress the day of the wedding. I'm getting choked up.

We wish we could arrange things so we didn't need a car. But unfortunately we're going to need wheels. We buy the smallest compact in the line up from a chain-smoking car salesman. Now we have both an auto loan and Laura's student loans. She knows how much I hate going into debt and we agree to make double payments to get rid of the liability as soon as possible. We have an efficiency apartment in the new city and I need to find employment. Unfortunately, the economy is in a deep recession thanks to the mismanagement of our country's fearless leader, the former movie star fascist residing in the White House. I'm back on the street wearing out shoe leather applying for jobs. In my hometown I could always rely on working at Leroy's shop as a backup. Those days are over.

Thanks to the math classes I took in college I land a position as an accountant for a department store. I have a desk where I sit from 8AM until 5PM crunching numbers that must balance to the penny. There are several secretaries here and the highlight of the day is going out for lunch in the food court of a mall. But I try not to eat much. I feel like my body is atrophying into a mush ball. Usually when people think of hard work they think of backbreaking physical labor. But sitting at a desk inside all day is just as bad for your mind and body, maybe worse. I'll keep this job for now, but start applying elsewhere.

I'm hired on at a landscaping company. The job is sunup 'til sundown six days a week cutting sod, laying down river rock and planting trees and shrubs. The work is hard and the hours long, but I still prefer it over sitting on my butt in a white shirt and tie inside an office all day. This city has a nice system of trails where Laura and I take walks after work. We dream of owning our own home someday and discuss the attributes of the various houses we pass by.

The nesting instinct is strong in newlywed couples and we long for a home of our own, but we have no money for a down payment and we don't want to be house poor. We do splurge once a week, trying out new restaurants with a "2 for 1" meal coupon book Laura got at work.

Winter comes and I'm laid off at the landscaping company. I send out resumes with my college transcripts. I'd love to land a gig in journalism but that doesn't pan out. So, I find work at a country club doing catering. I feel underemployed and would really like to go back to grad school but can't swing it financially right now. This country doesn't do enough to help young people pursue education. All I'm offered is loans and we have too much debt already.

It's Sunday and I'm fishing at Big Creek with my Uncle Bill. He is a retired union steamfitter who lives in a trailer west of town. I love the old guy dearly. We catch no fish, but this is a happy day I will always cherish after my uncle has passed away. When I get home, Laura has big news. She has been recommended for a job in Speech Pathology at a hospital in Idaho. I don't know what to say. I've been a Midwest flatlander for so long. Heading west sounds exciting but I'm apprehensive. We sit down and make a list of the pros and cons of moving to Pocatello. Moving wins out.

When I was in college, I had so few possessions I could move with my backpack. When we moved here to the capitol city, everything fit in our compact car. Now for the trip out west we must rent a small U-Haul. Household stuff accumulates! On the way, we encounter a severe wind storm. I'm afraid the boxy van will tip over in a gust so we stay overnight in Sheridan, Wyoming. The next day we arrive at Idaho State University.

Laura will be making more at the hospital and we can afford the tuition for me to attend grad school here. I've got a transcript full of science classes so decide the best course of action is to get certified to teach science. As an undergrad I used to take some courses just for fun, subjects that I was interested in, but were not required. Not anymore! All the classes I register for are required education curriculum.

We move into student housing. The digs are not bad. Our place sits on the side of a big red rock hill. From our door we can hike into the high desert mountains on BLM land and the Caribou National

Forest. One of the best things about the western USA is all the public land. Back home in the Midwest there was little of the natural prairie preserved in parks and you had to ask permission from farmers. Here in Idaho, we can walk for days on public land that we own as much as the next person.

I get a job assisting special needs students with their personal and educational needs. I have a university van that I use to transport students in wheelchairs. Every one of these young people is unique, courageously striving to overcome limitations most people never think of. I consider it an honor to serve them.

Most of the people in town are members of the Mormon or LDS church. They occasionally give Laura and I copies of their holy book. We are getting quite a collection of them on our bookshelf. The Mormons tend to be conservative politically, but most are decent folks. Like any sect or race or religion or ethnic group, most people are good-hearted, and the ones who aren't are usually exceptions.

I'm thrilled to live here in Idaho. The Rocky Mountains used to be a place where I might get to go rarely on vacation for a week. Now we can go on adventures camping or trout fishing in new scenery every weekend. As part of the outdoor program Laura and I chaperone trips with challenged students. One young man with cerebral palsy dreams of captaining a whitewater raft. No one else volunteers so Laura and I head down the Snake River with him giving orders. We did pretty well actually, all things considered, although we run a few rapids backwards or sideways.

Sadly, our little bird Perchy dies. We find his ball of feathers in the bottom of his topless cage. At least he got to fly free in his life with us. We bury his lifeless body on Red Hill looking over the college campus. Strange how you can grieve for a pet, like it was a person. Perchy was part of our family. We wipe away the tears and wonder if we will ever have children. One of Laura's friends at the hospital is expecting a baby. We figure we'll try when I finish my program. In the meantime, we're careful in the bedroom. I even get stuck at the cash register for a price check when buying a box of condoms at the drug store. Very embarrassing.

I focus like a laser on my classes now. I'm no longer on scholarship and we are working to pay all the bills. I'm hoping for a rewarding career as a teacher. When I attend classes I wear a pager so the special needs students in my care can contact me any time they need assistance. It's a juggling act but I love the work. My boss's name is Dak. He's an ex-football star who sometimes pages me when he sees me studying in the union, just to watch me jump up and get ready to dash out to the van. I suppose everyone needs a little humor in their lives.

This Saturday Laura and I will testify at an environmental impact statement hearing for a special isotope separator. Basically, this project is a boondoggle, a pork barrel project contrived by our far-right Idaho senators to bring millions of U.S. tax dollars into the state. There's already a glut of dangerous plutonium, which causes cancer, has a half-life of 24,100 years and can be used to make a nuclear bomb. Yet these yokels want to spend millions of tax dollars tearing up a big chunk of Idaho nature building a plant to separate out more Pu239.

Laura and I love the natural beauty of our new home here in Idaho. So, we have joined a bevy of conservation and environmental groups like Trout Unlimited, Idaho Conservation League and the Snake River Alliance. We prepare carefully for the hearing. Our testimony goes well. One of our group gets weird and dresses up like a human ballistic missile but despite that silliness, we win and defeat the damaging SIS project.

Sadly, the Trout Unlimited group is not as successful in the effort to protect the Portneuf River, a blue-ribbon trout stream here. There are both cold and hot springs in the river so trout can migrate to exactly the temperature they like and the trophy fish grow huge. Fly fishermen come all the way from Japan and Germany to wade these waters for lunkers. But ranchers overgraze the riparian areas, caving in banks under which the trout like to hide and causing massive erosion and manure pollution to the point where only carp can survive.

I get a notice to see the manager at the post office. Apparently, there is some sort of special letter he needs to talk to me about. Hey, maybe I won a contest, a dream home or a new car. I go to the window and they direct me to an office where I speak to the postmaster. He seems apologetic. What the heck is going on? He hands me a letter postmarked three years ago in West Palm Beach, FL. Some letters that got misplaced were recently discovered. Mine was one of them. I step outside to read it.

The note was written by Nedra after the Europe trip. She wanted to see me. I'm kind of stunned how fate or chance or luck or physics or whatever forces rule the universe can be so unpredictable. My life could have taken a very different path had that letter arrived on time. I go home and write Nedra a reply explaining what happened and that I'm married now. I try to be very complimentary and positive as I don't know if she'll even believe me that the letter was lost for three years, that's so weird.

When I think about it, everything must happen for a reason, because I'm so happy with my partner Laura. She's the best friend I could ever ask for.

Another congressional election has come and gone. Laura consoles me. Along with a group of college students I worked hard for progressive candidates, but this is conservative territory here in the west. Some republican potato farmers tell me all the problems are caused by eastern liberals. Having lived south of LA as a kid, I tell them I'm from California and to me, they're just eastern liberals. They become angry. I feel so outnumbered here. I fear for the future of the country. Using lies, trickery and a butt load of corporate PAC money the fascists win again. I'm glad I have in Laura a partner I can talk to openly about these concerns.

CHAPTER THIRTY-NINE

*L*ife is good. I'm crushing all my classes. I take school very seriously. The education courses are not as hard as some science courses I've taken, but the content is applicable for the new career I'm hoping for. Laura is working diligently providing speech services for her patients who have suffered head injuries and strokes. She is so conscientious and caring with her patients. I'm so proud of her. We don't have a lot of money but are steadily paying down loans. It's Christmas time and we don't want to spend money on a tree. But I find a tumble weed and we decorate it instead. Poverty is relative. We are deeply in love. We've never been happier in our lives.

Hard to believe but here I am, in student teaching. My education advisor recommends several host teachers but I want an assignment within walking distance of campus because Laura needs the car for work. In hindsight, I should have listened to my advisor. My host teacher at the nearby school isn't very talented. He uses lots of worksheets and not many hands-on experiments, but I stick with it and finish the program. Now I'm certified to teach junior high and high school science. The schools are short on science instructors and I start subbing right away.

I haven't seen my parents for a long time now. They've been living in a trailer in Arizona. Over spring break Laura and I go visit them. The desert is such a unique place. We hike among the saguaro cactus watching tiny lizards scamper across the volcanic outcrops. Leroy buys tickets to the Rose Bowl game and drives us to California. My mom wants to see the house where we lived south of LA when I was a kid. I remember going to the ocean, watching surfers, hotrods and listening to Beach Boys music. Our house was located near orange groves and grape vineyards. They made the world's best popsicles out of fresh juice. But Leroy has trouble finding our old place. The citrus groves and vineyards are all gone, replaced by freeways and strip malls. California is being ruined by human overpopulation.

The day of the big game has arrived. We have a hard time finding seats for the Parade of Roses. It seems everyone was out partying last night and there's a lot of puke on the curbs. Leroy buys a Wall Street Journal and lays it down for Mom to stand on. In the bowl game that follows, my alma mater gets beaten by UCLA. I swear one of the players on our team was paid off by bookies. I hear he showed up back on campus driving a new Mercedes. A federal grand jury probe finds the running back accepted illegal payments from gambling agents.

I have to leave the game early anyway, the roar of the crowd is too loud for my damaged ears. My hearing problem has hamstrung me my whole life, interfering with work, school and communication with others. I'm teaching science, and I love teaching, but the writing is on the wall once again. Because of my hearing loss I have trouble fielding questions from students. All the work and effort put into a teaching degree and I have to admit it is not the right fit. I talk to the education advisor and they recommend working as a librarian where the environment would be quieter.

I register for a maximum load of library science classes at the university. I'm supercharged with motivation to get through this program. I felt so defeated when science teaching didn't work out. I was stunned for a couple of days and felt like quitting college and getting a job doing manual labor. But I can't give up and let my hearing problem defeat me. Instead I accept my limitations and move forward. Besides, Laura got one of those home pregnancy kits and tested positive. She had it verified at the hospital. We're going to be parents. I feel responsible for another human being now. I have to get through this library media program and get a steady job.

With the baby on the way we're going to need more room. Fortunately, during this recession, cheap two-bedroom apartments are plentiful. We find one on the edge of town where we can easily hike up into the sage-covered hills. I need help moving our couch and bed. There's a note on a bulletin board advertising a handyman with a truck. I figure it will take an hour to move our stuff. The fellow arrives in a dilapidated old pickup that breaks down in our parking lot. I spend the rest of the day helping him fix his engine.

This handyman tells me he has a family, a wife and two children. They have been homeless but found a cheap motel now where he works remodeling rooms in exchange for rent. After we finally get the furniture moved his truck breaks down again. He asks for a ride back to his motel. I feel empathy for him and pay him double for his work. He thanks me and asks to stop at a convenience store on the way. I figure he needs milk or bread for his kids. He comes back to the car with a 12-pack of beer and a carton of cigarettes. Drugs and alcohol ruin so many lives, and nearly ruined mine too.

Now that we're moved into the new apartment Laura works on transforming the spare bedroom into a nursery. We buy a crib and a dresser onto which she stencils little teddy bears. Her stomach is getting big! I'm getting anxious.

I've gotten to know some Shoshone-Bannock Indians. We go on outdoor adventures together. They know much about nature and have a different outlook on things. I ask them if they want to go rafting Saturday. They look at me like I'm crazy and reply, "yes, let's go rafting *on the next sunny day.*"

Saturday comes and it is storming. A whole bunch of other groups get rained out. Instead I am patient and go with the Native Americans on the next sunny weekend. I say I'll meet them at 8AM. They show up after 10AM. They have a totally different concept of time that takes some getting used to. After the trip we go back to the "res" for buffalo burgers.

During the week I sub and take library classes. Two required courses aren't offered on campus this semester, cataloging and reference. I arrange to take them from another college through distance learning. The professor is excellent, but I have to say virtual education is nowhere near as good as in-person learning. When I look back on all my college years and the personal interaction I had with students and professors, I wouldn't give that up for anything. The social goals of education can only be accomplished with in-person learning.

Laura and I attend childbirth classes. She awakes during the night and starts having contractions. Then her water breaks. I nervously drive her to the hospital. The baby's head is starting to emerge. The nurse puts a heart monitor on. The beat slows and the mood becomes tense. The baby comes out with the umbilical around its neck. Our Mormon doc quickly untwists the cord. The baby cries out. We have a healthy boy. I want to name him Strider after the character in Lord of the Rings. Laura vetoes that and we agree on Tyler.

Our baby boy is a funny little guy. Sometimes we let him lie in the sunshine of the apartment window. He lets out a sound like a tiny donkey. I just love this little one so much. I'm glad Laura can breast-feed. This is so important for a child to develop proper immunity. I'm super-energized. I sub to make extra income and burn through my final classes becoming a fully certified library media specialist.

Having a child makes us want to be closer to our parents. In our case the grandparents are crazy about kids. So, it's a no brainer to move back to the Midwest. Laura and I really hope we can both find jobs in the same town so we won't have to commute. Reducing our carbon footprint is still a big priority for us. But we are unable to pull it off. I land a job in a rural school district supervising two libraries serving preschool through twelfth grade. Laura will be working as a speech-language pathologist in several different schools. We purchase a rebuilt Honda since we'll both have to commute now. Darn!

Laura and the baby fly back to the Midwest. It's hard to be physically separated, I love them so much. Leroy comes to Idaho to help me move. We clean the apartment 'til it shines. Leroy even loses some skin cleaning the oven with ammonia. But after all that work the landlord doesn't give the damage deposit back. What a rip off.

Laura and I now have enough stuff that I must rent the next larger U-Haul. It seems every time we move, I must get a 5-foot longer truck. The man at the rental counter asks me if I want insurance for the trip. I say no and I'm about to leave but go back and buy it. Who knows with my luck?

I say goodbye to Idaho. It's been fun and exciting, watching Olympians like Katarina Witt practice skating in Sun Valley, trout fishing in Henry's Fork and cross-country skiing through buffalo herds in West Yellowstone. We're off on the long trek back to Iowa. I'm thankful for Leroy's help. We drive straight through, 18 hours, taking turns piloting the moving van. A half hour from the little farm town Laura and I will be calling home I'm at the wheel. I notice a huge buck deer jump a fence and head toward the road. I slow down and pull over on the shoulder, doing everything I can to avoid a collision.

The big bruiser stag rams smack into the side of the aluminum U-Haul crunching it in like giant pop can. Leroy and I watch as the wounded animal limps into a hay field and lies down. We take note of the mileage marker and continue on our trek. After unloading the van, we call the highway patrol and ask for a trooper to meet us at the scene of the accident. Sure enough, the huge antlered animal is still lying in the field.

The trooper arrives and we explain what happened. On inspection we find that the deer has a compound fracture of the leg and other injuries. Unfortunately, the wounded animal must be put down. I assume the patrolman will dispatch the deer with a shot to the head from his side arm. But the trooper opens the trunk of his cruiser explaining that due to the use of automatic weapons by drug gangs all highway patrol officers now carry a fully automatic rifle in their trunk so they won't be outgunned. He's never had a chance to fire the weapon and asks if we mind that he tries it out now.

Together Leroy, the trooper and I walk through the hay until we reach the big buck. It's too wounded to run away. I feel horrible about what happened but I did my best to avoid hitting it. Now it's time to do the humane thing and put the poor creature out of its misery. Money is short with me and I ask the trooper if I could have the deer for meat. The trooper agrees and aims his assault rifle at the deer's head, about to pull the trigger when a truck slams on its brakes and screeches to a halt back on the highway. A man jumps out of the car waving his arms yelling for us to stop.

I'm thinking the fellow is probably an animal protectionist who doesn't want the deer killed. I love animals too and can relate to people who care for them. But in this case the animal is suffering and there is no chance for recovery. The man reaches us and explains that he is a taxidermist and wants to mount the deer's head.

During hunting season bucks have scrapped all the skin off their antlers. The deer I accidentally hit has a massive rack and the antlers are still completely covered in velvet. The taxidermist explains that he has never gotten an opportunity to work on a specimen like this before and asks if we would avoid shooting it in the head. That's fine with me and I direct the trooper to shoot the wounded beast in the heart instead, which he does, only with a multiple shot burst from his machine gun that ruins some of the meat.

The taxidermist gets out his knife and begins to cape the head while Leroy and I get knives and start field dressing the buck. The trooper stands over us holding his assault rifle watching while we work. I happen to glance back at the interstate highway and notice that cars are backed up as far as I can see.

It's obvious what's happened. The deer is laying down in the grass where the people in cars cannot see it. All they can see from the road is a state trooper holding a machine gun and three fellows clutching knives with blood up to their elbows. The commuters must think they have happened upon a bloody crime scene! I alert the trooper who hurries back and, after putting his weapon away, he starts to direct the snarled traffic.

The taxidermist thanks me and takes off with the deer's head. Leroy and I drive the remaining body to a meat locker where it will be made into sausage, burger and loin steaks. I'm very thankful. That's enough meat to last my family for a year. We return the smashed van to U-Haul. I luck out again. The insurance I bought has no deductible. I can walk away without any charge for the damage.

Laura and I found an old house to rent for cheap in a small farm town nearby. The landlady, Marge, is sweet and kind. She lets us plant a garden in the backyard. We've had gardens everywhere we've lived, but usually they were only small plots in a community garden. In Idaho friends let us use space in their backyard, but the soil was very rocky. I had to go to a stable and get loads of manure for anything to grow. Here in Iowa the soil is thick and black. We will be able to grow lots of vegetables at our new home, and the freezer is full of venison.

Since Laura and I must both work to pay our bills we need to find a daycare for Tyler. We are so fortunate. There are many Mennonites and Amish in the area and they have a daycare in their church. Tyler receives wonderful loving care from a Cambodian refugee woman named Yen at the church. I really admire the Mennonites. They are industrious and yet so generous. Many other people I have met say they are Christian, but they don't seem to pay any attention to what Jesus actually taught. These Mennonites walk the walk. Many are conscientious objectors who learn from their faith, what I had to learn the hard way in the army: that war is morally wrong and peacemakers are blessed.

I'm totally amped about my new library position. I love helping students find books and do research. I have story hour for preschoolers and help seniors with term papers. The district has constructed a new high school building. I spend my entire Christmas "vacation" moving 15,000 books, shelves and equipment to the new school. I'm working my hardest to make my new career a success. Most of the teachers here are friendly and competent. One old teacher, Mrs. Hinkle, falls asleep during her class. Her room is a disaster. She tells me that being a librarian is a good job … for a woman! I dismiss her sexist remark. There's always some interpersonal politics like this going on at school, but I concentrate instead on doing my best for the students.

With both of us working Laura and I have now paid off all of our loans and even purchased a washer and dryer. This may not sound like a big deal, but we've been going to laundromats ever since we moved out of our parent's houses. We've been using cloth diapers instead of disposable with the baby to reduce environmental impact and having these appliances makes laundry so much easier.

An audiologist comes to our school to do hearing tests for students. I talk to her about my own ear problems. She suggests I look into hearing aids. I've always wanted to try those little electronic gadgets but they were always too expensive. For some reason in the United States health insurance does not cover hearing devices. This seems unjust to me, one of the last frontiers in handicapped discrimination. I contact the lawyer I met while I was an undergrad. Tom McDonald remembers me, "the last time I talked to you, some young girl was trying to jump your bones."

The amiable lawyer helped me procure funding for an ear operation through workmen's compensation. Now he is able to go to court and get money for hearing aids too. I have to admit I feel a little self-conscious wearing the devices at first. But with the support of my wife and best friend Laura, I stick with the remedy and find that hearing aids are like a miracle cure, a real game changer for me. I can hear people socially and at work so much better. No longer do I need to ask people to repeat themselves or have to guess what people are saying.

Summer break arrives and I'm back on the college campus again! Nights, weekends and summers I take courses towards a master's degree in education. Grad school is very different from undergrad. I have to say a lot of the charm, excitement and magic are gone. The coursework is all serious business. But I do enjoy my fellow students and the material learned helps refine my skills at school. For a thesis I conduct a study on reading comprehension in 4th grade students, electronic versus print. Basically, I find there is no statistical difference in comprehension when students read from a computer screen or print up to about 600 words of text, after which comprehension gradually drops off when reading electronically displayed material.

Thanks to our teacher's union our district has a pay scale that rewards educational achievement. Both Laura and I have master's degrees now so our income has increased. We decide we can responsibly support another child. We understand that overpopulation is damaging the world's ecosystem and reducing the quality of life for humans and other living things. We hope for a girl so that we would have one child of each sex. If we do have another boy, then we will try again in the future for a girl. But three children would be the maximum justifiable family size for us. That seems logical to me, we'll try for one of each, a boy and a girl, but if the first two are same sex, we'll only try one more time, and then quit.

Laura becomes pregnant and carries the baby like a pro. Even the labor goes well. We're walking around the hospital hallways right up until delivery. We totally luck out and have a beautiful baby girl! We're done having kids. I want to name her Daisy. Laura objects and we agree on Anna. This is such an incredibly happy time for us. Our baby girl is an easy one. She rarely cries and is so amiable. What pure joy life is.

CHAPTER FORTY

With our improved income we have saved enough money to buy a dilapidated old house of our own for $23,000 in cash. The house needs basically everything redone. Fortunately, working in the schools, we have winter, spring and summer breaks. We work after school, on weekends and during vacations rebuilding the old fixer-upper. Laura and I strip walls down to bear studs. Sometimes it seems we're replacing the entire house, one board at a time. We will live in this remodel for a while when it's finished, and then try to flip it for a profit.

I love my job. Being the district librarian, I can collaborate with teachers in every grade level. I help with experiments in science erecting small wind turbines and solar arrays, invite Holocaust survivors to speak in social studies and bring rocks, fossils, Indian artifacts and wild critters like snakes and opossums for the elementary students to study. I enjoy assisting teachers with units in every subject area. I've finally found my niche, a career in which I can excel.

Of course, no job is perfect. There are minor irritations, like the parent who wants to ban Harry Potter books from the library. Or the occasional student with discipline issues, crawling under tables in the library to look up girl's skirts or vandalizing computer equipment. But most of the young people are genuine and really fun to work with. I encounter resistance from some administrators who dislike change, usually citing funding issues. So I concentrate on writing monetary grants.

I realize education in this country is underfunded. Our small rural district is always strapped for cash. But I'm able to bring in thousands of dollars more in grants and awards than my district pays me in salary every year. The science class gets new water testing equipment. The art classes get reproductions of famous paintings. The new building gets landscaping. The technology lab gets new computers. Along with others I encourage our forward-thinking superintendent to work with the utility company and our schools become the first in the nation to be powered by solar photovoltaic electric and geothermal heating and cooling.

Truly, having children is the highlight of my life's journey. Our toddlers are so much fun. I'm amazed at how much love these little ones give. What a joy sitting in a rocking chair in the moonlight singing them to sleep while we hold each other tight. And I'm doubly blessed because I also get to interact with 500 other wonderful children as their school librarian. I know all the struggle and study and hard work and sacrifice was worth it now. I have the rewarding career, and life, that I hoped for.

But I worry about the children's future. The government is building hundreds of new nuclear weapons. A nuclear war could end all life on earth. What can I do to resist the arms race? During summer vacation I arrange to go to Nevada with a group of anti-nuclear activists. We will have a protest and civil disobedience at the nuclear weapons test site in the desert there.

Laura and I pack the kids in the car and head off to Las Vegas, the closest city to the test site. Our anti-nuclear organization has arranged for a special room rate at the Excalibur Casino. Many of the members of our protest group are Catholic, several are priests and a whole bunch are nuns. Las Vegas is a wild and somewhat seedy place and it seems odd to be staying at a casino here with a bunch of nuns. Our toddler Tyler enjoys the jousting match in the motel basement and even gets knighted, Sir Tyler.

Up and down the strip outside they openly advertise for hookers, as prostitution is legal in Vegas. The nuns get wind of this and have some flyers printed up against human sex trafficking. They are out there now handing out information to passersby.

In the morning I leave Laura and the kids at the motel and head out to the nuclear test site. There we encounter a group of Bannock Shoshone Indians who explain that the test area is located on their ancestral land. They thank us for coming to protest. I knew many of their relatives back in Idaho and they give me a prized possession, a "get and go" pass that states that I'm always welcome on their reservation, as long as the wind blows and the grass grows.

When we reach the barbed wire perimeter of the base, we encounter security personnel dressed in black. I recognize their rifles as updated models of the M-16 I carried in the army. The soldiers warn us not to cross the wire boundary. I'm not sure what to do. But the nuns don't even hesitate, they tumble over the perimeter en masse. Then they fan out across the wide desert test site hiding behind rocks and cactus.

It's the first time in my life that I truly appreciate nuns and priests and their vow of celibacy, which I always before considered too restrictive and unnecessary. I have a family waiting for me back at the casino so I decide to wait and witness what happens, rather than go over the fence and get arrested. But the religious, they have no family to worry about and follow only their conscience, refusing to give in to the evil of nuclear madness.

It's now late afternoon and the soldiers have rounded up the last of the nuns from their hiding places. The lawbreakers are placed in a giant cage from which they are processed out one by one. I cheer and greet one of the nuns. She holds a summons in her hand to appear back in Vegas a month from now for her trial. She is from a convent in New York and I ask her if this is going to be a hardship, to have to return for the trial. She whispers in my ear not to worry; she gave the authorities a fake name and has no plans to return. Nuns are cool!

Back in Iowa, Laura and I are able to flip our fixer-upper, doubling our investment. We use the money to buy 4 acres and an uncompleted house project in the country. The previous owner was unable to finish the home because of a death in his family. I've not forgotten the warnings about global climate disruption of my college science profs. Laura and I work on creating a sustainable homestead. The house is finished as an earth bermed, passive solar design with geothermal backup heat, cooling and hot water. We install solar photovoltaic panels and a wind turbine for electricity.

Our orchard, greenhouse and gardens provide food. We raise horses, sheep, cattle, chickens and bees. Building a barn from scratch is our crowning achievement. This place in the country provides a great pastoral setting for our son and daughter to grow up surrounded by nature. We have a woods, a pond stocked with fish, a root cellar and tree house. We purchase electric car. Even our wood stove has a catalyst so we can gather round a warm fire in the winter without worrying that we are polluting the air.

We had to compromise and get a bank loan to complete the project. But we will have the debt paid off in less than 3 years. We're overjoyed with the way our sustainable, nature-friendly homestead turned out. We frequently bring groups of students from the school here for field trips. Our lives are busy but, we feel, full of purpose.

Of course, everything is not perfect. Our son has problems with ear infections and we must take him to the doctor. Our homestead is a postage stamp of green surrounded by big Ag operations. Occasionally the pesticides they use kill our bees. The erosion from their row crops muddies our pond. It's hard when some people belittle or look down upon your life's work. We encounter disrespect because we are "tree huggers" or "just educators" working in public schools. But Laura and I both know we have a positive impact on young people and that is worth more than status or fortune to us.

I believe in life-long learning and I never stop studying, taking continuing education classes at colleges and workshops all over the state and country. This way I can keep current on the latest educational practices. And, I have to admit, it's fun too. I go to Montana to search for and study dinosaur bones. I travel to Massachusetts to observe innovative science fair projects. I obtain a grant to interview a Nazi war crimes prosecutor in Florida. The state's rock quarries pay for me to help develop new curriculum to teach earth science. Experiences like these keep my teaching lively and relevant.

I'm back at my old undergrad alma mater today for a class on the latest in adolescent literature. I strive to keep my library collection current for students and teachers. It's a marvelous summer day with a gentle breeze and plenty of sunshine. My mind wanders back to my very first semester on this beautiful green grass and limestone campus. It seems like yesterday, I was so idealistic and resolute then, a hardcore environmentalist who rejected modern transportation. It's true, I've mellowed out and let go of some of those rigid values since then. However, I do look back on that person I once was with a lot of sentimental respect and admiration. My heart was in the right place. I was acting out of a love for nature and my fellow human beings.

In order to survive, people need to change. Sometimes we have to compromise, when we have no other choice. But we should always strive to do our best to live up to our highest ideals. You can choose to include, or exclude, other people from your life, but the solid fact is there's one person you always have to live with, and that is yourself. If you compromise too much, then you can become uncomfortable in your own skin. If you compromise everything, all your most deeply held, core values, you will be unable to live with yourself. Then there is no escape. That situation always results in a tragic ending.

With some people, you can never win. Had I stayed living in a teepee on my parent's spare lot years ago, hunting and gathering wild food, yes, I would have had very little environmental impact. But people would have harshly criticized that lifestyle, with the "you'd have us all living in caves with no plumbing" thing. So now I drive an electric car that I charge with solar PV panels and a 3.5 Kw wind turbine and some people rant about the copper wire in the car's engine or that a bird might fly into the blades of my turbine. (For the record we've never found one single dead bird or bat under our wind turbine). We're just doing the best we can.

I veer off the sidewalk now leaving behind all the normies scurrying like ants on their way to classes and start traipsing down the railroad tracks behind the English/Philosophy Building. It's the shortest route to my adolescent lit class as the crow flies, so I take it. My mind wanders back to that other time, as a freshman, when I was walking down these tracks in this exact same spot wondering what would ever happen to me and asking myself in the future: Did I graduate from college? What did I end up choosing for my career? Did I get a good job? Did I meet someone and get married? Will I have children someday? What is my life like then?

The ability to talk to yourself in the past or future is a valuable treasure indeed. I carefully place my feet on each railroad tie and make a mental effort to communicate to myself back then.

"Yes, don't worry man, everything turns out fine. You not only graduate with honors from this college, you finish graduate programs at two more great institutions after this one. You'd have never guessed it, but you have a successful and rewarding career as a teacher and librarian. You meet and marry a fantastic partner, beautiful inside and out. You have two healthy children, a boy and a girl, with curious, inquisitive minds. You live in an environment friendly, sustainable homestead and life is great!"

The course of my life has been erratic, unpredictable and often discouraging. There are so many times when I could have simply given up. I freely admit I've made many mistakes, have some regrets and I've often felt like an oddball. My views on politics are very progressive, definitely out of the mainstream. My longing to live in balance with, and to protect, nature is radical compared to most people. I reject war, violence and militarism in a way, and to an extent, that most people do not.

I couldn't afford to go to college in the way that I thought was normal, having the experience I thought other students had. My romantic life was either a feast or a famine, mostly famine. Some would say the year-long romance with my marriage partner was too short. But, when it is right, it is right. The path many of us take to a career and committed relationship can be tangled and convoluted. But I can see now that this is the substance of life itself. There are no guarantees, and no perfect choices and no one right path. And ultimately, THERE ARE NO NORMIES. I'm going to stop thinking of other people like that. Yeah, I'm a little weird and freaky sometimes, but so is everyone else, no matter how thick and elaborate a façade they display publicly.

I wish every living thing on this planet the very best in this endeavor of life. You never know where you'll end up. But that keeps it all interesting and worth continuing to see what happens next. When things get rough, we can remember the good times. There is much that is wrong with the world, but there is also much that is good and beautiful.

Peace and love,

Bert Jay Miller

Bert Jay Miller was born on September 11, 1956 at the University of Iowa hospital in Iowa City, IA. His social father, a mechanic, stone cutter and cement worker was unable to have children. His mother, who worked as a cook and secretary, underwent artificial insemination at the University of Iowa Hospital. The biological father, John H. Randall, was a research scientist, doctor and head of the obstetrics and gynecology clinic at the hospital.

Miller lived with his parents in Iowa City until 1962 when the family moved to southern California. His mother eventually grew homesick for the Midwest and the family moved back to Iowa City where Bert attended public schools graduating from Iowa City High School in 1974. In a farm work-related accident while detasseling hybrid corn Miller was thrown from a truck fracturing his skull and suffering severe hearing loss and tinnitus.

Bert Miller worked for many years with his father and brother pouring cement and stone cutting in their family business. Miller received an honorable discharge from the U.S. Army/National Guard 209th Medical Battalion serving 100 days before being injured during a training exercise at Ft. Leonard Wood in 1983. He worked his way through college at the University of Iowa, graduating in May of 1985 with a BS pre-medical degree in General Science. He was nominated for Phi Beta Kappa by the late Howard Laster, Dean of the College of Liberal Arts and professor of physics and astronomy.

In August of 1985 Bert married his life partner Laura whom he met while living in the River City Housing Co-op. At the time Miller worked as a staff writer for the award-winning Daily Iowan newspaper.

After moving to Johnston, IA in 1986 Miller worked as an accountant, a food caterer and in landscaping.

The couple moved to Pocatello, Idaho in 1987 where Bert earned a science teaching endorsement and library media specialist certification from Idaho State University while working as an assistant to special needs students. They had their first child, Tyler, in 1989 and a daughter, Anna, in 1992. After moving back to Iowa, Miller worked as a Pre-K through 12th grade library media specialist for 30 years.

Bert Miller received the Roy J. Carver Educational Technology Award in 1993, the Friend of Education Award from the WACO Education Association in 2001, the National Education Association Innovation in Education Award in 2005, the Glass Apple Award for outstanding teacher librarian in the state from Iowa First Lady Christie Vilsack in 2006 and the Lemelson EXCITE Teacher Award at the Massachusetts Institute of Technology in 2007 along with more than forty other grants and educational awards.

Bert and Laura created a sustainable solar homestead in Iowa where they lived until retiring in 2020. In 2021 they built a solar home on the front range of the Rocky Mountains of Colorado in order to be closer to their son, Tyler, a professional mountain climbing guide and their daughter, Anna, a nurse practitioner in the area of women's health. The Millers enjoy nature and outdoor pursuits including rock climbing, kayaking, hiking and bicycling.

Bert Miller is a member of numerous peace, social justice and environmental conservation organizations and the author of three easy children's picture books (Jump to the Moon, Acorns for Lunch, The Farmer Wouldn't Sell), one early chapter book (Pennwick), one adolescent novel (Muscle Car Wars), and one science fiction novel (The Moons of Gemini). Joe College is Miller's first new adult novel.

ALSO BY BERT J MILLER

The Muscle Car Wars

Moons of Gemini

www.ingramcontent.com/pod-product-compliance
Lightning Source LLC
Chambersburg PA
CBHW051546030726
47592CB00001B/160